Gold Star Chance

Also by CJ Murphy

The Bucket List

Frame by frame

Gold Star Chance

CJ Murphy

Desert Palm Press

Gold Star Chance
(Five Point Series – Book 1)

By CJ Murphy

©2019 CJ Murphy

ISBN (trade) 978-1-948327-28-2
ISBN (epub): 978-1-948327-29-9
ISBN (pdf): 978-1-948327-30-5

For permission requests, write to the publisher at lee@desertpalmpress.com or "Attention: Permissions Coordinator," at

Desert Palm Press
1961 Main Street, Suite 220
Watsonville, California 95076
www.desertpalmpress.com

Editor: CK King
Cover Design: TreeHouse Studio, Winston-Salem, NC

Printed in the United States of America
First Edition May 2019

Acknowledgment

This series was created for my wife, Darla, as a tribute to an incredible woman with a distinguished career. She never got the retirement sendoff she deserved for her years of dedicated service. Sadly, she never got the earned 'job well done' for planning, building and paying off a state of the art 911 center, for being the first line of emergency response rarely seen or thanked, for the nights of watching river levels, or the countless hours of preparing 5000 residents for the inevitable natural or man-made disaster. Darla, this is for you, for all you've done for so many and for loving a Murphy like me.

When I decided to write an emergency services series, I wanted to put it in a place that would offer the reader some of the best of my home state. Wild and wonderful aptly describes West Virginia's mountains, valleys, rivers and streams. The state offers residents and visitors the chance to enjoy the four seasons as they play outside in the rainbow of spring, the green of summer, the scarlet and ginger of autumn, and the pristine white of winter. Tucker County boasts a variety of options: two state parks, two ski resorts, five rivers for fishing, rafting and kayaking, the Blackwater Canyon and Dolly Sods for hiking, biking and camping as well as an area known as Otter Creek used by the US Special Forces to train. Once you add in the quaint towns, microbreweries, and fantastic restaurants, Tucker County becomes the perfect setting for the Five Points Series.

My wife was the former emergency manager and 911 director for the county this series is set in. In addition to that, I've spent over twenty-five years as a career and volunteer firefighter. With sixty years of combined emergency service work, my wife and I have a treasure trove of experience to draw on. My fictional emergency responders will have many unique adventures based on real life rescues, natural disasters, and law enforcement incidents that we've experienced. I hope you'll enjoy getting to know Sheriff Chance Fitzsimmons and her K9 Zeus as the pair protect the innocent while serving as the thin blue line between order and anarchy.

Chapter One

SHERIFF CHANCE FITZSIMMONS OPENED the rear door of her black Yukon and spoke in Dutch. *"Laden, Zeus."* The Belgian Malinois effortlessly leapt into the rear compartment, tongue darting in and out as he panted from their vigorous run around the Canyon Loop trail. Her K9 partner was her constant companion and had been trained at one of the finest institutions for producing police dogs. He was striking with his dark fawn coat and sable mask.

"Let's go home, boy." Using a towel pulled from the front seat, she wiped the sweat from her face, then vigorously rubbed it through her short grey-streaked short brown hair.

It was mid-May, and the mountain air was still cool in the early morning. Several people in the parking area pulled mountain bikes off their vehicles, in preparation for tackling part of the canyon. She walked to the window and ran a hand over the velvet ears of her companion. She'd traveled all the way to Holland to form her bond with the two-year-old. Leaner than a German shepherd, the breed was distinctive. Common traits were confidence and extreme intelligence. The Belgian Malinois was known to bond tightly with its handler and was loyal beyond question. Those qualities were exactly why she'd chosen the breed and him. Of one thing she was certain; Zeus would jump in front of a bullet for her and she'd do the same for him.

"Good run boy." Chance and Zeus had run the loop three times that morning for a total of seven and a half miles. Without conscious thought, she looked at the make, model, and license plates of each vehicle, committing the state and six to seven-digit number and letter combination of each plate to memory. *Subaru Outback, West Virginia tags 17J-654, Dodge Durango Maryland specialty tag, BAL 8765.* More than once she'd averted calling out the cavalry for a lost hiker by remembering where she'd last seen the vehicle of the missing person. A quick drive to the location of the last known sighting had frequently led to the discovery of the overdue individual. Normally, that person had underestimated the difficulty of the trail and time that it would take to hike back out.

Beyond her job as Sheriff of Tucker County, Chance also held the position of Operations Chief on the countywide search and rescue team. Her team was well versed in locating lost or injured visitors that failed to heed posted warnings or overestimated their wilderness savvy. During the summer months, they averaged one or two calls per week for overdue hikers, bikers, or anglers. In the winter months, finding a person who might have fallen from a tree stand or off the face of one of the canyon walls before temperatures fell below zero added to the adrenaline surge.

"Ready to go have breakfast, buddy?" The answering bark from the rear compartment echoed off the interior of the vehicle, as Chance slid her key into the ignition and started the engine. As was her routine, she picked up the mic for her radio and depressed the talk button. "SD-1 to Comm Center."

A disembodied voice came out of the speaker mounted in a utility compartment near the windshield. "Comm Center to SD-1. Go ahead."

"SD-1 is clear T1."

"SD-1 clear T1. Comm Center received."

Chance had made this contact call a part of her morning run routine after the day Dee fell ill and had to be transported to the hospital while Chance was out of communication. The location varied and was given to the communication center in code as T1 through T7. She used this code to avoid announcing to the always curious 'scanner land' where she and Zeus were having their morning run. Now, if something happened while she was in and out of cell phone coverage, the communication center knew where to find her. Currently, she frequented seven trails for these outings at five every morning. Her days as a Forest Service smoke jumper were certainly over. The necessity of being able to run full tilt through the woods as if the devil himself were chasing her was not.

Ten minutes later, she opened the back door of her home to see Maggie Fitzsimmons standing in her kitchen. The walls of the log home shone a honeyed hue and added to the comfort the house offered. The smell of black coffee and bacon assaulted her senses.

Maggie curled her nose and pointed to the hallway. "Shower first, I can smell you from here."

"You're a feisty broad first thing in the morning. I haven't even come close enough for you to smell me over that bacon." Chance grabbed at the plate, only to have Maggie peer at her over her glasses while she pointed toward the bathroom with added emphasis.

Maggie used a fork to turn over the bacon in the cast iron skillet. "I didn't raise you to sass me. I turned you over my knee when you were twelve, and I'll do it again. Don't push me to see if I'm kidding. Go. I'll feed Zeus."

Chance risked kissing the silver-haired woman on her way past and toward the shower. "You'd have to catch me first, old lady." Chance deftly avoided the swipe of the dish towel that came off Maggie's shoulder with speed belying her age.

"Old lady my ass. If you don't get in the shower and back to this breakfast table in seven minutes or less, I'll feed your breakfast to Zeus. Go, you ungrateful heathen."

"Love you, Mom." Chance often thought that if her hair turned the same color as Maggie's, she'd happily avoid a relationship with Miss Clairol. Maggie's silver hair had a beautiful shine to it. Chance looked at her own chestnut locks and reached up to touch the silver at the temples. She growled and shook her head at the shock of silvery white that had grown out in the front when she was very young. *This getting old sucks.*

The shower knob slipped in the beige-tile enclosure, as she turned on the water to let it warm. "One more thing I need to fix." She stripped out of her running clothes and stepped inside. Hot water pounded against the top of her head, and she stretched her neck from side to side to allow the massaging pulsations room to relieve the tension that settled there. She sang an off-key version of Janis Joplin's "Mercedes Benz," as she scrubbed her hair and body.

The bacon smell forced her to rush, and within minutes she climbed from the shower to dry off. Steam obscured the mirror and she wiped a hand across it, as she pushed open the small window to cool the room. Her stomach growled. "I hear you, girl. I'm hurrying." She raised her left arm and rubbed the towel along her side. The rough scar tissue that ran around her left bicep and down her flank was red from the heat of the water.

Years ago, she'd parachuted into a wildfire and been forced to deploy her emergency shelter. The aftermath had left its mark. She liberally applied cocoa butter to keep the skin supple and allowed the smell to fill her senses. The emotional scars from that day continued to fade as she excelled in her new career. As she brushed her teeth, she looked into the mirror. Fierce, gunmetal-blue eyes met her stare in the reflection. Once she spat out the toothpaste, she repeated the words she'd said every day since she left the burn ward. "Steel is tempered by fire, and gold is refined by it." She walked to her bedroom and dressed in a jog bra and boxer briefs before slipping on her tactical pants and steel-toed boots. She pulled on her black T-shirt and finger combed her hair on her way to the kitchen.

Zeus rose to meet her before dutifully sitting by her side when she took a seat at the breakfast table. Maggie placed the platter of bacon in the middle of the table and handed Chance a plate with two eggs, sunny side up. Maggie pointed to the yellow bottle near the salt. Chance used her fork to chop the eggs, then liberally squirted them with mustard before she mixed the overly yellow concoction. As she brought the first bite to her mouth, she saw Maggie shake her head.

"What?"

Maggie wrinkled up her nose. "The things your father taught you. How can you even taste the eggs?"

"With my tongue." Chance childishly gave a disgusting view of her food.

Her mother rolled her eyes. "Fifty-four going on seven. Eat, and get your ass out of here. You have that meeting at ten."

Maggie Fitzsimmons had been Chance's staunchest supporter and the only parent she'd had for forty of her fifty-four years of life. Chance's mother died giving birth to her. Years later, her father, Maggie's brother, died in the line of duty in the county where Chance was now Sheriff. Deputy Ray Fitzsimmons had found himself on a domestic call between an enraged husband and the wife he was intent on killing. Bulletproof vests don't stop gunshot wounds to the head.

With no other living relative, Maggie Fitzsimmons had stepped up and raised Chance to be a strong woman. Maggie and Dee ran a small real estate agency consisting mainly of rental properties they managed for others plus a few they personally owned. Maggie was well known and respected in the county, having served more than one term as county commissioner and head of the economic development authority.

"That meeting is with you and Dee, so I'm not really worried. Why do I need to be at the chamber of commerce meeting anyway?"

"Because Dee asked you to be there to help organize the fund raiser. Come on, Chance, it's for the girls' basketball travel fund. You know how it is; their budget is half what the boys' is. You owe this to her for putting up with your antics all those years she coached you to the championships."

Maggie's wife was a force of nature. Tall with a head of red hair,

Dee Fitzsimmons juggled all the elements of their life and still managed to look thirty years younger than her age. She served as president of Tucker County Chamber of Commerce as well as the girls' high school basketball and softball coach. She was also one of Chance's best friends.

"Yeah and because of her, I have no knees." Chance shoved a strip of crispy bacon in her mouth. She picked up another piece and reverently bowed her head. "You are the queen of bacon. I salute you."

"God, you are so full of shit. You have no knees because you spent twenty years jumping out of an airplane and you know it." Maggie picked up her coffee cup and used it to point to Chance. "Eat and get out of here. Leave me to my peaceful morning before I have to go deal with that jackass."

"Maggie Fitzsimmons, would you be casting aspersions on our esteemed county commissioner?" Chance knew that Maggie had no patience or compassion for the man holding her former office.

"How that jackass ever got elected still amazes me. I still swear that election was fixed."

"You act as if he kept you from winning. You didn't even run. As a matter of fact, he was running unopposed, so I'm not sure you could say it was fixed...unless he threatened everyone to not run against him. I told you to get your name on that ballot, but you said you'd done your sentence. If he pisses you off that much, you can always put your hat back in the ring. Floyd wouldn't stand a snowball's chance in hell against you."

Maggie narrowed her eyes and sipped her coffee. "Eat."

Chance chuckled and wiped up the last of her egg mixture with a piece of toast. She sipped at the coffee her mother had served in her favorite mug and checked her buzzing phone. It was a message from her second in command, Taylor Lewis.

Call me, ASAP. Issues at the barn.

She mumbled to herself as she stood and put on her uniform shirt. She walked to the closet that held her work gear. She grabbed the bulletproof vest with her badge pinned to it and slipped it on. After a deep breath, her hands smoothed down the Velcro. She adjusted the vest for comfort, before she donned her gun belt and threaded the belt through the buckle.

In the closet, Chance rolled the numbers to release the lock on the small safe that held her service revolver and backup weapon. With her left leg elevated on a low shelf, she slid the backup gun into the boot holster and grabbed for the black Stetson she favored with her uniform.

The mirror on the door gave her the opportunity to check out her appearance. When everything was in place, she grabbed Zeus' bulletproof vest, with his own badge sewn on the side, and slipped it over her partner's head. Once she'd adjusted the fit, Zeus shook and bounded over to the door, ready to go to work.

Maggie met her with a full travel cup and smoothed her hands over the uniform shirt and kissed her on the cheek. "Be safe, Chance." She looked down at the dog. "Zeus, keep her under control, do you hear me?"

Zeus answered her with a quick bark and a tail wag.

"We promise, Mom. See you at ten, unless Taylor isn't exaggerating that we have a problem at the barn. I'll call you."

"*Laden.*" Zeus vaulted into the back. The use of the foreign language commands helped with two things. One, the dog could distinguish commands from conversation. Two, suspects would not know what the dog was being told to do and were unlikely to be able to give the dog commands to counteract her own. As soon as she turned on to Appalachian Highway, she used the voice activation to call Taylor.

"Hey, Taylor, what's up?"

"Morning, Sheriff, sorry to call so early. Sabrina seems to be a bit lame this morning, and I thought you should know. I noticed some swelling in her leg."

"Taylor, don't ever worry about calling early. I'm on my way. Grab the Epsom salts and a bucket. I'll be there in fifteen minutes."

"Will do."

Chance's next call was to give Dee the heads up that she might not make the fundraiser meeting. As the phone dialed through, Zeus paced from window to window surveying the scenery. "See anything, boy?"

Her question was answered with a whine. She knew he'd much rather be out of the vehicle. He was a working dog, and his job was to follow any command that Chance gave him.

A deep, gravelly voice answered her call, "And what can I do for you, Five Points?"

"Morning Dee, thanks for bird dogging Mom on me at o-dark-thirty."

A deep chuckle rumbled across the line. "Hey, you know her, nobody tells her what to do. She's determined for you to eat breakfast. Coffee and a package of your favorite little coconut doughnuts doesn't rank as breakfast in her book. She misses you, so you should expect her to be there at least three times a week for a while. She's got that empty nest thing going since our last little bird flew off to school for the summer session."

Dee was referring to their adopted and former foster child, Kendra, in college over in Morgantown. "I did enjoy the bacon. How's Kendra doing at WVU?" Chance flipped on her blinker and turned onto the tree-lined road leading to the stables.

"You know her, rarely says a thing. She sounded good in our last phone call. I think she'll be fine. I know you didn't call to talk about the kid who idolizes you enough to find a school she could attend on a criminal justice scholarship. I'm sure she'll call you in a few days. I also know you didn't call to gloat about the bacon Mags fried you and keeps denying me. So, what's up?"

Chance pulled up to the stables and put the vehicle in park. "Hey, don't hate me because my cholesterol is well under the limit. I'm sorry, I might have to miss the meeting. Taylor called and Sabrina's come up lame. I'm pulling into the stables now. I'll try to make it. I just need to make sure she's okay and see if the vet will have to be called. That's a mess too, because ole Doc Hendricks retired. I haven't managed to find a new, large-animal vet closer than Deep Creek. I'll know more after I get there. I hate to bail on you if I don't have to."

"One more wise crack about my cholesterol and you'll see how well I've recovered from that heart attack."

"Yes, oh wise one."

"Oh, wise one, my ass. Go see about your horse. Don't worry about the meeting. I'll pass on your regrets."

"And then ask me to write a bigger check."

"Exactly. Bye, Five Points."

Dee had called her Five Points since she'd helped win the basketball championship with five points in spectacular style. She hit a long, three-point shot, then drove to the basket for the winning lay-up at the buzzer. As she went up, she took an elbow to the jaw—broken in three places and wired shut for almost two months. Milkshakes, broth, and soup became her 'friends.' Still to this day, it turned her stomach to even spell the word soup. Now, she was Five Points because of the badge she pinned on every morning. Chance could still see her ten-year-old self sitting on the front porch steps with her dad after work. She'd held his badge in her hands and asked him a question.

"Daddy, why are there five points on your badge?"
"Well, honey, the points mean different things to different people.

To me they mean honor, duty, courage, integrity, and empathy. The empathy part is the hardest as an officer. It's a hard one to find balance for. Someday, when you're wearing the badge, you'll understand."

His words frequently drifted back to her now that she was an officer of the law. Every day, she could still hear his words and now understood what he'd meant. He'd also told her life would offer her a gold-star chance at some point, professionally and personally. *'You have to be ready to grab it, kid. Grab it and hold on for dear life. You'll know it when you see it.'* She was sure she'd finally found it professionally. The personal one seemed to have passed her by many years ago, slipped through her fingers like fine sand.

Chance opened the back door. Zeus vaulted out and took his place at her side, as she stepped from the vehicle. Together, they strode up to a modest but well-equipped barn. The single-story wooden structure was painted red and trimmed in white. A nice corral they used for training was attached to the west side. Taylor was in Sabrina's stall. Her K9 partner, Midas, greeted Chance and Zeus.

"Find anything in her stall that she could have injured herself on?"

Taylor stood patting Sabrina's neck while she held the halter. "Not that I could see. It looks like she kicked the door there. That's a fresh strike."

"Easy girl," Chance cooed, as she approached the mare and ran her hand down the haunch, feeling each muscle and tendon. When Chance went to inspect her hoof, Sabrina pulled away and skittered sideways. "I think I found a sore spot. It might be just a stone bruise or that strike." Chance ran her finger along the U-shaped indentation in the wood of the stall door. "Let's try to soak it and see how it goes in the next few days. If it doesn't get better or gets worse, I'll call for a vet to examine her." Chance stood and wrapped an arm under Sabrina's neck and patted her. "Don't worry girl, we'll have you fixed up before you know it. I'll go get some hot water if you'll hold her. I know you should be getting off about now."

Taylor rubbed Sabrina's nose, and Midas came to sit by her leg. "We're not leaving my girl, so I'll be here."

Chance tipped her hat, grabbed the rubber bucket, and filled it with hot water. She stuck her own arm in to test the temperature. When it was just shy of uncomfortable, she took it back into the stall and poured in the Epsom salts. She mixed it with her hand to dissolve the salt, and then slowly directed Sabrina's hoof into the bucket while rubbing her flank.

Sabrina tried to pull away again, but Taylor, who stood just an inch shorter than Chance's five foot nine, held her steady and rubbed her cheek. "Easy girl, this will make it feel better."

"I couldn't see an abscess. Doesn't mean there isn't one, but let's watch it. Now promise me, after it soaks for twenty minutes, you'll go get some sleep. I know you're back on tonight. Don't make me call your wife."

Taylor laughed and shook her head. "My wife is your secretary, so she knows what's going on. I'd tell you to kiss her good morning for me, but then I might have to kill you."

Taylor's wife, Penny, had worked for Chance since the day she took office. Taylor and Penny had been happily married for just under ten years and were as close as any couple Chance knew. She was grateful that both of them had agreed to be part of her inner circle when she was elected as Sheriff.

"If I kissed her, you wouldn't have to worry about killing me. She'd do it for you. Did you get a chance to feed the rest of them?"

"I did. Before I go home, I'll let them out into the pasture. I'll keep Sabrina in her stall to rest that foot." Taylor nodded her head. "Bosley there can keep her company."

The big yellow and white cat jumped up and walked across the shelf right outside the stall. He plopped down, licked a paw, then shut his eyes. Chance reached out and stroked across Bosley's head, summoning a deep rumble from the cat.

"Big help he's going to be. I bet he's asleep in five minutes. Being a good mouser is tough work, huh Bosley?" She'd found a tiny, soaking wet kitten on the side of the road two years ago. He now ruled the barn and kept the mice out of the sweet feed.

"Okay, I'm going to try and make Dee's meeting. Call me if you need anything."

"You got it, Sheriff." Taylor touched the tip of her hat and went back to patting Sabrina.

The dogs sniffed each other, as Zeus followed Chance out of the stall before she secured the gate behind them. She stopped to wash her hands and take in the equine smells of the barn—hay, leather, and manure. She finished and they returned to her vehicle for their ride into Davis.

A few minutes into their trip, she saw the black Dodge Durango from the Loop Trail parking area peeking out of the driveway of one of their suspected drug dealers. *Maryland specialty plate with a Baltimore Orioles theme. What are you doing there?* She picked up her mic to call in the plate. Before she depressed the button, she thought better of it and used a scratchpad on her center console to jot down the numbers. She'd run them later to avoid radio traffic. Chance checked the dashboard clock and thought she could still make it to the meeting. No one would mind her being a few minutes late.

Her radio crackled to life, and a different dispatcher called her unit number. "Comm Center to SD-1."

"SD-1. Go ahead."

"SD-4 is out on River Road with an abandoned vehicle in the water. Passenger compartment is visible with no sign of occupants. Fire Department has been alerted. SD-4 has no communication and went to the campground to call it in."

"SD-1 received. I'm responding. Contact a wrecker service so we can start working to get that thing out of the water. Has SD-4 gone back to the scene?"

"Affirmative, SD-1. You're responding River Road."

A vehicle in the river on a summer night was nothing unusual. The driver had probably attempted to use the low-water river crossing and flooded out before making it to the other side. *Let's just hope the only swim they took last night was back to the bank and not downstream.* Several areas on the mountain had experienced heavy rains for the last two nights. The feeder streams that led down into the three rivers that formed the Cheat were nowhere near flood stage. The problem was that certain areas of the river could be deceptively deep. A novice driver or a dislodged rock could easily high center a vehicle, allowing it to stall out.

"SD-1 to Comm Center. Do we have a plate number on that vehicle? If so, text the information to me."

"That's affirmative, Sheriff. The wrecker service has been notified. One of their operators lives close by. He'll be there in ten minutes to assess what equipment will be required."

"That's received." Chance heard her phone ping with a text and let the onboard Bluetooth system read the information to her. An automated voice relayed that the truck belonged to a local resident, someone she knew well. Given the age of the owner, she assumed it was more likely that Mr. Davis's grandson, Tommy, had been the driver attempting to traverse the low-water crossing. Tommy had probably gone for a ride with the two other young men he tended to hang around with. She'd had more than one run-in with the boys, who ranged in age from eighteen to twenty. She'd save the drive to Mr. Davis's place until she had more information. Harold Davis was likely to be unhappy with the bill his grandson's joyride was going to produce.

She waved at several cars that passed by her, as she pulled up beside the other Sheriff's Department vehicle. Kenny Ness and his dog, Tyson, approached as she and Zeus stepped out. When she'd made Sheriff, she'd found enough grant money to purchase K9 dogs for five units. Chance's father had died when he deemed the situation required immediate engagement without backup. It could take assistance up to forty minutes coming from the other side of the county. She was determined that her road officers wouldn't face down a dangerous situation by themselves while they waited. K9 units were expensive, but a portion of every citation they wrote was designated for the care of the animals.

"What do you have Kenny? Any sign of the occupants?"

Kenny pushed his hat up off his forehead and wiped at his brow. He pointed to slide marks in the mud on the bank close to them. "Both side windows are down and water's flowing through them. I spotted shoe prints in the mud there. At least two different tread styles and some handprints like they climbed up from the water. When they ran the plate, it comes back to Harold Davis up in Red Creek."

"I'm betting it's his grandson. Now that I've seen evidence that suggests someone got out, I'll call up there and see if Harold had the truck out or if Tommy was driving. It's always possible it was stolen, but I'm betting against that."

Bob Watson pulled up in his wrecker. After exiting the vehicle, he pulled off his greasy ball cap and smacked it against his leg. He walked up to the group. "I'm guessing my boy's going for a swim to get that thing hooked up. Hell of a time to try and cross there." Bob put his hat back on and shook his head. "It's going to beat the heck out of that undercarriage getting it back to this side."

"I don't doubt it, Bob. How many trucks do you think you'll need?" Chance took her notebook out of her cargo pocket to jot down any instructions. "I'm going to go out to Harold Davis's. I can call back to the shop for you when I'm in range."

"Thanks. Tell Mike to bring the big, flatbed wrecker. I'm going to need the winch with the longest cable, and it's hard to say if the tires will hold to put it on the hook. Oh, and tell Mike to bring his swim trunks." He laughed at his last remark and shook his head.

Chance grinned. "I'll pass that on. Kenny, if you've got this in hand, I'll go make some calls."

"It's not going anywhere fast. I did see some oil on the water down below there, in the shallows, you might call the DEP while you're out."

"That fine won't be pretty. I'll add that to the list." Chance made another note and slid the notebook back into her pocket as she called Zeus. Ten minutes later, they made it to an area where she had decent cell coverage. Once she'd called the wrecker, she stopped by Harold's and determined that Tommy had indeed taken his grandfather's truck. Harold hadn't seen him since. She filled in the eighty-year-old man as to where they'd found his truck and what the procedure would be. He promised to find Tommy and make him call into the Sheriff's Department.

"Thank you, Harold. I'm sorry to deliver such rough news."

"Well, at least he didn't take my new truck. Not sure what his mother will do to him when she catches him. He'd better hope I find him first."

"Tell her not to kill him. I'd hate to have to arrest her." Chance watched as Harold laughed and started to cough. "You okay, Harold?"

A final forceful cough and he assured Chance that he was fine. "She might like the peace and quiet jail would offer. Between Tommy and those other two grandsons of mine, I'm surprised she hasn't lost her mind."

Chance left Harold with the intention of heading to her office. She still wanted to check on the plates from the Dodge Durango she'd spotted at the Kurst property. She'd make a call to the regional drug task force and pass on the information. Her office had limited resources for long-term drug investigations. A group of federal and state officers made up an undercover task force with an ongoing mission to stop the drug trafficking drawn by the tourist population. In the summer, hikers, anglers, and bikers of both the gasoline and pedal style abounded.

She looked at her dash clock. "Good Lord, twelve thirty and I haven't accomplished a damn thing."

The backwoods drive from Red Creek to the county seat was full of abundant wildlife, small streams, and tall, hardwood trees. The county was decked out in shades of green and a brilliant, blue sky dotted with fluffy, white clouds. It would be a perfect day for a trail ride with the horses later in the afternoon, if she could sneak it in.

Once she'd made it back to the more populated area of the county, her cell phone chimed in with a variety of text and voice messages. Her radio crackled with the traffic of other officers and a medical call to the lodge at Blackwater Falls. "All in a day's work."

Zeus led the way into her office, as she pushed open the door and greeted Penny. "Hell of a way to start the day. Can you call this plate in up to the Comm Center? I didn't want to put the traffic out over the air, if you know what I mean."

Penny Lewis stood up from behind the counter and placed her hands on her hips. "Good morning to you too, Sheriff." She held out her hand for the papers Chance clasped and narrowed her eyes.

Chance took a deep breath. "I'm sorry, Penny. Good morning. How are things?"

"Well, given it's after lunch and you're just making it in, I'd say busy. I hate to say it, but it's about to get busier. Brad stopped by and wanted to see you. He had to run over to the courthouse, said he'd be back in about fifteen minutes."

Chance shook her head. "That can't be good. I haven't had near enough coffee to handle whatever his complaint of the day is. Did we get his uniform order wrong again, or is his radio not working this week?"

Penny poured a cup of coffee and handed it to Chance. "Hard to say, but you are about to find out. He's coming out of the courthouse now."

"I'll be in my office." She held up the mug. "Thanks. You didn't happen to slip in a sedative to help me cope with whatever it is this time, did you?"

"No, but I'll make your favorite sandwich as an incentive."

Chance laughed and walked back to her office. "Tell him to wait and that I'm on a call. He's on my time. That should give me a few minutes to put up my best bullshit shields. Did Taylor make it home or is she still at the stables?"

"At the stables. You know her; she won't go rest until that horse seems better. I'll hold him off."

Chance ushered Zeus into her office and hung up her hat as she closed her door. She released a heavy sigh, as she sank into her chair and fired up her laptop while she called Taylor. "How's our girl?" Chance scanned her calendar and email for anything pressing.

Taylor sighed. "She's still holding it up, off and on. I let it soak a good while. I'll do it again after I go get some sleep. I'm headed home now."

"Think I need to call for a vet?"

"Might be worth making a few calls to line someone up if she's not better after the next treatment. Maybe just find out who's available."

"Okay. Get out of there and go to bed. I'll check in on her on my way home. Don't get up any earlier. She can wait until I get there. I'll turn on the Wi-Fi camera and keep an eye on her. Maybe by now, Doc can tell us if anyone has bought his practice. Get some sleep."

"Thanks, Sheriff. Let me know if you notice something. I can be at the stable faster than you can from your office."

A smile spread across Chance's face at her officer's concern. "I'll do that. Now get your ass home." She pulled up the webcam and looked in on each horse.

"Roger that."

Chance disconnected the call and opened an email from U.S. Fish and Wildlife Officer Quade Peters, her former colleague and close friend. She'd barely read one line when her door banged opened and Deputy Brad Waters strode in. Zeus stood quickly and alerted, baring his teeth. He reacted instinctively on the intrusion. She held up her hand to stop Brad and called out. "Zeus, *blijven!*"

Deputy Brad Waters stopped midstride and stared at Zeus, who was standing right in front of him.

Chance could see his hand shaking. "Zeus, *hier!*" Chance spoke his command to come back to her. "*Zit,*" put the dog into a seated position at her side. "Damn it, Brad! You're lucky he's as well trained as he is. You know better than to walk through a closed door without invitation."

"I'm sorry. I wasn't thinking." Brad said, never taking his eyes off Zeus.

"Zeus has one job, and that's to protect me, and he does it well." Chance gave the command for Zeus to lie down, but the dog never took his eyes off Brad. *You don't like him at all do you boy? Can't say that I feel any different.*

"I'm sorry, Sheriff." Brad looked contrite, and like Zeus, his gaze was fixed in place.

Chance didn't make the offer for Brad to sit down, but he took the liberty. "What's so urgent that you needed to see me?"

"I didn't hear you on the phone, so I figured there was no reason you couldn't see me now." Brad's tone was smug and condescending.

"Not that I have to explain myself to you, Deputy, but I'd just hung up the phone. It's customary to address a superior officer by their rank. The last time I checked, I'm your boss, not the other way around."

"Yes, Sheriff." Brad's words were spoken through gritted teeth.

He'd run against her the year she'd been elected. An embarrassing loss hadn't endeared her to him.

"Now, what is it that you so urgently need to discuss with me on your day off? Since you approached me and I did not call you in, understand that you will not be paid overtime or compensation time for this meeting." Brad had once tried to claim a casual conversation as a meeting on his timecard. "Understood?"

Brad glared at her for a few seconds. "Understood."

Chance waved her hand for him to proceed.

"With my seniority and years of service, I've earned the position of chief deputy. It's not..."

Chance held up her hand. "This is the last time I'm discussing this with you, Brad. The chief deputy serves at the will and pleasure of the sheriff. In my department," she stopped to lean forward on her desk and stare him directly in the eyes, "and this is *my* department as the duly elected and sworn-in Sheriff of Tucker County, I make the decision who my chief deputy is, not you. I don't care about your years of service or the fact that you served as Chief Deputy under the previous administration. You took that position to run a campaign for this office two years ago. That move left you without civil service protection." Her gaze was steady, as crimson rose out of the neck of his wrinkled T-shirt. "I allowed you to rejoin the rank and file when I took over, because of your service."

"Mighty nice of you."

"If you are unhappy with your position, I'll be waiting for your resignation to hit my desk. You're the one that asked me to fill the open slot when Larry went back to active duty in the army. I didn't seek you out. I agreed because I knew you needed the insurance for your family. If this arrangement doesn't suit you anymore, feel free to look for other employment. If not, then understand that I will not entertain this conversation again. Taylor Lewis is my chief deputy and will remain so until one of us decides we don't want it that way. Do I make myself clear, Deputy?"

Brad scrambled up out of his chair. His girth prevented him from clearing the arms without difficulty. "Crystal."

Chance watched him limp out of her office and down the hall, sure his gout was acting up again by his uneven gait. Bailiff duty prevented him from being on patrol and gave him weekends and holidays off. No K9 was assigned to him, because he was unable to complete the vigorous training and regiment required. He was currently on vacation.

Chance pulled his employment file out of her desk to make a note of the confrontation with a time and date stamp. She didn't trust Brad Waters, and she had good reason. The chair creaked as she leaned back, allowing her hands to rest on the arms. She started a slow rocking motion and looked up to see Penny in the doorway, holding a small plate with a sandwich on it. The door was still open from Brad's exit, and Chance waved her in.

Penny smiled and set down the peanut butter and banana sandwich. "I laced this with Advil. You shouldn't notice, given the thick layer of crunchy peanut butter." She tilted her head as if she were examining Chance critically. "That bad?"

"Somewhere, he got the idea that I was in the market for a new chief deputy."

Penny narrowed her eyes. "My wife decides to take another job somewhere and forget to tell me?"

Chance loved Penny's humor and was extremely fond of the woman who ran her office. They'd met at a Fraternal Order of Police Christmas party, while Taylor was still working with the Marshals Service. Chance had developed a friendship with the couple, and they'd even doubled dated with one of her previous girlfriends, a local television reporter.

"Not that I know of. Zeus almost made lunch out of him when he came through the door unannounced. You should have seen Brad's face. All the K9s around here, and somehow he forgets how protective of their handlers they are. I thought Brad was going to piss himself."

Penny ran a hand over the dog's head. "Don't bite him, Zeus. The new vet hasn't opened her doors yet, and you'd certainly get food poisoning."

Chance caught the part about the new vet in town, a female vet. *Could it be? No, no it couldn't be. Too many years had gone by.* "We have a new vet in town?"

"Seems so. Doc Hendricks didn't give a name or a date when she'd be taking over his practice. Give him a call."

"Well, my lucky Penny, this is good news. Keep your fingers crossed that if Sabrina doesn't look better by tonight, the new Doc will be willing to see her first patient tomorrow." Chance took a bite of the sandwich in front of her and chewed. "What else do you have for me today?"

"Quade wants you to call him. He sent you an email with some paperwork, but he needs to talk to you. Something about renewal certifications? I don't know. Said he'd be back in his office around one.

Other than that, this stack of papers needs your once over and signature."

Chance looked at the stack that seemed to grow daily, even if she made sure that corner was empty by the end of each day. She grimaced and took another bite of her sandwich. "You might need to add a side of Jim Beam to these sandwiches if you're going to keep burying me in paperwork. I'll get on it after I call Quade. Thanks Penny."

"Anything for you, Sheriff, except the Jim Beam here at the office. You'll have to stop by the house if you want that."

"I'll keep that in mind." Chance chewed as she dialed Quade.

"U.S. Fish and Wildlife, Officer Peters speaking."

Chance smiled at the familiar phone etiquette. "Hey Quade, keeping those fish safe and sound?"

"Keeping them away from the likes of you. By the way, we need to drop a line soon. It's been too long since we've hit the Cheat together. How are you, Chance?"

"Doing my best to serve and protect. What can I do for you, my friend?"

Chance could hear papers shuffling in the background.

"Seems I have formal notification that you passed all your recerts. Anytime you want to come back and play on the federal side or pick up a Pulaski again, I've got papers that say you are fit for duty."

Chance nearly choked trying to swallow the peanut butter. "I saw the attachments to your email. I'm happy to help out on a call basis anytime. Although I appreciate the offer, no thanks. I've become pretty accustomed to being my own boss and enjoying this plush office."

Quade's laughter was contagious. "Chance, I've been in that broom closet you call an office, and plush is not exactly how I'd describe it. When are you supposed to get your new digs?"

Chance let her head fall back against the office chair. "And leave the beautifully artistic, water stained ceilings in this high-class joint? I make sure Penny's office is water free and comfortable. I'd rather be on the road than sitting at this desk. I could use that Pulaski to dig my way out from under this pile of paperwork though. My old one is on a set of hooks right above the door. I need to move it closer so I can dig a line to keep anything else from making its way in here."

The axe with the adze on the back of the blade was, at one time, as familiar to her as her own hand. Years as a smoke jumper had taught her all the things this specialized tool could do when fighting a forest fire. "We need to do lunch soon, the fishing will be harder to find time for, given your schedule. Call me and I'll take a vacation day if you get some free time. Until then, I need to keep Penny on my good side and practice my penmanship. It was good to talk to you, Quade. Stay safe, brother."

"Right back at you. Tell Mags hi for me, and I'll watch the calendar."

Quade signed off, and Chance washed down the last of her lunch with a swig of cold coffee. The first three documents on her desk required no signature. They were bench warrants for a few of the locals who had failed to appear for their court dates. The papers she held mandated that she locate the subjects and take them forthwith to jail. The court would sort it out later. With those documents acknowledged, she moved on to invoices for the stables and ammunition, and several legal notifications she needed to take care of as the chief tax collector for the county.

Last in the pile was a uniform request from Brad Water's for new pants. *Pain in my ass.* Clicking on a folder on her computer, she pulled up the uniform budget to see how much was left in Brad's allowance. There, in black and white, was an invoice where she'd ordered him three new pairs of pants less than four months ago. His uniform allotment was depleted for the year. She opened a word document and supplied the dates of his uniform requisitions showing the depletion of his account. Along with that, she copied and pasted the department's uniform policy, which clearly stated that any request over and above the allotment was the responsibility of the individual. Only uniforms damaged during the performance of their duties would be replaced with discretionary funds. Seventy-five percent of the policies she had to write were because of Brad Waters. The man knew how to work the system and tested the limits every chance he got. The printed copies of the document were retrieved and signed. She would give Brad his copy and make him sign that he'd received it.

Penny spoke up from her desk. "Firing him would be less paperwork."

Chance grumbled over her shoulder. "How did you know what I'm doing has to do with him?"

"Anytime you deal with him, you get a tic in your cheek and your ears get beet red. I assume you saw his uniform request?"

Chance nodded her head.

"Hand me that and I'll have him sign it tomorrow when he comes in." Penny shook her head in disgust. "I have no idea what makes one man so miserable. You know he only does this to see how much he can piss you off."

"I regret ever giving him a job when Larry left. What's done is done. I was trying to help his family."

"Talk about biting the hand that feeds you."

"You don't have to give this to him. I'd rather he try to undermine me and leave you alone. Not a thing he can do to me but piss me off."

"Suit yourself, I offered."

The base radio on the shelf broke their conversation. "Comm Center to SD-1."

Chance picked up the mic. "SD-1 to Comm Center, go ahead."

"We have a report of an injured hiker out at Lindy Point. A child has fallen into a crevice and is unable to climb back up. The parents are with her but are unable to reach her."

"SD-1 received and responding. Alert the SAR team. I assume you're alerting fire and medical?"

"That's affirmative. They're being dispatched now."

"I'll call in for more detail."

"Comm Center received. SD-1 responding."

Chance grabbed her hat and headed for the door. She walked back to her office to retrieve her portable radio from the charger. The rest of her gear was in the Yukon. The tactical team would bring the rescue gear. Zeus loaded into the back, and Chance flipped on her lights and siren. As she headed to the stables, she called the Comm Center.

"Hey Pam, this is Chance, fill me in."

"Thirteen-year-old female, hiking with her parents. She's conscious and talking to them, but they have no way to get down to where she is. From what she's told them, her leg might be broken. They had someone in their party run all the way back to the lodge to alert us. He did give me GPS coordinates. I've sent them to your phone. I know you want the tactical team, and we've sent out the page. Any other resources you want?"

"Get the helicopter on standby. I'm going up to get Kelly and ride out there. I can make much better time with her. Call Taylor and let her know what's going on. She probably hasn't had enough sleep yet, but I doubt I can keep her home. Tell the fire department I'll contact them on Tac one with details."

"Will do. Be careful."

"Always." Chance disconnected the call and made her way up the mountain quickly. The stables were only about another fifteen minutes away and close to the park. Once she was on horseback it would be a ten-minute ride up the trail to the state park and likely another thirty to forty minutes out to Lindy Point. She'd check her GPS coordinates when she got to the stables to confirm. "Hang on, little one, I'm coming."

Chapter Two

CHANCE PULLED INTO THE stable and wasn't surprised to see Taylor's Yukon. She and Zeus entered the stall where Taylor had already thrown Kelly's saddle on and was tightening down the belly strap. Chance grabbed the bridle, slid the bit into the horse's mouth, and pulled the leather over her head.

"I'll get Jill ready and be right behind you." Taylor held up her hand. "Before you ask, yes, I've had enough rest. I left Midas at the house."

"I trust you. I know you'd rather be on Sabrina. She'll be miffed at you for riding Randy's horse."

Taylor led Kelly out of her stall. "I'll slip her a few more carrots. Can't take a chance on her injuring that foot more. Pam gave me all the info. SAR may need to bring the equipment out there by horseback if this kid is where I think she is. No way to get an ATV out there."

Chance retrieved a few pieces of hardware and a bag of rescue rope and slipped on the backpack containing her helmet and rescue harness. With one foot in the stirrup and pulling on the saddle horn she swung onto Kelly's back. Zeus pranced around beside them, ready to go. She entered the GPS codes from the Comm Center into her small, handheld unit. After checking the general area, she was headed to, she pulled on the reins and started Kelly away from the stable.

"Meet me at the main part of Lindy Point. What I'm seeing with these coordinates tells me she's out past that. We'll have to do the rocks on foot."

Taylor nodded. "I'm right behind you."

Chance urged Kelly into a trot on the gravel road and entered the woods left of the main road. A well-beaten path wound through the tall oaks and maples. Everything was green and lush this time of year. It was still warm this early in the afternoon. Once the sun crept toward the horizon, the temperatures would begin to fall. It was imperative that they rescue the girl before they lost the light. It was after two in the afternoon, leaving them about seven hours of daylight. The injured girl was in an area where some of the rock crevice were over sixty feet deep. Until she arrived, Chance had no clear picture of the rescue obstacles

"You doing okay, Zeus?" Chance looked at her K9 and was rewarded with a bark as he bounded beside her. It had taken many hours of training to ensure both her horse and her dog were comfortable working with each other.

The trail began to climb. She passed a small stream, taking time to allow Zeus and Kelly a quick drink before they started off again. The path ahead wasn't easy, and there would be no open water source nearby. Two canteens traveled with her to be used on arrival. Taylor would care for both horses when she got there. Chance would continue to push toward the girl.

Squirrels and chipmunks chattered out their annoyance, and a few deer were spooked from their grazing, as she rode on through the forest. Her radio had been relaying information about the responding units. Chance took a second to give an update on her progress.

"SD-1 to Comm Center."

"Comm Center to SD-1, go ahead."

"I'm about ten minutes from Lindy Point. SD-2 should be about fifteen minutes behind me. Any updates?"

"SD-1, your tactical team responded approximately fifteen minutes ago with SR-5. They'll get as close as they can and await your instructions. You should be able to reach them now on Tac one."

"Okay, Comm Center. I'll advise when I reach the scene." Chance thought about the equipment on Search and Rescue Unit Five. The gear needed for a high-angle rescue would be difficult to transport out to the scene. She might need help from the equine community. It would take time to get those resources to an access point. Although she hated to activate them without having eyes on the situation, daylight was burning. "Comm Center. Call the equine volunteers. See if they can mobilize to transport personnel and equipment. Once I get there, I can advise if I need them to start the transport of resources."

"Comm Center received. Equine unit will be called."

Chance patted her horse's neck. "Okay, Kelly, let's find that kid." The horse gently nickered a response and pushed on.

The laurel bushes were everywhere. Twisted branches and roots created thick cover that was difficult to maneuver through or around. After another ten minutes, Chance had to dismount and lead Kelly through what openings she could find, as she tried to meet up with a trail that would bring her close to the point. From there, she would need to walk in to find the trapped girl. Chance prayed the frantic parents hadn't injured themselves in an attempt to get to the girl.

Zeus lagged behind slightly as they approached the area she'd need to traverse on foot. When Kelly reached an impasse at the grey field of large granite boulders. Chance pulled out a collapsible bowl and poured one of her canteens into it. Kelly's burden had been greater, so Chance held the bowl as the horse drank. Zeus got his share when she set the bowl on the ground, allowing her K9 several long laps. She tethered Kelly to a tree to ensure her safety, then pulled off the length of rope she'd brought and threaded it over her head to rest on her shoulder.

"Okay, Zeus, it's you and me from here. Stay, Kelly." She patted the horse's nose and noted the GPS coordinates where she was leaving her mount. She knew Taylor would follow the same path and wind up near here, where she would secure both horses before making her way to the incident scene. Chance was grateful that Taylor would need little instruction. That was one reason why she made such a great chief deputy.

Her eyes checked the placement of each foot, as she made her way across the craggy surface. Zeus effortlessly leapt from one rock to another. The sound of a child's cry floated to her on the wind, and she picked up her pace until she was looking at a nightmare. A fortyish-year-old man was trying to make his way down the side of a boulder, while a frantic woman lay face down on the top, murmuring down into a crack in the rocks.

"Sir! I'm Sheriff Chance Fitzsimmons. Please stop and make your way back to me. I'm going to throw you a rope. Tie it around your waist, while I anchor you and bring you back up. You won't be able to make it to her that way and will cause us to have two patients in need of rescue."

The woman lying on the rocks startled and jerked her head toward Chance. "Please, help us!"

"I will. I need to bring him back to safety. Keep talking to her. Sir, I'm going to need your help back here." She yelled to the man, as she tossed him the rope. He shook his head no. "Listen to me, I've climbed those rocks, and you'll never make it without a harness and rope. You'll be more help up here with me." Chance tied the rope to a nearby tree and watched the man acquiesce. "Tie it high, up under your arms, and I'll help pull you back up here."

The man did as Chance instructed, and she helped him back to the top. Tears stained his face, as he collapsed on the ground, completely spent. "Okay, I'm Sheriff Chance Fitzsimmons. What are your names?" She indicated the woman still lying near the large crack between two huge boulders.

The man was pale and near frenzied. "That's Amy...a...nd...I'm St...Steve."

Chance handed him a pair of gloves from her pack. "Okay, Steve. What's your daughter's name?"

Large tears rolled down ruddy cheeks, and a sob escaped from his body. "Cassie."

She reached out and put a hand on his shoulder. "We're going to get her out. I need you to stay focused, okay? Cry happy tears when we've got her back up here with you."

He wiped at his face and put on the gloves. "Okay, what do you need me to do?"

"I'm going to put a stronger anchor over at that tree. Take my bag over near your wife, and I'll be right there. I'll need to see what's going on, so I can call in more resources. We're racing daylight, but you know how long it took you guys to get out here, so try to be patient. It will take time."

Steve grabbed the backpack and walked over near the crack in the rock. Chance tied a tensionless anchor by looping the rope around the tree several times. This allowed an even distribution of the weight on the rescue rope. With the anchor firmly in place, she walked to the edge. Zeus paced beside her, as she took out her harness and slipped her legs inside the loops. "Amy, I'm going to see if I can get down to her. What's Cassie been saying about her injuries?" Amy stared down into the crack, not acknowledging that she'd been spoken to. "Amy, I need you to help me. Come on now." She knelt beside Amy and touched her on the shoulder.

"She...she thinks her leg is broken. It's tucked underneath her. Cassie's been crying, but she's gotten quiet over the last fifteen minutes. I hear whimpers but not much talking."

The rough granite abraded Chance's elbows, when she lay down on the stone to peer into the opening. "Cassie? Cassie, can you hear me? My name's Chance. Can you talk to me, Cassie?"

Chance listened, hearing nothing more than soft crying far below her. To her right, the crack opened up slightly and appeared to give her a better option for dropping over the ledge. Two years ago, she'd rescued a dog out of the crevice a few feet farther to her right. She mentally mapped out her descent and reached for her radio. "SD-1 to

SR-5."

"SR-5, go ahead Chance."

"I've got a thirteen-year-old girl down in that same crevice where we rescued that dog a few years ago. I'll send coordinates to pinpoint. We're going to need a tripod, rigging, and the Sked stretcher. Bring a Sager splint in. I haven't started down in yet, but the family reports the girl's leg is bent underneath her. Has the equine unit mobilized?" Chance knew they would need a protective stretcher that was flexible enough to maneuver up the walls and out the top. The Sked fit that description. The thick plastic was protective and easy to haul.

"That's affirmative. The new vet has arrived to help with any injuries to the horses. We have an ambulance in staging, and the medevac helicopter is on standby. They'll head our way as soon as we give them the go-ahead. Do you have any other orders for us?"

Chance recognized the voice on the other end of the radio transmission. Sarah Riker was a rope rescue technician and had all the training and knowledge needed for this type of high-risk rescue. At the sound of Zeus's bark, Chance looked up to see Taylor walking out onto the rock near her. "No, that's all, Sarah. SD-2 just arrived. I'm going to start a rappel down to the girl to see if I can assess and stabilize her condition. SD-2 will be operational command out here and will make contact with you on this channel. SD-1 clear."

"We read you, SD-1. SD-2 is operational command. We'll start working our way to you."

Chance took a quick GPS reading and called in the coordinates to dispatch. "Taylor, if you'll man the rack, I'll try and get down in. If I remember last time, getting over the lip was the worst of it. After that, I've got to make my way over some narrow outcrops to where she is, so I don't come down directly on top of her. I can't see her to know if she's hit the bottom, so I'm going to have to take it slow." Chance put her hat on the ground and slipped on her helmet.

"Okay, let me check you over." Taylor checked all the knots and Chance's seat-harness straps. "I'm not even going to tell you not to hurt yourself. Last time you did this, you looked like you rolled around on glass, even with a long-sleeved shirt. I'll have the first aid kit ready."

Chance tapped Taylor's helmet and leaned back against the rope. "On rope." She made her way over to the opening and tried to gently maneuver over the edge. Without the ability to gain elevation, there was no real way to avoid the initial drop and the subsequent smash into the face of the rock. She managed it with only a hit to her knee. She could see Zeus staring at her over the top of the ledge. "Zeus, *af.*" He backed from the edge and lay down, and she heard Taylor tell him, "Good boy."

"Slack." Chance needed Taylor to feed the rope and lower her. The initial rappel she'd planned had been replaced with this lowering maneuver once Taylor arrived to help her. Chance felt the rope slowly allowing her to descend the wall. The first narrow outcropping was hiding Cassie from her view. Working her way around it wouldn't be easy, and she expected to lose several layers of skin on her cheek. "Ouch, shit."

"Chance, you all right?" Taylor's voice echoed off the walls.

Chance cursed softly. She shut her eyes and pushed away from the outcrop twenty feet down from the top edge. "Yes, I'm fine. Just keep that first aid kit handy. I'm probably going to need it. Slack." Once she cleared the ledge, she could see the red-headed girl about twenty-five feet below her in a narrow wedge. The space wasn't uniform across the opening and funneled in the area where Cassie was wedged.

"Hold." She eyed the patient and could see her chest rising and falling. "She's breathing. I've got about another fifteen feet to reach her. I have to shift my position. Slack." Chance needed to move over to an area of the rock face that widened out to the right of Cassie. The rope continued to feed out, dropping her down until she stopped to push off and around an obstacle. "Five feet."

A few more seconds, and Chance's heart broke at the sight of the young girl's tear-stained and dirt-smeared face. She detached her harness carabiner from the line, to allow her better movement. The crack narrowed below them to less than six inches, removing the danger in disconnecting. "Off rope!" From this distance below the top, she needed to yell to be heard. Removing the backpack she'd let dangle below her on the descent, she pulled out a stethoscope and blood pressure cuff. "Cassie, can you hear me? My name's Chance, and I'm going to get you out of here. Where are you hurt?"

There was a small whimper coming from the child, as Chance leaned in to see her patient's injuries. *A, B, C, Chance. Airway, breathing, circulation. Get the basics done.* She could tell Cassie was breathing, though she wasn't sure how patent her airway was at the time. A few major abrasions were dirt encrusted and oozing blood. A, B, and C were at least reasonably intact. She cleared some dirt from Cassie's eyes and was rewarded when they opened slightly. "Hey there. I think we need to figure out a way back to the top. What do you think?"

Cassie barely nodded and began to cry again. "My leg hurts."

"I'm sure it does. How about anywhere else? Can you tell me if your arms hurt or your back?" Chance unrolled the child-sized blood pressure cuff. "I'm just going to check a few things and see how you're doing, okay?"

Cassie nodded.

"Try not to move your neck any. Just say yes and no if you can."

"Okay."

"Good, now hang on while I listen." Chance wrapped the cuff around the girl's arm and took a reading. The values were in normal range, though her pulse rate was up. That was to be expected given what she'd been through. The problem was that the heart often tried to compensate for a major injury, and the symptoms were masked until the heart could no longer maintain normal function. Then the patient would begin to crash. Chance wanted to get Cassie up and out of the crevice before that happened. Her radio crackled to life. "SD-2 to SD-1 in the blind, search and rescue has arrived, and we're setting up a retrieval tripod. Let us know when you need anything. Sarah will be coming over the side as soon as she can to help with packaging."

Chance had her hands free enough to be able to answer. *In the blind* meant that information was being relayed without making a confirmed connection first. "SD-1, message received. Don't send anyone bigger than Sarah. It's a tight fit where we are. The two of us can package. We'll need the Sked." She watched as her rescue rope pinged off the sides on its ascent back out of the crack in the rock. "I haven't been able to put a collar on or get access to check on that leg." She waited for Taylor to repeat the message before she turned back to Cassie. "Okay, try to move as little as possible while I check you over. Let me know if something hurts."

"I'm scared," Cassie quavered. The sliver of light coming from the top made everything seem dark above them. The only other illumination came from Chance's headlamp.

"Would it help if I made it so you could see better?"

"Yeah."

Chance pulled out several glow sticks from her cargo pocket, bent them to release the chemicals, and shook the tubes. A greenish glow filled the crevice and let Chance and Cassie push the darkness back. "Okay, is that better?"

"Uh huh."

Chance began a gentle head to toe assessment, making note of any area Cassie said was painful. Her leg did appear to be broken. The lower part of her left leg was bent at an odd angle, hinting at a closed tib-fib fracture. Chance used her body to protect Cassie from the small rocks and fine dirt that fell on them from Sarah's descent.

Within minutes, her frequent rescue partner was on the other side of the funnel. Chance could see she was standing with one leg up on a rock and the other on a small patch of the bottom. "Off rope!" Sarah unclipped and looked at Chance. "What do you need?"

"Hey, Sarah, this is Cassie. Cassie, Sarah and I are going to put some equipment on you, so we can keep you from injuring anything else on the way out. Okay?"

"Please hurry."

Sarah met Chance's eyes. "Cassie, I'm going to help Chance, and we'll do this as fast as we can."

Chance pulled a cervical collar out of her trauma bag, and Sarah reached from the other side to help fit it around Cassie's slim neck. "Sarah, let's pass my rope under her arms and back. That will let us form a loop they can pull from the top. Once we get her out of the wedge, we can pass her to this side where I have more room."

"Sounds like a plan." Sarah moved into position.

Chance relayed the plan to the rescuers on top and said she would advise when they needed to raise the line to free Cassie. Once the loop was secure, Chance looked at Cassie. "Not going to lie, kiddo, your leg is broken. When we lift you to free it, it's going to hurt. You grab my arm here and squeeze as tight as you need to until we get you lying flat on your back." Cassie nodded her head, and Chance keyed her radio. "Go ahead and haul, nice and slow."

Chance tried to hold Cassie's neck, cradling her head with her forearms. "Haul, slowly!" The rope around Cassie went taut, and Sarah tried to support her leg as it was released from the rock. The girl's scream incited a cacophony of noise above them.

Sarah pulled out her radio. "Okay, she's free. We've got to get her to Chance. Be ready to lower." They moved Cassie over to Chance's side, and Sarah scrambled up and over to them before she keyed her radio. "Lower."

Chance grabbed the little girl and placed her on the confined space board Sarah had brought down with her. "Let's splint the tib-fib fracture. Radio up top to get that Sked down here as soon as you can." Sarah nodded and transmitted the order, as she pulled out a moldable splint to stabilize the fracture.

Chance held protective hands around Cassie's neck, as she asked her simple questions. "Do you know what day it is?"

"It's Tuesday." Cassie's small voice was broken with sobs.

"And who is the president?"

"Mommy says we have to be respectful, but I don't have to say that guy's name, do I?"

Chance and Sarah both laughed. "No, I guess you don't. How about where you were before you fell down here?"

"We were hiking at Lindy Point. I tried to jump the crack and slipped. That's how I ended up down here."

Sarah put her hand on Cassie's arm. "Cassie, we have to splint this leg. It's going to hurt again. After I'm done, it will feel better, because it won't be able to move around okay? Grab onto Chance's arm."

Cassie did as instructed. As predicted, she yelled out in pain as the splint was applied. They maneuvered her onto the spine board and stabilized her for transport with head blocks and straps. A Sked hung above them, and Chance watched as Sarah grabbed the tag line attached to the bottom of the device. Sarah maneuvered the equipment down to them. The same tag would help them keep the stretcher from getting snagged on the way back up. When everything had been retrieved, Chance watched Sarah put a small helmet and a set of safety glasses on the child. The two deftly picked up the board and slid the Sked under Cassie, before closing the webbing protectively around her. The unique stretcher would allow them to haul Cassie out vertically, making it easier to navigate the rocks.

"I'll go up with her." Chance announced, as she fastened the carabiner to her harness. "You belay us from here."

"I got you. Get her back to the top, her parents are pretty frazzled. So is Zeus for that matter. Taylor has him by the collar."

"That's my boy. Okay, Cassie. Let's get out of here. Sound good to you?" She smiled as Cassie poked her fingers out in the 'okay' sign. Small tears were still running out of the corner of her eyes. "You've been very brave. It's almost over. Sarah, get that chopper in the air. By the time we get to the top, they should be able to land that bird as close as possible."

"Will do, Chance." Sarah grabbed for her radio and relayed to the crew up top that Chance and Cassie were on rope, as well as the other instructions for patient transport.

A few seconds later, Chance felt the slack go out of both ropes that led out of the crevice. Slowly, she and Cassie made their way up the rock face. They had to stop occasionally to work around those jagged outcroppings, one of which cut a deep laceration into Chance's arm. Twenty minutes later, the Sked made its way out of the hole and was pulled to the surface. Once they cleared Cassie out, they brought Chance up and lowered the retrieval line for Sarah.

Up top looked like an equipment trade show. Rope, rescue hardware, and slings lay positioned on a tarp ready for use. Years of practice for this type of rescue made Chance very glad to be working with these volunteer professionals.

"Off rope." Zeus crept close to her and licked her hand. "I'm okay, boy. Thanks for keeping watch for me."

Taylor stood at her side, holding first aid equipment in her hand. "Never took his eyes off that ledge. How bad?" She pointed to the gash on Chance's arm.

"It's just a flesh wound, Chicken." The Black Knight skit from *Monty Python and the Holy Grail* was a frequent quip thrown out when she hurt herself.

Taylor grabbed Chance and made her sit on a nearby rock, where she began to pour sterile water over the laceration.

Chance winced. "Ow, that smarts."

"I'm betting you're going to need stitches in this. You've got a hell of a scrape across your cheek too. Lean your head over." Chance pulled off her helmet and allowed Taylor to flush out the abrasion.

Chance looked up to see Steve and Amy beside Cassie, tears of relief running liberally down their faces. "She's a lucky little girl. About fifteen feet to the left and she'd have been another thirty feet down." She watched as Cassie was loaded into a basket so the rescuers could carry her back out to the landing zone. "It's going to take at least an hour to walk her out of here. Better get some fresh relief staged along the way. Luckily, she probably only weighs ninety pounds or so."

Taylor smiled. "Already staged. I had Max get Kelly and Jill to bring them over to where they left the rest of the horses. We'll ride back out to the ambulance and get you checked out. There's Sarah coming up." Taylor motioned with her head to the tripod. "How come she doesn't look like she took a header off the rocks?"

"Well for one thing, there was more help to get her over the edge, smartass. If you're done mother henning me to death, I'd like to go check on Cassie."

Taylor handed over her hat. "You're as patched up as I can do for now. You'll need a trip to Urgent Care for stitches in that arm, Chance.

No arguments or I'm calling Mags."

"Good Lord, don't do that. I'm betting she's already at my house listening to all this traffic." They made their way to Cassie's side, where Amy hugged Chance and Steve shook her hand.

"We can't thank you enough, Sheriff." Amy covered her mouth when her voice broke.

"Cassie did all the work. I was just along for the ride. Take care of yourself, kiddo. Let me know how you're doing, okay?"

Cassie gave her a thumbs up and closed her eyes as the crew started to carry her out through the laurel bushes and trees.

Chance rubbed the top of Zeus's head. "Let's go home, boy."

Zeus barked, and both Taylor and Chance started walking behind the personnel carrying Cassie. A crew behind them began to pack up the equipment.

Chapter Three

IT TOOK CHANCE NEARLY an hour to make it back out to the staging and incident command post. Numerous agencies had mobilized, as well as a local television reporter from the nearest station, almost three counties away. As soon as Mya Knolls saw her, the unmistakable gleam of attraction shone in the seductive woman's eyes. Chance had dated her for a very short time, and Mya made it no secret she was more than ready to try again.

Mya's dream was to be a reporter in a large city on the east coast. Her ambition was well known, even if her sexuality was not. Chance knew there was no future with someone whose dreams pulled her far away. Chance was a true homebody and had spent enough time away. As Mya came toward her, Chance swung down from Kelly's back and put up her hands to stop her.

"Go see my public information officer, Mya. I have no comment at this time."

Mya put her hands on her hips and grinned. "I think we've gotten past the point of needing a go between, Chance. I think I've earned hearing it from the source."

"Well, this source isn't talking. The PIO is." Chance tried to hide her annoyance at Mya's flirtation. When she was working, Chance kept things all business. She would never be accused of using the uniform to attract anyone. This was her profession, and she intended to keep it all business when she was representing her office.

Mya glared at her and swung her blonde waves off her shoulder as she turned on her low heels and walked away from Chance and Taylor. She stumbled in the gravel when a heel got caught. She righted herself and tried to appear unfazed.

Taylor let out a low whistle. "She might have been a bitch, but even I'll admit she is easy on the eyes, my friend."

Chance glared at Taylor. "I wonder if Penny would agree with that statement."

"Hell yes, she mentioned that more than once on our double dates.

If she only had the personality to match." Taylor shook her head. "Let's get you over to the medical tent. See if they can clean out that laceration on your arm."

Chance had resigned herself to the fact she'd soon be sporting stitches, or at least skin glue, to close the wound. She was busy listening to some traffic on the radio, as they led the horses to the rehab area. She felt a sharp elbow to the ribs from Taylor.

"Check that out."

Chance scowled and rubbed her side. "Check what out?" She looked in the direction Taylor's head was leaning. A woman in dark-green canvas pants, work boots, and a light-green polo shirt was bent over the horse hoof between her knees. She was digging something out from beneath the shoe. The chestnut gelding nickered, as the woman released his leg and patted his side. When she stood up, her gaze locked on Chance. Jacqueline St. Claire stood with the hoof pick still in her hand. She didn't move for several seconds, then broke the stare down and returned to the horse she was helping.

"Jax," the word escaped Chance's mouth before she had a chance to put up her internal mask.

"I hear that's the new vet Jacqueline St. Claire. Word is she's old Doc Hendricks—"

"Niece." Another word floated past her lips without conscious thought. Chance was eighteen again and floating on an inner tube in the Cheat River. A gorgeous woman in a red, white, and blue bikini top and cutoff jeans floated beside her. She wore Chance's ball cap. Her black hair pulled through the hole in the back. The ponytail was so long, it dipped into the water. Her shapely arms draped over the sides; her fingers barely trailed the water. Long, tanned legs floated in front of her. Mirrored aviator sunglasses Jax had stolen from the dash of Chance's truck covered pale, almost ice like, green eyes.

"Chance?" Taylor interrupted her pleasant trip down memory lane with a slight touch to her arm.

"Wha...?"

"Are you okay? You're as pale as the sheets on Mag's clothesline. You look like you've seen a ghost."

"I have. I haven't seen that woman in thirty-six years."

Taylor whistled and looked back to the makeshift corral. "I'm guessing there's some history?"

"You could say that. Come on, I'll introduce you." Chance led Kelly, with Zeus hot on her heels. Taylor followed with Jill in tow.

"With the look she's giving you, I think I'd better go find my fire gear. Holy shit, Chance."

"Let it be, Taylor. That was a long time ago."

"I don't think it's me that needs reminding."

"Shhhh." Chance couldn't hold back the smile pushing up the corners of her mouth. "Jacqueline St. Claire, as I live and breathe."

"Chance Fitzsimmons. I was wondering when I'd see you. When Uncle Marty called and said the equine team was going out for this, I thought it couldn't hurt to tag along in case one of them got hurt. Looks like it wasn't only the horses that sustained injuries on this incident." She pointed to Chance's elbow and the blood drips landing on top of her boot.

"Just a scratch. I'll have medical look at it. Jax, this is Taylor Lewis, my chief deputy. Taylor, this is Jacqueline St. Claire, or as I knew her, Jax. Do you still go by that or did you go all formal at the University of California Veterinary School?"

"It's still Jax. Jacqueline is my mother and too damned long to write on paperwork day after day. Nice to meet you, Taylor. How are you, Chance? God, it seems like a lifetime since I've seen you. How long has it bee—?"

Chance cut her off. "Thirty-six years since you headed off to school." She looked the woman over as discretely as she could. "I thought maybe I'd hear from you back then. Although, I can't give you too much hell, I spent about twenty years away from here as a smoke jumper. One too many close calls took me out of commission." She held up her left arm where the scar tissue was still corded and raised.

Jax's hand flew to her mouth. "Chance, are you all right?"

"You know me. Takes more than this," she motioned with her head, "to keep me down. We got rolled over up in Montana. They don't make those baked potato bags for two. I was hanging out a little."

Jax stepped forward and gently put a hand on Chance's arm. "Marty said you were a smoke jumper. He told me you're the county sheriff now. Congratulations."

Taylor laughed. "You might want to offer condolences instead." She looked at Chance. "I'm going to go check in over at command, see if they need any help. Jax, with the horses we use for the department and the dogs, I'm sure we'll be seeing a lot of you." Taylor tipped her hat and walked Jill away from the two.

Chance shook her head and settled her Stetson a little straighter. "Shocked as hell to see you here, Jax."

Jax laughed. "Why don't you let me clean up that wound and wrap it again for you? We can chat."

Chance squinted at her. "Aren't you a vet? Zeus seems to be fine. You can check him over if you're looking for something to do."

"He's very handsome. Belgian Malinois make great K9s. Nice to meet you, Zeus." She held out her hand and let him sniff.

"You know your breeds. I'd be lost without him. He knows me better than I know myself."

"I don't doubt that. There's a special bond formed when you work that closely. I witnessed it when I was on the SWAT team out in California as a tactical medic. Hence my ability to clean human wounds."

"Tactical SWAT team?"

"You know how it is. Dad wanted my brother to follow him into law enforcement. Mom wanted me to be a doctor. I tried to find a foot in both worlds after Jennings."

"Jax, I'm sorry about your brother. I truly am."

Jax's brother and his wife had been killed in a freak accident while hiking on part of the Appalachian Trail. They'd left their two small kids with Jax's parents.

"Hard to believe that was twenty-two years ago. The twins are all grown up. Jessie went into the air force, and Jackie is a stay-at-home mom with two little ones of her own. They were only five when Jennings and Lynn died. Dad and mother raised them as if they were their own. Second-chance family you know?"

"I know it about killed your Uncle Marty and Aunt Mary. Mags kept a close eye on them. Now you're back here to take over his practice?"

Jax smiled and put her hands in her back pockets. "I am. I needed a change, and Marty wanted to retire. I spent a lifetime out in California in the rat race. I'm looking for a slower pace and clients who appreciate my services."

"Well, speaking of that. I've got a mare with a sore foot. Might be a stone bruise, but I'm betting abscess. After this all dies down, will you take a look at Sabrina?"

Jax reached out for Chance's hand. "How about I take a look at you first, then we talk about me coming to see Sabrina?" Chance followed her to a stool just inside the makeshift stall partitioned off with ropes and tarps.

"Sounds like a plan. Where are you staying?"

"Uncle Marty's for now. I need to look for someplace of my own. I love him, but I'm not sure I can live with him very long. He's pretty set in his ways."

"Your Uncle Marty…set in his ways? That's the understatement of the year. Ouch!" Chance flinched, as Jax tried to pull away the covering on her wound.

"Sorry, let me soak that dressing with some sterile water." Jax stepped away and returned with a full kit.

Chance looked over the clear plastic pouches. "You sure this is for humans and not for horses?"

Jax shook her head. "Whether I use it on my four-legged or two-legged patients, sterile water is sterile water. Now be quiet, you big baby."

Chance let her soak the dressing Taylor had applied and gently pull it from the skin. With a syringe, Jax squirted the water all around the wound, before she pulled out a small piece of stone with a pair of tweezers.

"You're going to need this debrided and some stitches. Does the scar tissue bother you much?"

"Diminished sensitivity. The dressing was stuck to the open part of the laceration. It has some sensation in certain areas. The nerves got pretty toasted." Chance continued to watch Jax work.

"I can't even imagine the pain when it happened." Jax began to apply another dressing over the wound, then wrapped a roll of cling around it.

"Well, with it being third degree and having a lot of morphine, I made it through. It was the recovery that hurt like hell. The debriding and the grafts were a bitch." She picked up her arm and turned it over to examine the bandage job.

"You really do need stitches."

"I'll go to Urgent Care once I know everyone is out of the woods and all the equipment is back in service."

Jax placed her hand on Chance's cheek. "I'm glad you survived your injuries."

"Yeah, me too." Chance rose from the stool. "So, about Sabrina?"

"How about nine tomorrow morning? I'll bring my mobile office and take a look."

"It's a date, Doc."

"Oh no, that's Marty. I'm just Jax. And about that date, I'll take you up on one sometime, if you're still single."

Chance toed the ground and met Jax's sparkling green eyes. "I've been waiting a long time to take you on another date."

A voice from her radio broke the gaze. "Comm Center to SD-1."

"You know where the stables are?" Chance reached for her radio.

"I do. See you tomorrow, Sheriff." Jax waved her off. "Go."

Chance grinned and keyed her portable radio. "SD-1 to Comm Center, go ahead." She raised a hand to wave to Jax and walked toward the center of the activity.

The command center was still buzzing, as Chance walked in. She glanced at the command board and noted that all personnel were reported back at staging. She made her way to Incident Commander Ike Roth, chief of the county fire service. There were four stations located in strategic areas around the county. Each was run by a deputy chief, with Ike handling command of the larger incidents that required countywide resources.

"Chance, did you get checked out by the medics?" Ike gestured toward her arm with roll of paper.

"Jax took a look at it. It's going to require stitches. It's fine for now. All my people out?"

"Yeah, the last horse rode in about five minutes ago, carrying the tripod. No major injuries, some small scrapes. The girl was flown down to Ruby, and we have someone taking the parents back to their car. One of our folks will drive them down to the ER. Lucky kid. This could have been disastrous. I'm glad you made it out there when you did. Sorry you got banged up."

"Comes with the territory. Need anything else from me?" Chance looked at her watch. She was going to have someone drive to the stables to get her truck and trailer to take the horses back.

"No, but if you're looking for a ride, Taylor will be back in about fifteen minutes with the trailer. She was thinking the way you taught her." Ike winked.

Chance grinned at him. "And now you know why she's Chief Deputy at thirty-seven."

"Smart woman. Find good people and let them do their job."

Chance wandered through the command center checking in with everyone. She turned at the sound of a horn. Chance watched Taylor pull the fifth-wheel horse trailer into the lot. Zeus barked a greeting, as Taylor stepped from the truck.

Taylor walked over to where Kelly and Jill were tied. "How about we get these girls home and you can get to Urgent Care before it closes?"

Chance shook her head in agreement. "I'd say that's a good idea."

She loaded Zeus in the truck and helped Taylor secure both horses inside before climbing into the front seat. "I want you to take tonight off, Taylor. You've been up all day. I'll call in someone from the reserve, or maybe Carl will want an overtime shift while he's on vacation. He didn't go anywhere that I know of."

"I'll take you up on that offer, Sheriff. Penny's texted me six times about asking you for the night off. You'll make her a happy woman by making me stay home tonight. Let's head to the barn.

"Wagons ho, my friend."

Chapter Four

MAGGIE AND DEE WERE BOTH waiting at Chance's house when she drove in. She let Zeus out of the back and watched as he ran over to accept a vigorous rub down from Dee.

"Traitor." Chance laughed. She held her hands up. "Before you ask, I'm fine, and yes I've seen a doctor. Faith put seven stiches in my arm. You wouldn't have brought dinner, would you?"

Dee walked up to her and wrapped an arm around her shoulder. "Mother Hubbard over there isn't about to let you waste away, Five Points. She brought your favorite." Dee smiled and took two steps away from Chance. "Chicken broth and a milkshake."

Chance jabbed her right fist out, catching Dee in the shoulder. "Funny, smart ass."

"Just making sure they didn't remove your funny bone. She's got a giant steak and baked potato for you, and a fucking piece of dried up chicken for me."

Maggie stood with her hands on her hips. "Hey, do you kiss your mother with that mouth?"

Dee walked up and wrapped her arms around Maggie's waist. "My mother is dead, but I do kiss my wife with it." Dee pulled Maggie into her arms and gently brushed their lips together.

"Yuck, mushiness." Chance teased.

"Go get a shower. Dee will take care of Zeus. I'll have dinner on the table in fifteen minutes. If you aren't back by then, Zeus will enjoy the steak."

Dee put her fists on her hips. "You'll give Zeus the steak instead of me? What the hell?"

Maggie patted Dee's cheek. "Zeus doesn't have high cholesterol and didn't suffer a heart attack less than a year ago. You'll eat chicken and live to see another twenty years with me if I have anything to say about it."

Chance laughed at the bickering. She walked over to the closet and stored her weapons and her vest. On the way to the shower, she stripped down to shirt and jog bra, forgetting about the bandaged stitches in her arm. "Son of a bitch that hurt!"

Maggie called from the kitchen. "You okay?"

"Yes, just tried to remove my brand-new stitches. I'm fine." She made her way to the shower, stripping off the rest of the clothes before climbing in. She knew she probably shouldn't be showering, but she was too dirty to bathe any other way. The water felt good, and it let her mind relax to the last time she'd seen Jax St. Claire. They were in the swing on the back porch of Doc Hendricks's house, Jax nestled in Chance's arms. They'd talked for hours about their dreams and where life was taking them. Seeing her today had stirred everything up, all those old feelings. There were no bad memories, no angst-filled goodbyes, but several kisses that lingered in the dim glow of the porch light and a promise to keep in touch. That promise had disappeared the same way the dirt from her body swirled down the drain. They hadn't seen each other since then until today. Doc hadn't said anything about Jax to Chance in years.

"Did you fall down in the shower or what?"

Chance heard her mom's voice outside her room. "I'm coming. It's harder to maneuver when I'm trying not to get that bandage wet." She shut off the shower and dried off. A pair of comfortable shorts and a T-shirt would have to do for her dinner attire. The smell of steak on the grill drew her into the kitchen, as she finger combed her hair back off her forehead. Her cell phone sat on the table and began to vibrate off the edge. She lunged to catch it and fumbled with the screen password.

"Sheriff Fitzsimmons."

"Sheriff, this is Willa at Comm Center. I have a gentleman from today's rescue requesting to talk to you. Want me to patch him through?

"Sure, Willa. Thanks."

The sounds of a connection being made signaled someone new on the line. "This is Sheriff Fitzsimmons. How can I help you?"

"Sheriff, this is Steve Arnold. You rescued my little girl today."

"Oh, yes. We were a little busy to get last names when we were out there. How's Cassie?"

"Doing well. They took her to surgery to set her fracture. She has several good scrapes all along her forearms and chin. The doctors say she'll do just fine. I wanted to thank you for what you did today. I don't know what I'd have done if you hadn't shown up. I was terrified climbing over those rocks."

"I'm extremely glad you didn't become victim number two. You tell Cassie how proud I am of her. She was very brave."

"I certainly will. Thank you again, Sheriff. You saved my little girl. I'll be forever grateful."

"It was my pleasure, Steve. Now go be with your family."

They said their goodbyes, and Chance made her way outside to a table set with a meal that would greatly replenish the energy she'd expended that day. She took a long, grateful pull on the beer she found waiting for her. Her head fell back against the chair, and she rolled to face Dee and held up the bottle.

"Thanks. This has you written all over it, since that one," she pointed to Maggie with her bottle, "is too refined for beer."

"Is it a crime to like wine instead of beer? If so, then arrest me. I never could drink that swill." Maggie pointed to Dee. "Two, no more, I mean it."

Dee held up her hands. "I hear you. I'll have my second with my delectable piece of chicken." Dee spoke out the side of her mouth to Chance. "It might help me choke it down."

Maggie turned and put her hands on her hips. "I heard that."

Chance nearly strangled on her beer. "Momma D, I'd quit while you're ahead. Take my word for it; sleeping by yourself gets mighty lonely."

Maggie put a plate down in front of Chance, with a large steak grilled to perfection. "Speaking of being lonely. I ran into Mya downtown today."

"Don't remind me. She wanted inside information on the rescue. I told her to go talk to the PIO. She wasn't amused. The exclusive will go to Rick and Tess at *The Advocate*. Mya will just have to get her information from someone else."

"I also ran into the new veterinarian."

Chance took a deep breath and chewed a bite of her steak. The beer bottle felt cool in her hand, and she wanted to run it across her heated cheeks. Maggie and Dee knew what Jax meant to her, and she wasn't ready to talk about it yet. "Let it go, Mom, please?"

"For now." Maggie put a plate in front of a scowling Dee and kissed the top of her wife's head. "I only do this because I love you. Eat."

They finished dinner and cleared the dishes, before settling onto the loungers on the porch to watch the sunset. When Chance built the house in Canaan Heights, she'd positioned it so that her bedroom would see the sunrise through large, French doors. The living room and patio faced the sunset. She'd done most of the work herself, once the logs were in place. She was the owner of twenty prime acres up on the peak and spent her spare time riding her horses.

Zeus put his paw on her thigh and whined. It was like he could read her mood. Chance scratched him behind his ears. "Glad to know you can read my mind. I'm okay boy." As the sun dropped below the horizon, Chance tipped back the last of her beer and thought about the dark-haired woman she was sure would haunt her dreams.

***

The next morning, Chance and Zeus made their way to the barn to check on Sabrina after their run. Once again, Taylor had beat her to the barn. The barn was filled with the sound of horses moving in their stalls as they enjoyed their breakfast. Kelly nickered as she passed, and Chance scratched down her forehead before entering Sabrina's stall.

"How is she?" Chance ran her hand down the horse's flank only to have her flinch like she had the day before.

"No better. I think it's time you call that new vet, what's her name again?" Taylor fed Sabrina a carrot from her pocket.

Chance pushed her hat back off her forehead. "Jax St. Claire. She'll be here at nine to check on Sabrina."

"How is it you know her again? Don't try to bullshit a bullshitter. I saw the reaction you had when you laid eyes on that tall drink of water. Damn near brought a blush to my face with the amount of heat coming off you two."

Chance couldn't help but chuckle. "Jax used to spend summers here, and well," she hesitated, "we used to hang out."

"Hang out, huh?"

"It was a very long time ago."

"I don't think it matters if it was thirty-six years or thirty-six days ago. There's something still there, Chance."

"Thanks for the advice. I'll be sure to let your wife know you are keeping up on my love life."

Taylor shook her head. "Let her see you two in the same room, and she'll be planning your wedding. Not kidding, my friend. You two were shooting sparks when you looked at each other. Deny it all you want."

Chance waved Zeus out of the stall. "Thanks, Dr. Ruth. I'll be back in about an hour. I have a few things I want to look into."

Chance picked up a flake of alfalfa and slipped it into Kelly's holder.

"I'll be back, girl."

Taylor was perceptive. The moment Chance saw Jax, it was as if the heavens opened up in the middle of a storm cloud to display a single beam of radiant light. For many years, she'd fantasized about seeing Jax again. She'd have to wait and see where it would lead. A lot of years had passed in their separation. It would take time to figure out who Jax was now, the same deceptively innocent temptress, or someone totally unknown? *I know the reason she gave for coming back. I also know there is a lot more I want to know, and I'm eternally grateful for the opportunity to find out.*

She and Zeus got on the road. As she passed the Kurst house, she spotted another unfamiliar vehicle with Maryland plates. "Something's up there, boy. I need to check in with the task force again." She jotted down the make and model, along with the plate number. The last thing she needed was a drug ring operating under her nose.

The Kurst brothers were known to occasionally sell marijuana and deal in pills. Chance had busted them more than once, but only with small amounts that were constantly pled down in court to misdemeanors. Larry Reap, the local prosecutor, was closer to retirement every day. Chance couldn't wait until he quit running for reelection. The Reaps were a powerful family within the county. Larry had been prosecutor for the last fifteen years. His father had held the position before him, and one of his brothers held a magistrate office. They had a stranglehold on the scales of justice, and Chance truly looked forward to new blood in those offices someday.

Chance pulled into the Canaan Valley Store. The place was a regular stop for her and held all the essentials a community without a grocery store could use. It was also a place tourists could buy souvenirs and the only gas station on this part of the mountain. She waved to the clerk on her way by and poured herself a travel mug of coffee. The bell on the door jangled when another customer entered, as Chance stepped to the counter to pay.

"How about letting me get that with mine?"

A shiver woke every nerve in her spine, as Chance recognized the rich alto voice and looked up into the same eyes that had captivated her the day before. "Morning, Jax. How about you let me buy the new vet in town a cup of coffee instead? It'll be a welcome back present."

Jax walked over, filled a tall thermal cup with dark roast, and carefully attached a lid. "If you let me repay the favor and buy you lunch later."

Chance glanced out at the Yukon to ensure it was still running. She hadn't planned to be in the store long and hadn't brought Zeus in with her. "That can be arranged. I checked in on Sabrina this morning. That foot is still sore. Taylor's with her now. I was doing a little patrol before you make your visit."

Chance paid for their coffees, and the two women walked out. Jax leaned against a dusty, dark blue Chevy Silverado dually. "I was using the time to drive around out here in the valley. I'm looking for a place to rent until I find something to buy. Living with a widower leaves a lot to be desired. Everything is exactly as it was when Aunt Mary died. He hasn't changed a thing in fifteen years. Trust me, it could certainly use a woman's touch."

Chance let out a laugh. "Just not yours?"

"It's a bigger job than I want. I love him, I do. Living with him is another thing. I was thinking of calling Maggie to line up some places for me. Think she would have time to see me later?"

Chance let a smile sneak out. "I think I can put in a good word for you."

"I'd appreciate it. Now, how about we go see that horse of yours. I know it's a little early, I doubt Sabrina will be unhappy."

"No, I'm sure she'd like to be out of pain. Taylor is there soaking her foot now. Follow me."

Jax climbed into the truck, and Chance followed suit in the Yukon. "I'm in trouble, Zeus. Trouble I don't want to find my way out of." Zeus barked his agreement and looked at her with soulful eyes. "Yeah, so are you."

Within minutes, both vehicles pulled into the stables. Chance watched Jax pull her bag out of the king cab, along with a set of muck boots. Jax dropped the tailgate and gathered her long hair into a ponytail that she tucked into the back of her shirt. She pulled a pair of well used leather chaps out of a tack box and expertly fastened them around her legs as she slid into the muck boots.

Chance stood transfixed. *Damn.*

"Lead the way, Sheriff."

Zeus barked, and Midas answered from inside the barn. Taylor met them at the stall gate.

"Welcome, Dr. St. Claire. Thanks for taking the time to check in on my girl. It's a little better today, though not much."

Jax extended her hand to Taylor. "It's Jax, Dr. St. Claire makes me sound old. Who's this?"

Taylor let her hand drift to her K9 partner. "This is Midas."

Jax let him sniff her hand and rubbed his head. "Hello, Midas. Nice to meet you. Let's check Sabrina out. "

Chance held open the stall door and watched as Jax approached the horse, talking softly and running her hand across her flank and over her muzzle. Even when they were kids, Jax had proven to be quite the horsewoman and obviously still was. *She's still as beautiful as the day I first saw her.*

"Hey, girl. Let's see what we can do about this sore foot okay?" Jax bent the knee back and tucked the hoof between her thighs, as Taylor held Sabrina's head.

Chance noticed the gentle touch Jax used to prod around the area with a hoof pick.

"I think we need to take off this shoe and see what's going on under there." Jax reached into her bag and pulled out a few farrier tools, then used them to remove the horseshoe. A stone fell free and Jax examined the area under where the shoe had sat. After a few minutes, she pulled out a hook knife and sliced away a bit of the sole. "I think that stone caused an irritation. I'm pretty sure there's a developing abscess. You caught it early. I can put a poultice on the foot that should draw out the abscess quickly." She stood and chucked Taylor on the arm. "Good job."

Taylor's smile engulfed her face. "She's my girl, only the best for her. Well, her and every other horse in this barn. Chance makes sure of that."

Jax smiled up at Chance, as she stepped to the sink and pulled materials out of her bag. "I'd expect nothing less. How many horses do you have here?"

Taylor answered for Chance. "Four. Sabrina, Kelly, Kris, and Jill." Taylor stroked the large, yellow tabby that made its way up on to the bench. "Oh, and Bosley here watches over all of them. "

Jax turned to Chance and broke out laughing. "What, no Charlie?"

Chance joined in the laughter. "Charlie was always behind the scenes, remember?"

"You always did have a thing for *Charlie's Angels*."

"Hey, I wasn't alone in that obsession. Hell, Taylor here is too young to have seen the original series, but she knows who they are."

Taylor held up her hands. "Don't drag me into your debauchery. I didn't name them. You did that all on your own."

Jax pointed to Sabrina. "We'll leave it on for a few days. With this type of wrap, she'll be able to put weight on it. Hopefully the abscess will burst quickly, and she'll feel much better. Leave the shoe off for a while. I'd say she'll be good as new in a week or two."

Chance squeezed Taylor's shoulder. "You'll just have to share Jill and Kris for a while."

Taylor punched Chance. "You know, you could share Kelly every once in a while."

Chance blocked another punch. "I could, but Zeus and Kelly are a team. I use Jill if I have to, but she's not as in tune with Zeus. Sorry, pal."

"I get it, you're a one-woman rider." Taylor stuttered, "I mean, one-horse rider."

Jax laughed at both of them. "You two are too much. Taylor, will you hold Sabrina's harness while I put this on? Chance, I could use your help wrapping this."

"Sure." Chance climbed in the stall and helped hold Sabrina's leg, while Jax applied the poultice and molded the flexible boot over and around the hoof.

Honeysuckle. Chance was so close to Jax, she could smell her shampoo. The scent she always associated with her memories of Jax flooded her with the sensation of running her fingers through that dark hair.

Fifteen minutes later, Sabrina stood calmly in her stall, while Jax and Chance cleaned up. Taylor called to Midas and locked the stall behind his exit.

Bosley rubbed against Jax's leg, and she bent to pet him. "You're a sweetie. Take care of the girls, okay?"

"He does a great job of keeping everything running smoothly here." Taylor washed her hands in the sink, and Chance handed her a few paper towels.

"Well, I'll be back to check on Sabrina in the morning. How about the others? Are they in need of anything while I'm here?" Jax was packing up her kit.

Chance stood with her hands on her hips, the leather of her gun belt creaking slightly. "Not a thing. Your uncle was here last month and gave everyone a clean bill of health."

"Great." Jax pulled off her chaps and folded them across her arm, as she reached down for the case.

"I'll carry that." Chance reached down and took it from her. "Taylor, I assume you're on duty tonight?"

"I am. I've got some errands to run for Penny and the grass to mow. I'll check back in on her after that and again when I come on duty. Thanks again, Jax. I appreciate it."

"Glad to be able to help. This is my community now. I hope to get to know the K9s, too. Midas, it was nice to meet you." Jax spoke to the Belgian Malinois near Taylor's side.

"Trust me, if you're agreeable, I'd like you to handle all our veterinarian services." Chance held out her hand to help Jax up.

Jax smiled and accepted the proffered hand as she locked eyes with Chance. "It's very agreeable."

Taylor made her way out of the barn. "Chance, I'll call you later. Penny just sent me my next 'honey-do' list."

"Stay safe." Chance nodded at the hand Taylor raised in recognition.

Chance and Jax walked out to the Silverado, where she lifted the kit into the huge truck. "This thing is a monster. Do you have a camper?"

Jax shook her head. "No, I need it for the horse trailer. I brought two horses cross country with me. I have them boarded over on Clover Run until I get a place."

"Trail horses?"

"Two very good ones. I've been doing endurance races for about ten years. Back in California, I used to do a race almost every month when I had the time."

Chance thought about the time involved in training for that type of race. "You must have lived and breathed riding. Wouldn't leave much time to do anything else with a busy practice."

"Riding was my stress relief. Put me on a horse and everything melts away. If I remember right, I wasn't the only one."

"You remember correctly." Chance looked at her watch, grimacing at the time. "I need to get to the office. Still up for that lunch?"

Jax climbed in her truck. "I am. The Lion's Den, say twelve thirty?"

Chance shut her door for her. "I'll be there. Drive safely."

"You be careful out there, and I'll see you then."

Jax backed out of the space, as Chance put Zeus in the Yukon. "Zeus, that woman's back in my life less than twenty-four hours, and I'm losing my heart all over again."

Chapter Five

JAX ST. CLAIRE PUT her window down and rested her arm on the door to let the breeze cool her heated skin. She was flushed and she knew it. Chance Fitzsimmons still had a powerful effect on her, decades later. The broad shoulders and muscular frame were an enticing package. Chance had been gorgeous as a teenager, but the adult Chance was simply stunning. Jax had done her best to not stare at the scarred skin running down Chance's arm. Imagining the pain Chance had endured brought tears brimming to the surface.

She pulled her truck around the back of her new practice. The clinic needed a thorough inventory and a few updates, including a computer system that was to be installed that afternoon. New examination equipment would be delivered next week. Her plan was to remain closed this month to allow for the renovations; she'd do house calls when needed.

When she pushed through the door, she wasn't surprised to see her uncle standing with his hands on his hips. "Hey, Marty."

The wiry man ran his hand through his salt-and-pepper hair. "Never knew my place was so lacking."

Jax approached him and put her arm around his shoulders. "Uncle Marty, your practice survived fifty years. Your way wasn't wrong, and neither is mine. Just different. I'm planning to offer some services that you didn't and use some technology that I helped develop in my last twenty years of practice. I'm not fresh out of vet school. I had a pretty successful business out in California. When you talked to me about coming back here and taking over, you had to know I would do things differently than you. Not better, just differently."

Martin Hendricks rubbed the back of his neck, as he slid his arm around his niece's waist. "Don't mind me. I wouldn't have offered this place if I had any doubt about you taking over. I know we talked about it, but are you sure you really want to make this move? I promise, I'm not trying to be nosey. I'm thrilled to have you back here. Just tell me you aren't running away from anything you're going to regret."

Jax shook her head and hugged her uncle. "I didn't leave anything behind in California I'm going to miss. I know we haven't talked much about it since I got back, but I've never hidden anything from you. Lacey and I were together for a long time. We built a life and a practice together. I can't tell you exactly when we became more business partners than life partners. Along the way, she found she wanted something, someone, different. I never was good at sharing. I decided there wasn't anything holding me there except the practice. Your offer came at the right time."

"Your old Uncle Marty is probably the last person you want to talk to about your relationship, but do you still love her?"

"I loved who we used to be. Who we became was something less than friends and more like business partners. I'm over fifty, and I want something else in my life beyond work."

"And you think you're going to find that here in Tucker County?"

"When I think back to a time when I believed life was full of possibilities, it was here when I stayed with you and Aunt Mary. I had dreams. I could breathe. I think I let the smog and fast pace of life in California choke out any dreams of happiness or joy. When I asked Lacey for the divorce, I didn't know what I was going to do. That's when you called me. Some people don't believe in signs. I do. From that day on, I was more focused than I'd been in years." Jax closed her eyes and took a deep breath.

"Well then, I'd say we need to get moving on making this place yours, so you can get back to living." He stepped away from her and walked to what had once been his office. "I'll start clearing out things you're not going to need. What about the files? How do you want to handle them? I know it sounds old fashioned, but my record keeping was done with a number two pencil. We need to go over to Mike Lambert's soon to get the paperwork squared away."

Jax sighed and released her hair from the ponytail, only to gather it up again and fasten it back in place. "I wish you'd let me buy everything from you instead of just deeding it over."

Martin raised a gnarled finger in her direction. "We've talked about this. I have no children. Your mother doesn't want any part of this place, and that leaves you. You'd have gotten it in the end. Look at it as getting your inheritance while I'm still alive to stand back and boast a bit. I don't want to hear any more about paying me. Use the money you got from selling in California to bring this place into the twenty-first century. If you want to pay me, promise me a standing, Thursday-morning breakfast at the diner. That'll be payment enough."

"On one condition." Jax pointed a finger back at him. "Can you leave your diploma and the photos in there? I'd like to remember why I decided to become a vet. That's all your doing."

He rubbed the stubble on his chin. "Yup and your momma has never forgiven me for taking you on that barn call."

"I love you, Uncle Marty."

"Love you too, kitten." He smiled at her and turned to go into his office.

Jax slowly looked around the waiting area. "A new coat of paint, new tiles on the floor, and this place will have a new life." *Just like me.*

***

A few hours later, Jax was in the bathroom at her uncle's house, freshly showered and in a different outfit to meet Chance for lunch. She'd spilled a bottle of iodine down the leg of her jeans when cleaning out a cabinet. It was in the mid-eighties outside, and she'd decided on a pale-blue sundress and sandals. Looking in the mirror, she opted to leave her hair down. *Chance always liked to run her fingers through my hair.* She looked away from the mirror. *Whoa, where did that come from?*

She knew where. Denying the attraction to Chance was futile. She'd felt the flip in her stomach when she looked up to see Chance walking toward her yesterday. Years melted away, and she was back sitting close to Chance in a beat-up Chevy truck, a strong arm around her shoulders. They'd spent an entire summer dreaming and making out in the bed of that truck, floating down the Cheat River, and riding horses through the Monongahela National Forest. Even when she met Lacey in college, she'd never felt the overwhelming desire to just be in her presence the way she had with Chance. Lacey was the exact opposite of Chance. She was dark where Chance was light and light where Chance was dark in both body and spirit. Their outlook on the world was completely different. Chance was content to sit on the tailgate of a truck and drink a 'borrowed' six pack from Momma D's stash. Lacey had wined and dined Jax at the finest restaurants and swept her off her feet. Before Jax knew it, she and Lacey were spending every hour together in the classroom or the bedroom. When they'd graduated, they started their life and eventually, a practice together.

"If I'd only known then what I know now," she muttered to the mirror.

Twenty plus years and an unknown number of infidelities had left Jax empty and in need of a change. Her uncle's call had come out of the blue with a lifeline she'd been searching for. She could start over in fresh, though familiar, surroundings.

Marty was sitting on the porch drinking a glass of iced tea, as she stepped out. "Well, don't you look like a summer day."

Jax blushed and smiled at him. "I'm having lunch with Chance at The Lion's Den."

"The sheriff is one of the finest people I know. She's been through a lot. I can tell you Maggie and Dee are glad she's not jumping out of airplanes anymore. Though I'm not sure wearing a badge and a gun make her a safer bet."

"I saw the scar on her arm the other day. She told me she was in a burn over. How'd she end up back here?"

"Spent three months in the burn ward out in Montana. Maggie and Dee contracted a local pilot to bring her back home to heal up when they released her. Stubborn cuss worked her way into a lateral move into the law enforcement side when she was fully healed. Retired from U.S. Fish and Wildlife and ran for Sheriff. Won in a landslide."

"She certainly seems to love her job. The horses she has are gorgeous."

"Only the best for her. Trained them all herself. I've taken care of them for years. Her chief deputy is a crackerjack too. Chance stole her away from the U.S. Marshals Service. Overall, she's built a strong department, except for that jackass, Brad Waters. Lazy as they come. Not sure why she keeps him around. She's good people, and I'll vote for her as long as she can run. "

Jax kissed him and stepped off the porch. "I think she's good people too. You talking about voting reminds me I need to get on the ball about switching my permanent residence. Which also means I need to find a home."

"You know you're welcome to stay here. The house will be yours someday anyhow." He waved a hand. "I know, you need your own place. I'm just offering. Now get out of here. Tell her hi for me and to stop by for coffee some time."

She waved as she climbed into her truck. "Will do. Love you, Uncle Marty." The truck roared to life, and she backed out of the driveway on her way to lunch with a handsome sheriff.

***

Jax finished chewing her bite of club sandwich, as she watched Chance drown two fries in ketchup before shoving them into her mouth. "You always did love your ketchup."

"Still do. Mom put the kibosh to me putting it on my pancakes. I've evolved to pure maple syrup produced right here in the county. Now, my eggs, they still get the mustard my dad got me hooked on."

The story of how Chance's dad was killed was legendary within the county. There was a memorial plaque on the courthouse that Jax had walked by yesterday. Chance was honoring her father's memory in outstanding fashion by filling his very large shoes.

"Hey, where'd you go?" Chance touched Jax's hand.

"I was thinking about how this county hasn't changed much in thirty years." She pointed to her sandwich. "This place still puts more bacon on a club sandwich than any place I've ever been."

Pictures of local sports heroes and team photos took up every free spot on the walls of the small diner, while autographed memorial balls lined a high shelf around the dining room. She stared at a picture of Chance with a basketball net around her neck and a smile as wide as the Blackwater Canyon.

"Was that when you won the state championship?

Chance turned her head to the picture. "Sure is. You can't tell from the picture, but my jaw is actually broken." She rubbed a spot on her chin. "I wouldn't let them take me to the hospital until I enjoyed every second of the celebration. I'd earned it."

"No doubt." Jax watched Chance put another fry in her mouth. They ate and talked about the county and its residents. Twice, the bell rang as the diner door opened, and Chance was able to give her the rundown of the person that came in, including how many animals they had that Jax would likely be treating.

Chance sipped her tea, then brought up a related subject. "How's the move in going at the clinic?"

Jax wiped her mouth with her napkin and absent mindedly reached over to wipe some stray ketchup off Chance's chin.

Chance laughed and picked up her own napkin. "Maggie would approve; that's usually her job. One time I stopped by her office and about gave her a panic attack, because she thought she saw blood on my badge. It was only a remnant of my burger from lunch."

Jax nearly doubled over with laughter and tried to not spit Coke out her nose. "Oh my God, Chance." She looked at the strands of silver that blended in with the chestnut-brown hair. She still had the shock of white in the front she'd had when Jax knew her. "I'm sure she worries about you."

Chance used her thumb to clean a few crumbs from the table, dropping them onto her plate. "They both do, too much if you ask me. When I quit smoke jumping, they'd hoped I'd go for something a little more sedate. It's just not my style. I have to be doing something to fix a problem, whether it's on fire or against the law."

"That always was your style, even before you settled on a career. I remember you were always volunteering to help with something."

"I have to believe that a difference can be made."

"I have no doubt you do that in spades."

"What about you? Your Uncle Marty told me you finished school out in California, then it seemed like you fell off the face of the earth. I'll assume you were making a life treating animals and digging your toes into the sand. Only thing beach-like around here is a sandy riverbank."

Jax pushed a piece of sandwich crust around her plate. "You're half right. I graduated and opened a practice, only not near a beach. I was up in the Napa Valley area. Wine country instead of sandy beaches."

"Ah, so I assume I can ask you for recommendations on good vino?"

"Sorry, that would be my ex's specialty. I can tell you the best microbreweries."

"Your ex was a wine maker?"

"Her family was. We went to veterinary school together. We set up a practice near her family's vineyard. I specialized in large-animal vet services, and she went into exotics. We treated everything from bearded lizards to prize racehorses."

Chance tipped her head sideways, then sat forward and rested her head on her interlaced fingers. "Sounds like it was a lucrative practice. A little different than the cats and cows you'll be treating around here."

Jax nodded her head. "True, but this place has its own perks and a lot less baggage."

"Sounds like that's a conversation better had over a few beers on my deck. I have a rescue squad meeting tonight, or I'd offer to make you dinner. How about tomorrow?" Chance asked, a note of hopefulness in her voice.

The smile Jax felt creep across her lips grew wider, as she contemplated the soulful eyes staring into her own. "I think that sounds better than a three-hundred-dollar-an-hour couch I was offered in California. I'll take you up on dinner as long as you let me bring the beer."

Chance reached across the table and clasped Jax's hand. "Deal."

***

Jax went back to the house and changed into a set of work clothes to head back to the clinic. On her way out the door she saw a man stood on the porch, hand raised as if ready to knock. "Can I help you?"

"I'm hoping you can." He held out his hand. "Matt Carson. I volunteer with the 4-H team as well as organize a few endurance races for the group here and the surrounding counties. I wanted to introduce myself and to find out if you might be interested in helping out with animal care needs, when possible."

Jax shook the man's hand. "Nice to meet you, Matt, that actually sounds pretty interesting. I've been doing endurance races myself, out in California, for years."

The man's face lit up. "Wow, that's great news. I'm part of the equestrian search and rescue group. I saw you the other day at the command post. I wanted to connect with you and say thank you for volunteering to look at the animals."

"Marty let me know about the operation when he couldn't go. I was glad to be able to help out. I'd like to do more than just offer veterinary services if I can. What's required to join the group?"

"Trust me, just show up at a meeting. I'm the local president. We meet the third Thursday of the month at the Canaan Valley Fire Department. We help them out, and they give us a meeting room to organize our group and events."

"The third Thursday, huh? That means you all are meeting this week. What time?"

"Seven thirty. I'll look forward to seeing you, Dr. St. Claire."

"Jax, please. Dr. St. Claire sounds way too formal. I'll see you there, and thanks again."

He turned and raised his hand to say goodbye.

Hum, endurance races and search and rescue. More time with a tall handsome sheriff. I'd say that's a win-win. Mac and Glenny need a good workout. Wonder if I can convince Chance to go for a ride soon?

She stopped her train of thought. Ever since seeing Chance at the rescue, she was trying to find opportunities when she could spend time with the woman from her past. Since the second she'd seen her walking across that gravel lot, her heart hadn't stopped pounding. Thoughts of Chance and those summer days of their youth had made an impression that stayed with her long after she'd immersed herself in life at UC Davis. Somewhere in those biology and physiology classes, Lacey Montgomery had entered her life and, for a time, stolen her heart.

It was sometime after that when her dreams of coming back to West Virginia and going into practice with her uncle vanished in a haze of lavish estates, BMWs, and vineyards. *Ten years in, my life was so deeply entangled with Lacey's not much else existed. I have no idea when being in love or being loved stopped mattering. I do know this. I refuse to live the rest of my life that way.* Jax shook off those memories, as she pulled into the clinic. Marty was loading his beat-up Ford with a few boxes. He leaned against the truck and waited on her.

"How was lunch?"

"The food was top notch, exactly as I remember it. Before I left the house, Matt Carson stopped by to ask about me becoming involved with their equestrian group. I think I'm going to take him up on it. I wasn't sure I'd find anything like that around here. I'm hoping it'll give me a good chance to meet a lot of the locals."

A weathered hand pushed grey hair back off his forehead. "You got a little taste of the group when you helped out on that rescue. Chance has really brought a lot of those groups together into a community that works well. Should be right up your alley with your experience. Did you tell Matt you headed up a lost-person team out in California?"

"No, I figured I'd save that for the meeting he invited me to. I don't want to be in charge of anything back here. I miss the days of being a spoke in the wheel. Being in charge kept me off the horses and in the command post most of the time. Enough of that. I see you've loaded up some boxes. Need help with anything else?"

Marty shook his head. "No, I started going through things and realized most of my material is really outdated. I've kept up with new techniques, but unless it was a special situation, what I was doing was working. I don't think any animal suffered under my care because I wasn't trying the latest or greatest. I know you've been practicing a long time and the way you do things will help so many animals. I'm over eighty, honey. It's time to turn it all over to you and spend time doing things I enjoy, like fishing. What I've left behind you can throw away, donate, or use as you see fit. This place is yours to do with as you will. I want you to be happy here and enjoy your practice. From what we've talked about, I don't think you ever enjoyed what you built out there."

Jax kicked at the dirt with the tip of her boot. "No, I didn't. It was high-pressure and high-priced veterinary service for people who saw their animals as trinkets and investments. Don't get me wrong; I had the privilege of working with some incredible horses. The stable workers were the ones who did most of the work. They were the only people who showed many of those animals any affection. This place will give me a chance to get back to the kind of medicine I wanted to practice."

"Did you get everything squared away out there?"

She took a deep breath. She and her uncle had always been able to talk. He'd known she was gay before the rest of her family had. He knew about Lacey and was the first person she called when she'd found out about the last affair.

"Lacey and I finalized the divorce and the dissolution of our business partnership. She bought me out of the practice and the house. Don't worry Uncle Marty, I didn't lose out. Her grandmother made sure of that. Madeline Montgomery was unhappy with the way her granddaughter treated me. In the end, she was one of the few Montgomerys on my side. I still talk to her. She was very supportive of me coming back here and being the kind of vet I'd always dreamed of."

He hugged her. "Well, you've got your whole life in front of you and plenty of time to figure it all out. I'm going home to unload these boxes into my office and grab my fishing pole. I hear they stocked Red Run." He climbed in his truck. "Will I see you for dinner?"

"I'll be home in time to cook whatever trout you catch, and I'll patty out some burgers in case you don't." Jax leaned in his truck window and kissed the grizzled cheek. "I love you, Uncle Marty."

"Love you too, kitten. Don't work too hard. Tomorrow's another day."

"Be careful and keep your phone on you."

He waved as he drove out of the lot. Jax walked through the door of the clinic and looked around. The place was neat and tidy, but she needed to clear away all the things be keeping in order for the contractor to come in and do the renovations she had planned. The computer technician was due any minute.

"Well Jax, it's not going to get done by itself. Time to get cracking."

Chapter Six

CHANCE WHISTLED LOUDLY IN order for the president of the Tucker County Search and Rescue Squad to call the meeting to order. The business side of the operation never interested Chance, unless it came to applying for grants. She'd become good at wording the narratives to key in on their unique terrain and frequency of visitors getting themselves into trouble. It probably didn't hurt that many state and federal bigwigs owned vacation homes up in the valley. They donated to the local causes as goodwill tax deductions.

After the business of the squad had been dealt with, the meeting agenda listed an operational debrief of the rescue. Chance stepped up to a white board and rolled a dry erase marker back and forth between her hands.

"First of all, I want to tell you all what an awesome job you did." Zeus barked his approval. "Thank you for that ringing endorsement, partner." She drew the incident scene and turned around when she heard a few snickers. "I never claimed to be an artist. Use your imagination." With all the pertinent details drawn in, Chance went on to describe her initial actions. "We were close to having a second rescue. If I'd had arrived a few minutes later, Cassie's dad would have been down on that ledge where we lost that guy a few years ago. He was near panicked. Those situations are going to continue to happen out there. Even with the warning signs, people still go over onto those boulders."

A list of the equipment they'd used lined the right-hand side of the board. "Inevitably, we end up using the tripod to gain some elevation to bring us all out. At our next drill night, I'd like to practice using a gin pole set up and see if we could stage something like that out there. If not, I'd like to find a way to leave a cache of equipment somewhere near that overlook. That alone would save us a great deal of time shuttling equipment out to the site. The Saddleback Equestrian team does a fantastic job of getting personnel out there, don't get me wrong. The problem is, it's time consuming to load those pack animals down and trudge through the woods with the equipment. That works against us if an incident occurs late in the day. If all we needed to do was transport personnel, we could get operations started much quicker. We were racing the sun on this operation, and time was of the essence."

Sarah spoke up. "That's happened to us a few times. People get a late start and then have to make their way back out to call for help when something goes wrong."

Chance looked around, and all heads were shaking in agreement. "Dave, you work for the state park. Do you think there's a chance they'd let us build some kind of small structure out there? Maybe we could camouflage whatever we come up with to store some of our larger equipment."

Dave Searles, a beanpole shy of thirty years old, pushed his ball cap back on his head. "We could talk to the superintendent. We'd need to get permission to put anything on state owned land. I'd like to leave things close to how God created them. That death out there with that guy you mentioned shook them up pretty good. I'd say with this rescue coming out as successful as it did, it might be the right time to ask. I'll see if we can get a meeting with them."

"Great. Give me enough leeway to be able to configure something aesthetically pleasing that will be serviceable enough to protect our equipment. We can use a push-button locking system so keys won't be needed. That would also allow us to change the code as often as we want." Chance made a mental note to do some research on options.

"Sure thing, Sheriff."

Chance went back to her white board. "I'd like to have a joint drill with the Saddlebacks. Several of us own horses, and it's always good to train together to make things seamless when we're working a scene. I'll try to set something up with them later next month. Okay, as well as it went, there are always lessons we can learn. Let's discuss what we could have done better."

For the next forty minutes, the squad dissected the operation. Everything from the callout procedures to the tactical operation were examined. Chance assured everyone that she would not have gone down into the crevice without having another team member on scene. She was a doer, but she respected the margins of safety and the need for backup in technical situations. It was important for her to show her younger members accountability for their own actions. She bore the scars on her body for what happened when something went wrong.

"Okay, are there any more questions?" Chance scanned the room filled with fifteen skilled team members. Heads were shaking. "Then, I would say thank you for coming. I'll let you know about details for our next drill night." Zeus barked on cue, and the sound of chairs being folded and stowed away filled the room.

Sarah walked to the front of the room. "How's your arm?"

Chance bent her arm at the elbow. "Hell, I forget about it most of the time, until I drag some piece of clothing across it."

"Did you fill out the injury form?"

Chance smiled. "That's on my list to do before I leave tonight. No workers' comp claim to file, I let my insurance cover the treatment at the clinic."

Sarah shook her head. "Let me guess, my sister sewed you up?"

"She did. I managed to get out of there with just a stern warning from Faith."

"If you're going to tell me my sister let you get out of there without a tetanus shot, I'm going to call bullshit. I know her better than that."

"There was discussion of a booster. My records show I'm up to date. That rusty nail I jammed under my fingernail two months ago sealed the deal on me not baring my backside."

Sarah stared at the ground. "I'm sure Maggie's taking care of you, while Dee's probably trying to convince you to let her take out the stitches."

Chance put a finger under Sarah's chin and raised it so their eyes met. "I'm okay, Sarah. I've got enough keepers watching out for me. How's Kristi?"

"She's at home, hanging out with Daniel. He's grown six inches since you last saw him. It's nice having him home from college. You know you are welcome at our house any time. Breaking up with Faith doesn't mean you have to stay away from us."

"I know that. I've honestly been busy. Faith and I parted as friends, and I've known Theresa for years through the basketball team. She's good for her. Faith needed someone who was less adrenaline driven. Theresa is a teacher and home every night. She doesn't get called away at the drop of a hat or shot at."

Sarah crossed her arms. "I'm well aware of all of that. None of it means you are absolved from being Daniel's godmother. We're family, Chance, regardless of my sister. We grew up together, and you got me into this crazy world of search and rescue. You've got obligations, and I'm holding you to them. It's been over a month since you've been to the house. We're cooking steaks tomorrow night. How about you come by?"

"Uh, I sort of have plans."

Sarah peaked an eyebrow. "Plans?"

Chance reached up and nervously pulled on her earlobe. "Dinner plans. The new vet, Jacqueline St. Claire, is back to take over Doc Hendricks's practice, and I invited her over for dinner."

Sarah bugged her eyes out. "Jax St. Claire from all those summers ago? That Jax?"

"How in the hell did you remember that? You were too busy sucking face with Kristi to know what in the hell I was doing."

"How in the world do you think I could forget? She and Kristi became friends when we all ran around together our senior year. Remember that float trip where you tipped out of your inner tube and pulled her out of hers? Then there was a missing red, white, and blue bikini top we had trouble finding the next morning when we camped down on the riverbank in the truck beds. Don't tell me I don't remember who Jacqueline St. Claire is."

"I certainly remember how she lost it. Best birthday ever." Chance couldn't help but laugh, as the pair made their way out of the fire hall, Zeus on her heels.

Sarah leaned against her Jeep. "I also remember someone moping around like a lost puppy for six months after Jax went off to school. So, she's back?"

"She is, and I did not mope."

"Bullshit. Even Mags and Dee had started to worry, then the basketball season started and you snapped out of it."

"We won the championship, didn't we?"

"Yeah we did, and you ended up with your jaw wired shut. Hard to pine away for someone when you're busy drowning yourself in chicken broth and milkshakes."

Chance shoved Sarah's shoulder. "Shut up or I'll arrest you. You know I can't even smell chicken broth to this day."

"So Jax St. Claire's back and you're cooking her dinner?"

Chance loaded Zeus in the vehicle and climbed in the front seat, grinning from ear to ear. "She is, and I'm grilling out for her tomorrow night."

"She still hot?"

"Smoking hot. The old saying some things get better with age. She proves it. Tell Daniel to come by the department tomorrow, and I'll take him to lunch."

"I will. Don't be surprised when he starts asking you when the test for Deputy Sheriff is."

"I can always use another good man on the force. Good night Sarah."

Chance drove away thinking of the boy who was like a nephew to her. She'd made him promise to finish college before he applied for a law enforcement position. He'd recently graduated and was ready to go. When she was with Fish and Wildlife, he'd sworn that's what his goal was. Now that she was retired from there and holding the position of sheriff, he'd changed his mind about being a federal officer. He called once a month wanting to know when the application period would open up. She had one officer close to retirement. Daniel's intelligence assured that he'd test high, and his physical abilities should propel him to the top of the list. His desire to become an officer concerned her, but she'd rather have him working for her than learning from someone she didn't know or trust. Sarah and Kristi were like sisters to her. *I'll call him tomorrow. Sarah's right, breaking up with Faith doesn't mean I broke up with them.*

***

Mist saturated the air, and the grass at the edges of the trail was heavy with dew. Chance's shoes were wet, and Zeus's belly dripped with moisture when they reached the Yukon in the parking lot. She'd reported in from T7, a trail off of Cortland Road through the nature preserve. There were no other cars at the trailhead. She pulled a water bottle and a towel from the seat. She poured most of it into a collapsible bowl for Zeus, then drank the remainder.

Once they were back inside the vehicle, Chance reported into the communications center that she was clear and pulled out onto Cortland Road. Sunlight broke through the morning fog and reflected off the side mirror of a vehicle parked off the roadway and hidden by some scrub trees. Chance turned the Yukon around and pulled up behind the Toyota Camry with blacked-out windows. There was no exhaust steaming in the cool morning air.

The mic in her hand, she contacted dispatch. "SD-1 to Comm Center."

"SD-1, go ahead."

"I'm on scene with a vehicle off of Cortland Road near the orchard.

Maryland registration—" Before Chance got the plate called in, a shot pierced her windshield. "Shots fired! Shots fired!" She rattled off the registration and threw the Yukon into reverse away from the vehicle. With the accelerator jammed to the floor, and her service weapon in her hand, Chance ducked low. The minute the tires bit on the pavement, she whipped the vehicle sideways and exited into a crouch. A slap to the hatch release button allowed her partner to join her, as she pointed her weapon in the direction the shot had come from. Zeus came to her side, blood pouring from a wound somewhere on his head. Immediately, she examined him before reaching in the vehicle and grabbing the mic.

"SD-1 to Comm Center, K9-1 is hit!" The sound of a revving engine made her drop the mic and grasp her weapon with both hands. The vehicle screamed out of the brush. "Stop. Police!" A green blur barreled directly at her, and she squeezed off four rounds into the front windshield before the impact threw her and Zeus across the road. The horrific sounds of crunching metal and breaking glass broke the early morning tranquility and hurled her into blackness.

***

Chance came to, hearing Taylor's voice screaming, "Officer down." She tried to dispel the queasiness and clear the confusion from her head. A memory of the blood she'd seen on her partner came roaring back. "Zeus! Where's Zeus?"

Chance had no idea how long she'd been out, but a wet tongue hit her face. She raised an arm to assure herself that he was still with her.

Taylor put a hand on her shoulder. "Lay still, Chance. I've got help coming."

"Asshole fired on me. Hit Zeus somewhere. Check him, Taylor." Chance spit a mouthful of blood out and tried to clear her pounding head.

"He's okay, Chance. It just nicked his ear. Right now, I'm more worried about you."

"The perp, did he get away?"

Taylor put both hands on her shoulders to keep her in place. "Perp's dead. Another unit checked the car. I've got an ambulance on the way for you and Zeus. Boss, you need to lay still. You took a hell of a hit."

"Why'd the fucker fire on me? I hadn't even got out of the truck yet. I was calling in the plate."

"Probably the drugs on the seat. The guy still has a tourniquet on and a needle on the floorboard."

"What the fuck? God my head hurts. Check Zeus...he was bleeding."

"Chance, listen to me." The wail of the sirens nearly drowned out her voice. "The ambulance and two troopers just pulled up. Lay still and let them take care of you. Zeus is okay. You're worse than him right now."

Through a haze of red, Chance tried to focus, as white-hot pain shot through her body. She could make out fuzzy features that looked familiar.

"Chance, it's Sarah. Lay still. I'm going to look you over. Where do you hurt?"

"Sarah, check on Zeus. He's bleeding."

"Taylor has him. Let me take care of you. You cracked your head on the pavement, and I'm pretty sure that left wrist is busted."

"I have to check on Zeus. Let me up." Chance struggled to get up off the ground and fell back in agony when she tried to push up with her hands.

Sarah pushed gently against Chance's shoulder. "You stubborn ass. I told you it looks like your wrist is broken. Now lay down. I mean it."

"The moms squared are going to kill me."

"Can't help you there. For now, let me try and fix you up so you'll be in good shape when they do."

Chance tried to laugh until she became aware of new pain so sharp and stabbing, it stole her breath on a gasp.

"Chance, talk to me. What's going on?"

"Get Zeus to Jax."

Sarah shook her head. "We'll take care of Zeus. I need to get a line started."

Chance grabbed Sarah's hand forcefully with her own. "Get Zeus to Jax, promise me."

"Dammit, Chance, I promise. Now let me help you."

"Sheriff, it's Taylor. I've got Zeus. I'll get him to Jax, then I'll meet you at the hospital."

Sarah and another EMT packaged Chance on a backboard, moved her to a gurney, and loaded her into an ambulance.

The last thing Chance remembered were blue and red lights bouncing off the inside surfaces of the ambulance, as Sarah's voice told her to stay awake. That, apparently, was one request she couldn't fulfill.

***

Jax heard her uncle answer the house phone as she was about to walk out the door to go work on the clinic. She perked an ear to make sure it wasn't for her. His excited voice brought her back to the kitchen, where he held an ancient, harvest-gold telephone receiver attached to a long, tangled cord.

"Uncle Marty what is it?"

He talked into the phone without answering her. Jax listened, unable to make out what the person on the other end of the line was saying. The look on Marty's face said it wasn't good.

He looked up at her while speaking to the caller. "We'll meet you at the clinic. Just wrap it up for now to control the bleeding. We'll see you in about fifteen minutes." He hung up and reached for his wallet on the kitchen table. "We've got work to do. There's a Sheriff's Department K9 that's been shot."

Jax grabbed his arm. "One of Chance's?"

"Not just one of them, hers. Zeus is on his way to us. From what Taylor said, it's not life threatening. A bullet caught him in the ear, and it won't stop bleeding."

Jax's radar went on high alert, as she asked the obvious question. "Uncle Marty, why was Taylor calling and not Chance?"

Marty put his hands on her forearms and held her. He looked her in the eyes. "Chance is hurt. Head injury from what I was told. They're transporting her to Garrett Memorial for evaluation."

Jax's stomach roiled, and her legs buckled beneath her. "Chance has been shot in the head? Why aren't they flying her out? That's crazy! Garrett can't handle an injury like—"

Marty raised his voice over her rising panic. "Jax, honey! She's not shot, just injured, from what I heard. Let's go do what we can for Zeus, so she can concentrate on making it through this. She's as close to that dog as anyone or anything in her life. I'll drive. No way am I letting you try to get there by yourself. I may be retired, but I still can do a thing or two. I know what she meant to you. We'll do our part. Now let's go."

Jax's feet felt leaden as she allowed her uncle to fold her into his arms and lead her to the truck. *You're wrong Uncle Marty, not meant. Means.*

Within minutes, they were unlocking the door to the clinic. Jax's focus shifted to what she needed to do for Zeus. Most likely, her uncle thought she'd be unable to concentrate on treating his injury. He would be wrong. Times like this made her focus laser sharp. All her years of practice and training kicked in as second nature. The crunch of gravel made her move to the door to hold it open as Taylor carried Zeus in, Midas right behind her.

"Bring him into the surgical room. We'll have more room to work in there." Jax pointed back down the hall, and her uncle followed behind. "What's it look like? I'm assuming that blood that's all over you is his?"

"Yeah, it looks like it took the top of his ear off. Can't seem to get the damn thing to stop bleeding." Taylor laid Zeus on the new stainless-steel table.

Jax stepped on the foot switch and brought the dog to a comfortable height. She hadn't thought she'd be using the new equipment this soon but was glad she had it. "Looks like one of the vessels doesn't want to close. She stepped back and measured Zeus's weight using the built-in scale, then moved to the medicine cabinet to draw up the appropriate dosage of pain medicine to relax the dog. "You think he'll bite if I leave the muzzle off?"

Taylor smiled. "In pain or not, he won't bite without Chance's command. I'll hold his head if you'll feel more comfortable."

"No, it's fine. I have no doubt he's been expertly trained. This medicine will help with his pain and let me clean it to get a good look. I think I need to tie off the bleeder or cauterize it, at least." As Jax leaned over the dog to examine him, she became covered in blood. She gave Zeus the shot and stroked his neck to his shoulder. She motioned for her uncle. "What do you think, Uncle Marty?"

Zeus whined and twitched, as Jax flushed the wound. Marty pulled out a few supplies from a drawer. "He got the big one. I think a few sutures right there will stop the bleeding. After that, we probably can stitch it all the way across and close it. There's no way to save the shape. You'll need to excise it and make it smooth across that area. We'll tell Chance it doesn't take away from his good looks. That ear has character now. We'll probably want to put him under for that much work.

"Okay, I agree. Let's get him ready. Taylor, what's going on with Chance?" Jax moved around the room gathering an intubation kit.

Taylor was looking at her phone and scrolling. "How much do you already know?"

Jax donned a gown and tied it at the back. "Only what you told

Uncle Marty."

Taylor rubbed the back of her neck and pulled her phone from her pocket. "She was checking out a suspicious vehicle. As she was calling in the registration, the guy opened fire on her. The shot went through the windshield and apparently," Taylor pointed to the injury, "caught Zeus in the ear. Chance managed to get the Yukon in reverse and move back onto the roadway. She'd gotten out to shield herself with the vehicle, when the guy tried to escape by ramming her. She was able to fire before the impact. Unfortunately, it threw her across the road. When she landed on the blacktop, she hit her head. It looked like she broke her left wrist. They took her to Garrett Memorial. I just got word she's having a CAT scan now." Taylor put her phone back in her pocket. "If it's okay with you two, I'm going to step out and check on Maggie and Dee. I sent a deputy to get them."

Jax acknowledged with a headshake. "Shouldn't take us long. I'll let you know in a few minutes how he is. Tell them we're taking care of Zeus."

"Will do." Taylor left the room, Midas at her side.

Jax and Marty methodically worked through medicating and intubating their VIP patient. It was as if they'd worked together many times, as each found a rhythm in the task they were performing. Jax focused on her sutures and tried not to let her mind stray to thoughts of Chance lying in a scanner. With the procedure finished, they moved Zeus to a recovery area to allow him to wake up slowly.

"He's not going to be happy with the cone of shame. I don't want him scratching his ear, so he'll have to live with it for a while." Marty closed the cage and stood back.

"They always hate it. We don't need him opening that back up. His hemo count was good when we checked. I'd prefer he didn't lose any more and keep it that way."

Marty put a hand on her shoulder. "He's young and healthy; he'll do fine. I'll stay here and watch him. You go get an update on Chance."

Jax removed her disposable gown and threw it into the trash. "Thanks. It was all I could do to concentrate on Zeus." She walked out and found Taylor pacing in the waiting room. "Any word on her yet?"

Taylor looked up from her phone. "How's Zeus first?"

"In recovery. Marty's watching him. We were able to close the wound easily."

"That will relieve Chance's mind. Okay, this is what I know, which isn't much. She's out of the scan and back in the ER. No word on the results. They're evaluating the rest of her injuries. I'm coordinating with the state police. We've got press crawling all over my wife at the sheriff's office. I'd like to head to the ER. Unfortunately, as Chief Deputy, I've got too much to do here, right now. Sarah's there with her. Maggie and Dee rode over with Randy. I'll head there after I go check in with Penny and try to formulate a statement for our public information officer. The one trooper that was on scene is a good friend. We'll need to coordinate what we release to the media. I'll say this, I'm grateful Chance is a very good shot.

"Do you think..." Jax hesitated, "that Maggie and Dee would care if I came to the hospital? I could give Chance an in-person update on Zeus. Maybe that would ease her mind, so she can concentrate on her own health."

"I'm sure they'd appreciate that. If Chance is awake, Zeus is all she's going to be able to focus on. Are you okay to drive?" Taylor looked at Jax with what could only be construed as concern.

"I'm fine. I'll feel better if I'm there."

"I have no doubt having you there will be good for Chance. Be careful and call me if you need anything." Taylor handed her a business card. "I wrote my personal cell number on the back."

"Thank you, Taylor."

"It's me that needs to say thanks for taking care of Zeus. He's an important part of this department and, well, he's family."

Jax smiled. She'd worked with other police officers and knew the devotion between K9 handlers and their dogs. She watched Taylor and Midas leave the office, and then turned back to the recovery area. Marty was repositioning Zeus's head to make sure he could maintain his own airway.

"Is he starting to wake up a bit?"

"Some. He's still pretty groggy from the anesthesia on top of the pain medicine. I'll stay with him. You headed to the hospital?"

"I thought I'd go home and change. I don't think she'll want to see me covered in Zeus's blood. I'm going to take a few pictures of him with my phone to show her how he's doing. Maybe it will calm her nerves." Jax walked over and opened Zeus's cage. The dog's eyes were open. "Hey buddy. Your mom's going to be asking about you. Can you give me a good picture, so she won't worry so much?" Zeus huffed, as Jax pointed her cell phone at him, zooming in on the surgically repaired ear first. She took a few of him resting comfortably, along with a short video of her talking to him.

She stood and put the phone in her pocket, as she walked over to her uncle. He kissed her on the temple. "I'll have to take your truck to go home and get mine, can you call someone for a ride home?"

Marty nodded.

"We'll be fine here. He's going to sleep, and my new edition of Fins and Fur arrived. Drive slowly and call me with an update on Chance, doctor's orders."

Jax kissed him on the cheek. "Thanks, Uncle Marty. I love you." With that, she strode out of the clinic and climbed in her truck. *Now that I'm sure one Fitzsimmons is on the mend, let's see how the other one is faring.*

Chapter Seven

CHANCE LAY IN THE bed of her Chevy pickup, Jax snuggled in close to her. A million stars danced overhead, as the peepers croaked out a love song. The water lapped against the riverbank in a soft rhythmic slap. A slight nip to the side of her neck brought everything alive in her body.

"Jax, you know that drives me nuts."

Jax bit her neck again and moved her hand under Chance's black, basketball T-shirt. "You don't say."

The light scratch of fingernails against her stomach muscles made Chance's body jerk with arousal. She flipped Jax onto her back and let her own body lie down on the soft flesh beneath her. Jax wore a pair of cutoff jeans and that red, white, and blue bikini top that turned Chance into a complete mess of desire. She was eighteen and had touched only one other girl, when she was a junior, and nothing to this extent. As a senior, her focus would be on her grades and basketball. Right now, all she wanted to concentrate on was getting those shorts down Jax's long, silky legs.

"God, you feel good," Chance murmured.

"I'd feel a whole lot better if you took your clothes off...mine too while you're at it. Especially now that you're legal and I won't be considered a cradle robber."

Chance laughed and bit Jax's lower lip softly. "Happy birthday to me, and you're only nineteen, hardly a cradle robber." She unbuttoned Jax's shorts and slipped her hand inside. Jax was so wet for her.

Jax reached behind her own neck and put the tie for her bikini top in Chance's mouth. Chance moved her head until the string came lose, then used her teeth to move the fabric enough to take a tanned nipple between her lips.

Jax groaned beneath her and ran her hands in Chance's hair. She pushed Chance's head tighter to her breast and let out a gasp.

Chance looked up at her, the nipple still in her teeth. "I want you," Chance whispered.

Jax held her face and looked into Chance's eyes. "Then take what's yours." Jax helped push down her shorts.

Chance let her fingers trail down the taut stomach muscles again, before she allowed her fingers to run through Jax's wet center. She let her fingers brush Jax's clit with a feather-soft touch, and Jax bucked into her. Chance was breathing hard and heard Jax gasp as she moved to be inside of her. With utmost tenderness, she entered her and felt Jax clamp down around her fingers. Their eyes met and she uttered the words she'd never said to anyone who wasn't a family member.

"I love you, Jax."

Serious pain abruptly pulled Chance from the first night she'd made love to Jax, the first night she'd declared her love. Sounds disoriented her, and there was a pounding in her head. The bright lights of the room felt like knives stabbing behind her eyes, forcing them closed. The noise in her ears reminded her of the last time she'd walked by the shooting range without hearing protection. The ringing had lasted for hours.

Her stomach flipped, and she felt the urge to throw up. "I'm going to be sick." A basin was forced beneath her chin as she was flipped onto her side, while she emptied the contents of her stomach.

"Chance, don't move around so much. Let us do the work. That wrist is broken."

The voice was familiar. The sensations bombarded her and kept her from thinking clearly. Pain and noise overwhelmed her. *Jax? Was that Jax? No, not Jax. Who?* A terrifying memory hit her.

"Zeus, where's Zeus? He was shot, bleeding. Have to find Zeus!" Chance tried to rise from her supine position, only to be held down. The voice came again.

"Chance, settle down. Zeus is fine. He's at the vet's office. Let us take care of you. Please, Chance." It was clearer now. She knew that voice and heard the trepidation in the plea. "Faith? Where am I? What's happening?" She tried to focus, but the lights were too bright and sent her stomach into convulsions again.

A confident blonde stood at the side of the bed in navy-blue scrubs, concern written all over her face. "Chance, you're in the emergency room at Garrett Memorial. Zeus is with Doc Hendricks. Taylor says he's fine. Maggie and Dee are in the waiting room." Faith bent down. "You have to settle down before you hurt yourself. I can't sedate your ass or I would. Now I mean it, lay still. Don't make me go get Maggie to ground you."

The thought of Maggie and Dee's distress settled Chance down. Zeus was fine; he was getting treatment. She needed to figure out what the hell had happened and how she'd gotten there.

"Okay, okay. Stop yelling, my head is killing me." Chance reached up with her right hand to feel a row of stitches above her right eye.

"I'm not yelling. It's the concussion. Leave those stitches be. You've got a few more battle scars for your collection. You're damn lucky. You have a grade three concussion, and your left wrist is a mess. We have an orthopedic surgeon coming in to evaluate."

Chance opened an eye cautiously and tried to figure out where she was. "What are you doing here? This isn't the clinic."

Faith lifted an eyebrow. "Unhappy with my treatment, Sheriff?"

Chance tried to shake her head but stopped abruptly when the nausea hit. "No, no, that's not what I meant. I thought you only worked in the clinic."

"I started taking shifts here at the ER last month to help out when they're short staffed. I want to thank you for not tearing up my previous work. Now lie still. The nurses need to clean up a few more patches of road rash. I know Maggie and Dee are chomping at the bit to get to you. Taylor's been calling here about every three minutes asking for an update." Faith leaned over Chance and aligned her body so that Chance didn't have to turn her head. "You were lucky, Chance. This could have been a lot worse."

Chance took a few deep breaths and tried not to be frustrated with her ex-girlfriend's concerns. "Faith, I'm fine. Battered and bruised, I'll admit. I've been through worse."

"One of these days that isn't going to be true, and I'll be leaving flowers on your grave."

"Faith, we've been through this. Please don't, not now."

"And now I remember why I'm you're ex. I'm going to go talk to Maggie."

Faith started to pull away, and Chance reached for her with her bad hand. Her mind was too muddled to realize the consequences. The pain rolled through her. "Fuck! Damn it, Faith, please." Chance tried not to throw up again. She took a deep breath and steadied herself, as she struggled to maintain control. She risked opening her eyes to look at the woman she'd shared nearly five years of her life with. "I'm sorry. I appreciate all you're doing for me. I just can't do this right now, okay? Can we call a truce for once?"

Faith studied her, then nodded. "I'm going to go get your real family."

Chance felt the blow as surely as if Faith had issued an open-handed slap. Faith was now in a healthy relationship with someone who loved her. Chance still felt guilty from the breakup. The most dangerous thing Faith's wife did was take on members of the girls' basketball team in one on one. Faith was right, they were no longer bound together as family, and the disagreements that led to that reality were old and not worth repeating. Chance could no more change who she was than Faith could change how she felt about it. The darkness closed in again, and she drifted off into the peace.

***

Chance woke to soft fingers pushing back the hair off her sweaty forehead. It might have been minutes or hours later, she had no idea. She carefully opened her eyes to see a face similar to her own. "Hey, Mom."

The lines on the forehead of the woman who raised her released slightly. "Hey, yourself. You gotta stop scaring me like this, kid. Dee's already had one heart attack, and I'd like to avoid having one myself. I know you're tough. You can stop proving it to me any time." Maggie leaned over and kissed Chance's forehead.

"I'll see what I can do. I'm sorry I scared you. Scared the shit out of me too. How's Zeus? They just keep telling me he's okay."

"Well, I'll let his doctor tell you herself. Jax went for coffee."

Chance looked around the room. She was no longer in the emergency room but in a private hospital room. Dee sat with her head propped on her arm napping. "What time is it?"

Maggie looked at her watch. "A little after ten."

Chance furrowed her brow, confused that such a short amount of time had passed since the end of her morning run and the shootout. "Ten? I thought it'd be a lot later."

"Honey, it's ten o'clock in the evening. You've been in and out on us all day. Jax should be back any minute. I'll see where she is so she can give you an update. Be right back."

Chance lay in her bed thinking about the fact she'd lost sixteen hours of the day. She could only remember bits and pieces. She looked down at her casted arm. *At least it's not my gun hand, or for that matter, the hand I wipe my ass with. No way in hell I'd let Maggie or Dee handle that job.* There was only a dull thud in her head, and she was grateful they'd kept the lights down low and the blinds shut. She needed to know how Zeus was and what was happening with the investigation. *Where's my cell phone?*

A light rap on the door announced her visitor. Jax walked past a still-snoring Dee to stand by the bed. She cautiously leaned down. "Hey, you."

Chance tried to muster up a grin. "Hey, yourself. How's my boy?"

Jax pulled out her cell phone and showed a picture of Zeus lying on the floor beside her uncle's chair. "Taylor stopped by the house and sent me this. He's resting comfortably, although not happy at all about his cone of shame. Uncle Marty didn't feel right about leaving him in an empty clinic overnight."

"What were his injuries? I haven't heard how he's doing since I came in this place."

Jax reached out a hand and touched Chance on the forearm of her good side. "He's missing the very top part of his ear. The bullet took most of it off. When we got him, the damaged section was hanging on by a piece of tissue. To avoid infection, and a host of other issues, we went ahead and removed it and sewed the wound up. He's doing well. He keeps trying to scratch at the wound. Thus, the cone."

"Take good care of him please. That dog...well, he's more than a dog."

Jax leaned down, allowing Chance to look directly in her eyes. Without a light shining in them, she didn't experience the blinding pain. She felt Jax take her good hand. "That I can promise you. He'll stay with Uncle Marty unless you want Taylor to pick him up."

Maggie stepped forward.

Chance closed her eyes. "No, Taylor is going to have her hands full trying to figure out who the guy that shot at us was. Maggie might have to come and feed him, unless Taylor stops by. There are only a few I've trained Zeus to know as safe.

"I do remember someone telling me the suspect is dead. Other details are pretty fuzzy."

Maggie shook her head and stepped over to Dee. "When he's able, I'll have him brought to me. Until then, I'll go feed him. I'm going to get this one home. She turns into a pumpkin after nine."

Jax turned to look at the two women. "I can take you home."

Maggie waved her off. "Our secretary and her husband brought our vehicle over. Chance, we'll stop over to Marty's tomorrow and visit with Zeus. I'll bring you something other than those hospital things if they're going to keep you, or something easy to put on if they're going to release you." She helped Dee from the chair.

Dee scrubbed her face and walked over to Chance's bed. "Five Points, you sure keep the blood pumping through my system. Can we try to stop seeing how well those stints are doing? Love you. See you tomorrow." Dee bent down and kissed Chance.

Maggie followed her and cupped Chance's face as she held their foreheads together. "Try to get some rest. We'll be back in the morning. I love you, honey."

Chance held on to Maggie's hand for a long time, holding her close. "I'm all right, Mom. You okay to drive home? I can have one of the deputies come. I..."

"You worry about healing up. Maybe they'll release you tomorrow. If they do, I'll fry you a plate of bacon that will need sideboards."

Chance chuckled and kissed her. "Deal. Now go home. I'm doing fine."

Maggie and Dee left the room, and Jax moved closer. "You scared the shit out of me."

"I promise, that wasn't in my plan."

"I don't want you to worry about Zeus. You just concentrate on getting better. You owe me dinner. In case you've conveniently forgotten."

"No, that's something I *do* remember.

Jax scooted a chair close to the bed. "Faith was in a few times. She seems nice and very competent."

Chance drew in a deep breath and blew it out slowly. "I'll assume Maggie told you she's an ex?

"She did and said you parted on friendly terms."

"We did. Are you sure you want to even hear this?"

"What I want is for you to get some sleep. I've made arrangements to stay here tonight. With the way they've remodeled these rooms, there's a couch over there that will do just fine as a bed."

"Jax, you don't have to stay. I'm fine. Go home."

"Nice try. Not going to happen, so you might as well quit arguing. Maggie and Dee will feel better with me here. I'm a paramedic, remember? Not that you're going to need my skills in here. It helps to have someone right here to help, without you having to hit a call button." Jax squeezed her hand. "Let me do this for you, and for me, please?"

Chance sighed. "Okay. I really need to talk to Taylor. Being in the dark is driving me crazy."

Jax held up a hand. "I have a message from Taylor for you. She said rest up and she'll be here first thing in the morning with a detailed briefing. All the appropriate people have been notified. She did tell me to let you know that Trooper Harley Kincaid is heading up the investigation and everything shows it was a justified shooting."

"Harley is great trooper and a good friend who would put her mother in jail if she broke the law." Chance rubbed her eyes.

"How about you close your eyes and try to rest? That's what your body needs most. Tomorrow's another day, and there isn't anything you can do tonight anyway. Sleep, and I'll be right here."

Chance looked at Jax who sat there with her long hair braided across her shoulder. "Thanks for coming. I'm sure having you here helped ease Maggie and Dee's mind."

"They were good to me all those summers ago. I think the world of them. They were pretty worried about you."

"They're really the only parents I ever knew. After Dad was killed, they gave me a good life."

"I don't think they regret a minute of it. Nice to have parents that accept you exactly as you are."

Chance drifted and jerked awake. "Still no change on that front for you?"

Jax squeezed her hand. "We'll save that for a few beers and the deck with my other stories. For now, I want you to get some sleep. I'll be right here when you wake up."

Chance started to say something that was just on the tip of her tongue. Her mind was muddled. Memories of making love with Jax at the riverbank made the events of the day fade into the background. She tightened her hand on the soft one in hers and fell asleep.

***

Three days after she was released from the hospital, Chance was close to losing her mind. Not being able to go back to work or be part of the investigation was making her cranky and foul tempered. The headaches were slowly becoming less severe and shorter in duration. The photophobia, caused by the concussion, had her wearing sunglasses from the moment she woke up until the sun went down. A mild case of double vision and a wonky feeling made walking around a challenge, as she was never sure what step was the real one and which one was its mirrored twin. Zeus whined at her side.

"I know buddy, this sucks." With Chance able to watch him,

combined with his drive to obey her commands, she was able to leave off the cone of shame until bedtime. His ear was healing nicely. Jax had been by several times to check on both patients.

"How about some iced tea and a sandwich? It's time for your medicine, so I brought that out too." Maggie walked out on the deck and handed her a glass. She set the plate down on the arm of the Adirondack chair. Thick slices of turkey poked out from between slices of homemade bread.

"Mom, don't you have better things to do than play chef and nursemaid? I'm fine." She threw back the pills and took a drink.

Maggie sat down beside her. "Are you getting tired of having me around or just unhappy with my cooking?"

Chance rolled her head to the side and gave Maggie a crooked grin. "I'm not tired of having you around. I know you have things to do and a wife who has probably snuck down to McDonald's for lunch, since you've been spending yours with me. I'm on the mend. I apologize for being cranky."

"You never were good at being sedentary. When you were twelve, I thought I was going to have to staple the ass of your jeans to the chair to get you to do your schoolwork. I guess that's why you've always chosen the jobs you have. They've all kept you moving and on the go. Penny says you're the perfect sheriff, as long as you don't have to sit at your desk for more than an hour at a time."

The laughter brought a dull thump to Chance's head. "Please don't make me laugh that hard, it makes my head hurt."

"Truth hurts. If you really are tired of having me around, all you have to do is say so. It's not a hardship on me, trust me on that. I don't want to make you feel like a child, even though I want to protect you because you *are* my child."

Chance reached out her uncasted hand and took Maggie's in hers. "I truly am sorry for scaring you. Tucker County is usually a pretty safe place to be a law enforcement officer." Chance pushed her sunglasses to the top of her head. "We also know the opposite can be the truth. Our family has lived with the reality of that since Dad was killed." She let her words sink in for a minute. "I'm careful, you know that. I also make sure I'm well trained. That incident was a fluke. I spotted that car after my run. Before you say it, I know I didn't have my vest on. I wasn't expecting to get into a gun fight. I was checking on what I thought would be a simple abandoned vehicle, stolen or ditched. The windows were tinted and kept me from seeing the occupant. I'm glad I didn't pull any closer, or I might have more than a concussion, and Zeus might be missing more than just the tip of his ear. I'm admitting all this to you so that you'll understand that I've already evaluated my actions and won't make the same mistake twice."

The woman she'd always considered her mother turned her head and looked out at the view. Chance pulled Maggie's gaze back to her. "Talk to me."

Maggie took a deep breath and let it out slowly. "Chance, you're the most conscientious officer I know. You've tried to plan for every contingency. You made sure the patrol officers have K9 units so they are never working alone. You've bought them the best equipment your budget will allow and given them the best training out there. The one thing you can't predict is how the bad guy is going to react. I worry about you every day you put on that vest and strap that gun to your side. When you were smoke jumping, Dee and I tried to put it out of our minds that you were hurling yourself out of a perfectly good airplane into a place that was on fire."

"Mom..."

"Let me finish, Chance. When you got burned, we prayed to every god who would listen to us that you'd live, and later that you'd thrive. Those prayers were answered, and I'm forever grateful. Even with your position with Fish and Wildlife, we knew some crazy poacher or hunter could try to hurt you. Now that you're the boss of your own department, you have more than just yourself to worry about."

Maggie shifted in her chair. "Your dad and mother gave you the name they did because you were the answer to the *chance,* they took to try to get pregnant and what they considered their greatest gift. It was a risk for her, but she wanted a baby so badly they had to try. Neither of them really got to see the incredible person you'd become. When they died, your name took on new meaning to me. You gave me a chance at the child Dee and I never thought we'd have. I know I didn't give birth to you, but that hasn't stopped me from looking at you as the daughter I always wanted," she laughed, "and the son I didn't."

She squeezed Chance's hand. "Dee and I've been proud to fill in for your mother and dad. To be honest, I'd like to have been a grandparent." She held up a hand to Chance. "Relax, I gave up on that a long time ago, unless your sister, Kendra, decides to have children someday. You've always been determined to keep moving like when you were twelve. Your spirit could never completely settle. God bless Faith for trying to make you hang up your gun. I told her she was trying to catch water with a sieve."

Chance rubbed her forehead. "I'll give her that. She tried everything she could think of."

Maggie rose from her chair and knelt in front of Chance. "What I'm trying to say is that I'm proud of who you are. I always have been. I'd like very much to live out my life without burying my child. You're like a cat that's used up a few of its nine lives." She stopped and took a breath. "Don't say anything else. I'm not asking you to quit. I'm only asking you to do everything, and I mean everything possible, to make sure you grant my wish. I love you and so does Dee." She rose and wiped at the tears that continued down her cheeks. "Now, I'm going home to plan a nice, healthy dinner for my wife and give you some time to rest. If you need anything..." She bent and kissed Chance on the head.

"You're on speed dial, Mom. I love you, and I'll think about what you said, I promise." Chance watched the silver-haired woman walk away with one hand on her back and the other covering her mouth to stifle the sob Chance could tell she was holding back. *I'm such a jackass.*

Chapter Eight

JAX CONCENTRATED ON HER cards. They were sitting on Chance's back deck playing gin. She'd finally removed her sunglasses, which allowed Jax to evaluate her face for lost sleep or illness. Her face seemed relaxed and pain free. Jax breathed a sigh of relief. Supper had been a flavorful affair, thanks to a special marinade Jax used for the pork chops. The sun dipped lazily below the horizon and painted the sky a soft, orange Creamsicle color.

"Gin." Jax fanned out her cards and quirked the side of her mouth into a tiny arch.

Chance tossed her cards on the table. "Dammit, how'd you do that? Again, no less?"

"Uncle Marty and I play almost every night. He taught me the game when I was young, and my skills only got better with time." Jax handily beat Chance five games out of seven.

"Okay, I surrender. Uncle."

Jax raised her arms in triumph and let out a whispered "Yes!"

"How about I get you a beer as your reward for stomping my ass?"

"To the victor go the spoils."

Chance grabbed the table edge with her uninjured hand and grimaced as she got up. Jax's gut churned with concern. With a hand that trembled, she reached out. "Are you all right?"

Chance nodded. "Let me go get that beer for you."

Jax watched Chance make her way back into the house, waiting for a misstep or a stumble that never appeared. *Warriors never show weakness.* A few minutes later, Chance reappeared with an uncapped bottle of amber ale in her hand. She held it out to Jax, who took a deep drink.

Jax looked at the label. "This is really good. How long ago did Tucker County become the microbrewery hub of the region?"

"Mountain State Brewing Company is one of the oldest distributing microbreweries in the state." She pointed to Jax's bottle. "Their Almost Heaven Amber Ale is a particular favorite."

Jax wiped a few drops of condensation off the label. "I love the caramel finish."

They grew silent for a few minutes, enjoying the sounds of the evening. Cicadas trilled off in the trees and a whippoorwill sang its repetitive tune. Sweet hints of honeysuckle drifted in as the breeze picked up.

Chance broke the silence. "Spend many nights like this in California?"

Jax answered almost immediately. "I wouldn't even be home yet, and I'm not talking about the time difference. Most mornings, I left the house at seven and I didn't make it home until nine. I ate dinner alone in my office frequently. I'd shower when I got home and fall into bed. The next morning, I'd start all over again. The only break I got was on the weekend. Saturdays, I'd head to the barn to spend the next eight to ten hours doing something for myself, on the back of a horse."

She took another pull on her beer, letting the smooth finish please her tongue. She swallowed down the rising bile at the back of her throat over the insanity of her former life. "I'd work out Mac and Glenny on the trails, where I could gratefully lose myself. Now, I see it was more like I was trying to find myself." She let her words trail off and ran a hand through her long hair.

"Sounds like you got out of there just in time."

Jax tilted her head in Chance's direction and drew her brows together at the insight. "What do you mean?"

Chance leaned forward, resting her elbows on her knees, supporting her casted hand with her good one. "I mean, it sounds like California was sucking the life blood out of someone I vividly remember, who enjoyed pushing the envelope, diving into the deepest water and reaching for that hand hold that was almost impossible for anyone else. The woman I'm looking at right now has all the same intelligence, all the same mannerisms, all the same beautiful features she did when we were young, except..." Chance hesitated.

The air evaporated out of Jax's lungs, as she waited for the coming judgment. All the things Chance said were complimentary. The fear of what she didn't like nearly froze Jax, as crippling dread moved through her veins like ice forming on a creek in the middle of February. *She's not interested in me anymore. I'm too late.*

"It worries me that I don't see that zest for life, that fire I always saw glowing brightly in your eyes. It's like one of my old smoke jumper teams parachuted into your fire and dug everything away that could keep a fire burning. The light in your eyes doesn't seem near as bright."

Jax focused on Chance's casted arm, not truly seeing the black wrap, as she digested Chance's analysis. For the first time in years, someone truly saw her beyond her physical attributes or her occupational endeavors. Chance had taken off the watch face to see what prevented the clock from keeping time. The abrasive grit in the precision gears had worn away their inner workings. She realized that Chance saw her affliction in a way only Uncle Marty had been able to diagnose accurately. He'd described it as a dog that had been starved for food and affection, willing to accept whatever attention its irresponsible family was willing to provide. She was quiet for a long time, afraid to voice her thoughts, until she felt a light touch on her arm.

Chance dipped her head. "Jax, I'm sorry. Did I say something wrong?"

The touch was warm and tender; Chance's thumb rubbed lightly on the inside of her forearm. Jax brought her eyes level with Chance's warm, gunmetal-blue ones. She brought a hand to Chance's cheek and used her thumb to trace a shadow under Chance's eye.

"No, you didn't say anything wrong. As a matter of fact, you've given an accurate portrayal of exactly who I became. Now you know one of the reasons I came back here when I left California. It felt like everything that made up who I truly am had been replaced with who I was expected to be. The real me...the girl who loved to ride in a beat-up pickup truck to the riverbank to spend the day fishing or floating and spend the night in the bed of that same truck...wasn't good enough, even to myself. The only thing I held on to was the love of horses."

Chance leaned in closer. "And you think that by coming back here, you can find the woman you were?"

"I think by coming back here, I can wake up the woman I used to be."

"Like Sleeping Beauty?"

Jax focused on Chance's lips. "Well, it took something extraordinary to wake her up." Chance moved in closer, until Jax could smell the mint from the iced tea on her breath.

"It did. True love's kiss."

Chance's face was too close for Jax to focus on anything but her lips. She wanted so badly to feel them on her own. As if granting permission, she tilted her head slightly and leaned it to one side.

"Maybe that will work in this case," Chance said.

"I'm willing to try if you are."

Jax moved in until even the slightest movement, on either of their parts, would find them kissing whether they meant to or not. And Jax meant to. She leaned forward until her lips met Chance's. It was a feather-soft brush at first, hesitant and fleeting. The second was less tentative, with an increase in both intensity and duration. Hunger drove Jax. It had been decades since she'd felt the slightest desire to touch anyone, or to be touched.

Her hand shook with desire and found its way to the side of Chance's face. She let her fingers slide around the back of the strong neck. Jax groaned in pleasure when she felt Chance mirror her movement. Fingers wove into her hair and pulled her even closer. When her tongue snaked out to enter Chance's parted lips, she had a flash of a summer evening around a campfire at the riverbank. The same warmth she remembered radiating off the fire was now burning through her body, nearly incinerating her. Somewhere in the haze, she realized the heat had receded, as if she'd backed away from it.

"Jax…"

Jax came back to her senses as the hunger quelled. She sat back and put both hands in her hair. "Holy shit."

"I'll second that motion." Chance met her eyes and reached out her hand. "I want you to understand why I'm slowing this down. I enjoyed the hell out of kissing you. I pulled back, because I want to make sure you're okay. It's been a pretty emotional few days. To be honest, I feel like it's 1984 again. My hands are sweating, and my heart is racing. The same beautiful woman is causing it all."

"Ditto and I'm right there with you." Jax rubbed a hand across her eyes. "I detect a but coming."

"No buts, only a promise. I promise I want more than my libido is telling me I want. I want time with you. Time to get to know you again for who you are now. I also want, no, I need you to know who I am now and how that all came to be."

Jax tried to process what Chance was saying. It felt like the woman before her was warning her off, while at the same time, telling her that she wanted something more than just a friendship.

"Since I saw you at the rescue operation, I've barely been able to think about anything else other than those days from our past. I remember that girl in her bikini top and cut off shorts. When I woke up in ER, I was having a vivid dream of our first night together. I can honestly tell you I think you're more beautiful now. Back then, you completely stopped my heart from beating. I'm damn sure the woman

I'm looking at is capable of even more than that."

Chris Cornell's cover of *Nothing Compares 2 U* floated out of the hidden speakers on the deck. Jax thought about the irony of the song. No one had ever compared to Chance. Jax blushed profusely, remembering the outfit she'd painstakingly picked out in an attempt to seduce Chance. It had worked a great deal better than she'd hoped for back then.

"Chance, I can promise you I don't look that way in a bikini anymore. You remember me as that nineteen-year-old." Jax stood and turned away from her and faced the yard. "I may have all the hallmarks of that girl from the past, unfortunately, I'm also battered and bruised."

"That's why I dumped a bucket of icy water on both of us. You're not the only one. I'm battered and bruised too. Jax, those scars aren't limited to the outside of my body. It's also likely I'll have a lot more of them before I take my last breath."

A flashback of the scars she'd seen on the backside of Chance's left arm flitted across Jax's memory. "I'm not afraid of scars, Chance. Are you?"

Jax was turned and pulled into a muscled chest by a well-defined arm. She took her first unrestricted breath in years and melted into the embrace. She wrapped her arms gently around the torso she knew had taken a beating just a few days ago.

Chance nuzzled her hair. "No, I'm not. I want you to truly know who it is you're thinking of letting down your armor for."

Jax said nothing, as she absorbed the subtle scent of leather and sweet feed, pure Chance. She melted into the security of the arms around her. "It's been such a long time since I felt accepted. You make me feel safe to be myself."

"You can always be yourself with me, Jax. I expect nothing less. I'd like to have a word or two with whoever the hell it was that ever made you believe you weren't good enough."

"That list would be too long to even put together."

Chance pulled back and squinted. "Not Marty, right?"

"After Jennings died, he and Aunt Mary were the only people who made me feel like I mattered."

"I'm sorry, Jax. I know that had to be devastating. I can't imagine anyone making you feel unworthy. You deserve better."

"Well, that's all water under the bridge. I've lived with the judgments of my mother and with what my ex-wife and her family thought of me." She stepped back from Chance and walked to the edge of the deck.

Chance moved up beside her. "Did you have anything that made you happy all these years?"

"My horses and the endurance racing we participated in. When we were out on a trail, I could lose myself. "

"Well, when my ribs heal up, we'll have to go riding, if you don't mind sharing that time with me?"

Jax turned and placed a soft kiss on Chance's cheek. "That's an offer I'd never refuse, after you're healed up."

"Yes, doctor."

Jax leaned on the railing, her arm touching Chance's. She remembered those summer nights when they'd spend time together doing nothing more than watching the lightning bugs dance in the tall grass. The silence was as reassuring as the strength Chance displayed. Jax felt like she was creating a whole new life for herself with building blocks from the past. She could live with her new reality, one that she sought out and that she would be wholly in charge of. It was time she reclaimed who she was always meant to be. Starting today, she was going to do exactly that.

Chapter Nine

EARLY THE NEXT MORNING, six days from her injury, Chance slowly made her way to the door to let Zeus out. She yawned and looked up to see Sarah standing on the other side of the door with a Tupperware container in her hands.

"Hey you. How are you? Thought you could use breakfast. This will give Maggie a break from being your chief cook and bottle washer. I bring you cinnamon rolls from my best half."

Chance pushed the door open with her hip. She looked out at the yard to check Zeus. "Your best half makes killer cinnamon rolls. Feel free to drop by with those as often as you'd like."

"Kristi thought you'd say that. Now tell me the truth, how're you feeling?" Sarah set the container on the kitchen table. "And don't bullshit me."

"Scout's honor I'm being good, and things seem to be healing up as expected." Looking at her friend she knew that wouldn't be enough. "My arm thumps when I let it hang down. As long as I don't make any quick movements, the ribs don't bother me too much. Headache is abating, though the light still bothers me. Double vision is clearing out. Now is that enough no-bullshit detail for you?" Chance poured them both a cup of coffee and handed one to Sarah.

"You're such a pain in my ass. Yes, that's enough detail. How about we take these out on the deck?"

Chance carried her cup by the handle in her good hand and walked out the French doors. "Sounds good. Zeus is in the yard doing his business."

"How's his ear doing?"

"As long as I keep him from shaking his head, pretty good. Doc Hendricks and Jax have been stopping by to take a look at him off and on."

Sarah took a sip of her coffee and opened the Tupperware container. "Don't tell my wife I ate one of these. I got the these-are-for-Chance-you-hear-me speech as she held the container out of reach. I swear to Pete. She likes you more than me."

Chance let out a laugh. "She does like me more, but she loves you. It was good to see Daniel when he stopped by to check on me. You were right. He's a giant now." Chance reached out to take Sarah's hand. "You're a great mom, you know?"

"Kristi deserves the medal for that one. She raised both of us. She's got the patience of Job which, as you know, I have very little of. Our twenty-fifth anniversary is coming up, and I'm trying to figure out what to do."

"I can't believe you guys have been married that long. Although there are times when I get out of bed that I have no doubt we are that old. It seems like just yesterday you two started dating right before our senior year of high school. When she moved to town, you were hooked from day one.

"That I was, my friend. She's still the most beautiful woman I've ever met. How I convinced her to be with me is still a mystery. She'd never even thought about being gay until I swept her off her feet. My life was never the same, and twenty-five years later, I'm still as in love with her as I was back then. I will say that my body tells me all the time how old we are. My ankle still swells from where I broke it playing basketball with you."

Chance rubbed her jaw. "I'm with you there. Some mornings my jaw still aches."

Sarah laughed. "When you got hurt, Kristi wanted to make you some soup. I ixnayed that immediately."

With a hand on her stomach, Chance groaned. "No soup, ever again."

The pair took a seat at the table overlooking the scenery of the valley. "Speaking of our glory days, how is Jax?"

Chance couldn't have hidden her grin even if she'd wanted to. "We're a little older and a lot more jaded, but she still sets my heart off on a run of V-tac. She took care of Zeus for me and came to the hospital. And she stayed. That has to mean something doesn't it?"

"If I remember right, it was a chance meeting that brought you two together all those years ago. You had that horse that got a gash on her flank. Doc Hendricks showed up to take a look at it. When he got out of his truck, he wasn't alone."

"I was gone from that moment on."

"Do you think she's part of why you and Faith could never make it last?"

Chance stopped midsip and looked at her best friend and the younger sister of her ex-lover. "I'm sorry, Sarah. We've been friends for so long that I forget when I talk to you about things like this, it could be seen as disrespectful to her."

"Chance, I appreciate that, although that's not what I meant. Faith is happy. I guess what I'm trying to ask is if your feelings for Jax kept you from being truly committed to anyone?"

"I don't know. I don't think so. Faith and I first spent time together because of my relationship with you and Kristi. When we started dating, I was with Fish and Wildlife. Things didn't seem so complicated. After our first few years together, that changed. The issues between us didn't have to do with my feelings for anyone else. I promise, Sarah, I was all in with Faith. It came down to the fact she couldn't stand worrying about me every time I went out on a police call or search and rescue. She wanted a life without that stress, and I couldn't offer it. Jax is an entirely different situation. We're both pretty beat up in a variety of different ways. She was in a long-term relationship with someone who didn't value her."

Chance took another drink and a bite of her cinnamon roll. The two women who'd held her heart for longer than anyone else were as different as where the sun rose and where it set. Trying to compare the two women was impossible. The only thing they held in common was being a doctor, one of human medicine and one of veterinary medicine. *Red hair to ebony, blue eyes to ones of the lightest greens Chance had ever seen. Pale skin to...*

"Earth to Chance?"

"Huh?"

"You were gone. What were you thinking about?"

"The difference between night and day my friend, night and day."

Another hour passed, as the two friends checked in with each other after a shared trauma.

"Seeing you lying there on the pavement scared the shit out of me, Chance. I'm not going down the road of trying to tell you not to do what you do. I only ask that when you do it, be as careful as you can. You're well trained and have reflexes I'd have died for when we were playing basketball. I'm just asking that you be alive long enough to have an opportunity for some real happiness. Kristi and I haven't made it twenty-five years because it's been easy, safe, or even comfortable. We've made it because we decided life was better together than it was apart."

Chance nodded in acknowledgment of her words. "I'm not discounting anything you've said, my friend, I promise. I really tried with Faith, Sarah. You know me as well as anyone on earth. I really tried. I compromised as much as I could. I cut back with the wildfire group, only going out when they couldn't get anyone else. I dropped out of the drug task force and turned all of that over to Taylor. I couldn't stop being who I am. If I'd done that, we'd never have made it as long as we did. I gave her one hundred percent of what I had to give. I never asked her to give up anything except the hope that I'd leave law enforcement. I couldn't do that Sarah, not for Maggie or Dee, and not for her without being an unhappy bitch. Eventually that unhappiness would have poisoned us. She's happy now, and for the first time in a long time, I'm looking forward to possibilities."

They sat in comfortable silence for a long time, watching birds on the feeder and a large red squirrel hard at work on an ear of corn jammed on a nail at the rail fence. Zeus sat with his eyes focused on his domain. His head turned to the house when Chance heard the kitchen door open. He stood and wagged his tail, as Maggie made her way onto the porch.

"Good morning, girls. Sarah, good to see you."

Sarah rose and hugged her. "Nice to see you too, Maggie. How's Dee?"

Maggie rolled her eyes. "Fighting me tooth and nail on this low-cholesterol diet. Worse than trying to get that one to even try soup."

Chance covered her eyes. "Again, with the soup!"

"I take that to mean you aren't interested in any?" Maggie's grin was infectious.

Sarah laughed as Chance grimaced.

Chance held up a hand in Maggie's direction like she was stopping traffic. "Not even if you grounded me and made me sit at the table until it was gone. No soup!"

Maggie crossed her arms. "You big baby. How are you by the way?"

"I'm bored. I'm starting to go stir crazy."

Sarah stood and handed Chance the last cinnamon roll before putting the lid back on the container. "And with that, I'm out of here. Years ago, when she said she was bored, it meant we were about to go climb something or build something. Occasionally, it was build something to climb." She kissed Maggie on the cheek as she passed.

Chance held up her cinnamon roll. "Tell Kristi thanks for breakfast."

Sarah snapped her fingers. "Tell her yourself when you come for supper next week after your birthday. Oh, did I forget to mention that was a condition of giving you the cinnamon rolls? Must be getting old. My spawn wants to show off his archery skills for you. Bring Jax if she's available."

"Good thing I love Kristi and Daniel. You," she paused, "are just a royal pain in my ass. I'll be there. I'll have to see about Jax."

Sarah waved as the screen door slammed behind her. "Call if you need anything."

Chance called after her. "Will do."

Maggie handed her a bundle of mail. "I figured I'd bring that in. How'd you sleep?"

Chance stood and drew her into a hug. "First, let me apologize for making you worry so much."

"Chance..."

"Let me finish, please. I know what you've been through, what I've put you through. I haven't been fair. Having a kid like me probably wasn't any picnic either, and I grew up to be an older version of that headstrong kid. All I've ever wanted to do was make you, Dee, and Dad proud."

Maggie put a hand on Chance's cheek. "That's all you've ever done. Forgive an old woman for being a worrywart. You are who you are, and I expect nothing less. Dee and I love you, and Kendra idolizes you. It took everything I had to keep her in school when you got hurt. She had one foot in the car before I could get her stopped. She's taking those summer classes to try and finish a year ahead of time."

Kendra was the little sister Chance never had. They'd talked every day since she'd been released from the hospital. Chance had convinced her to stay put.

"She said she's coming home for my birthday. It'll be good to see her."

"I'm sure she needs to see for herself that you're fine. It shook her up pretty bad. I'm grateful there were a few of her close friends nearby when I had to tell her."

"I've been informed she's planning to stay at my place, whether I like it or not."

Maggie looked up. "Will that be a problem? Her room is just like she left it. She can stay with us."

"No, no. It's never a problem to have her here. She told me she's anxious to talk about a few of her law enforcement classes."

"And eventually, I'll have two of you to be worried about."

"Kendra's going to make a better officer than I've ever been. She's smart as a whip. I look forward to seeing what branch of law enforcement she chooses to share that brilliance with. Until then, let's encourage her to enjoy being a college kid."

Maggie released her and wrapped an arm around her waist, as they went back into the kitchen. "How about another cup of coffee, since you've already had breakfast?"

"You're on."

They followed Zeus into the house and talked over coffee for the next hour. Another knock at the door brought Zeus to his feet, his tail wagging.

Chance saw her chief deputy with Midas, standing on the other side of the screen door. "Grand Central Station around here. I didn't know I was so popular. Come on in." Midas made his way over to Chance, and she scratched his face. Zeus whined. Taylor bent down and rubbed down his back.

"How are you boy?" Zeus wiggled in pleasure at the attention. Taylor laughed. "I know, you're as ready to get back to work as she is. "

"We won't lie about that will we, Zeus?" Zeus answered with a short bark and went to the coat closet as if he expected they would be going to work that very minute. Chance smiled and called him back, patting him on his side. "Soon, I promise. Sorry, boy."

"What are you doing running around over on this side of the mountain?" Chance gingerly got up from her chair and poured a cup of coffee, beckoning Taylor to an empty place at the table.

Taylor waved at the other occupant of the kitchen. "Hey, Maggie."

"Nice to see you, Taylor. Now that your next babysitter has arrived, I have to get to work." Maggie stood and headed to the door.

Chance grabbed her hand on the way past. "Thanks for bringing in the mail."

"I'll call you later, Chance. Try to behave."

Chance looked at her. "Tall order. I promise, I'll try."

Maggie shook her head and walked out.

Chance sighed, knowing she was making Maggie worry too much. She turned back to Taylor. "How's Sabrina?"

"Doc Jax stopped in to look at her this morning. Said she's good as new."

Chance smiled at the mere mention of Jax. She seemed to be doing that a lot these days. "That's great news, did she put the shoe back on?"

"She did and made a recommendation about a few things we might try in order to prevent some of the small issues we have. Said she'd tell you about it the next time she sees you."

"I'm sure that'll be this evening when she comes by to check on Zeus. I miss riding. Hell, I miss running. I feel like I'm sitting here spinning my wheels."

Taylor smirked. "Faith still hasn't given you the okay to go back to work, has she?"

The icy stare Chance threw at Taylor could have frozen the Cheat River solid. "What do you think? Everyone's mother henning me to death. You know me; I can't sit still for five minutes unless I'm asleep. I'm not built to sit around and recover." Chance made an air quote with her uncasted hand. "At least if they'd let me go to the office I could do paperwork. Our grant is coming up for the K9 training, and I need to finalize all the quotes. I'll bet you can't even find my desk with all the things your wife needs me to sign. Even Zeus is tired of me whining. I need to get back to work."

Taylor's chuckle finally broke through into a full-on laugh. "Petulant much? God, you're worse than a five-year-old who had their favorite toy taken away. Chance, you had a serious accident less than a week ago. You need time to allow that arm to heal."

"Wrist, damn it."

"Wrist, arm, either way, you are out of commission until Faith signs your release form. As Chief Deputy, I order you to enjoy your deck while you are off on sick leave. That also means I want confirmation from Maggie before you step one foot back in your office. I'm sure she'll be happy to zip tie your ass to the chair if she has to. Damn it, Chance. You scared the hell out of all of us. If the shoe was on the other foot and I was acting like you are, you'd kick my ass, then send Penny home to babysit me. You've always said you won't have your deputies do anything you wouldn't do. If any of our deputies were in the condition you are, you wouldn't let them back on the job until they were one hundred percent. How do you justify bending the injury rules for yourself?"

Chance held up her hands in defense. "All right, all right! I'll shut the fuck up about venting to any of you. Every one of you knows what I've been through before, and I know myself pretty damn well. I'd never endanger anyone, and I'd never let any of you down by trying to be a half-assed back up. I'm battered, not broken." She looked at her broken wrist. "Figuratively speaking. Now I'm done talking about this. Do you have anything else we need to discuss? I'm sure it's time for my nap."

Taylor leaned forward and dragged both hands down her face until she covered her mouth. "What do you think you have to prove, and who in the hell do you think you have to prove it to?" Taylor rose out of her chair and headed to the door.

Chance started to speak, but Taylor held up her hand. "Come on, Midas. We're not doing any good here."

"Taylor, come on." Chance rose, but the kitchen door was already closing. She stood and watched through the glass. Taylor loaded her dog in the vehicle. She started the engine and sat with both hands on the steering wheel, then rolled down the window.

"I'll call you later. I've got a mound of paperwork on your desk to clear off." Taylor rolled the window back up and turned the vehicle around to leave.

To her credit, she didn't spin a single tire or throw any gravel in the driveway. Chance put her head back and closed her eyes. "Shit, piss off all your friends and family, why don't you?"

Zeus stood beside her, panting softly.

"Well boy, as long as I don't piss you off, I guess I'll have one friend."

The restlessness was getting to both of them. She'd been ordered, by Faith, not to drive for at least a week, or until the concussion symptoms abated. That order had been backed up by both Maggie and Dee. If the double vision persisted, she'd be grounded for an even longer period of time and ordered back to the neurologist. Her department-issued Yukon had been totaled in the incident. She'd have to rely on her personal Toyota Tundra until the insurance claim worked itself out and she could outfit a new one.

"Zeus, I'm going to go nuts sitting here in this house."

The stables were only a few miles away. She could check on the horses. If Maggie caught her, there would likely be a verbal smack down coming. Not like she hadn't been getting those since she was twelve. She could call Taylor and beg a ride back to the house after their walk. It would give her a chance to apologize for being an ass.

"Well, Zeus, it's better to ask for forgiveness than permission. Let's take a walk."

***

Jax met Maggie at her office to discuss a list of properties that were available. Living with Marty was starting to wear on her. She wanted a little breathing room and to stop living out of her boxes in storage. It was time to find a home. She pushed through the door of the real estate office and was greeted by a wide smile.

"Well hello there, stranger." Maggie came from behind her desk to embrace Jax.

Jax accepted the hug and dropped into the chair Maggie directed her to. "I think we're past the stranger part. I've seen you more in the last few weeks than in thirty odd years. Have you talked to the patient today?"

"She's lacking."

Jax furrowed her brow. "Lacking? In what? Does she need something?"

Maggie let a chuckle out. "Yes, a bucket load of patience that she's short on. She's like a caged animal, pacing the house and yard. Taylor called a little bit ago...said Chance bit her head off."

Jax grimaced thinking about a confrontation between the two friends. "Oh, that can't be good."

"It isn't. This is her first major injury since, well." Maggie didn't finish the sentence. Instead, she pointed to a vivid photo of Chance on the fire line, dressed in a yellow, button-up shirt. A red, brimmed hardhat was cocked sideways on her soot-stained face. She dug at the ground with a Pulaski, while a line of pine trees blazed behind her like giant wooden torches against the evening sky.

"I saw the scars on her arm. She briefly mentioned it when I cleaned her up from that rescue out at Lindy Point. That photo is terrifying."

"Dee and I did more praying in those years than ever. She tried not to let us know how dangerous it was. Didn't matter, we knew. When she got caught in that burn over, she was trying to protect a ten-year-old boy and his dog. She put them in her fire shelter with her. She was given the Chief's Honor Award for her bravery. It cost her the career she loved. Thankfully, the boy and the dog survived. They had some injuries too, but not as bad as Chance's. I thought we were going to lose her. I really did."

"I can't imagine what she went through. I'm really glad she survived."

"Enough about that. Chance is always going to live up to her name. She even likes to say, 'there's always a Chance.' Anyway, she's never been able to sit still. Has to be doing something, says it feels like she'll jump out of her skin if she isn't moving."

"I told her, as soon as she gets the all clear, we'll go for a trail ride. That should lift her spirits."

"True. Let's get down to business so we can go see a few places." Maggie shared printouts of several houses and properties for sale, as well as rentals.

"This one has a barn, a large garage, and a good bit of land with it so you can pasture them. The land alone sells it."

Jax picked up the paper. A small brick home stood beside a barn that looked new. She studied a few other papers and saw something she liked in almost all of them. Maggie was good at finding what her clients were looking for.

"I like them all except for this one. It's too close to the main road for me. I want some privacy."

"I can certainly understand that. How about we take a ride and look at them up close?"

"Let's do it."

The pair headed out to Maggie's Toyota Four Runner and drove into Canaan Valley. Ten minutes into the trip, Maggie leaned forward in her seat and squinted at the windshield. "Damn her, I'm going to kick her ass. What the hell does she think she's doing?"

Jax had been looking at the print outs and pulled her head up to see what Maggie was fussing about. It took less than a second for her to take in the tall figure walking along the side of the road with a dog at her heel. "Uh oh."

"Uh oh, is right. I'll tan her hide." Maggie stepped on the accelerator and brought the vehicle alongside the pair. She rolled down her window. "Chance Raylynn, you're grounded. What in Sam Hill do you think you're doing? Get in this vehicle this instant."

A contrite Chance leaned on the open window. "We're just taking a walk. I can't drive, and you know I can't sit. I've worn a path down to the pond. Zeus suggested we go see the horses. I agreed and there you have it."

Maggie looked down at Zeus, then back up to Chance. "Get in the vehicle."

Chance sighed and opened the back door. "Laden, Zeus." The K9 climbed into the back seat and she followed.

Jax sat with her hand covering her mouth in a desperate attempt not to laugh. She did not want to draw the wrath of Maggie. "Hey, Chance."

Chance pointed a finger at her. "Don't laugh, smartass."

Jax shrugged her shoulders. "You are so busted."

"Chance," Maggie held her hands to the sides of her head, "you are going to drive me to drink."

"Pour enough for two."

Jax couldn't hold back her laughter any longer. "Not much has changed around here. And you still can't keep out of trouble."

"What fun would that be?"

Maggie turned and glared at Chance, who winced and held her hands up in defense. Jax was nearly bent over in her seat, tears running down her cheeks.

"Congratulations, you've earned yourself a babysitter for the rest of the day. You'll accompany us to see a few properties. Once we finish there, we'll go to lunch, and I'm dropping you off to Dee. She can take you to the stables. Don't argue. Don't say one word. You hear me?"

Chance said nothing.

Maggie's voice rose. "Answer me!"

Chance threw up her arms. "You said not to say a word. Now which is it, answer you or don't say one word?"

Jax tried desperately to bring herself under control and was losing the battle. The giggles turned into body shaking cackles that eventually spilled over to both of the other occupants, until the entire vehicle was shaking.

Maggie sighed. "Now look what you've done, messed up my mascara. Damn you, Chance. You are infuriating."

"And that's why you love me." Chance leaned forward and kissed Maggie's cheek. "I'm sorry, Mom. I really am. I'm going stir crazy and didn't think a walk over to the stables would hurt. I've been good for almost a week. I'm pretty sure that's a record. I promise you, I was going to call Taylor to take me back home. It would have given me an opportunity to say I'm sorry for being a bitch earlier. "

Maggie turned to her and shook her head, then looked at Jax. "Kids, big or small, they're still a pain in the ass. Remember that."

Jax bit her lip to hold back another outburst of laughter. "I'll try. I'll even take a turn on watch. Instead of bothering Dee, I'll stand guard over the patient. You leave her to me when we finish up."

Maggie looked over at Jax. "I don't offer hazard pay. Are you sure?"

"Hey!" Chance indignantly crossed her arms and looked at Zeus. "Do you hear how they're talking about us?"

Maggie turned completely around in her seat and faced Chance. "Zeus is smart enough to know I'm not talking about him."

Zeus barked at the sound of his name.

Jax grabbed her side. "I think she's got you there. I'd quit while you're behind."

Maggie put the vehicle in gear, and the four of them headed off in the direction of the first property.

***

Two hours later, the three women picked up Jax's vehicle and drove to Maggie's for lunch. Jax remembered the meals she'd been privileged to share with this family so many years ago. Maggie was an excellent cook. Before long, Jax pushed back from the table that sat on the deck. "Maggie, that was scrumptious."

"You're welcome here any time, Jax. With or without that pain-in-the-ass kid of mine."

Chance blushed.

"Well, you act like a child. If the shoe fits, wear it." Maggie cleared plates from the table and headed inside to the kitchen.

"How about I run you over to the stables to see the angels?" Jax took the last drink of her tea and stood up.

"I'd like to go see them. Taylor said Sabrina is doing better and you reshod her."

"It looks great, and she doesn't seem to favor it at all now. On my endurance team in California, we were using Razer shoes. They allow for a little flexing. It made a big difference. It might be worth trying a set to see if you like them."

"I'll do some research and see what we have in the budget. If it'll be better for the horse, I always try to find the money." Chance picked up her glass and carried it to the kitchen.

Jax watched her walk, noticing how the worn jeans fit Chance's ass. *She just gets better with age.* She watched as Chance walked up and hugged Maggie. The affection between the two was so evident. Jax knew Maggie worried about her from the conversations they'd had while Chance was in the hospital. Her scolding had been given out of love and concern for her welfare.

Maggie dried her hands on a dishtowel and turned to hug Chance fully. "I do love you, pain in my ass or not. Do your best to not turn me into someone who needs to be medicated." She turned to Jax. "I'm leaving her in your care, because I know you will make her behave. For the next few hours, I can relax. Think about those offers I showed you.

The one with the barn has been on the market the longest because of the price. It also includes the mineral rights. Rare in this day and age. It might be more land than what you want, I know. I worry the other one won't be big enough for you to have room to ride. Either way, if any of those aren't what you're after, I know of another place that will come on the market in a few months. If you can stand living with Martin that long? It's the old Richards place." She turned to Chance. "You know the one I'm talking about. It's beside your place. I talked to his nephew last week. Stan Richards is in a nursing home and suffering from dementia. His nephew has his power of attorney and told me Stan won't ever be able to come home. He's trying to get the affairs in order."

Chance's face glowed. "That place is spectacular. If I'm not mistaken, we share a corner at the far western point. We'd be neighbors."

Chance's smile heated Jax's whole body. The thought of living beside Chance was as enticing as kissing her. She wondered if she could hold out another few months. *Living with Uncle Marty isn't unbearable.* She'd need to see what the place looked like before making a decision. She doubted Chance would have said that the place was spectacular if it wasn't. "Well, is there anything preventing us from seeing the place from the outside?"

Maggie turned her head and appeared to be thinking. "Probably not. Once you've seen the property, I can talk to Adam. If you like it, I'll see if he'd let you have first look at the place once he's ready.

"We'll take a drive by on the way back to my place. Can't hurt." Chance kissed Maggie's temple and held up two fingers to pledge her Scout's honor. "I promise...to do my duty...to not drive you crazy."

"Thank you, dear."

Jax and Chance made their way to the door. Before Chance let it shut, she stuck her head back inside. "For the rest of the day." Chance slammed the screen door and headed for Jax's vehicle at a fast clip, Zeus ahead of her.

Jax watched her hunch her shoulders at Maggie's loud protest. "You are such a shit, Chance."

Chance grinned. "She wouldn't want me any other way and neither would you."

Jax backed the vehicle out of the drive. "Truth time, how are you feeling?"

"Restless. That's the truth. I feel fine. My arm hurts a little if I let it hang down too much. The rest of me is okay. I need to apologize to

Taylor. She stopped by this morning, and I vented a little. She used her authority to shut me down. Informed me I can't go back to work until she gets a signed release that has to come from, not just Faith, but Mom as well. Everyone keeps telling me to stop acting like a child, and I would if they'd stop treating me like one. I'm over fifty years old. I've been taking care of myself for a very long time. I'm fully capable of doing it for another fifty."

"Maybe they want you to have the chance to do just that. I get it. I fell off my horse once and broke my ankle. My office staff coddled me to the point I was ready to fire all of them. Constantly telling me to sit down. The work wasn't going to do itself, and the practice was busy. Lacey was gone on a six-week teaching trip to London, or so she said, and there was no one else to pick up the slack. I get it, Chance. Honestly, I do. The difference is, you had a head injury, a grade three concussion. If it was just your arm, no one would be bitching at you half as much. You were unconscious, and that puts the concern at an entirely different level."

"So, she wasn't in London to teach?"

Jax glanced over at Chance and slowly shook her head. "Out of all that, you zeroed in on that piece of information? No wonder you drive Maggie crazy." She laughed. "She was there to teach, except that wasn't the whole story. I can't tell you which affair this was, in all honesty. A British counterpart that she met at a seminar asked her to come and teach on exotics. I didn't think anything of it until a mutual friend sent me an email with a photograph of the two of them sucking face in a London night club. It wasn't the final straw, only one more on the camel's back. She apologized, and we went to therapy. The next affair was with one of our office staff. That was the final straw. It was time, and I didn't want to try any more. She obviously didn't think I was worth being faithful to, so, I decided to come back to where I felt I could make a difference."

"That's some pretty heavy baggage, Jax. I don't know how you did it for that long. I had a girlfriend that cheated on me once, while I was out on a jump. I came back early from a deployment and stopped by without calling first. I used my key to get into her place, flowers in hand. I walked in on her and a local police officer. I didn't say a word. I put the flowers on the counter with my key and never went back." Chance scratched lazily under Zeus's chin and shrugged. "She showed up at my work trying to find out what happened. I told her to drop off whatever she still had of mine to my office. She was none too happy. She was pitching a fit, until I showed her the photo on my phone of the gun belt and uniform strewn around her apartment. I got my stuff and I never heard from her again."

"Oh, Chance, you've got to be kidding?"

"I swear on Dad's badge."

"I was fortunate enough to only see the flirtation. Thank heavens I didn't witness the actual act. No one deserves that. What an ass she was."

Chance stared out the side window. "Yeah well, according to what her friends told me later, that's what happens when you leave someone alone over and over. It wasn't like I went on vacation without her. I was working. In the end, it was better to find out before I made a commitment I wouldn't break."

They spent an hour at the barn. Chance visited each horse before they headed over to the Richards farm. "Take that next left, let's go see the place together."

Jax did as directed and drove up a tree-lined road. A canopy of leaves shaded the gravel, until a simple, two-story farmhouse came into view. The front porch had two wooden swings that hung from the ceiling on long chains, and several wooden rockers. Two large, red barns sat forty yards or so from the farmhouse.

"Oh, I love it already! The barns are stealing my heart. Anything in the house can be fixed. Hell, if it's that bad, I'll tear the place down and build. I wonder how much total land is with it?"

Chance laughed. "I'm sure Maggie can tell you. Think you can stand living with Marty a while longer?"

"I can if it means I get this place."

"You don't even know what they're going to ask for it."

"It won't matter. Let's just say, price isn't an issue. Remember, Lacey bought me out of a multimillion-dollar practice. Given what I could have told and proven to her family, she was very generous with our split. California's a no-fault divorce state. The family scandal would have been worse than the amount of money they offered me to go away. Trust me, it was a drop in the bucket."

"Damn, girl."

Jax winked. "There's a lot you don't know about me, Chance. I hope, with me living here, you'll have plenty of time to fix that."

Chance's grin swallowed her face. "Count on it."

Jax followed the circular driveway back out. More than once she caught Chance looking at her. "What?"

"You're even more beautiful than when we were kids. Back then, you turned every head, male or female. Mine especially."

"How about now? Do I still turn your head?"

"You don't just turn my head. You turn my whole body around and into a raging inferno."

Jax furrowed her brow, "What?"

"Jax, I need to kiss you and feel your skin on mine."

Jax's entire body heated, and she jerked the wheel. "You can't say things like that to me, I'll wreck us."

Chance turned fully to Jax. "You've been wrecking me for over thirty years, in my dreams."

Jax quickly pulled off the side of the dirt road. A cloud of dust enveloped the vehicle. She released her seatbelt and grasped Chance's face in her hands. "I'll second that emotion. Now shut up and kiss me."

Their lips met with an almost palpable hunger. Jax threaded her hand into Chance's hair, anchoring her in place. She plunged her tongue into the warm mouth. Chance met her with equal fervor, and Jax felt a hand possessively cup the back of her neck. After what seemed like an eternity, the two broke apart. Chests heaving, they let their foreheads touch, as each breathed in the exhalation of the other.

Jax could barely speak. "Wow."

"Yeah, what you said. Some things don't change. You still turn me into a pile of mush."

Jax traced Chance's lips with her finger. "I'll take that as a good sign."

"It's a very good sign that I'm still crazy about you."

"That feeling is more than mutual. I also know it grows harder, every day I'm around you, not to touch you. I'd like that to be more frequent than it is now. The being around you, I mean."

"Nice to know I'm not alone in that. I'm on fire, Jax. Every cell of my body is crying out for you. The day I looked up and saw you at the command post, someone threw gasoline on the torch I've carried for you deep down in my soul. Hell, when I woke up in the ER, I was down at the riverbank, reliving my eighteenth birthday with you."

Jax put a hand up over her mouth. "You're kidding."

"I swear! You were just about to give me my birthday present when I regained consciousness. Do you have any idea what it's like to wake up from an erotic dream of one of the best days of my life, in the presence of my ex-girlfriend?"

"Oh Chance, that is so wrong."

"You bet it's wrong. We hadn't even got to the best parts yet. I'd just untied your top." Chance smiled and gave her a toothy grin, clicking her teeth together.

Jax squirmed uncomfortably. She remembered holding that tie to Chance's lips and letting her pull the knot out. The smirk Jax couldn't contain reached her toes.

Chance ran a finger down the side of Jax's face. "I think you remember that moment as much as I do."

Jax held up her hand. "I plead the fifth."

"I was legal and so were you. It wouldn't have mattered if we weren't. I'd never wanted anything or anyone that badly in my life. The minute I saw you again, it was as if years melted right into the ground."

"Not going to lie, I felt the same way. You walked out of my dreams. I had no idea whether you'd even want to see me." Jax cupped Chance's cheek and ran her thumb over the soft lips in front of her.

"I have an empty house not far away. I think we should get started on a reenactment."

Jax couldn't help but laugh. "You think so, huh?"

Chance leaned over and kissed her with enough heat to melt the polar icecaps. "Nope, I know so. Drive, Dr. St. Claire."

It took Jax a few minutes to bring her pulse rate back down, allowing the blood to flow back into her brain. "Kiss me like that again, and I'll recreate your birthday present right in the bed of this truck."

Chance leaned over and nipped at Jax's earlobe, causing her to shiver in pleasure. "I have so many more things I want to do with you beyond kissing you senseless. Put the truck in drive, Jax."

Jax needed a few deep cleansing breaths to clear the red haze of arousal and desire from her eyes. When she could see clearly again, she moved the gearshift. With great restraint, she pushed on the accelerator.

It took only minutes to reach Chance's from the Richards property. They stumbled into the house, leaving Zeus in the yard. Jax spun Chance against the wall and kissed her with the desperation their separation fueled. She pushed her hands under the tight, black T-shirt and ran her hands up the hard-oblique muscles that rippled under her fingers. She wanted this woman badly enough that if they didn't find a bed, she'd take Chance right there against the wall. Back then, she'd been the more aggressive of the two of them. She'd always felt Chance was holding back, afraid to be too forceful because of her larger frame and strength.

"Let go, Chance. I won't break. You take me to your room, or I'm stripping you down right here in your kitchen."

She watched something flash across the flinty blue eyes. Chance's pupils dilated. Before her eyes, Jax saw the passionate girl she'd fallen for turn into a beautifully powerful woman. With one quick motion, Chance turned Jax to the wall and bent slightly. Jax felt a strong arm, slide under her ass.

"Hold onto me. Don't think, hold on."

Jax did as asked. She wrapped her arms around Chance's neck and her legs around her waist, as she felt herself being lifted into the air.

"Holy shit, you're strong."

"You ain't seen nothing yet, baby." Chance marched through the house and down the hall. "Wait until I have two good arms."

"I'll keep that in mind. For now, take me to bed, Sheriff."

Chance walked into her bedroom and kissed Jax, as she gently placed her on the bed and covered her with her own body. "You have entirely too many clothes on."

An arched eyebrow was the only warning Jax gave before she pushed Chance over onto her back to straddle her. With crossed arms, she grabbed the bottom of her T-shirt. Once her long hair pulled through the neck, she tossed it to the side. "Your turn." She pulled the shirt from Chance's shorts and slowly began to pull the fabric up over her torso. Her eyes locked with Chance's. She let her fingers play along the center line that separated the abdominal muscles, scratching lightly. Chance arched into her touch.

"Oh God."

Chance flinched slightly when Jax used a sensuous touch to slide her fingers along the raised lines of scar tissue that randomly intersected up her left side.

Jax bent and kissed the juncture of her shoulder. "You're so damn sexy."

Chance ran the back of her hand across Jax's chest forcing a sharp intake of breath as she popped the front clasp on the black silk bra, releasing her breasts. "From my vantage point, you're the sexy one. Do you know how long I've waited to feel you straddle my hips again?"

"About as long as it has been for me, a lifetime." Jax leaned forward and held herself above Chance. "And too damn long. Sit up so I can get that shirt off you."

Chance complied, and Jax pulled the T-shirt and jog bra off her body. Chance reached up and explored Jax's shoulders with featherlight touches. She traced the collarbones that bordered the prominent hollows that joined with the muscles of her neck.

Chance groaned, as Jax bent and took a nipple in her mouth, sucking it in. She reached up to cup the back of Jax's head, pressing her lips harder into her flesh. "Shit, Jax."

"I'm through waiting to touch you and make love to you. It has been too damn long. I have no intention of waiting one more second to be with you. We still have too many clothes on and this going slow is killing me. Off, now!" Jax's tone broached no argument.

***

They struggled to divest themselves of the rest of their clothes, before Jax resumed her position straddling Chance. The incredible feeling of this beautiful woman's wet center felt like liquid heat as it met Chance's skin. She put her hand over Jax's breast and squeezed, gently at first, before pinching the nipple, making the lithe body arch into her touch.

She cursed her casted hand. "I've waited for this for so long. I'm dying to touch you."

"Then do it. Nothing's stopping you and it's well past time." Jax stared into her eyes, her pupils so dilated, they looked like black pools of ink, liquid and fathomless.

Chance moved her right hand between their bodies. Without any further foreplay, she buried two fingers deep inside Jax. She felt her lover rock back and forth. With each movement, her fingers pushed deeper inside. The feeling was exquisite, and passion burned with the intensity of a flashover, as she watched Jax put her head back.

"Don't stop, Chance. Don't stop."

Chance knew in her heart, she'd give Jax anything she asked for. She rolled them over until the most beautiful woman she'd ever seen lay beneath her, rocking her hips to meet Chance's thrusts. She leaned on her left elbow, as she tried to hold her weight off of Jax. The heat of their reunion burned her skin, as she closed her lips around Jax's nipple and bit down. She felt fingers weave into her hair and hold on tight. She needed to taste her, and she was determined to make that happen as she kissed down Jax's body until she lay between her thighs, hovering above her center. Chance lowered her mouth and felt Jax buck against her so hard that teeth met pubic bone. Worried, she pulled back to look at her lover, but Jax pushed her head back down.

"Please, I need you. Now."

Those words lit a fire inside of Chance more powerful than the wildfire that had seared her skin so many years ago. As Chance took Jax's clit between her lips, she sucked until she felt Jax's back arch off the bed. When she added a third finger and crooked them, she felt the tremble start in Jax's thighs. Chance reveled in the feeling that transported her back to a place she hadn't been in a long time.

"Chance!"

The flood of Jax's climax filled Chance's mouth, and she drank as greedily as if she'd been in the desert, dying of thirst. Still wanting more, Chance coaxed her lover to a second orgasm by flicking her tongue back and forth across the still hardened clit. Jax trembled beneath her touch, yet never asked her to stop, encouraging Chance to continue as she met Chance's thrusts. The feeling of Jax's center clenching hard around her fingers, made Chance feel safe and at peace. It'd been a gift to touch her all those years ago. She held this moment with the same reverence. When the spasms subsided and Jax's legs trembled, Chance climbed back up the body beneath her and collapsed into Jax's arms.

"My God, you are so beautiful, Jax."

They were both gasping for breath as Chance gently withdrew her fingers, leaving them cupped over the heated center. Jax reached out and held Chance's face in her hands, bringing her closer to kiss her. Chance turned over and pulled Jax in close to her. "What did you do to me?" Chance asked.

Jax laughed. "What did I do to you? I think it's the other way around, honey."

Chance raised her head to look into the pale-green eyes that stared back. "I guess, we came home." She reached over and hit a button on a remote by the bedside. The room filled with the first few notes of a familiar song. Roberta Flack's *The First Time, Ever I Saw Your Face*, played softly in the background.

Chance rolled on top of Jax and used her good hand to trace the contours of her face. She ran a finger over strong cheekbones, then traced softly over plump lips, before tenderly sliding down to her jawline. She thought about that first time she'd ever seen this beautiful woman. The ground had fallen away, and Chance slid into an abyss she had no desire to climb out of. That very second, she'd become lost in eyes of sea foam green, deep and soulful. There was a wide smile that hinted of mischief and passionate kisses. That impression had proved itself right the first time they'd come together. That same woman, somehow even more beautiful, was now lying in her arms again.

Jax was quiet, and Chance saw a tear slide down her temple into her hairline. "Hey, hey, what's wrong?"

Jax cupped Chance's cheek. "Nothing. Absolutely nothing is wrong. This song brings up so many memories of us. We made love to an entire mixtape of love songs you put together just for that night. At this moment, I truly feel like I am exactly where I'm supposed to be. Home is where you are. I'm so sorry I ever left."

Chance rested her chin on Jax's chest. "There were journeys we both had to take to find our way back to the things that are important. "

Jax surprised her as she pushed Chance over. "What I really find important is my current need to touch you. I intend to do just that." Hours later, they lay with their arms and legs tangled together. Their bodies fit together perfectly.

Gentle fingers traced the raised scar tissue on Chance's left side. "Do they bother you?"

Chance drew in a breath and sighed as she kissed Jax's forehead. "Not really. I try to keep them as supple as possible with cocoa butter lotion and some daily stretches. It took a long time to get them stretched, but they don't restrict my movements now. Years ago, they had to do a few scar relief procedures to release one that kept me from having full range of motion in my shoulder. The one on the back of my arm gets noticed when I wear a sleeveless T-shirt. Other than that, they're just part of my every day, part of my skin."

Jax looked up at her. "I don't mean just physically."

"I've made my peace with them. Every morning, I repeat a phrase 'steel is tempered by fire, and gold is refined by it.' I believe in that."

"If I'd known, I'd have been a basket case."

"You'd have done exactly what you did when I got hurt this time. You'd have been there. I won't lie; there were plenty of days I wished I hadn't survived. Between the debridement and skin grafts, the docs kept me pretty medicated. Trust me, it barely touched the pain. I don't know what I'd have done without Mags and Dee. They never let me give up. When I was at my lowest, they were right there every day until I made it home."

"I should have been there with you. I wish I had been."

Chance pulled her in tighter. "You're here now. That's all that matters. We can't change a second of our past. The future, that's different. All I ask is that we keep living in the here and now and keep walking into our future."

"I'll second that notion. Unfortunately, we're going to have to get up. I'm fixing dinner tonight at Uncle Marty's."

"Well then, I suggest we take a shower together, you know, to conserve water. I'll give you a pair of my shorts and a T-shirt to wear home."

Jax smirked. "Conserve water my ass. However, I won't argue the logic. Come on, Sheriff." She pulled Chance up from the bed. "Let's get moving. We need to wrap that cast on your arm. I don't want you getting wet."

"Too late for that."

"Smart ass, you know what I mean."

Chance couldn't help the snicker that turned into a full belly laugh. Jax dug her finger into Chance's side and smacked her arm. "Go."

A few minutes into the trip to Marty's, Chance blurted out an idea. "How about Zeus and I hang out and help you get things settled at your office for the rest of my recovery? We'll even go handle barn calls with you."

Jax held up one finger. "On two conditions. One, you promise to behave and not overdo." She held up a second finger. "And two, you have dinner with me frequently."

Chance brought her good hand to her chin and rubbed her face. "You drive a hard bargain. Deal." She held out her pinky. When their fingers wrapped together, Chance brought the knuckles to her lips and kissed them.

With each mile that passed, Chance patted herself on the back over her negotiation skills. *Personally, I think I got the better end of this deal. I get to spend time with one very sexy vet, and she's going to feed me. I call that winning.*

Chapter Ten

A FULL EIGHT DAYS vanished into the past before Chance even blinked. She'd accompanied Jax on several calls and assisted her in the next steps of getting the vet clinic ready to open. She swirled the ice in her Coke while she listened to Jax tell Marty about Adam Richards's asking price for the farm. Chance was looking forward to having Jax so close to her. She was sure Jax was tiring of their trips to the storage shed to 'find something.' Warm hands snaked around her shoulders from behind.

Jax kissed her cheek. "Dinner's about ready. Are you hungry?"

"I am. Whatever you're cooking in there smells fantastic."

"It's a slow-cooked carne asada on a huarache. It's a tortilla that resembles a sandal sole. I've also got a tomato and avocado salad. I sometimes forget that getting good avocadoes back here isn't as easy as it is in California."

"Sounds like a Greek gyro without that yogurt sauce. What's that called? I can never remember."

"*Tzatziki* sauce. I love that stuff. I'll have to look that up and we'll have gyros one night."

"I could go for that. There's a Greek restaurant over in Morgantown. We'll have to go sometime." Chance leaned her head back, and Jax kissed her upside down on the lips.

"I'd like that. An evening away from here with you? Let's see what's playing at the Creative Arts Center. Maybe there's a concert or something."

"I think that can be arranged. I'll check with Kendra, since she's going to school there."

"I'm sure we can find it online. Either way, let's do it. Come on, time to eat."

Chance rose from the chair and followed Jax into the kitchen. Marty was already seated at the table, his napkin tucked into his shirt collar.

The rest of the evening they enjoyed dinner with laughing and talking. Marty enticed them into a game of Russian Rummy and was thoroughly wiping the floor with them. Around nine o'clock, Marty went to bed and Jax drove Chance home. The night air was warm and smelled of the laurel flowers that grew all over Chance's property.

Chance leaned back on the headrest. "Do you know how badly I want to ask you to stay?"

"Probably about as badly as I want to say yes."

"It seemed so much easier back then. We just did whatever we felt like and worried about nothing. Now we're adults who worry about everything."

"The price of growing up." Jax turned up the driveway and stopped in front of the house.

"Well, just once, I'd like to go back to those days on the riverbank with you. Not a care in the world beyond watching your skin turn golden brown."

"The summer isn't over. You get that cast off your arm, and the riverbank will be waiting." Jax leaned over and kissed her again. "And so will I. Pick you up at eight tomorrow morning? We'll take Zeus's stitches out if the ear looks good, then you can help me shop for a new vehicle."

Chance opened her door, then snuck back in for another kiss. "We'll be ready. Come on Zeus." Her K9 companion jumped out, and the two of them watched Jax disappear up the driveway. "There goes the best thing that ever happened to me, Zeus. I'm lucky enough to get a second chance, and I'm going to make the most of it."

Zeus barked, and it made Chance laugh. "Glad you agree."

***

The next morning, Jax had coffee with her uncle over huevos rancheros. She'd taken up the cooking duties and noticed Marty seemed to smile more every day. Given her growing relationship with Chance, all the things in her life were positive. She was back here with them both, and felt she had her life on track.

"I'm picking up Chance and Zeus this morning, and then going shopping for new wheels. I need something other than my beast to get around these back roads. I think I still want a truck to carry the farrier equipment and the things I need for the large-animal practice. Seats that I can just wipe down and not worry about would be nice."

Marty took a sip of coffee. "Sounds like you know what you're looking for. Chance should be able to help you. She can tell you what dealerships to stay away from. I'm glad to see you two spending time together. I think you're good for each other. I like to see you smile, and you've been doing more and more of it."

"I'm not the only one who's smiling more. I've seen your eyes crinkle quite a bit since I got home."

He chewed a bite of his breakfast then sipped his coffee. "Well, it could be because my favorite niece looks happy and maybe a little smitten."

Her laughter almost made coffee come out her nose and she coughed. "Smitten?"

"In my day, being smitten with someone was a good thing. That's how I felt about your aunt." He pointed at her picture with his mug. "From the moment I met her, I thought she was the most beautiful woman I'd ever met. I did everything I could to catch her attention until she took notice. Your advantage is, Chance is already on the hook. You set it years ago. If you ask me, she's been waiting years for you to reel her in."

Jax could only smile, as she took her dishes to the sink.

"Go on, I'll get those. Love you, kitten."

She kissed his cheek on the way by and grabbed her keys. "Love you, Uncle Marty. See you later." She stopped and turned around quickly. "Oh, if necessary, can you stop by the office and accept a delivery of equipment? I should be back, but something might come up."

"Just call, I've got nothing planned." He grinned. "I'm retired, remember? I've got a young hotshot vet taking over my practice. Word is, she's pretty good." He grabbed the paper and shook it out. He looked over the rim of his glasses at her. "Time will tell."

"Now I know where I got the smartass part of me that drove Mom crazy."

He pointed a finger at her. "Don't let you mother fool you. When she was growing up, she wasn't the angel she expected you to be. I promised I'd never tell those stories, but maybe someday I'll start losing my mind and a few might slip."

Jax slipped past the screen door. "Oh, I'll be right at your side for that. Trust me. Love you."

"Love you too."

A few minutes before eight, she pulled up to find Chance sitting on her front porch with a travel mug in her hand, Zeus at her side. Jax rolled down the window. "You two ready to hit the road?"

Chance got in and leaned over the consol. "He'll be one happy dog."

"Would it be okay if we go truck shopping after? Uncle Marty said you'd know where to go."

Chance stared at her, and Jax flushed. "For a kiss, I'll buy the damn truck."

Jax leaned in and softly kissed Chance's lips, lingering longer than was necessary and lightly biting her lower lip. "What will that get me?"

"Drug out of this truck and into my house. Holy shit. Are you trying to kill me?"

"Just reeling you in a bit."

"Honey, get the net."

Jax laughed and pushed Chance back into her seat. "Come on, you nut, we need to get on the road."

A few hours later, they were roaming row after row of shiny new vehicles at the Toyota dealership in Fairmont. Zeus was missing his stitches and had been completely released from the cone of shame. They walked around the lot checking out each model.

Chance stepped up to a jet black one and Zeus sniffed around the tires. "I love this color. Sadly, they're a mess to keep clean."

"I used to have a black BMW, and it always looked dirty. "

Chance looked at her with a raised eyebrow. "A Beemer huh? I'd have taken you for a Corvette, but I wouldn't have guessed a BMW."

Jax rolled her eyes. "It was always about image to the Montgomery's. The only time I drove it was when Lacey wanted me to take her someplace. She refused to ride in the truck. The rest of the time, I drove a variety of everyday vehicles, depending on what I had to do. Honestly, I lived a privileged life. The problem was, I wasn't happy with it. Any of it, in fact. I've been happier here since I left California. Now, let's go talk to the saleswoman you know. Nothing here on the lot has everything I want. Let's see if I can order one. I think the metallic silver would be best. What do you think?"

Chance stood beside a truck of that exact color. "It's definitely a sharp color and won't show dirt as bad as the black or navy."

"I want a long bed that will let me put in a roll-out tray, where I can put a couple of cabinets. Cover that up with a fiberglass topper, and I'll have a mobile office."

Chance smiled. "Better count your pennies."

"I did that a long time ago. Chance, I don't have to worry. The honest fact is, I wouldn't have to work another day in my life if that's what I wanted. I'll use the money to buy my new home and vehicle and set up the practice the way I want. After that, I'll start a Marty Hendricks scholarship for veterinary students. Even with all that, I still wouldn't have to work. I will, because my sanity requires it, and...Marty wants someone to continue what he started."

"Seems we both want to honor the people that made us want to become who we are."

Jax thought about Chance's words. They made sense to her. "Indeed. Let's go order a truck."

It took a few more hours to make all the decisions, sign the paperwork, and write the check. They picked up subs so they could eat in a local park with Zeus. They ate until they were stuffed, then Chance threw a tennis ball for Zeus before they started home. Chance's cell phone rang when they were about twenty minutes from the county line. Jax could only hear one side of the conversation.

"Sheriff Fitzsimmons."

A pause.

"I'm fine...I know...I'm not doing anything stupid...Give me a break. I'm *fifty*-four not four! I wasn't aware I had an appointment, at least not one that I made. Yes, I can stop by."

Another pause. Jax could hear a feminine voice but didn't know who it was for sure. She had an idea that it was Faith, the doctor who'd taken care of Chance and was her ex-girlfriend.

"Enough, I said I'd be there."

Chance pushed a button to end the call.

"Let me guess. Faith isn't happy you're out running around."

Chance was silent for a few minutes. "I miss the days when you could slam down a receiver on someone you were pissed at. I'm far from being a child, regardless of what 'mom squared' says."

"I'm going to take a wild guess and put my money on the fact that you were not talking to either of those two women and instead to one who used to play a big role in your life. That was Faith, right?"

"You guessed correctly. She's complaining that I haven't been in for a checkup since I got out of the hospital. I've been to my orthopedic surgeon. I'm not sure what her issue is. We broke up over four years ago. She's married to Theresa, and according to Sarah, she's happy."

"You're pretty unforgettable, you know?"

Chance sighed and looked over at Jax. "I get it. Our breakup doesn't mean she doesn't care. That's all well and good. Life goes on, and we have to deal with the here and now. I'm beyond grateful for her concern. What I need is that concern not to bleed over into unwarranted overprotectiveness. It's like taking those stitches out of my arm yesterday. It was time. Hell, I've stitched myself up when we've been deep in the wilderness on a fire."

Jax shook her head. "Taking stitches out is one thing. A concussion is another." Jax reached over and rested her hand on Chance's cast. "Let's get you over there so she can lay eyes on you and see for herself that you're on the mend. It will probably ease Maggie and Dee's mind too."

"Fine. She said the clinic wasn't busy. Let's do it now, if you aren't busy?"

"Works for me."

Jax turned the vehicle in the direction of town. She thought it might be a good opportunity for Faith to see that Chance wasn't dealing with this injury on her own. If there was ever to be something long term between her and Chance, the thin, spider web threads of the past needed to be broken. Friendship was one thing. She'd noticed more than once, during Chance's hospital stay, that Faith acted more like a lover than someone adhering to the ethical line of an attending physician. Chance's words revealed a great deal to Jax. She still cared about Faith, though it seemed she had transitioned into the friendship role more easily than Faith had.

In the parking lot of the clinic, Jax turned off the vehicle and shifted to face Chance. "I'll wait here for you."

"Oh no, you won't. I want a human witness for the inquisition from Mom and Momma D. Zeus, for all his abilities, can't do that for me." Chance rubbed her forehead with her right hand. "To be honest, I want Faith to see you with me. My life is changing, and you're the reason. It's time people got used to it."

"People, or Faith?"

"Both."

Jax climbed out of the vehicle and walked to the clinic door. She paused to allow Chance to open it for her with her typical chivalry and followed Zeus in. Chance checked in at the reception window and came back to sit with her.

"Shouldn't be too long. She's finishing with a patient."

"We aren't on any timetable."

They sat watching a rerun of *Jeopardy* and answering the questions, each attempting to beat the other to the buzzer.

"What is the prime meridian?" Jax answered.

"Cheater." Chance scowled.

"How is that cheating?"

"You didn't wait for Alex to acknowledge you."

Jax rolled her head to the side and glared at Chance.

"What is the Mesozoic era?" Chance grinned with an overly wide smile at her own exuberance.

"Now who's cheating? And how did you know that?"

"Remember me telling you about the little boy Maggie and Dee fostered? Well Eddie was a dinosaur freak. I can tell you everything you need to know about T-Rex, Diplodocus, or Triceratops."

Jax's eyes widened. "Remind me not to challenge you in a dinosaur category."

"I'd wipe the floor with you."

The nurse came through the door that separated the waiting room from the treatment area. "Sheriff, can you follow me to Exam Room 2?"

Chance looked at Jax. "Here we go. Come on."

"Are you sure?"

"Very."

They were led to a hallway, where Chance stopped and told Zeus to wait in a small conference area with just a hand signal. After her vitals were recorded, they were directed into a small exam room. Chance climbed up on the elevated table and sat with her cast in her right hand. Jax chose to stand in the corner. Her previous interactions with Faith had been professional and cordial. She could tell that Faith cared for Chance beyond the doctor patient relationship, and she was concerned how Faith would take her presence during this checkup. Jax vowed to stay silent and allow Chance to handle the interaction.

A rustle outside the door and a brisk knock preceded Faith into the room. Without looking up, Faith washed her hands and read through the chart before tossing it on the counter and crossing her arms. "Nice of you to stop by."

Jax watched, as Chance sat up stiffly and squared her shoulders. "Pretty sure it was at your demand."

"The last time I checked, I am your doctor. I think that entitles me to be a bit perturbed that you have yet to make an appearance in this office since you were released. It's not my job to call you for an appointment."

"Faith, take it down a notch. I've been to the surgeon that fixed my wrist. It's not like I've been without medical care.

Jax wondered where this was going. The tension between the two was thicker than morning fog on the mountain. She decided to remain quiet until she had no choice.

"I'm your primary physician. I'm the one who makes medical decisions about your care." She pointed to her chest. "Me. They know you over this one incident. I've been making sure you're fit for duty for a long time."

"Once again, your need to exert control over my life is more about your need, not mine. I think it's more about the fact you no longer have any say in what I can and cannot do." Chance put a leg over the side and began to climb down from the table. She turned to Jax. "Let's go."

Faith stepped in front of the door and held up her hand to stop her. "We've only started this exam, and I'll be damned if you are going to dismiss my concerns like I don't matter."

Jax could see crimson creeping up the side of Chance's neck toward her ears. She watched as Chance tilted her head.

"I'm not even sure I know who the hell you are right now. I haven't dismissed your concerns. I have yet to step back into my office, and I've been very conscientious to take care of myself. So, step out of the way."

"You're not going anywhere. I'm far from being done."

"Are you holding me against my will? Because trust me, you're done."

Zeus whined and let out a sharp bark from the other side of the door. His protective instincts toward Chance fascinated Jax.

Faith threw her arms in the air. "As if I've ever been able to stop you from doing one damned thing you wanted to do. Why start now?" She stepped aside and dramatically waved at the door. "Understand this, I'm not signing off on you. Go if you want to, you're still not going back to work."

Chance stepped closer to her. "You have no..."

Jax stepped between them. "Ding, ding, ding. Round one. Go to your corners." She pointed to opposite sides of the room and hoped that her humor would help defuse the nuclear bomb about to explode in the small room. "Chance, please sit down. Faith, settle down." She spoke in the direction of the door. "Zeus, it's all right." Jax watched Chance's jaw clench and unclench.

Both women turned to Jax with astonished faces, then complied. "Rewind. Doctor Riker enters the exam room and greets Sheriff Fitzsimmons. Take two. And...action." Jax brought her hands and arms together to mimic the scene clapper used in the movie-making business.

Everyone chuckled, releasing some of the tension that had nearly boiled over.

"I'm okay boy, lay down. I'll be right there." Chance backed up a step.

Faith took a deep breath. "Your vitals look fine. Any recurring headaches or blurry vision?

"No to both. I feel fine."

Faith pulled a corded device off the wall and clipped a black plastic cone on the end. She looked in Chance's ears. After she discarded the disposable item, she used the bright light to look in Chance's eyes. "Any nausea or motion sickness?"

Chance blinked rapidly when the light was removed and shook her head. "No."

Faith ran through a detailed concussion protocol, asking memory and orientation questions. Chance sat relaxed, answering the questions and performing each task as it was given. Jax was no expert when it came to human head trauma, but she'd read the protocol and was silently scoring Chance's responses. From her limited knowledge, Chance was doing well.

"Can you recall the words I gave you?" Faith stood resting her back on the counter.

"Elbow, wagon, lemon, monkey, and candle."

Jax looked at Faith and a small smile showed.

"Pretty good. You don't seem to be having too many lingering effects from the concussion. You still have a bit of failure to obey commands. Sadly, I don't think that's related to the concussion. Let's take a look at those stitches I put in from your rock-rescue adventure." Faith opened a cabinet.

Chance rubbed her face. "I took them out."

Faith turned, tipped her head up, and shook it from side to side. "Of course you did. Why am I not surprised?"

Jax covered her mouth to avoid laughing.

"It's no big deal, the cut was healed, and the stitches were constantly snagged on my shirt." Chance had her head bowed and was swinging one leg back and forth.

"Honestly, Chance, you are going to drive me to drink."

"Well then, you can join Mom, she says the same thing."

Jax again held up her hands to stop the impending blow up. "Okay, okay. Simmer down and let's see if we can get the medical exam out of the way before we get on to the mental evaluation part."

Faith appeared to expel her frustrations with a measured breath. "You're right, Jax. Thanks for being the mediator here. Fine, let me look at it."

Chance bent her arm at the elbow, then tipped it back until Faith could see the area where the stitches had been.

"It looks clean."

Chance put her arm down. "Now can we discuss me going back to work?"

Faith again threw her arms in the air and pointed at Chance. "You're not quite two weeks out of the hospital. You're not ready to go back to work!" Faith pointed to Jax with one hand and indignantly jammed the other on her hip. "Talk some sense into her. My years of medical school apparently don't qualify me to make patient-care decisions for the superhero here."

"Let's talk about this like the adults your driver license claim you are." Jax gathered her thoughts as quickly as possible, attempting to form reasonable arguments that might appeal to the other occupants of the room. "First, Chance. Did you send Zeus back to work after he was shot in the ear?" Jax heard Zeus whine at the mention of his name.

Chance's brow shot up. "Well no, but..."

"No buts, did you? Simple question, simple answer."

Chance looked at Jax, bewilderment in her eyes. "No."

"And did you keep Sabrina off that rescue because she had the abscess?"

Chance protested. "That's different."

"Again, simple question, simple answer." Jax tilted her head and caught Faith trying to hide a smirk. Jax pointed at her. "No smirking over there. I'll get to you in a minute."

Chance weaved her head back and forth, as she produced a 'so there' glare.

"Not done with you yet, no smirking from you either. Did you hold Sabrina back from something she would normally have gone on, because she wasn't one hundred percent?" Jax watched the resignation cross Chance's face.

"I didn't want her hurting herself more."

"I'll take that as a yes. Okay, we are making some progress here. Now, Faith, is her head injury worse?"

Faith cleared her throat and stood straighter. "No."

Jax nodded. "Is there anything physically that will suffer if she sat at her desk for say, four or five hours a day?"

"Well, it might strain her neck from having her head up her ass." Faith sighed. "No, she won't cause any physical damage. You can go back for partial days as long as the headaches don't return. I don't want you on the street patrolling." She pointed to Chance. "It's too soon for that. You aren't one hundred percent no matter how well you fake it."

Chance raised her hand and Jax acknowledged her. "Go ahead, briefly."

Chance's mouth dropped open. "What if I went to the office from ten in the morning to two in the afternoon? No patrolling. With me out, Taylor has been pulled into admin and it screws everything up to take her off the street. Deskwork, phone calls, and meetings only. Will that satisfy you?"

"Possibly. If you overdo it, you'll delay your recovery. I mean it, no emergency situation that requires you to endanger yourself."

"Understood. And I can drive, right?"

Faith nodded her head. "No road patrol. I mean it."

Chance saluted Faith.

Jax stepped forward between the two. "Faith, be honest. Are your concerns based more on your medical evaluation, or does your worry go beyond the professional, despite the fact you two are no longer together? Truth time."

Faith took a deep breath and chewed on the side of her cheek. "A good deal of both. There can be complications if her brain isn't given the time to heal properly. Her belief that she's bulletproof has put another dent in her armor. I'll also admit, ex or not, I still care. Married or not, I haven't stopped caring. I assure you, it's likely to happen again. This is the third head injury she's had since I've known her. A fist, a two by four, and now a moving vehicle have left their mark on what's inside that thick skull. The brain can only take so much. None of which factor in the likely concussions she's had when she was jumping out of airplanes onto the fire line."

"Point taken." Jax shook her head.

Chance stood and stepped to Jax's side to face Faith. "Look, we parted as friends, and I'd like to keep it that way. Although there's no one I trust more, maybe having you as my doctor isn't so good for our friendship. I promise to take it easy until you give me a full release." She stepped forward and grabbed Faith's hand. "I know you worry. I need you to remember that my mental well-being is as important as my physical one. I need to work. To do that, I need you to sign a release so that Maggie, Dee, Taylor, Penny, Sarah, Kristi, and that one," she pointed to Jax, "will stop worrying and treating me like I'm a newborn chick." Chance took a deep breath. "Please?"

Faith shook her head, then turned and wrote out the release. When she turned to Chance, she held the slip out of reach. "This has restrictions. No gun, no patrolling, no chasing bad guys or rescuing damsels in distress for at least another week. I want to see you again to release you fully. Deal?"

Chance put out her hand to shake Faith's. "I'll agree to everything except the gun. I'm still the sheriff, and not everyone likes me. I have to be able to defend myself. Deal?"

Faith rubbed her temples then nodded her agreement.

Jax clapped her hands. "Well done you two. See, that wasn't so hard. A little give and a little take. Compromise isn't a loss for either side." Faith and Chance both glared at her. "All right, all right. My mediation skills are firmly back in the bag."

"This one's got your number, Chance. You'd better be sharp and watch yourself, or you'll find a ring on that finger yet."

Jax blushed profusely, thinking of what the future would hold for them. She needed to deflect the attention and held up Chance's casted hand. "She can't, her finger is too swollen."

Faith winked at Jax. "Well then, I guess you'll have to keep working on that one in her nose."

All three broke out into fits of laughter as they left the room. Jax mentally licked her finger and put a tick mark in her win column. It was turning out to be a very good day.

Chapter Eleven

JAX STOOD IN FRONT of Dee with her hand up, swearing an oath. Chance stood back and chuckled at the conversation. Dee was examining the release with a magnifying glass.

"Momma D, she's swearing on her horse's lives. You know Faith's signature as well as I do. Jax was there. I can go back to work from ten in the morning until two in the afternoon. No road duty. I swear, I promised to be very good. I don't need another ass chewing."

"She's telling the truth, Dee. It wasn't easy. It nearly came to blows at one point." Jax still had her right hand raised.

Dee squinted at Chance. "I swear, if you do anything to hurt yourself, I'll kill you myself."

Chance pulled at her hair with her good hand. "Dee."

"All right, all right. I'm letting it go. You're on notice. Mags is going to shit a brick."

"That's why I stopped at the liquor store and bought her a bottle of Scotch. When I drive her to drink, she'll have plenty of good stuff on hand."

Dee glared.

Jax hugged Dee. "My office isn't that far from hers. I'll check in on her, and you know that Penny will keep her in line."

"That might be. She's still going to have a fit."

Maggie came through the door off the deck. "Who's going to have a fit?"

Chance swallowed hard. "You are. Listen to me first. After that, feel free to throw a hissy."

Maggie crossed her arms. "I'm listening."

"I had a follow up with Faith, and she said I could go back to work."

"Bullshit!"

Chance went closer and put her arms around Maggie. "Not full duty and only part time. I need to work. Other than this cast, I'm fine." She held her tighter and pressed her lips to her temple. "Mom, I'm all right. You have to trust me on this." Chance felt the stiffness in Maggie's body gradually release. Hoping this was a good sign, she blew a raspberry.

"You're such a little shit."

Chance sighed. "Not exactly accurate. I'm taller than you, so I'm a big shit." She felt Maggie chuckle against her chest, and delicate arms came around her waist.

"You're going to be the death of me, you know? Jax, are you sure you know what you're getting into?"

Jax let out a full belly laugh. "She doesn't seem like she's changed that much. Always was a smart ass. Seems to me she came by that pretty honestly."

Maggie pointed a finger at Jax. "Please don't encourage her. She's hard enough to live with. Unless I miss my guess, you'll find that out for yourself eventually. Oh, by the way. Adam called again. He was able to work through a few things with his lawyer. He wanted to know if you'd like to proceed with the sale sooner than had been discussed."

Chance relished the smile that delivered Jax's answer. "Oh, that would be fantastic. I miss having the horses to visit with every night. When does he want to meet?"

Dee chuckled. "Yeah, it's the horses you want to be able to visit with. Don't bullshit a bullshitter. Living less than a mile from tall, dark, and irresistible can't hurt either, right?"

Chance and Jax both blushed as Jax answered. "Well, let's just say having good neighbors is the icing on the cake. I hear she's pretty good with a hammer when she has two good hands."

Chance pointed a thumb at herself. "Consider me hired. Now that everyone isn't pissed at me, can we have supper? I'm starving."

Maggie smacked her arm. "I swear to God, there's a tapeworm in your gut. Dee, the chicken's been marinating in the fridge, time to work out those grill-master skills." She pointed to Jax and Chance. "You two, set the table on the deck. The rest I've got."

Chance straightened her back, puffed out her chest, and saluted sharply. "Yes, Ma'am."

The four women spent the next few hours enjoying dinner and conversation. Dee couldn't help telling several stories of the predicaments Chance had found herself in over the years, including getting stuck out on the A Frame Road with a young lady, when a tree fell across the access road behind them.

Dee wiped at tears in her eyes and was barely able to talk with the laughter. "It was one in the morning, and she's calling me to bring the chain saw."

Chance frowned and waved her arm indignantly. "It was midnight and too far to walk out for help. I'm lucky I found enough signal to get a call out. Thank God for the power of a bag phone back then."

Jax was nearly doubled over with laughter.

Chance stood and took her empty beer bottle to the kitchen. "Jax, I think it's time to go, before they completely ruin my reputation."

Jax made her way out of the chair and hugged the women, who followed them into the kitchen. "Thank you for a wonderful evening. I don't know when I've laughed that much."

Zeus barked, and Chance looked down at her partner. "You're a lot of help, buddy."

Maggie walked up and hugged Chance. "Now, promise me you won't overdo it tomorrow. Did she release you to drive?"

Chance sighed. "Yes, and I promise I'll call it quits at two. I had to have six copies of that damn release made so that every one of you had your own. As a matter of fact, sign Penny's so she knows that you're aware."

Maggie laughed. "Oh, don't worry about that. When Penny sees you walk in the office, I expect my phone will ring immediately."

Chance grumbled indignantly and mumbled under her breath. "One mother gave birth to me, and now I have seventeen looking after me. Again, I'm fifty-four, not four."

"When you start acting your age, maybe we'll recognize it. By the way, what do you want for your birthday next weekend?" Maggie patted her cheek.

Jax brightened at the question. "Oh my, your birthday is next Saturday. My calendar would have sent me a message this week."

Chance turned her head slowly toward Jax and warmed at the thought that her lover remembered it all these years later. "You have a reminder in your calendar about my birthday?"

Jax looked at her with soft eyes. "I do. Your birthday always happened while I was visiting Uncle Marty and Aunt Mary. I remember some epic bashes on the riverb—"

Chance covered Jax's mouth with her good hand. "Nah, nah, nah, nah." She could feel the grin under her fingers.

Maggie had her hands on her hips. "Oh really? Sometime when your editor isn't around, you'll have to wander down memory lane with me."

Jax pulled Chance's hand away and went to hug Maggie. In a loud stage whisper to a cupped ear, she elaborated. "Maybe when we sign the sale papers."

Chance pulled Jax away and put her arm around her shoulders, ushering her to the door. "Good night you two."

Dee hugged Chance as she passed by. "Night, Five Points. "Remember to throw in the chainsaw." Love ya."

"I've got a house now. No chainsaw required. Love you too, Momma D."

Chapter Twelve

THE NEXT DAY, CHANCE woke up to the smell of waffles and sausage. She peered at the clock, and noticed it was a little after five. *Has to be Mom.* She sat up and stretched. Zeus was not at the side of her bed. Folding back the sheet, she climbed out and stepped into her well-worn Birkenstocks. A quick look in the mirror showed she'd worked all night on the stellar creation that sat on top of her head. She stretched her scars and repeated the mantra that had become second nature.

"Steel is tempered by fire, and gold is refined by it." A yawn escaped. Nothing short of two cups of coffee would make her alert enough to tackle her bad-hair day. She grabbed a ball cap sitting at the end of her dresser and pulled it on. *That'll do for now.*

Mags had her favorite mug on the table. Chance dropped unceremoniously into a chair at the table and took a cautious sip. Zeus came to stand beside her.

"Why didn't he bark when you came in?"

"He knows what's good for him."

Chance raised an eyebrow.

"And I brought him two homemade dog biscuits. He can be bribed. You just have to know the code."

Chance shook her head and laughed, as she took another sip of her coffee. When she looked at her K9 partner, she rubbed his head between his ears. "Traitor. Making me breakfast at five in the morning didn't come up in conversation last night that I remember. Did I miss something?"

Maggie turned around, spatula in hand. "Are you complaining, again?"

"No, I just figure it would save you some time if you come out and tell me what you want to say or ask what you want to know."

"Fair enough. What's going on with you and Jax? Is it serious?" She turned back to the stove and removed a waffle from the griddle.

"It's headed in that direction. Why?"

Maggie sipped her own coffee. "This one never really left your heart, did she?"

Chance eyeballed the plated waffle and three links of sausage placed in front of her. "No, she didn't. I didn't understand why she disappeared back then. Now, all that matters is she's back."

"And here to stay, if the way she's cementing herself in is any indication. Hopefully, we'll be signing the papers on the property in the next few days."

Chance swirled a piece of waffle in the maple syrup. "I hope so. She's planted herself in my heart pretty deep."

"I don't think you have much to worry about. The way she came running into the hospital when you were hurt told me all I needed to know. She was afraid of losing you. Enjoy this time, honey. When you dated before, there was always the knowledge she was going away at the end of the summer. Now, she's come back to make this home, forever."

Chance chewed on her thoughts as much as she did the bite of waffle. Images of Jax as a young girl flitted through her mind. She could picture them dancing on the riverbank to Lita Ford's gravelly voice. She'd closed her eyes and wished it would all remain the same forever. That song lingered for years in Chance's mind. She'd cried at Webster Concert Hall in New York, when she heard Lita and Lzzy Hale sing it together back in 2016. It's how she'd held on to Jax. She'd worn out several cassette tapes back in the day, as she allowed the lyrics to transport her back to nights in the bed of her pickup. Jax's body beneath her and the soft hands that burned themselves into her skin were embedded in her soul.

"Chance? Are you all right?"

Chance had no idea how long she'd been lost in memories of a younger Jax and the incredibly passionate love they'd made. She smiled at Maggie. "I'm fine, lost in all the things I have to do." She wasn't lying. Making love to Jax had been on her mind since touching her for the first time. They'd made love as often as they could, and she was looking forward to the next time they could be together.

"Don't scare me like that. I thought you were having a stroke."

Chance reached across the table and took Maggie's hand. "I'm fine. You know me, my mind goes in a thousand different directions at once."

"Yeah, I do. The blush in your cheeks tells me work wasn't the thing running through your mind." Maggie cleaned up the last of her breakfast preparations. "I'll let you off the hook and not make you confirm my suspicions. Don't forget, Kendra will be here later tonight.

It's taken everything I could think of to make her stay at school during your convalescence. She was ready to drop out of the summer class to come home and take care of you. I told her you had plenty of tender loving care already."

"Did you tell her about Jax?"

"I didn't have to. You forget...she keeps in touch with Daniel. Since he was home, she trusted him to give her his honest opinion about how you were doing." Maggie squeezed her shoulder before running a hand around Zeus' face. "You two try to stay out of trouble. I'll be checking in with Penny. Don't think you can get away with anything. I've got to go. If I don't fix Dee's oatmeal, it will be full of syrup and brown sugar. I swear, sometimes I think you're more related to her than to me. You're both terrible patients."

"Mom, Dee and I are fine. Don't put yourself in the hospital worrying about us. I'll be home in plenty of time to have dinner with Kendra. Come on over when you guys get off work, and I'll grill for all of us. And before you ask, yes, I'll invite Jax. Love you. Tell Momma D I'll call her later. If I don't, I know I'll have her up my ass too. Now go."

Maggie's laughter cackled through the house as she left.

***

Chance pushed open the glass door and chuckled as Penny nearly sprayed coffee over her desk when she saw her. Zeus made his way over to the desk. Chance stood at attention at the reception counter and addressed the real administrator in charge. "Sheriff Chance Fitzsimmons reporting for limited duty, ma'am."

Penny patted Zeus while frowning at Chance. "God, you're a pain in the ass. You whine about having to stay home for a full two weeks after you're found unconscious on the road. Freaking Brad calls off because his hemorrhoids are inflamed."

Chance came around the desk and knelt down beside Penny to look her directly in the face. "Penny, I'm well on my way to mended. This cast and Faith's lingering overprotection are the only things preventing me from being back to full duty. I promised almost everyone in the damn county I'd sit at my desk and leave by two in the afternoon." She touched Penny on the shoulder. "Come on Penny, look at me."

"You scared all of us, Chance. We like working for a boss that gives a damn about her employees. That boss also happens to be our friend. Seeing you like that nearly broke Taylor."

"And that's why I've promised to be very good until I'm one hundred percent. Taylor has enough to do keeping the road deputies safe under her supervision. I'm here to do what the citizens hired me to do...be the sheriff. Everything is going to be all right. Now, is Taylor's ass in my chair?"

Penny stood with Chance and hugged her. "Yes, and she's chomping at the bit to get out of it. I doubt I'll ever have to worry about her running for office."

"If I can help it, six years from now, she'll be wearing this badge." Chance pointed to the gold, five-pointed sheriff's badge on her uniform shirt. "I'll try my best to win my next election. That will give me the two terms West Virginia law says I can have. After that, we'll see. Taylor is a natural at this job. I know you guys are young. I remember my thirties, when the world was full of opportunities. She's a great chief deputy, and she'll make a better sheriff than I can ever think of being. Taylor has time to warm up to the idea. As far as I'm concerned, she's Chief Deputy until she says she doesn't want to be. For now, I'm going to my office, so you can call Maggie and confirm my release."

Chance watched Penny's face pink up. Penny narrowed her eyes and clucked her tongue. "How do you know that's what I was going to do? That blow to the head make you psychic?"

Chance pointed down to the desk. "No, but you have her number pulled up on your cell phone." Chance laughed and headed back to her office with Zeus. "Go ahead, she told me this morning that she'll be waiting for the call."

As she stepped to her office door, she could hear Penny chuckle. Zeus brushed past and greeted Midas with a tail wag and a sniff. Chance took a minute to look at her shoebox of an office. Accolades of her current and former professions were all around the room. Several pictures from her smoke jumper days lined one wall, her and her crew, soot-stained and smiling. She remembered those brave women and men she'd stood at the gates of hell with. A few had paid the ultimate sacrificial price, and that fact still churned her gut. A news article displayed a picture of her with Richie Allbrandt and his dog, Topper, the two victims she'd protected inside her fire shelter in Montana. Richie was now serving as a Montana state trooper. His parents sent her a Christmas card every year, along with dog treats for Zeus. She and Richie talked on the phone every few years, usually on the anniversary date of the fire. She leaned against the door frame and accidentally disturbed a picture of her and retired DEA agent, Scott Ross, on one of their marijuana eradication operations, a huge pile of plants behind them.

Taylor sat behind Chance's desk on the phone. "Brad, I don't care if you have a doctor's excuse. You are out of sick time. You'll have to either use vacation time or go without pay. It's your choice. Read section three of the employee's handbook. It's all there in black and white. I've got your shifts covered for the next three days. If you're going to be off longer than that," her eyes cut up to Chance, "you can talk to the sheriff about it, since she's back."

Chance glared at the cheesy 'so there' grin. She hadn't missed dealing with Brad's infuriating attempts to game the system. She was grateful that Brad would age out in another two years. At sixty-three, he was on borrowed time and he knew it. It was one of the reasons he'd run against her for Sheriff.

"I've got someone waiting to speak to me, Brad. This conversation has been documented along with the excuse the doctor's office faxed. Go soak in a hot bath and buy some Preparation H." She hung up the phone with a little more emphasis than was necessary, and then gave it the middle finger.

Chance leaned in the doorway chuckling. "The only way he's going to get rid of those hemorrhoids is if he bathes in it and drinks it by the gallon. That guy is one giant pain in the ass."

Taylor laughed so hard, tears started to form at the creases in her eyes. "Ain't that the truth? I don't know how you do it every day. I'll take the HR issues with every other one of our deputies combined, over dealing with that guy."

"And that's why I don't make you. Good or bad, it's my fault he's still here, and I deal with the consequences. So, how's that chair feel?"

"Tight and uncomfortable like that set of dance tights my mom tried to get me into when I was five. I'll take being a road deputy any day over these mounds of paperwork." Taylor picked up a stack and let it fall back on the desk with a thud.

"Well, like I told your wife, you'll have six years of reprieve if I have anything to do with it. After that," she pointed to Taylor, "I expect to come and visit your ass in this office as the newly elected sheriff. No pressure, but you've got the skills for it. You also have the time to watch me to see how you want to do it differently when you're in that chair for eight years."

"Chance, I'm not a politician."

"No, you're a good law enforcement officer who's made a good name for herself in the county, as well as in the LEO community. You'll have plenty of people doing most of the campaigning for you, long before your name is on the ballot. Before you vacate my office, I need to say a few things."

Taylor rocked in Chance's chair. "I thought you were saying a few things?"

"No, those are things about the future. The things I need to say are about the past. I was an ass the other day. Cranky and restless. I apologize. I was being pretty selfish, not thinking about you being there when I got hurt. I don't mean to take your loyalty, or your friendship, for granted.

Taylor started to interrupt. "You didn—"

"Yes, I did. I put you in as Chief Deputy, because there is no one I trust to have my back more than you. We've always been straight with each other. Well, relatively speaking." Chance grinned and caught Taylor doing the same. "I trust your opinion. I should have been listening instead of railing against the injustices of my situation. You didn't cause it and you were doing all the right things. I gave you hell for it, and I'm sorry."

Taylor continued rocking in the chair, and then pushed up on the arms to stand. She came around the desk to face Chance. "When I came here from the Marshals Service, I did it because I wanted to work for someone who believed I could make a difference. I signed on as Chief Deputy, knowing there would be flack because I came from somewhere else and didn't come up the ranks. You wanted to shake things up, and you demanded that those serving under your leadership follow your guiding principles." Taylor held up her right hand and turned to a picture of Chance's father in his uniform that sat with a triangular folded flag, framed in dark walnut.

Both of them recited the words Chance's father had taught her and that she'd passed on to Taylor. "Honor, duty, courage, integrity, and empathy."

"Chance, I followed you here, because you live those principles. I'm proud to serve under someone like that. You're the gold-star example, Chance. Forgiving you helps me exercise that empathy principle." She patted Chance on the shoulder. "Now, let me get you up to speed, so I can get the hell out of this office."

Chance nodded and followed Taylor back to the desk. For the next hour, they worked through scheduling issues with Brad's medical leave, tax collection paperwork, several subpoenas for deputies to appear in court, and finally, a stack of concealed carry applications.

Taylor held one up. "This one piqued my interest, Leland Kurst."

"Hell, he just moved back here with his dad right before I got hurt. None of that group needs to be carrying around a gun where I can't see it. If it smells like a skunk, it probably is. Do a triple-I background check on him. Call Pam and have her put on her investigator cap. Dig up everything you can. If he had a traffic ticket for jay walking in Baltimore, I want to know about it."

Chance wanted to see everything that the Interstate Identification Index had on Leland. He'd been living out of state for the last few years, and she doubted he'd been able to keep his nose clean. She was sure his rap sheet would prove her point.

Taylor nodded. "I'll get right on it."

A knock on the office door made Chance look up to greet the visitor. She was pleasantly surprised to see the olive-green-uniformed officer standing at her door.

"Hey there, Harley, come in."

Sergeant Harley Kincaid stepped through the door, removed her campaign hat, and sat down in the chair Chance pointed to. "Morning, Sheriff. Good to see you back." She looked over at Taylor. "Had enough of riding the pine in her place?"

"And how. Speaking of that, I'm out of here." Taylor turned to Chance. "I'm going to go get that check started." She pointed a warning finger at Chance, "Remember, Penny has Maggie on speed dial."

Chance grinned at her and pointed to the door. "Get the hell out of my office and get to work."

After she'd left, Chance brought her attention back to the polished officer who sat across the desk from her. "I assume you've brought me an update?"

Penny walked in the door holding two cups of coffee.

"Thanks for being a mind reader." Chance held her hand up to accept the liquid gold.

"All part of my jailor duties. Nice to see you again, Harley. Chance, Taylor's taking me to lunch a little early. Behave and don't make me put in a bad report to the warden."

Chance bit her cheek and pointed to the door. "Go."

Harley sipped her coffee. "Oh, that's good. Better than the swill at my office. Let's get down to business. I came to give you the lowdown on the guy from your accident."

"Accident my ass, he shot at me and rammed me on purpose."

Chance stopped. "Forgive my short fuse. I'm still a bit edgy. You know what it does to me to be out of the loop."

Harley laughed and pulled a notebook out of her uniform's breast pocket. "The guy was Dennis Cooley of Baltimore, Maryland. Small-time criminal with a rap sheet of the usual...larceny, possession, and theft of services. The guy was stealing cable and internet from his neighbor."

"What the hell was he doing here?"

"Well, if I had to make a guess, I'd say making a delivery. With the amount of product we recovered from his vehicle, we might have a problem brewing."

"What did the guy have?"

Harley raised an eyebrow and leaned forward. "High quality heroin."

"Good God, we don't need that around here. We barely have enough resources to bust the meth labs and oxycodone sales. That means some heavy hitters are moving in before the start of the busy season. Watch and see how fast our overdose calls start going through the roof." Chance sat back and scratched at the top edge of her cast. "This thing is going to be the death of me. I damn near knocked myself out last night."

"My daughter broke her arm a few years ago. We taped up a wire coat hanger, after she tried to get to an itch using my mother's knitting needle."

"By the way, how's Meg doing at the academy?"

Harley's grin covered her face. "Really well. Top of her class."

"Chip off the ole block. Will she come back here or take an assignment wherever she can?"

"Meg wants to come home. In the last few years, they've been trying to station new troopers closer to home for retention purposes. I'd like to have her back here, so I can keep an eye on her. They won't put her in my command for obvious reasons. Maybe Elkins."

"You did a great job raising her as a single mother."

"Yeah well, a few years ago, that might have been debatable. Thank God for my own mother. I'm pretty sure she kept me from killing her."

Chance shook her head. "No, she's a great kid. Hell, I guess she's not a kid anymore. Meg will make an outstanding West Virginia state trooper, just like her mom."

"Thanks, she's made me extremely proud. Now, back to this druggie who put you out of commission. We're doing some backtracking on his financials and trying to figure out who he was here to see. We doubt that he was here to sell on his own. We've got to get a handle on this before it's out of control. It won't be long before ski season, when we have a lot of well-off, out-of-town visitors strapping two by fours to their feet. I just wanted to tell you in person that it was a justified shooting and that's what went into the report."

Something ticked in Chance's mind. She picked up the concealed weapon permit and handed it to Harley. "According to this, Leland Kurst is back in town. The address listed is his dad's place. I called in a bit of information to the task force about an out-of-state vehicle at the Kurst's not too long ago. Blacked out Dodge Durango with a personalized Maryland plate. I'll have dispatch fax that license check over to your office. You know as well as I do, if they have visitors, it's not because someone just stopped by. I've busted those boys so many times I've lost count. With Leland back in town, we might need to see if there was any connection to this Dennis Cooley from Baltimore. I'll call over to the task force and give them a heads up so their undercover officers can start watching for any links. I'd love nothing more than to put that whole family away. They've done more than I can ever prosecute them for. I look at it this way, Capone went away for tax evasion."

Harley rose from her chair and slipped her hat back on. "I'll have my troopers keep an eye out too. Get healed up. We need you back on the road."

Chance stood and walked her to the door. "I'll do my best. Keep me informed. I know Taylor's working with you, but I'd appreciate being kept in the loop."

"You got it."

Chance went back to her office and started pouring over the various stacks on her desk. The hours ticked by quickly. She was so engrossed, she didn't notice Zeus get up from her side to greet a visitor.

"Good thing I'm not a bad guy. I'd have had the drop on you, Sheriff."

Chance looked up to see the shapely figure she'd spaced out thinking about that morning. Jax stood running her hand over Zeus's ears. Chance's entire chest swelled with warmth. Jax was still the most beautiful woman she'd ever seen. "Trust me, my partner there knows you're not a bad guy, or he'd have ripped your throat out. The last time Brad stepped in my office, it took all my training to bring him to heel."

Jax walked in and sat down in the chair across from her. "How's your first day back?"

Chance picked up her incomplete work pile, then pointed to the few things she had managed to get done. "It sucks. I have all this to go through yet."

Jax got up and shut the door to Chance's office. Eyebrow raised, Chance's eyes followed Jax around the desk, before she leaned down and kissed her softly.

"Rome wasn't built in a day. The paperwork will still be here Monday." She looked at her watch. "It's almost two and time for you to go home. Did you even eat?"

Chance was still reeling from the tingling in her lips. "Uh, Pen...Penny brought me back a sandwich when she and Taylor went out."

Jax pointed to the coffee cup. "How many of those have you had?"

Chance squinted, trying to remember. "I have no idea. I think I've poured two, and Penny brought me the first one."

"And I will assume you had at least one when Maggie fixed you breakfast and a travel cup on the way in? Am I right?"

Chance tried to think. "Good guess. Your point?"

"My point is, your knee was bouncing up and down so hard, you were vibrating the floor when I came in. All that caffeine and no way to burn it off in a system like yours? Recipe for disaster. So, you are going to put the pen down, follow me to your house, and we're taking Zeus for a walk together."

Chance sat back in her chair and consciously tried to steady her knee. "We are, are we? Do I have any say in the matter?"

"You do. You can say yes now, or two minutes from now. Either way, your choice."

Chance's laughter made Zeus look at her. She held up her hands in defeat. "Okay, then yes. Let me finish this one form, and we'll head out."

Jax opened the office door and winked at her. I'm going to go talk to Penny and get a full report on your activities for Maggie." She looked at her watch. "You've got ten minutes, Sheriff. Best get pushing that pencil."

***

Chance held the door for Jax, whose arms were laden with groceries as she stepped into the house. "We need to get those steaks marinated."

Zeus ran in past them and jumped up on the slender young woman standing in the kitchen. "Hey boy. How's my boy?"

Chance helped Jax set the groceries down and spoke to Kendra Fitzsimmons, her adopted sister. "You snuck out early, didn't you?"

"Hey, I was good and stayed at school when you got hurt. That killed me. Professor Ross said it was okay for me to miss class this once." The young girl wearing blue jeans with ripped-out knees and a maroon-and-white, archery-club polo stepped forward to stand in front of Chance.

Chance drew her into her arms and hugged her, as the girl buried her face in Chance's shoulder. "Given that I worked with Ross on several cases, years ago, I'm not surprised, once he found out who you were coming to see. Honest kiddo, I'm okay. Now, I'd like you to meet someone, someone important to me." Chance turned them. "This is Jax St. Claire. She's Doc Hendricks's niece and is taking over his practice. She's also buying the Richards place. Jax, this is my little sister. She's a criminal justice major at WVU."

Kendra stepped away from Chance's arms and extended her hand. "Hi, Kendra Fitzsimmons. Nice to meet you, Jax."

"It's nice to finally meet you, Kendra. This whole family has told me so much about you."

Kendra laughed. "Don't believe everything they say. They tend to exaggerate."

"Holding a 4.0 in a criminal justice major and a technology minor is bragworthy, Kendra. Be proud of that." Jax came over and put a hand on Chance's shoulder. "I don't think this one was exaggerating when she said you were an exceptional young woman. I trust Chance's judgment."

"That might be your first mistake. She did manage to leave me in a store one time."

Chance threw up her hand. "For two minutes, two minutes!"

"And I was ten!"

Jax started to laugh hard enough to make both of them look at her. "I'm sorry. Listening to you two is like listening to a conversation between me and my brother. One time, Mom made him take me on one of his movie dates. Let's just say they went into one and sent me to another. I came out and they were gone. They were so," she paused, her words choking to a stop.

Chance pulled her in tight and held her. "You okay?" She felt Jax relax against her and shake her head.

"Chance, they were in such a hurry to, well, get busy, they forgot all about me for twenty minutes. When he finally came back to the theater, anything I wanted was on the table if I didn't tell Mom."

Chance pulled her closer.

Kendra's look of shock was comical. "And what did you ask for?"

"He had to pick me up from school every day, let me read his comic books, and take me for ice cream for a whole month."

Kendra put her hands on her hips and let her mouth slack open. "I got robbed. All I got out of the deal was a pack of Sour Patch Kids and a milkshake from McDonald's. I demand a redo, or I'm telling Mom."

Chance pulled back to look at Jax. "Stop giving her ideas. I get in enough trouble with Mom without your help."

Jax leaned up and kissed her lips. "That you do."

"Okay you two, these groceries aren't going to unpack themselves. And if I'm not mistaken, 'mom squared' will be here at seven, expecting dinner. What do you need me to do?" Kendra dug through the bags.

Chance handed her a box of rice. "How about you put this stuff away for me."

"I can do that. It's about all the brain power I have left."

"By the way, how are your classes going?" Chance went over and opened a cabinet. The glass baking dish she wanted to put the steaks was beneath two others and a stack of bowls. She started to reach up before a hand touched hers.

"Let me help the afflicted, before I have to clean up the mess you're going to make when all your glassware hits the floor." Kendra pulled down the baking dish and slid it toward Chance.

Chance put a hand over Kendra's. "I promise, I'm ok, Bullseye. I wouldn't lie to you. Jax will back me up." She watched as her little sister teared up. "Come here." Chance pulled her close and enveloped the young woman in her arms, allowing her the safety to cry.

Kendra wiped at the tears that hadn't made it to Chance's shirt yet. "You haven't called me Bullseye since my senior year."

Chance looked over to Jax, who stood quietly in the background. She nodded her head when Jax pointed outside. "You act like that was ten years ago. You'll always be Bullseye to me, even if you never let another arrow or basketball fly."

"You scared me to death. I had my car packed and was headed home. The 'rents were trying hard to keep me there. If it hadn't been for Daniel's call, I would have. He swore you were okay."

"You trust Daniel, so trust me. I'm okay. Unfortunately, it's an occupational hazard." Chance led her to the table and held her hand as they sat. "I know the fear, Kendra. You and I share a set of parents because that hazard became a reality for my dad. It's something you'll face in your own career, if you continue to pursue law enforcement. Once they pin that badge to your chest, I suspect that Dee's visits with Ms. Clairol still won't be able to cover up the white hair we're going to give her. Why do you think Mom stopped trying? Hell, it's already happening to me, look at this." Chance pointed to the white shock of hair near her forehead.

Kendra laughed. "I've seen pictures of you when were young." She reached up and tugged the streak. "You had this in high school."

"Well, I was imagining you back then. I always wanted a little sister. Lucky, I only had to wait thirty-nine years to get you." Chance cupped the back of Kendra's neck. "You okay now?"

Kendra shook her head and wiped at the remaining tears. She looked toward the deck. "So Jax, huh?"

"Yup, Jax."

"The Jax?"

Chance nodded.

Kendra whistled low and looked outside again. "The one in the red, white, and blue bikini top in that picture with you? Damn, she's still hot."

"Get your eyes back in your head. Yes, she is, and she's no cougar. Don't even look at her like that, or I might have to ground you."

"I've got my own prospects, thank you. Doesn't mean I can't admire a thing of beauty."

Chance flipped her ear. "Remember, I have arrest powers. I can hold you for twenty-four hours with no bail."

Kendra rose. "As if. Mom would ground your ass. I'm betting you've been chomping at the bit to go back to work. How'd you get Faith to release you?"

"That's a story for another time."

Kendra looked hopeful. "Over a beer?"

Chance squinted at her. "Unless someone screwed up on your birth certificate, in another year we'll discuss it over a beer. I have no doubt you've already tipped a few. Hell, I can't say I didn't have anything before I was twenty-one, but I'm not contributing to it. Maggie would kill me. Be careful. Don't let anything derail the path you decide on."

Kendra shook her head. "Not a chance in hell. I'm going to be one of your deputies before you're out of office. I've got three years of college left or the 'rents will kill me. Two and a half, if I can find a way to do it. You just make sure you're still around to pin that star on my chest, you hear me?"

"God willing, I'll do my very best. I love ya, kiddo. Let's get the prep work done before they get here. With or without Professor Ross's permission, be prepared to take a grilling as to why you're home early. Now, put those groceries away for me while I go check on Jax. That story about her brother stirred up a few things for her. He and his wife died in an accident. You remember how to make that marinade I taught you?" Kendra nodded. "Okay, make sure to run the tenderizer over the steaks before you put them in to soak. I'll be right back."

"Thanks, Chance."

"Anything for you."

Chance left Zeus with Kendra and found Jax down by the pond. She walked up and put her arms around the woman facing the water. "You'd never be able to prove that kid in there isn't related to me by blood, she acts like I did back then. She even wanted to know if you were the woman in that picture we took together down at the riverbank."

"Oh, did she?"

"Yup, said you were a thing of beauty and hot."

"Optimum word, *were*."

Chance turned Jax until she could kiss her. She let their lips and tongues come together until she felt Jax soften and relax in her arms. "Wrong, she said *still* hot. I saw her give you the once over a few times."

"All I care about is what you think." Jax bunched up Chance's shirt into her fists.

"What I think is you're an incredibly beautiful woman that I am more than glad to get a second opportunity to be with." Chance kissed her again. "Are you okay? I know that story about Jennings made you laugh. I also know it made you choke up."

Jax didn't say anything for a few minutes. "Losing Jennings was like losing my champion. Dad never stood up to Mom. Jennings always did, when it came to me. I don't know how many times he intervened when Mom went off on me about my *choices*. After he died, few people ever got who the real Jax was and was happy with her. That's why I used to come up here and spend summers with Uncle Marty. I could get away from *Mommy Dearest*."

"I remember your second summer here, when she dropped you off. She was none too pleased to meet me. Said she knew my dad and mom. She didn't seem to like me. Hard to believe she grew up in this county."

"I know. She almost didn't let me come back after she talked to her spies around here. Told me to steer clear of you for reasons she wouldn't elaborate on."

Chance laughed. "I can tell you why. She caught me checking out your ass when you left that first year."

Jax play slapped Chance's belly. "You are so bad."

"I can't help it. I'll freely admit that I loved both your brain and your body back then."

Jax tilted her head and brought Chance's lips down a bit to meet her own. "How about now? What will you admit to?"

"I'll readily admit that you have my heart in your hand. I never stopped loving you. I'll admit that we have a lot more to learn about our years apart and that I want nothing more than to spend time working toward a future together. I love you, Jax. I always have." She put her fingers to Jax's lips. "Don't say anything now unless you plan on figuring out a way to kidnap me and cast a spell to suspend time. The moms will be here any minute, and Kendra's spending the night."

Jax nodded, as Chance gathered her in her arms. If Chance had her way, she'd pull the woman she loved inside her own skin. If there was one thing she knew, it was that she never intended to let Jax go, ever again.

Chapter Thirteen

JAX WALKED ARM IN arm with Chance, back up to the house. She was a little in awe. The young woman she'd fallen for so many years ago had matured into this personification of duty and honor. What was more amazing, was that this synthesis of strength and mischief was still in love with her. Jax wanted nothing more in her life. Chance hadn't let her say the words that were right on the tip of her tongue. The next time she had the opportunity, she would return that sentiment in spades. *Or hearts as it may be.* With Kendra staying the night at Chance's, Jax knew that their next assignation would have to wait. Jax was in desperate need of the one touch that still burned inside of her like a blacksmith's furnace.

"So, tell me about Kendra's past. How did she end up with Maggie and Dee?"

Chance sighed. "I don't have enough time to tell you the whole story. Let's just say when deputies were called for an overdose, they found five-year-old Kendra fending for herself. Her mom wasn't fit to take care of a hamster. Her dad tried to burn the house down with them in it. She came to Maggie and Dee when child services called them to see if they'd be willing to do an emergency foster. Eventually, after a long court battle, they were awarded full custody and eventually adopted Kendra as their own. I'll tell you more about it sometime, when she's out of earshot. She knows the whole story. Unfortunately, it brings up really bad memories for her. It messes with her sleep for months when we talk about it."

Jax shook her head. "It always makes me sad. So many people out there that want kids and can't have them. People like Kendra's parents have them at the drop of a hat and don't take care of them. Thank God for people like Maggie and Dee."

"They're the only real parents Kendra has ever known. She's one tough cookie."

"And wants to be just like her big sister."

"I'm younger than the moms. I can keep up with her."

Jax laughed. "I think it goes much deeper."

Once they were back in the warm and well-equipped kitchen, Jax helped Chance and Kendra fix dinner until the crunch of gravel alerted her to visitors. Jax looked out the window. "They're here."

She turned in time to see Chance and Kendra standing at the sink. The image nearly took her breath. Both women were tall, although Chance towered an inch or two above Kendra. *They both have to be just under six feet. Gunmetal-blue eyes to Kendra's sky-blue ones. Definitely the same cocky attitude and swagger.* Jax noticed they even stood alike. She could envision a younger Kendra studying Chance's every action to copy it to her own internal hard drive. That's what Uncle Marty had always been to her, a hero she wanted to emulate. The opening of the door drew her from her musing to greet Dee. Maggie followed closely behind with a covered pie pan.

"Kendra Jo Fitzsimmons, how long have you been here?" Maggie set the pie down and looked at the clock on the wall. Dee walked over to hug her. "You shouldn't be arriving for another hour since your last class should have ended at three."

Jax chuckled, as Dee mumbled "busted" just behind Kendra's left ear.

Kendra hid behind Dee and pulled Chance's arm to form a barrier, using Jax to secure the right flank. "Mom, before you lose your cool, Professor Ross gave me permission to miss class. He was interested in hearing how Chance was doing, and I promised to give him all the details on Monday." She peeked out between the shoulders of her protectors. "Come on, tomorrow's Chance's birthday, and I stayed when you told me to. Can you cut me a little slack?"

Maggie's arms were crossed over her chest, and one eye was nearly squinted shut. "Only if you stop cowering behind your human force field and give your mother a proper hello."

Kendra's grin smothered her face and she came out behind from Dee to wrap Maggie in a bear hug. "Missed you, Mom."

Maggie clung to Kendra while looking at Chance. "You're forgiven, if you feed me."

Kendra tickled Maggie, then ran back behind Dee. "Five Points has that covered."

Chance held up her hands. "Bullseye did most of the work."

Maggie's hands were now on her hips. "You two do remember you were given proper names?" She pointed to Dee. "The nicknames were all your fault."

Dee stepped forward and pulled Maggie into her arms. "Yes, my little steel magnolia, I remember."

Maggie slapped her on the shoulder. "You are incorrigible." She kissed Dee softly then pushed her away. "I need wine, and you're closest to the refrigerator. Fill the order."

Dee laughed and turned to follow her wife's directive. Jax watched it all with amusement and hadn't noticed Chance sliding closer to her until she felt an arm around her waist.

"Welcome to what life's been like around here. Aren't you glad you missed it?"

Jax turned to her. "No, the exact opposite. I wish I'd have been here for every second."

Chance pulled her tighter. "Well, you don't have to miss another minute. You're one of the family, so expect to be duly initiated. Maggie will have plenty to say about the rest of your life, trust me."

"Chance Raylynn, are you over there bad mouthing me?" Maggie stood with her hands planted firmly on her hips.

"No, ma'am."

Jax laughed, as Chance pushed her between Maggie and herself then ducked behind her left shoulder. "Coward."

"And proud of it."

Maggie rolled her eyes. "How long before supper? I'm going to go sit on the deck and listen to Kendra tell me how school is really going. Come on Dee, she might need you for backup."

Chance let her laughter peel out into the room. It was like music to Jax's ears.

"Let me throw the steaks on the grill, and I'd say we can eat in about fifteen minutes. Kendra threw the baked potatoes in the pit about fifteen minutes ago."

Maggie waved them off as she herded the other two out the sliding door. Jax wiped away tears of laughter. "Chance, you have no idea how I've missed those two. Laughter at Mom and Dad's house was always severely lacking."

"How about your own home, no laughter there either?"

Jax pondered the thought for a moment. "To be honest, no. I think that stopped the minute I said '*I do.*' Life changed, she changed. Eventually, so did I." Jax leaned back on the dark granite kitchen counter.

"Interesting that I don't really see the change. You're still the beautiful, intelligent woman you were then. I'm glad you found the smile you lost out there. Let's get these steaks on before the natives get restless."

Chance carried the meat, and Jax brought two beers with her. She used the bottle opener attached to the porch post with *Coke* stamped into the metal. Remembering an old, red-and-white cooler Chance had during their summers on the river, Jax pointed to the bottle opener. Chance's smile lit up her face as she nodded. "Yes, that's off that old cooler."

Jax nodded. "I thought so."

"That opener and I are old friends. The cooler met an untimely death. Putting the opener there seemed right."

A loud sizzle rose when the thick cuts of beef hit the grill, and every head turned. Within minutes, the smell of seared steak filled the air and had Zeus sniffing from his place by Chance's leg. With the steaks nearly done, Kendra retrieved the baked potatoes from a small fire pit near the deck and unwrapped them from the foil. Jax and Maggie put plates and utensils out for everyone. Dee jumped up and helped Chance distribute the steaks, as the group found their places at the table. The chatter stopped as everyone took their first bite. One by one, groans of pleasure escaped each diner.

"I think I've died and gone to heaven," Dee confessed.

"I'd enjoy that slowly, because that's the last beef you're getting for a month."

Dee went slack jawed as she looked at Maggie, who continued to chew with a smile. Kendra sliced another piece of her steak and rolled her eyes in pleasure. Chance tried to hide a smirk behind a drink of her beer.

Dee wagged a finger back and forth at her daughters. "You two wait. Your time will come. Enjoy that metabolism now."

Maggie leaned over and kissed Dee's cheek. "I'm just trying to keep your words from becoming a self-fulfilling prophecy. You'll die and go to heaven when I'm damn good and ready for both of us to walk through the gate together. Got it?"

Dee shook her head and kissed her wife. "From your lips to God's ears."

Jax watched the slow smile and the look of absolute devotion on Dee's face. When she turned to look at Chance, she saw a gaze nearly as intense staring back at her. Deep in her chest, Jax's heart skipped a beat and her center pulsed. Her desire for Chance grew every moment they spent together. She wanted what Maggie and Dee had. After a lifetime of never being enough, she wanted to be everything to someone. Not just someone, she wanted to be everything to Chance. A soft touch on her forearm brought her attention to the eyes that drew her in.

"Where'd you go?" Chance asked.

Jax let the smile she felt inside show. "A little trip to the future." Jax covered Chance's hand. "I'll tell you later."

They finished dinner and listened as Kendra told them about her classes. "Professor Ross is tough. He's also an awesome instructor. And just so you both know, he let me go early to come home since he knows Chance. He told me you saved his ass one time."

Maggie pinched her lips tight. "Language, young lady."

Kendra rolled her eyes. "He said Chance saved his butt. Is that better?"

Maggie nodded.

"Anyway, he said it was when you were with Fish and Wildlife. He didn't elaborate much. He told me that he's still alive to teach me how to become a good officer, because you stopped the bleeding. What happened?"

Chance took a drink of her beer. Something told Jax reliving the memory wasn't going to be easy. She watched for any sign of distress. When Chance tugged at her earlobe, Jax had her confirmation.

Chance ran her hand down her face. "We'd done some aerial reconnaissance in our marijuana eradication program. During one of our passes over the refuge, we saw that telltale color we look for. The visible footpath told us it was a tended growth."

Jax was surprised. She'd seen the helicopters fly over in California. None of her experiences gave her a clue how they helped locate illegal drugs.

"We made a notation of the GPS points whenever we found patches. We had ground teams ready to go in and do the eradication. When we landed, I joined up with Ross to make our way to the location. These guys were no amateur growers, and it wasn't a personal use patch. This had all the earmarks of a distribution operation. We managed to avoid a few booby traps. We weren't expecting something like a claymore buried in the path. Scott Ross stepped on one, and the blast took his leg off below the knee."

Jax, drew in a sharp breath and grabbed Chance's hand. *It could have been her.*

"He was losing a lot of blood. I pulled him back and threw a tourniquet on it. A few years before, I'd taken a continuing ed course on how to stop major hemorrhaging. I'd started carrying a few tourniquets with me in my tactical vest. I threw one of those on and called for his evacuation. We were about a mile back in the refuge and completely inaccessible by vehicle. Sarah and her crew brought a collapsible litter that we used to carry him out to a clearing, where they loaded him for the flight to the hospital. There wasn't enough of his lower leg left to save. Fortunately, he's alive to teach punks like you." Chance threw her balled up napkin at Kendra, who caught it easily.

"He has an awesome prosthetic. He has a habit of putting his leg up on a chair and leaning on his thigh. That's how I saw it the first time. I asked him a question about it, and he told us part of the story. I didn't know all of it until now."

Kendra dropped her head. Jax recognized the hero worship Kendra had for Chance. She knew a little about that feeling, as she was carrying a great deal of adoration in her own heart for the strong woman whose hand she held.

"I honestly didn't know if he was going to live or die that day. When we got back to base, most of us wanted to head to the hospital. I'm not saying I didn't. My focus was to get the guys who injured him. I knew he would want that more than anything, so I made it happen. We brought in a couple of ordnance guys, who took care of the rest of the explosives. There were four more in different areas around the grow site. I turned that place over until we found a single, faded gas receipt. When we busted down the door to Fred Wendell's place, they were none too happy to see us. We arrested five of them with enough cash, weapons, and drugs ready for distribution, that we didn't have any trouble getting a conviction. We put them away for a long time for the attempted homicide of a federal officer. After we added the narcotics trafficking charges, they'll be lucky to see the outside of a prison before they need a walker." Chance abruptly rose. "I'll be right back." Zeus followed at her side.

Kendra rose to follow until Maggie put a hand on her arm. "Jax, I think maybe she needs you, more than any of us."

Dee got up and walked over to Jax and knelt beside her. "There is very little that bothers Chance more than having a fellow officer injured on her watch. When she was burned, one of her crew tried to outrun the burn over and didn't make it. She blames herself each and every time someone working with her is injured. Even if she isn't in charge of the operation, it digs into her gut. Chance is a leader, and a leader like that wears her honor on her sleeve. I think you understand that part of her."

Jax nodded and followed in the same direction Chance had gone. She found her in the front yard throwing a tennis ball for Zeus. She joined Chance without speaking. After the third throw, Zeus brought the ball to Jax and dropped it at her feet. She bent and scratched his ears before she let the ball sail.

Chance whistled. "You've got quite the arm."

"I played intramural softball at UC Davis." She tapped her knees. "Catcher. That's why I don't have any knees and have this spike mark on my calf."

"Were you blocking the plate?"

Jax smiled and raised an eyebrow. "I was at the plate. She tried to slide in. Let's just say she didn't make it." She slid an arm around Chance's waist. "I tag what I'm going for."

Chance reciprocated with an arm around Jax's shoulder and pulled her into her chest.

"You okay?" Jax questioned.

Chance sighed. "I am. It should be me missing my leg. I stopped to tuck in my bootlace that kept snagging on briers. Scott Ross stepped in front of me to take the lead."

Jax gripped Chance's shirt tightly in her hands. "If it'd been him in the lead that stopped, would you have taken over for him?"

"Yes, that's not the point. It should have been me."

"You could fill the Blackwater Canyon with 'should haves.' All you can do is deal with the reality of what actually happened. From the sounds of it, that's what you did. According to Kendra, he credits you with saving his life. You had the training to stop the bleeding. Did he?"

"I have no idea."

"Well then, let's look at the positive side of it. You knew what do to. In the end, both of you are alive to teach future officers how to save the life of their partner." Jax waited without saying anything else and felt Chance relax in her arms.

"How do you do that?"

"What?"

Chance tipped up her chin. "Know what I need even when I don't."

Jax chuckled. "Magic."

"Ah. You're definitely bewitching."

Jax pulled back and took her hand. "Come on, it's family time, and that's a pretty great one out there on the deck."

"I'll second that. You know I count you as family."

Jax squeezed her hand as she led her back through the house. She prayed that someday she'd feel like a true member of the Fitzsimmons clan. "Remind me to give you your birthday present the next time we're alone."

"If it's anything like my eighteenth birthday present, I'll tell them all to get the hell out right now."

"We'll see, Sheriff. We'll see."

Chapter Fourteen

CHANCE SAT AT THE breakfast table with a cup of coffee and the newspaper in her hand, when Kendra plopped down heavily into a chair, a loud yawn nearly swallowing her face. "Coffee?"

Kendra sat zombie-like, rubbing her eyes. Chance couldn't help but laugh at the strand of hair sticking straight in the air. When Kendra put her head face down on the table, Chance let out a snicker and Kendra flipped her the middle finger. Chance grabbed a mug and added an overgenerous pour of the flavored creamer she kept for her sister.

The young woman grabbed it with both hands and greedily sipped.

"One of these days, you'll realize that more coffee in relation to the creamer in that cup will be helpful in waking you up. How do you drink that stuff?"

Kendra mumbled something unintelligible, and Chance shook her head. After another sip and a stretch, Kendra finally spoke. "I don't tell you how to drink your coffee. Leave me be. It's too early in the morning for meaningful conversation."

Chance looked at her watch. "Uh, it's nine. Good thing I'm not allowed to run, or your ass would have been up at five to go with me."

"Come on, Chance. Don't make me adult yet."

Chance could only laugh as she raised her cup to her lips. Sometimes when she looked at Kendra, she saw a younger version of herself. They were as close as any two siblings she knew, save the age difference. "Feel like dinner out at Sarah and Kristi's? Daniel will be there."

Another large yawn and a mumble covered Kendra's answer. The nod of her head was the only indication of actual acceptance of the invitation. Chance took her cell phone and her cup of coffee to the deck and took a seat in one of the Adirondack chairs to call the Riker home. When the call was answered, Chance laughed at the immediate scolding she took.

"I know, I know. I'm sorry I haven't been there in a while. Forgive me, Kristi. That's why I'm calling. Is that invitation still open for dinner?"

"It wasn't an invitation. It was an order and you know it. Daniel said Kendra is home, so drag her ass with you. Oh, and Jax better be on your arm."

"I haven't checked with her yet. If she's free, I'm sure she'll be with us."

"Any requests? This is your birthday dinner, you know." Kristi Riker asked.

"There isn't a single meal I've ever had at your house when I haven't stuffed myself to the gills. I love everything you make, except liver. You know me. No organs or innards. And no soup!"

Kristi's small laugh always reminded her of a baby's giggle. "Got it, no organs or innards. I was already scolded about the soup suggestion. How about barbeque ribs? Side dishes yet to be determined."

"You're making my mouth water. Can you throw in some lime pickles?"

"That's a given, honey. Make your way over here around seven. Sarah's working dayshift and will be home before you get here. Daniel can finish them on the grill."

"Thanks, Kristi. We'll see you then."

She hung up the phone and called Jax's cell phone. The sultry hello sent a shiver down Chance's spine. "Good morning, beautiful."

"Good morning. How are you this morning?" Jax asked.

"Bored. I miss my runs and riding Kelly. Taylor and the rest of the guys have been working everyone out to keep them exercised. I'm itching to get back in the saddle."

"Then I shouldn't tell you that I just came back in from a ride, should I?"

"Oh, that was a low blow. Anyway, I called to ask if you want to go to dinner with Kendra and me out to Sarah and Kristi's? Barbeque ribs are on the menu. Will you come?"

"What time?"

"I'll pick you up at six unless you want to do something else earlier?" Chance enjoyed spending time with Jax, no matter what they were doing.

"I've got some final things I need to do at the office. A delivery of some new equipment came in yesterday, and I want to get it installed. My plan is to open the practice full time next week."

Chance knew their opportunity to spend a great deal of time together was coming to an end. She would soon be back to full duty, and Jax would be busy running her practice. "Need any help?"

"If that help involves a tall, dark, handsome woman, then yes. I can always use the help. Thanks for offering Kendra."

"Oh, you are full of piss and vinegar this morning, which is more than I can say for poor Kendra. She's communicated mostly in grunts so far."

Chance watched Zeus sniff around the edge of the tree line and hike his leg on one of them. The morning air was quickly warming in the bright sunlight, and she turned her face to it.

"I remember when we were that young. Sadly, I was always an early riser. As soon as I could get out of the house, I did. I'd spend all day outside if I could. Jennings and I would take off and maybe make it home for supper." They grew quiet for a few moments. Zeus came to sit by Chance, and she bent down to put an arm around him.

"Enough of this trip down memory lane. Can I bring you breakfast, or have you already eaten?"

Chance smiled. "I had some toast earlier. I'll meet you at the clinic.
"

After a few more exchanges, they hung up. Chance found Kendra spreading peanut butter on a toasted waffle.

"I'm going to help Jax down at her office today. I think Mom needs some assistance with a few repairs to that one property they don't have rented. Can you make sure she doesn't hurt herself? I'll stop by there and pick you up about six thirty. Okay?" Kendra nodded and Chance grinned. "Maybe you'll be able to actually speak by then." She grabbed her keys and signaled for Zeus to follow.

Twenty minutes later, she pulled into Three Rivers Animal Hospital. Chance admired the sign and liked the new name. Three rivers came together to form the Cheat, down in Parsons. Jax's truck was there, as was another vehicle in the lot. Leland Kurst stood at the door, talking with Jax. Chance felt the Glock holstered in the small of her back and spoke to Zeus "Blijven." She watched his countenance change when he shifted into work mode with the Dutch command to stay alert.

Chance exited the truck and brought Zeus with her. She committed the Maryland registration to memory, as she made her way to the front of the building. Leland stiffened when he saw her.

"Thanks, Dr. St. Claire. I'll call you and make an appointment to get those shots."

"The office should be open full time here next week. By then, there should be a receptionist instead of an answering machine. Thanks for stopping by."

Chance approached so that she could see at least one of his hands. The other he'd slid into his pocket when Chance got out of the truck. Zeus was still on alert and in formation by her side.

"Leland, I heard you'd moved back. Come home for work?"

"Sheriff." He tipped his ball cap and moved the toothpick in his mouth to the other side. "Uh, no. Grandpa hasn't been well. Dad called and asked me to come home and help with the farm."

Chance nodded.

"I saw the doc pull in, and I wanted to ask about some shots for my dog."

Chance nodded again.

Leland slid his filthy ball cap down farther. "Well, I gotta be goin'. I'll call."

Chance watched Leland walk past Zeus, who never took his eyes off the greasy-haired man. When Leland made it into his vehicle, he pulled out and sped out of view. Chance turned back to Jax, who had her arms crossed over her chest like she was cold.

"Are you okay?"

'Yeah, I was so happy to see you pull in. He gave me the creeps."

Chance stepped forward and drew Jax into her arms. "His family is bad news. I don't believe him for a second that he came back home to help work on the farm. I don't want you to be alone with that guy ever. If he makes an appointment, you call me and I'll be here at your office. Please?"

"I'll be more than happy to have my own personal security system."

Chance took the keys from Jax and unlocked the door. "Come on, let's forget about him. Don't let him ruin the day. We have work to do."

Jax shook her head and flipped on the light as she walked into the clinic. Chance stopped her and pulled her back. Her protective nature was on overload, and she needed to feel Jax safely in her arms. She brought their lips together and felt Jax's knees try to give out. She held her firmly to her own body. Jax slid her arms around Chance's neck and wrapped a leg around her calf. Their tongues danced, and Chance brushed her right thumb across Jax's breast, pulling a gasp from her. Their foreheads touched, as they stood breathing each other in.

"I will always be here to protect you. I'm not going to let anything happen to you, Jax. Ever."

"Do you have any idea how much I want to take you home and strip you out of every stitch of your clothing?"

Chance gasped, doing her best to bring her pounding center under control. She wanted nothing more than to feel Jax's skin sliding against her own. They hadn't been able to be alone together for a few days. Her internal temperature was reaching boiling point. A pinpoint of pain on her lower lip brought her mind back when Jax nipped, prompting another passionate kiss. "I have a pretty good idea. Actually, I'm imagining you with nothing on at all and taking great pleasure in being the one to get you that way. Unfortunately, Kendra is probably still at my place."

Jax dropped her head to Chance's chest. "And Uncle Marty is home too, damn it. I need to get that paperwork finalized on the Richards place. Then, no matter who's home where, we have a place to go where we can limit the traffic flow."

Chance kissed her nose softly. "I'm all for that. I'm scorching the rotors putting the brakes on so many times." Chance groaned and let Jax move away from her. "Let's see about getting this work done. Maybe by then, Kendra will be gone."

Jax winked at her. "Well, at least it's a plan we can work toward."

As Jax started to walk away, Chance pulled her in for one final kiss. "Plan your work, then work the plan."

Large boxes sat in the middle of the reception area. Jax got to work opening them, with Chance's help. Chance took the time to call the dispatch center and ask them to run the license plate and email her the information. They put together the new reception furniture and a new medication-dispensing system. Together, they put out a display of pet-safety equipment, including reflective collars and leashes.

Three hours later, Chance put down the small drill she'd been using to put the locking cabinets in place. "Hey, by the way, who'd you hire to be your receptionist?"

Jax carried in a packing crate filled with small instruments. "Lindsey Hawthorn. She'll be my receptionist and assistant. She graduated as a vet tech earlier this year. I stole her from an office in Elkins. She wanted to be closer to home and not have to drive in the winter."

"I know Lindsey very well. She dates Harley's daughter."

"Harley?"

"Sergeant Harley Kincaid. She's the company commander of the West Virginia State Police, Parsons Detachment. Her daughter, Meg, is at the academy right now. Meg and Lindsey have been dating since high school."

"Dr. Allen recommended her. He and Uncle Marty have been

friends for years."

Chance stood and stretched her back. "She'll do a great job for you. I coached her in softball. Hell of a pitcher. You guys ought to join the local league. You'd be ringers."

"Not so sure about that. College was a lifetime ago." Jax loaded the cabinet with supplies and laughed when Chance's stomach growled. "I think I'd better feed you before you pass out. You sound like you're starved."

Chance walked up and put her arms around Jax's waist. She bent and kissed the exposed skin of Jax's neck. "I'm starved all right. I can tell you food is low on my list. Your ass looks delicious in those jeans."

Jax groaned and melted into Chance's touch. She arched her neck, giving Chance more access and threaded her hand into the taller woman's hair.

"I want you so much. I'm not sure how much longer I can wait. Kendra sent a text that she's with Maggie working on the rental house. I'm supposed to pick her up from Maggie's to go out to Sarah's. That means...my house is vacant." Chance bit down softly on Jax's earlobe and reveled in the moan that followed.

"My truck or yours?"

"At this point, I could run there. Mine."

***

Jax climbed in through the truck door Chance held open for her. Waves of heat radiated from her center; desire pulsed with every heartbeat. With every mile that passed beneath them, she was that much closer to the woman she'd been dreaming about. She put her hand on Chance's thigh and ran her nail along the skin at the edge of her shorts. She smiled as she felt the muscle tense beneath her touch.

"Chance?"

"Yes?"

"Drive faster."

Jax laughed when she felt Chance's leg push on the accelerator. When they turned onto the gravel road that led to Chance's house, Jax felt her pulse skyrocket. The minute the gearshift slid into park, Chance jumped out and ran around to help Jax out. They were laughing so hard, they nearly fell trying to get up the steps.

"I haven't felt like this since the last time I touched you."

Chance was standing on the step below Jax. "Put your arms around my neck."

Jax protested. "Your arm."

Chance put her arm around Jax's waist. "For once, stop worrying. I'm all right. Just feel, Jax."

Jax relented and slid her arms around the strong neck before her. When Chance pulled her in, she wrapped her legs around the hips before her. This was becoming a pattern she was growing to enjoy. Chance opened the door and ushered Zeus inside. She locked it behind her and flipped the deadbolt. Jax greedily kissed her, as she ground her center into Chance. When they broke the kiss, Jax had only one word to say, "Bed."

Chance turned their bodies and walked directly to her bedroom. She tumbled them both onto the quilted surface. "I can't wait until I have two good hands to enjoy you with."

Jax flipped them. "Well until then, let me do the honors." She sat up, pulled her shirt out of her shorts, and began slowly unbuttoning her shirt. She watched Chance's eyes turn liquid. Her hand roaming across Jax's body sent shivers of pleasure through her. She dropped the button-up off her shoulders and let it pool around her arms. She leaned over and whispered in Chance's ear. "I love you, Chance. You are everything to me."

Chance cupped the side of her face and drew her down for a kiss. "The love I had for you stayed alive inside of me, tucked in a place no one could touch. If you'd never come back, that wouldn't have changed."

"That was true for me too. Thank God I made my way back."

Jax pushed up Chance's shirt and revealed the rippling muscles that lay there. "Damn you. No one should look this good at our age."

"Have you looked in the mirror?"

"Sheriff, I'm in shape, but I don't look like this." She drug her finger down the prominent center line that separated the squares of muscle.

"Well, all I can say is I love the shape you're in. You've got curves I love to run my hands along. You're so perfectly female."

"Yes, my love, I am all woman. A woman in love with another perfect woman." Jax began to rock against Chance. "A woman that needs you to touch me, right now."

"With pleasure."

Chance sat up, and Jax stripped her of the T-shirt she wore to perfection. Hands fumbled with buttons, clasps, and shorts until they lay stripped bare, skin to skin. When there was nothing between them,

Chance brought her hand to Jax's center and slid two fingers inside her.

"You feel so good. You've always known exactly how to touch me." Jax rocked hard against Chance's hand.

A third finger slipped inside, as Jax grasped her own breasts. "Damn that fucking cast. I hope you get that thing cut off soon. I need both your hands on me."

"I'm right there with you. Until then, come up here. I'll let my one hand wander over those perfect curves while my tongue reminds you what it's like to ride the rapids."

Jax slowly crawled up her body and poised above her. "It's been more than a long time since anyone's done this to me."

"Then you were married to a fool." Chance reached up and pulled her down.

Jax felt the first touch of Chance's mouth to her center and moaned. "I was the fool. This was where I held your memory closest to me. In every memory of you doing this. I was the fool for ever leaving you." Jax moaned, as Chance pushed her tongue deep inside her, making her legs quiver. She felt Chance brush her tongue across her clit. "Oh, my God."

Chance's tongue lashing continued with flat even strokes and small circles. Jax grabbed the headboard for stability. She never wanted this to end. She could feel the waves starting deep inside her. Warm waves that rippled through her until she could barely hold herself up. Chance held her in place with one strong arm as she licked and sucked her.

"Chan—"

She couldn't get her lover's name out as her climax hit hard, nearly doubling her over. Wave after wave of pure pleasure rolled through her until she could no longer hold herself up. She slid down and moved until she lay side by side with Chance.

Chance whispered a question full of concern. "You okay?"

Jax reached up and put a finger to Chance's lips. There was no way in hell she was ready to make complete sentences.

Chance said nothing more for a long time, as they lay together. Finally, Jax rose up on an elbow and ran her fingers lightly over Chance's chest in lazy patterns. She bent down and kissed Chance, lingering for a moment. "Don't ever leave me."

Chance raised a hand and crossed her heart. "I promise."

"Make good on that promise, Sheriff. I'm holding you to it, and I've waited a lifetime for it."

Chapter Fifteen

HOURS LATER, CHANCE STOPPED in front of Maggie's. Kendra lumbered out of the house and climbed into the rear door of the Tundra with a large case in her hand.

"Hey Jax. You two get the clinic ready?"

Jax let her hand continue to rest on Chance's thigh. "We did, mostly." She watched Chance out of the corner of her eye. "Chance is very talented." She tried hard not to laugh when Chance risked a smirk.

"I've heard that." Kendra muffled a laugh with a fake cough.

"Watch it smartass, I'll hang you up by your belt loop like I did when you were nine." Chance shook her head.

"I'd like to see you try. Remember, you're the one who taught me self-defense."

Jax laughed at the two. She'd seen, many times, that families of choice often carried bonds stronger than those forged by DNA. She remembered teasing like this with Jennings when they were kids.

They traveled to Laneville, where they turned up Edelweiss Drive. A large, timber-frame home came into view, smoke rising from a grill on the corner of the deck.

Kendra pointed. "Hey, there's Daniel." A tall, lanky young man waved with a set of barbeque tongs.

"He's been working on his archery skills. Don't be surprised if he kicks your ass, Bullseye."

Kendra cracked her knuckles. "When pigs fly."

Jax nearly snorted at Kendra's competitive nature. The truck came to rest beside Sarah's Jeep. Zeus barked, as a golden retriever jumped off the deck to greet the vehicle. The minute Jax exited, the dog planted his nose right in Jax's crotch, making her jump. "Hey there, handsome. Who are you?"

Sarah came to the steps. "Tucker, stop that! I'm sorry, Jax, we've tried to break him of that without much success. Welcome."

A woman who barely came up to Sarah's shoulder slid under her arm and waved at Jax. "Hi Jax, good to see you. It's been way too long.

Welcome to the zoo we call home. I hope you're hungry."

Kendra walked by them with her archery equipment and snorted. "I'll bet they're starving, because they worked so hard at Jax's clinic." She exaggerated the word "so" and made air quotes with her fingers, as she climbed the stairs and hugged Kristi before heading to where Daniel was opening the grill.

Sarah raised an eyebrow, and Jax covered her mouth with her hand. She couldn't hold the laughter back and turned into Chance's chest, her shoulders shaking. Chance wrapped her arms around her and laughed with her.

Sarah put her hands on her hips before waving them up. "Not much has changed. You two still can't keep your hands off each other."

Kristi held her arms out for Jax. "It's good to see you. I know we're a little older. Still, it's nice to know we turn their heads the way we did back then. How've you been?"

Jax stepped into the hug. "Much better now that I'm back here. I worked on my tan and spent too much time around vineyards. I figured it was time to come back to the mountains and ice-cold beers."

Kristi put her arm around Jax's waist. "Well, let's see if we can find one for you. We've graduated from our days of Pabst Blue Ribbon. We've got great local breweries over in Thomas and Davis. We love the amber ale from Mountain State Brewing."

"Can I get one?" Chance raised her hand.

Kristi squinted and looked at her then back at Jax. "Is she on any medicine she shouldn't be drinking with?"

This caused another fit of laughter from Jax. "No, not that I've seen." She looked at Sarah. "I'll bring them."

Kristi smacked her arm. "Don't spoil her, she can come in and get enough beer for her and Sarah. Want to help me in the kitchen? It'll give us time to catch up while the adrenaline junkies commiserate."

"I'd love to. What needs doing?"

"You can do the salad, while I put the corn on."

"Put me to work, I can take it." Jax looked back at Chance and winked.

Kristi rolled her eyes. "Oh my God, you two. It's like you never left."

"I never should have."

"Jax, we all have regrets. It's what we do now that counts. My advice to you is let it all go. Live in the here and now. Come in here and catch up with me. We haven't had a good girl chat since those days on the riverbank."

Jax followed her in, and Kristi set a pie and a knife in front of her. "That's something we need to do when she gets that cast off. A good river float would be a great idea."

"I'm all for that." Chance walked by them, grabbed two beers, and retreated to the deck.

"I agree. Once Daniel figures out what he's doing, I'll have a little more time. That boy keeps me hopping."

Jax put the knife in the sink and wiped her hands on a dishtowel. "I still can't believe you two have a son old enough to have graduated college."

"I know, and we waited to get pregnant until we felt certain we could afford to have him. It wasn't easy. I can tell you. I still wouldn't change a thing. He's determined to go to work for Chance. I'd like to see him do something outside of law enforcement, but he has his heart set on working for her. For better or worse, those two," she pointed out to the grill where Daniel and Kendra stood, "think Chance walks on water. I'm relieved we could get him to finish school first. He almost quit when she became Sheriff. The only thing that kept him from quitting was there weren't any positions open. Chance said she wished she'd never hired Brad and tested for the vacancy instead."

"I met the guy. I can't see how he can even be a police officer. Certainly doesn't seem like he's out to protect and serve."

"No, and he's a royal pain in Chance's ass. He ran against her when she was elected. Personally, I think he stays to be a thorn in her side."

"Like she needs an internal issue with all the outside problems."

Kristi put corn in the water to boil. "Daniel should have the ribs done in a few more minutes. Let's have a beer." Kristi grabbed two longnecks from the refrigerator and handed one to Jax.

Jax saw the label and smiled. "This is good. I had this at Chance's. I think I've found my new favorite beer."

"Our friend, Vickie, runs the place. She's a master brewer and tends bar there at the tap room. Most of the time, we get it in growlers. Sarah found it in bottles over in Elkins the other day."

"We'll have to find some time to go to the taproom and try the rest." Jax stopped and grinned. "So many things I look forward to, now that I'm back here."

Kristi pulled out a chair at the kitchen table. "I think Chance smiles more now than I've seen in years. When she was with Faith—" She stopped abruptly.

Jax reached out a hand and put it over Kristi's. "It's okay. I met her at the hospital and more recently at a checkup. It must be hard for you guys, not having them together."

"Not as much as you think. Faith is Sarah's sister, and we love her dearly. When they were together, we enjoyed doing things with them. Unfortunately, there was always tension. Those little town criers on their sides tend to interrupt plans." Kristi pointed to the small boxes with knobs clipped to both Chance and Sarah's waists. "Over the years, I've learned it's part of who Sarah is. Faith couldn't stand competing with Chance's need to protect and serve. There is no difference in Chance on or off duty. Faith wanted to be Chance's only focus."

Jax looked at the radio Kristi spoke of. She'd heard its alert more than once. While Chance was recovering, she was on limited duty with the rescue squad in a consultant only role. "Out in California, I headed up an equestrian search and rescue team. I hold a paramedic license to use during operations. I never had the need to jump on an ambulance. My skills were more for fieldwork when we reached the patient. I understand that calling. Matt Carson approached me after that call out to Lindy Point. I was supposed to sign up for the squad and then..." She stopped abruptly without finishing her thought.

"Chance got hurt and you had your own patient."

Jax nodded. "I've never been so scared. I could have lost her before I really got a chance to tell her how I felt. I missed my opportunity with her all those years ago. I won't do it again."

"Well, if the way Chance looks at you is any indication, I don't think you have much to worry about. In all the years they were together, I never saw Chance look at Faith the way she did at you when you guys got out of her truck today. She's happy, and that's important. Chance is family to us, with or without Faith. She's actually been my friend longer than Faith has."

"You two don't get along?"

"We do. Let's leave it as a different kind of relationship. I don't think she ever thought I was good enough for Sarah. Faith thought Sarah should have gone to medical school instead of starting a family. In her mind, I kept Sarah from being what Faith thought she had the potential to be. Faith loves Daniel, don't get me wrong. I think she wanted Sarah to be more than a paramedic supervisor working on an ambulance."

"I think Sarah has always been very capable of making her own decisions. As an outsider looking in, I don't see any regrets."

Kristi blushed. "She told me she was going to marry me the first day she met me. I wasn't even out of the closet." She held up her ring. "That didn't matter to Sarah. She made it so I couldn't live without her. I don't have any regrets either. I'm happy being a nurse at the Harman Medical Clinic. Faith tried to get me to come to work for her. I declined. That would be a little too much family togetherness for me."

"She certainly gave Chance a dressing down when I went with her for the checkup. I think she still has feelings for Chance." She held up her hands. "I know, I know. Everyone keeps telling me she's happily married. I can't help but see regret when I'm around her." Jax looked out the window. "Sometimes, it's the one that got away that you can't forget."

Kristi got up and took the corn out of the pot. "You should know, and I'm happy to see you working toward changing that outcome. Come on, grab that bowl. If I know those four out there, they're starved. And if you were busy," Kristi made air quotes, "with Chance today, you probably are too."

Jax bit her lip, stifling a laugh, as they headed out the door. Kristi put the corn on the large wooden picnic table. Jax put a spoon in the pasta salad and placed the pie she'd cut at the end of the table. Sarah regaled Jax with stories of the antics she and Chance had gotten into when they were younger, even as they admonished Kendra and Daniel not to get any ideas.

When the pie and ice cream had been devoured, the group made their way to the fire burning in a stone surround. The four adults leaned back, sated, while Kendra and Daniel set up the archery range.

Chance egged Kendra on. "Think you still got it?"

Daniel smirked. "I'll smoke her ass."

Kendra scowled. "My nickname is Bullseye, you jerk. We'll see who wipes the floor with whom."

Everyone chuckled at the inaudible sound of the proverbial gauntlet drop, as the two young archers stepped up to the line. Daniel's first shot missed the center. His arrow pierced the line that separated the rings, nudging him to a higher score.

"Jar-licker." Kendra zinged him using archery slang for the type of score he'd earned. She adjusted the quick release on her bow and drew the string back near her ear. When the arrow struck the center of the target, Daniel hung his head.

Jax put her hands over her ears, as Chance let out an ear-splitting whistle that echoed around the yard. Daniel adjusted his stance and let his next arrow fly, burying it directly beside Kendra's first shot. Sarah clapped and cheered her son on.

"Keep up, if you can." Kendra pulled her next arrow from her quiver and notched it on the string. As she released it, Daniel faked a cough in an attempt to throw her off. The tactic failed, and her arrow sank beside her first, dead center.

"Spider! Nice shot, Bullseye." Chance yelled and Jax clapped.

"Lucky shot," Daniel sneered.

"Lucky my ass. When that arrow splits the x, that's skill." Kendra bowed.

The shots continued to hit the target until the quivers were empty. When the scores were tallied, Kendra stood with an eyebrow raised and a smirk lifting one corner of her mouth. Daniel went to one knee and presented Kendra with his bow.

"Get up you jackass and start practicing more. Maybe someday you can be this good."

Sarah stood and clapped. "Chance would still smoke both of you, and you know it. If she didn't have that cast on, I'd put money on it."

Daniel and Kendra both turned and bowed to Chance, who waved them off.

Jax leaned over and kissed Chance. "I think you're still top dog, honey."

"Who do you think taught the likes of them?" Chance laughed and pulled Jax into her lap.

The rest of the evening was spent around the fire, making s'mores and telling more stories, before it was time to say good night. Zeus climbed into the back seat. Chance turned the truck around and looked at Kendra.

"Where are you staying tonight?"

"Momma D asked if I could help put down those pavers in the backyard, so I'll crash at home tonight."

"I'm sure it killed her to ask. It was more than likely on Mom's orders."

Jax laughed. "Oh, I'd bet money on it."

Chance stopped the truck and looked at Kendra. "If I wasn't in this cast, I'd help. I know if I even tried to pick up a shovel, I'd be henpecked. You know how scared we all were with her heart attack. Don't let Dee hurt herself. She's doing really well, and she's got most of her strength back. "

Kendra held up her hand. "Don't worry, I'll be the manual labor. She can be the brains of the operation."

"Now I really am worried how that design will turn out. Just watch her."

Kendra shook her head. "You think Mom won't be there supervising the both of us?"

"True. Let's get you home so you can be well rested." Chance let a grin show.

"Uh huh, getting Jax all to yourself has nothing to do with it. I'm twenty, not five."

Chance held up her hands and leaned over to kiss Jax. "I plead the fifth. I refuse to incriminate myself."

Kendra reached up and flicked Chance's ear. "Just drive, Romeo."

Jax leaned in and kissed Chance again. "Yeah, what she said. Drive, Romeo."

Chapter Sixteen

ONE WEEK LATER, CHANCE sat in an exam room to have her cast cut off. She hoped she would be cleared for full duty once she saw Faith in the afternoon. She needed to get back on the road. Even more importantly, Chance wanted two good hands to touch Jax with. The sound of the cast saw didn't bother her as much as the tickling sensation it caused.

"Let's get an X-ray. If it's completely healed, I'll send you on your way and release you to return to full duty." Dr. Alden watched the nurse use the spreaders to separate the two halves of the cast. "You know, I'd like to not see you like this again. We can get together for some burgers and beer instead."

Chance let her smile shine. "If I can help it, it's the only way you'll see me again." She left the orthopedic office and let Zeus in before she climbed into her truck. She was still waiting on her new department vehicle. She voice activated her Bluetooth feature to make a call. When Jax answered, Chance told her the good news. "One doc down and one to go."

"Everything looked good?" Jax asked.

"She gave me a lightweight, elastic support for a few days. Other than that, she said I should have full mobility. I might be able to predict the weather better than a meteorologist though." Chance turned out of the doctor's office parking lot and merged into traffic.

"Ah, a little weak is it?"

"The muscle tone will come back quickly. She told me if it persists, we'll look at physical therapy. Other than that, she said she'd rather meet for dinner than surgery. I agreed."

"Are you on your way back?"

"I am. I need to stop by the clinic and see if I can wrangle a get-out-of-jail-free card signed in blood by Faith, with six copies for interested parties."

"Need back up this time?" Jax chuckled.

"Nah, I think I've got it. I've been good, really good. I can tell you I'll be mightily pissed if she doesn't sign."

"You have time to run over to Fairmont after your visit? They called to say they found a truck with everything I wanted two states away and brought it over. I can either wait on mine to come in or take this one. I'm ready to stop driving the Silverado all the time."

Chance brightened at the thought of a road trip with Jax. "That's great. Want me to drop Zeus with Taylor? He sheds like a cat this time of year."

"Honey, I'm a vet. Every second of my day, I'm wearing some kind of animal hair. He's welcome to come. Though, I'd really like to take you to dinner on the way home."

"Good point. I'll leave him with Taylor. He needs some play time anyway. I'll drop him at the office when I take my return-to-duty slip in. Okay, I'm about twenty minutes out. I'll go by the clinic and give you a call after that."

"Sounds good. Marty is going to hang out here this afternoon and answer any barn calls. I don't have any more appointments. Oh, Maggie called and said the paperwork is all ready for me to sign on the Richards place. If we hadn't had that hiccup with the mineral rights, we'd have had this done a week ago."

"Great. Let me know where you'll be, and I'll pick you up either at your office or Mom's when I'm done. Oh, and Jax?'

"Yes?"

"Have I told you how happy I am that you're back?"

"Every day. I love you, Chance."

"Love you too. See you in a bit." Chance disconnected the call.

Having Jax back in her life made her feel alive and hopeful about the future. She knew there would be some conflict; no relationship was perfect. The difference was Jax had no issues with her job, her volunteer work, or the time either took. Jax had even joined up with the equestrian group as both a rescuer and a vet. Riding with Jax was something she was really looking forward to.

Every time Chance had mentioned getting on a horse over the last month, everyone and their stepbrother had a fit with her. She'd visited and groomed the horses daily. What she had yet to do, was to make her way back into the saddle. Submitting was not her favorite thing, but one concerned look from Jax and she was mush. If all went well today, she'd be riding by tomorrow. *Tonight, I'll take Jax home with me and let this hand become reacquainted with the woman I love. I still can't believe she's back and in love with me.*

The clinic didn't look busy, and Faith's Sequoia was in the lot. She checked in at the desk and was ushered back to the hallway. Faith stood at the counter writing in a chart.

"Well, well. I see that Rhonda freed you."

"I'm hoping to swing for the fences and be released from your watchful eye as well."

Faith pointed to a room and stepped in with her, leaving Zeus in the hallway in a sit. "There used to be a time when you wanted to me to watch over you. Guess that's changed too, huh?"

"Faith..."

Faith held up her hand and read over the paperwork from Dr. Alden that Chance handed her on the way in the room. "Rhetorical question, no need to answer." When she'd finished the report, she clipped it to the chart and threw down the folder. They stared at each other for a long time.

"Is the plan for you to snipe at me and then not let me respond?" Chance held up her hands in question.

"I'm trying to formulate my thoughts without needing to bite my tongue. Let's put this on the back burner while I examine you."

"I'm all for that."

Faith went through a series of concussion tests and examined Chance's wrist. At one time, Faith's touch would have ignited her core. She would have longed to feel those elegant fingers on her body. It was different now; it had to be. It felt as clinical as it should. She could nearly touch the tension in the room.

When Faith walked back over to the counter, Chance risked speaking. "Well?"

"That wrist is still too weak for me to release you. I wasn't crazy about your grip strength." Faith continued to write in the chart, refusing to look at her.

Chance took a deep breath. "Turn around, Faith." When she didn't, Chance stood and walked to her. "Faith, look at me." The woman before her hesitated, then moved across the room, her arms crossed tightly.

"You're not ready."

"I *am* ready. Rhonda gave me no restrictions with my wrist. She released me to full duty. I've had no headaches in over ten days. No dizziness, nausea or anything else concussion related. You can't continue to fight me on this."

"Then you'll need to find another doctor, because I refuse to send you to your death."

Chance straightened to her full height. She knew Faith still cared, and if she'd taken a job that removed danger from her life, Faith would have never left. That had been one thing Chance couldn't do. Faith moved on and was now married to someone else.

"If that's what you want, then I'll take your advice. Consider yourself relieved of any further responsibility for my health care. I'll call in as to where you'll need to send my records. As of now Faith, you are no longer my doctor. You stopped being in control of my life a long time ago, when you left and said I do to Theresa. You took an oath to do no harm. Trust me, you're doing plenty of harm to this friendship. We fought over this subject entirely too much when we were a couple. I certainly am not going to stand for it now that we aren't. Figure it out, Faith. We're godparents to a kid who will want us both there on his special days. I'd like to be able to say we can be in the same state when those moments happen." Chance pulled open the exam room door, startling Zeus, and strode quickly to the exit. She could hear Faith yelling at her to stop. She didn't until she was at the door of her truck. When she pulled on it, a hand pushed it shut.

"Quit acting like a jackass, Chance Fitzsimmons. Get back in the clinic."

Zeus growled when Chance removed Faith's hand and pulled on the door. "It's okay, Zeus." She turned slightly to be able to look her ex in the eyes. "You might want to look in the mirror if you're looking for a jackass. As of last week, I'm fifty-five years old. I've faced life and death for myself and been responsible for the death of others. I've been fortunate enough in this life to have been blessed with three mothers. I don't have an ad out for a fourth. Your former position of lover has been taken. Doctor and friend seem to be beyond your capacity, although you have plenty of qualifications for both. You figure out what's important to you and you get back to me, Faith. Until then, I've given you leave of responsibility to me for anything other than your vote. If you'd rather see Brad Waters in the job, then pick up a Republican ballot when you enter the polling place. I've got appointments I need to keep." Chance pointed back at the building. "And you have patients." She climbed in and started the truck, leaving a stunned Faith standing in the parking lot. Her patience was gone, and she needed to blow off steam. She knew exactly where to do it, too.

Chance dropped Zeus and her work slips at the sheriff's office, before she drove to the shooting range and walked into the facility. Weston Long stood at the counter.

"Hey Wes, can you set me up on a lane?"

"Sure thing, Sheriff. How's that arm?"

A sharp retort, laced with venom, was right on the tip of her tongue. He wasn't the issue. Faith was. Wes was a friend and a fellow member of the rescue squad.

"Finally got the cast off today. Thought I'd give it a little work out, get back to fighting weight, so to speak."

Wes shook his head. "Glad to hear it. We've missed you down at the squad. I'll set you up on lane six."

Chance waved at him and went to the locker she kept there. She'd had high hopes that Faith would be returning her to full duty today without protest. The harsh words that had passed between them filled her with regret. Her ex-lover's overprotective streak was rubbing Chance like eighty-grit sandpaper on a fresh burn. Maybe it would be best if Faith wasn't her doctor anyway. She was too close, and it felt like her judgment was based on something other than medical tests. Things had been fine until *Jax came back*.

She walked to the range and put her equipment down, before she donned her ear protection and pulled her Glock from the holster in the small of her back. Several calming breaths later, she stepped into her shooter's stance and smoothly fired off several rounds into a human-shaped target. All kill shots. It felt good to hold her weapon and feel the slight recoil in her hand. She recognized a slight twinge in her wrist. Nothing that worried her or made her uncomfortable. *Just need to rebuild my strength.* She reloaded and switched hands. The shots weren't as accurate, although they would still be deadly. She reloaded and adjusted her grip slightly before firing off several more shots. Chance removed her headgear and pushed a button to bring the target to her. She heard the door and turned before hanging another target, and recognized the woman walking to her.

"I'm fine, Sarah. The good doctor didn't need to call in a babysitter or a therapist for me."

"Faith didn't call me. Maggie did." Sarah stepped up to Chance's right in lane five. She pulled her own pistol out of the case and sent a target down range.

They both emptied several magazines before they stopped. They had the range to themselves and could speak freely.

"I know what you're going to say." Chance stopped and cleared her weapon as Sarah did the same.

"Oh, you're a mind reader now?"

Chance closed her eyes and composed herself. "From the moment we got together, she became overprotective."

"But you're not together now," Sarah shrugged.

"No, we aren't. That's the point. We aren't together, because I wouldn't do what she asked and stop being who I am. I'll admit I got hurt doing my job and made her nightmare come true. I'm healed up, and she's still trying to manipulate my life in order to stop me from doing what she never wanted me to do in the first place."

"What are you going to do about it?"

"What I should have done after we broke up. Find another doctor so she doesn't have that responsibility or concern." Chance disassembled her weapon and began to clean it.

"Well, that certainly is one way to remove her control. It won't do anything about her concern."

Chance stopped and threw down her rag. "The point is that I'm not her concern anymore. We aren't together, and I'm capable of returning to the duty I was elected to. When I got hurt, I relented and let her take care of me, because there was no one I trusted more. I trusted her judgment. Ever since Jax came back, her judgment seems more possessive and restrictive in nature than ever. She left, Sarah," Chance pointed to her chest, "not me. She walked away. She moved on. For fuck's sake, she's married!" Chance stopped and put her back against the lane divider.

Sarah put her hands in her pockets. "Yes, she is. You know as well as I do that she never stopped loving or caring about you. When you were in that shootout, her greatest fear nearly came to pass. She was scared that you'd be gone from her life forever." Sarah ran her hand through her hair. "I'm not here to argue her point, Chance. You're my best friend, and she's my sister. I'm closer to you than I've ever been to her. Hell, I'm her greatest disappointment. To you, I've always been good enough and damn good at what I do. I'm here for you right now, not her. She called Maggie in tears. Maggie called me to come and check on you." She pointed to the ground. "The fact that I'm standing here tells you where my loyalty falls. I didn't go to comfort her or come here to enforce her will. I came here because you and I are as close as two people can be without being lovers."

Chance wrinkled up her face at that notion.

"Yeah, exactly. Did Rhonda say you were good to go?"

"She did."

Sarah put her headgear back on. "Then I think you have all the release you need, Sheriff." She loaded in a fresh magazine and fired off a final burst, before she pulled off her hearing protection again. "Go to work and don't worry about Faith. She's got some demons of her own to face down. Her little sprint out of the clinic has tongues wagging. She'll have to explain it to Theresa, and I'm not sure claiming a physician's concern for your welfare is going to hold water. Theresa thinks the sun rises and sets in her ass. The one thing I do know is she won't play second fiddle to anyone." Sarah cleaned her weapon, then put it back in the case.

"So, we're all good?" Chance raised her eyebrows in question.

"We always have been. Now, I also know that Maggie was calling Jax, who isn't aware of your anger management hideaway like I am. Call her."

Chance pulled Sarah into a one-arm hug. "Thanks for having my back, Sarah."

"Always, Chance. Always."

Once she was back in her truck, she checked her phone and saw a notification from Jax. "Sorry I missed your call. Where are you?"

"I'm back at my office. I signed the paperwork for the house, then an emergency showed up in the office that I rushed back for. I take it from Maggie's call your meeting with Faith didn't go well."

"I'll tell you about it when I pick you up. I'm about ten minutes out."

"I love you. Drive safe. "

"Always."

"The Chance I used to date wouldn't."

Chance laughed. "I don't want to get a ticket. I hear the sheriff's a bitch."

Jax snorted. "I've heard that too. See you in five, Sheriff."

"I love you too, Jax."

On the way to the animal hospital, she took a side road to avoid a line of oversized vehicles carrying large pieces of a new windmill tower. The gravel road took her past the backside of the Kurst house. At least three newer model vehicles, all with Maryland license plates, were parked near a barn at the edge of the Kurst property.

"Way too much out-of-state traffic at that house." She couldn't make out the licenses with the naked eye. She pulled to the side of the road and removed her cell phone. Using the zoom feature, she snapped the license plates and drove away. Once she reached the Appalachian Highway, she pulled over and sent the pictures to Harley. Her phone rang a few minutes later, as she parked beside Jax's vehicle.

"Hey, Harley."

"I'm running those plates now. I really don't like the amount of traffic that place is getting. Looks like Leland brought some friends home for a sleepover. I think we have a major problem. I've had troopers watching that place, and we've seen about a dozen different vehicles, both Maryland and West Virginia visitors. A few Virginia plates as well. The task force has Leland under surveillance."

"He gave Jax the creeps the other day."

"Jax?"

"Oh, come on, don't play dumb, Harley. I know you and Taylor talk. I also have it on very good authority your future daughter-in-law is going to work for the Jax you don't seem to know anything about."

Harley's deep laughter came over the phone. "You always have been good at tying it all together. Okay, yes, I know who Jax is. So, what happened?"

Chance looked up to see Jax waving to Marty as she made her way across the parking lot to Chance's truck. She climbed in and kissed her on the cheek. Chance smiled and pointed to the dash to show her the active phone call. "I'll let Jax tell you. She's in the truck now."

Jax furrowed her brow. "Tell who what?"

Chance again pointed to the dash display. "Jax St. Claire, meet Sergeant Harley Kincaid."

Jax furrowed her brow. "Nice to meet you, uh, Harley. What can I help you with?"

Chance backed the truck out for their ride to Fairmont, as Harley and Jax conversed.

"I hope we'll get to meet in person someday. First, let me thank you for hiring Lindsey. I know my daughter will be glad Lindsey isn't driving back and forth in the winter. Secondly, tell me about your encounter with Leland Kurst the other day."

"Oh, that guy gave me the creeps."

Chance reached out and held her hand.

Jax slipped on a pair of sunglasses. "He just showed up at the office as I was leaving, wanted to talk about me seeing his dog. He made my skin crawl and kept trying to crowd me. Luckily, my own personal security system showed up. The guy turned white as a sheet. Eventually, he said he'd be in touch and left. I haven't heard from him since." Jax physically shivered.

Chance spoke up. "I did a little crowding of my own."

Harley laughed. "I'll just bet you did. I'll have to keep an eye on the clinic. Meg will lose her shit if he shows up when Lindsey's there. He was a pain in their ass when they were in high school."

"Tell Meg not to worry. The Three River's Animal Hospital officially has its own security professional." Chance rubbed the back of Jax's hand with her thumb. "I won't let anything happen to either of them. We need to figure out what the hell is going on at the Kurst's."

"I'm on it. I'll call the task force and give them the latest. Hey, are you back on the road yet?"

Chance looked at Jax. "I am as of tomorrow. Today, I'm taking Jax to pick up her new vehicle, then she's taking me to dinner."

"You two crazy kids have fun, while I'm slaving away protecting and serving. Okay, Chance. I'll call you if I find anything out. I'll fax copies of the license checks. Talk with you tomorrow."

Chance reached up to disconnect the call. "Keep your head on a swivel, Harley."

"Back atcha."

Chance disconnected the call and squeezed Jax's hand. "You look scrumptious. I like the little puppies and kittens on your scrub shirt. And your hair in that ponytail? All you need is my ball cap with those sunglasses."

Jax released Chance's hand and smacked her. "Sweet talker. Okay, tell me about your day."

Chance blew out a breath and started. "Well, you know Dr. Alden released me and I went to see Faith. That meeting was just as confrontational as the one you went to with me, maybe worse." She proceeded to tell Jax what had transpired. "I told her I wasn't in need of another mother, and the job of lover was taken." She grabbed Jax's hand and kissed it.

Jax opened her mouth then shut it. "You're kidding?"

Chance held up her hand as if she was testifying. "That's the truth, the whole truth, and nothing but the truth. She called me a jackass, and I shot back with look who's talking. The conversation didn't end well. I left and went to the shooting range to practice a qualifying round. I know Taylor will want that bit of knowledge to feel comfortable with me returning to full duty. Sarah showed up after Faith called Maggie."

"And Maggie called me. I don't get it. I'm confused."

"Sarah got a call from Maggie and figured out where I'd go, given that kind of a cluster fuck. She found me at the range. Let's just say it's a productive way for me to let off a little steam. Maggie's call was out of concern for both of us. She figured Sarah could calm me down."

"And did she?"

"To a certain extent. They put pop-off valves on propane tanks for a reason. Better to vent than to cause a BLEVE."

"A what?

Chance laughed. "Sorry, firefighter acronym. Boiling liquid expanding vapor explosion. BLEVE. Better to release the pressure than risk the explosion."

"Ah."

"Exactly. Faith's got an issue. An overprotective issue and a possessiveness she doesn't have a right to. I don't need it. Faith is a great doctor, but she's no longer *my* doctor in any sense of the word. I have clearance from Dr. Alden, and that's good enough. I'll take it easy for a while, but I'm going back to full duty and answering calls when needed."

Jax held up her hands. "You're a big girl. I think tonight we can work out some way to test that wrist strength. "

Chance glanced over at Jax and watched her lick her lips. "Oh God. Don't do that while I'm driving. I'll wreck and kill us both."

Jax put her hands back in her lap. "Okay, I'll be good for now. What are you going to do about Faith? You know, eventually, you're going to have to talk to her. If you don't, it will cause both of you more heartache. I won't lie. I'm grateful she was in the ER the night you came in. No one would have taken better care of you or given us greater access to you."

Chance took a few seconds to gather her thoughts. She had no idea what she was going to do. She shrugged her shoulders and reached out to grab hold of Jax's hand. "I really don't know what to do. We share godparent responsibilities for Daniel, and my best friend is her sister. Those are the only two things we have in common anymore. For now, I go back to work and be cautious with this wrist for a while. I need you to know I wouldn't put anyone in the public, my department, or myself in danger. I just got you back. I'm in no hurry to check out."

"I'll second that thought. Now let's go get my new truck."

Chapter Seventeen

JAY GAZED AT THE small farms and towns they passed by, through the haze of the afternoon heat rising off the pavement. She had no doubts about the way Chance felt about her, but she was concerned with Faith's lingering tentacles. When she'd arrived in town, she'd quickly been able to find out Chance's relationship status. Between what Marty told her and a few simple inquiries, she knew bits and pieces of the former couple's history. It would have crushed Jax to come back to Tucker County to discover a happily married Chance. She was more than grateful to have found her single.

"Where do you want to eat?" Jax pulled up a text from Marty telling her he was closing the clinic and taking calls from home to catch *Judge Judy* on TV.

"I'm thinking Chinese or Mexican. Those are two food choices that are lacking back in Tucker County. Which one we choose is up to you."

"Back in California, I could take you to some amazing little hole-in-the-wall Mexican places. This one near my old office had the most amazing tamales. Is there a good place in Fairmont?"

"Actually, there's a place over in Clarksburg that's in an old laundromat. Not the typical chain restaurant fare. Unbelievable food on the menu and prepared by personal friends of mine. It's a little farther out. Trust me, it's worth the drive."

"Then it's settled. Since I won't know where I'm going, I'll follow you. Hey, by the way, how's your new patrol vehicle coming?"

Chance rolled her head side to side. "The equipment is being installed. We salvaged as much off the old vehicle as possible to save costs. You know, light bar, radio, siren, and the parts that we add on to turn it into a cruiser. The unit had special technology installed to keep Zeus safe when I have to leave him in the vehicle. I didn't salvage that. If it failed, Zeus could die. If the air conditioner stops working, alarms get sent to my phone and the dispatch center. If all the systems fail and the temperature continues to rise, the door will open and he's been trained to get out. This time, I'm installing ballistic film over his area. He's already got one bullet hole. I'd like to never have that happen again."

Another twenty-minute drive brought them to the dealership. Jax admired her new truck sitting out front. Chance whistled. "That thing is smokin'. I'll have to put twenty-four-hour protection around you."

Jax rolled her eyes. "Yeah, a big, silver work truck is so sexy."

Chance scoffed. "With you in it? Damn sexy. Come on, let's get this over so we can go eat. I'm starving."

It took another hour to sign all the paperwork to release the vehicle. Jax followed her south on the interstate to Clarksburg, then west until they reached a small, residential neighborhood. Los Loco was a tiny, fluorescent-green building. Black and red *calaveras* adorned the cement block walls. The smiling skulls gave the place a festive, though out of place, appearance in the Victorian-style neighborhood. Chance led them beyond the cars parked three deep on the cracked blacktop to a street where she directed Jax to park in front of her. They walked back down and were seated by the waitress who served them a basket of warm chips and a bowl of salsa.

Chance held up two fingers. "Iced tea, please. No lemon."

A smile crept across Jax's lips. "You're like an elephant, you know. You never forget."

"Not when it's important. Everything about you was important, so I didn't forget anything."

Jax dipped a chip into the salsa. She pushed back in her seat and let out a groan of pleasure. "Oh my God, this is nearly orgasmic. I haven't had salsa like this since I left California. There's actually cilantro I can taste."

"The owners here immigrated several years ago. Their parents own a larger, chain-like restaurant in a busy shopping center. Pasqual and Anita wanted to have a small place of their own, serving more traditional fare."

"How did you ever find this place?"

"My rescue squad did some training with a group over here. We used a local fire station up the hill for the class work. This place was close, cheap, and serves great food. It's a well-kept local secret."

Jax nodded and loaded up another chip. "They make these, don't they? You can tell they aren't store bought."

"They do. Hopefully Pasqual or Anita will come over to the table. Everything is made fresh daily."

"I'm stealing this secret. Not that I'll have a lot of opportunities to come over here."

"There's always Christmas shopping."

"True."

The waitress set down their drinks and took their orders. While they waited for their meal, Faith came up in their conversation. Things would likely come to a head again, and Chance needed to talk out all the options. She had other physician friends, so finding another doctor wouldn't be hard. The greater concern was the wrath of Faith at gatherings that would happen as the year wore on. The tension would become uncomfortable when they were all together. Eventually, a woman approached the table and spoke in an accented English. Chance rose from her seat and bent to hug her.

"Fitz, good to see you. Too long, too long, yes?" Anita held her by the hands after releasing her from the hug.

"That it has been. Apologies. Anita Garcia, this is Jax St. Claire." Chance looked to Jax.

Anita reached for Jax's hand. "*Hermosa dama*. It's a pleasure to meet a friend of Fitz."

Jax blushed. "Thank you for the compliment. It's also a pleasure to meet a beautiful woman like you who can make salsa like that." Jax pointed to the table.

Anita grinned at Chance. "Oh, I like this one. You keep her."

Chance looked at Jax with all the sincerity she could muster. "I intend to do just that. I like her too."

They sat and talked with Anita for nearly an hour, before they went to pay the bill. Anita chastised Chance for offering to pay. She was able to prevail when she noticed Anita's swollen belly. "How far along are you?"

"Ah, six months. Next time, I plan better. Have the baby before summer."

"Which is why I'm paying for our meal. Soon you'll be needing diapers."

Anita patted her abdomen. "True, Pasqual is helping out at his father's restaurant as manager tonight. He'll be sorry he missed you."

Chance winked. "We'll definitely be back, soon. You be careful and don't overdo."

Anita waved at them. "My *abuela* had seven kids by my age. I'll be fine." She hugged Chance. "Jax, nice to meet you. You do your best to keep this one in line. Is big job, no?"

"That's an understatement. I promise to do my best. It was very nice to meet you. The food was unbelievably good...as good as I used to have in California."

"I'm glad you liked it. Safe travels, *mi amigas*."

Chance hugged her, and they made their way out.

"Ready to head home?"

"I am. Although I'm full as a tick. That will make me sleepy. Guess you'll have to keep me awake by talking to me."

Chance eyed her skeptically. "You do remember we're traveling in separate vehicles?"

"I do, and I know that both of them have Bluetooth. Get ready for an epic game of I Spy."

Chance's laughter startled a bird from its perch. "I'll see what I can do."

It was nearly nine when they reached Philippi on the way home. They stopped to fill Chance's truck with gas, and Jax got out and stretched her legs.

"I'm going to call home and check on Marty while we're here." Jax stepped away from the pumps and pulled out her phone.

"Okay, tell him hi for me."

Chance slid her credit card in and started the pump, as she placed the nozzle in the tank. She watched Jax's brows furrow as she held the phone to her ear. After she disconnected and tried the call again, Chance walked over to her.

"Problem?"

Jax looked up at Chance and looked at her phone again. "He's not answering his cell or the house phone."

"Maybe he had to go to the clinic? If he's driving, he probably won't answer his cell."

"Maybe. Let me try the clinic." Jax dialed and put it on speaker. The call rang through to the house answering machine. "The phone is still on forward. He doesn't normally go out after dark. His eyes just aren't that good anymore."

"Let me see who's on duty and have them run by the house. Maybe he's outside and didn't hear the phone or something." Chance pulled her cell phone from her pocket and dialed dispatch. When the call was answered, she recognized the voice. "Hey, Ron. This is Chance. Which one of my deputies is out?"

"Hey, Sheriff, Kenny's on duty."

"Can you patch us together?"

"Can do. Hold on."

The dispatcher put her on hold, and in a few seconds she heard him put her together with Kenny.

"Okay, Sheriff, he's on the line."

"Ron, stay on the call for a second. Kenny, I need you to take a drive over to Doc Hendricks' place and check on him. We can't seem to reach him, and he doesn't drive much after dark."

"Not a problem, Sheriff. I'm only about five minutes from there. I'll give you a call back once I get to the house."

"Okay. We're going to get on the road. I'm in Philippi now."

"Ten-four, Sheriff. I'll let you know."

Chance turned her attention back to the dispatcher. "Thanks, Ron. I wanted to put it on tape so you have record of the call for service."

"I've started an incident for a welfare check, Sheriff. Let me know the disposition, and I'll close the call when you tell me."

"Good man. Thanks." She hung up and looked at Jax. "Let's get going. I'll let you know what Kenny says as soon as he calls."

"It should only be a few more minutes. Can we sit still until he calls you? My mind is spinning."

"We can. Dispatch didn't say anything about a medical call to his place, and Ron would have told me if there had been any calls to either location." Chance was silently counting down the minutes, as she took Jax's hand in her own. "He hasn't had any issues of late, has he? Health wise?"

Jax clutched her hand. "No. For his age, he's in incredible shape."

"It's going to be okay, honey. No matter what the issue is, we'll deal with it."

Jax was shaking. Chance's phone rang, and she hit the speakerphone icon so Jax could hear. "What'd you find, Kenny?"

"Nothing, Sheriff. The house is dark, his truck isn't here. The place is locked up."

Jax shook her head. "Something's wrong. If he didn't leave the porch light on, then it was still daylight when he left, or he never got there. The last time I talked to him, he was going home. Said he'd handle anything from there, if need be."

Chance could see that Jax was near frantic. "Kenny, call dispatch and have someone go check the Three River's Animal Hospital. See if you find him there. We called and got no answer. The phone was forwarded to the house. We're about forty minutes out."

"You got it, Sheriff. If he's not there, I'll check the road between the two places and get back to you."

"Good plan."

They hung up and Chance looked at Jax. "You're in no shape to drive. Follow me over to the 911 center here in Philippi. We can leave your truck there and pick it up tomorrow."

Jax nodded, tears beginning to roll down her cheeks.

"Hey, it's going to be okay. We'll find him. Let's get moving."

Chance called the 911 center and asked to leave the vehicle on the premises. Five minutes later, Jax was sitting beside Chance. She needed to get them back to Tucker County and kept both hands on the wheel as she floored the truck. She hadn't heard from Kenny yet about the clinic. There was an area where she knew she'd lose service for about ten minutes. She'd use her portable radio to make contact with dispatch. Her focus needed to be on the narrow, winding highway, while the love of her life fell apart in the seat beside her. The helpless feeling she had was one of the most painful things she'd ever experienced.

Jax's voice was small. "Why haven't they called?"

"This is a dead zone." Chance picked up her portable. "SD-1 to SD-4." She waited for a reply, knowing there were shortcomings even with the statewide radio system. If the radio couldn't hit the tower, the signal went nowhere. "SD-1 to Comm Center."

"Comm Center. Go ahead, Sheriff."

She pushed the talk button on the side and held the radio to her mouth, hoping the signal would hold out. "Make contact with SD-4. Find out if he's made it to the clinic."

"Ten-four. Comm Center to SD-4."

There was a long pause before the communication center tried again with no response from Kenny.

Chance came up with another idea. "SD-1 to Comm Center. What trooper is working?"

"Comm Center to SD-1. State Police unit 207 is on duty."

"Call Harley and see if she's near there."

"Comm Center to SD-1. We were advised that unit was tied up on a stranded motorist call about twenty minutes ago. We'll make contact."

Chance pushed the vehicle. She didn't want to make a mistake and cause them to get in an accident. A whitetail deer sprinted across the road in front of her, reminding her that her driving skills still depended on her ability to avoid unexpected objects in the road.

"Jax, I need you to control the radio for me, so I can keep both hands on the wheel. Key that mic up for me if they call my unit number. Hold it to me the way I did."

Jax nodded. "Okay. Chance, I have a bad feeling."

Chance risked taking her hand off the wheel to hold Jax's momentarily, in reassurance. "We'll find him, baby. I promise you. We will." She noticed the small tear track running down Jax's face. "Hold the radio up for me. After I talk, hold it a second longer, then release. Okay?"

Jax nodded, and Chance put her hand back on the wheel. They were past the county line and headed back into town. Chance nodded for Jax hold the radio. "SD-1 to 207."

"This is 207. Go ahead, Sheriff."

"207, have you made it to the clinic?"

"I'm two minutes out. I was at the other end of the county."

"Okay, I'm at St. George. Have the Comm Center transmit your findings in the blind. They should be able to reach me even if I can't answer back."

"Ten-Four."

Chance weaved her way through the small community and started up the narrow back road. This route would cut off ten minutes and put them closer to the clinic. The curves were sharp. Thankfully, Chance had been driving these roads all her life. Headlights would alert her to oncoming traffic and allow her to take the center of the road.

The radio shattered the silence. "207 to Comm Center, officer down! Get an ambulance rolling to the Three Rivers Animal Hospital!"

Before Jax could offer the radio to Chance, the communication center set off the alarm tones that would bring every law enforcement officer with an active radio to attention. "Any available law enforcement, State Police Unit 207 is on scene at Three Rivers Animal Hospital requesting assistance. Officer Down, officer down!"

Chance grabbed the radio from Jax. "Harley, what's going on?"

There was no response for a few seconds, as Chance fishtailed the truck onto the main highway, five minutes away from the clinic. She listened as Taylor and several other officers from varying agencies marked up on the radio, en route to the clinic. Finally, she heard Harley's voice. "207 to Comm Center. I've got an officer down with a gunshot wound. K9 unit is secure. Get a helicopter in the air. Chance, Kenny's down. No sign of Doc Hendricks other than his truck."

Jax held her hand over her mouth. "Oh my God."

"I'm two minutes out, Harley. Watch your back." Chance was watching for any vehicle coming from the area around the clinic and saw none. "SD-1 to Comm Center. Have all law enforcement agencies watch for any vehicles coming from the area. How far out is the ambulance I heard respond?"

"Ambulance 36 responded from Canaan, and we have another crew headed to Station 2. They may get there sooner. We have Healthnet 6 coming from Buckhannon. Landing zone will be at Thomas Ball Field."

Chance skidded into the clinic and could see Harley bent over Kenny in the flashing red and blue lights. She slammed the vehicle into park and jumped out with Jax right behind her. Her weapon was in her hand. "Where's the wound?"

Harley looked up at her with blood pouring between her fingers. "Under his arm, right above where his vest is. Tyson's secure. I put him in my vehicle. He's got blood all over his muzzle. I'd say he got a bite of whoever did this."

Chance looked up to see Jax coming out of the clinic with an armload of supplies. She threw them down and pulled open Kenny's eyes as she tried to talk to him.

"Kenny, it's Jax. Come on, talk to me." She handed Harley a pressure dressing. "Chance, see if you can get a blood pressure on him. I don't like his color. The blood pool around him tells me he's lost a good deal of it. I've got some lactated Ringer's from my jump kit for the equine squad. I'm going to start a line." She tore open the packaging with her teeth and threw the clear plastic bag across her shoulder, while she pulled IV tubing out of another package.

Chance applied the cuff to Kenny's arm, as another law enforcement vehicle showed up. She saw who it was. "Get this place secured, Taylor. Harley, did you get a chance to look around?"

"No, there were no other vehicles here, and Tyson was sitting with Kenny. My focus was on getting the bleeding stopped."

Taylor held up a hand. "You take care of Kenny. Quade is behind me. We'll secure the scene." She had her weapon out and went over to coordinate with the U.S. Fish and Wildlife officer.

Chance put the stethoscope in her ears to listen for the pulse that would give her one of the vitals they needed to judge Kenny's stability. "His pressure's for shit. Eighty over fifty. Pulse is bounding."

Jax had a tourniquet on his upper arm and was slapping his forearm. "He's got no pressure. Hitting a vein is going to be a bitch."

Chance watched her palpate the skin, then deftly slide a needle into his arm. She watched for the flashback that would indicate Jax had been successful. It was slow, but there it was. Jax shoved the tubing into the port. She removed the needle and jammed it, point down, into the ground. Chance watched as she opened the flow and saw the clear liquid run through the bulb in a steady stream. She took a few minutes to look at the amount of blood that was soaking into the dusty earth. The volume she saw told her Kenny was critical.

"His breathing's for shit too. I'm betting the bullet caught a lung. I don't have anything to tube him. Hopefully the ambulance coming has a medic onboard. We need to get his vest off."

Chance pulled at the Velcro straps around his torso, then grabbed the scissors Jax had brought with her and cut through the shoulder straps so the vest could be lifted off. She cut his uniform shirt off and found his white undershirt covered in blood. She leaned close to his ear and whispered. "Kenny, you fight. We're with you. You keep fighting, dammit."

"We need to look for an exit wound. Feel around his back, Chance." Jax grabbed the stethoscope and put it to his chest, moving it all around. "I've got no breath sounds on that right side, and his trachea is deviated. That lung's down."

Chance looked up and saw Taylor running back to her. "Scene's secure. No one around." She grabbed her mic. "Comm Center. Scene is secure. Tell the ambulance to pull directly up to us." Taylor knelt beside Chance. "How is he?"

Chance met her eyes and relayed all Taylor would need to know with just a look. "We've got to get him out of here. How far out is the helicopter?"

"I'll find out." Taylor got up and walked away.

Chance felt across Kenny's back for any of the things she'd been taught in EMT class. "DCAPBTLS," she murmured, as her hand found no deformities and no penetrations. The rest of the acronym relied on visual observations that would take rolling him over and light to see clearly. Currently, they were working with a streetlight and the headlights of the vehicles around them. She could hear the sound of a federal siren that indicated one of the ambulances had arrived. Sarah jumped from the cab and reached into the side door, grabbing a large trauma bag before running to them. More police units were arriving. Chance listened, as Taylor began to give orders and coordinate the incident.

Sarah slid in beside her and looked at Jax, who was trying to start a second line in his other arm. "Jax, what have we got?"

"Single gunshot under his right arm. I think it must have hit a lung. His pressure's bottoming out. Chance did you find an exit wound?"

"No. I can't really see anything back here. I didn't feel one."

Sarah pulled out her radio. "36 to Comm Center."

"Go ahead, 36."

"How far out is the chopper?"

"Three minutes. Landing zone is ready."

She depressed her mic again. "Tell them to stay hot, we're going to load and go."

"Ten-four."

"Jax, did you get that second line?" Sarah put her hand on the carotid artery point.

"Just did. I've got two large bore's running. Good thing I've had a lot of practice starting these. His veins are crappy. We've got to go. His trach is deviated, and I don't have anything to get that lung back up."

A new voice broke into the mix, as Faith ran up to them. "I do. Let's get him in the ambulance." Faith looked at Jax. "What's his condition?"

Jax relayed everything, as they loaded Kenny up on the cot. Chance tried to take in everything going on around her and assessed the current issues. Kenny was shot and the shooter was on the loose. Marty's truck was there, but he was nowhere to be found. Two separate problems were somehow tied together, she needed to figure it out, yesterday. She looked down at her hands. They were covered in her officer's blood. She'd sent him on a welfare check. Kenny was well trained and very dedicated to his job. She walked back to the area where they'd found him. There was no weapon on the ground, and she couldn't remember seeing one in his holster. She looked over to see Kenny being loaded in the ambulance. Her current lover, her former lover, and her best friend were moving around in the box.

"Fuck!" Chance screamed at the insanity of everything and shut her eyes for a moment. When she opened them, she jogged to the ambulance before they closed the door. She had a few things she needed to figure out. "Is his gun in his holster?"

No one acknowledged her, while they hooked Kenny up to monitors. Faith was doing something to his chest with a needle.

Chance yelled into the enclosed ambulance body, "Hey! Is his gun in his holster?"

Sarah's eyes flashed with anger.

"It's important. I need to know if he drew his weapon or not. If he was shot under the arm, I'm assuming he had them up. I need to know if they were up like this," she formed a shooters stance, "or like this." She moved both hands up in the air. "I don't see his gun on the ground, and

Tyson bit someone. Now look at his holster, please, and I'll get the fuck out of your hair."

Sarah shifted up the cot, felt around his gun belt and shook her head at Chance. "No gun."

Chance slammed the ambulance door and walked back to Harley and Taylor. She grabbed a flashlight out of Taylor's Yukon and went back to the blood-soaked ground. She trained the beam in front of her in a sweeping pattern. She found what she was looking for, then walked to Kenny's vehicle. The ambulance took off, and Chance heard a radio transmission confirming the crew was headed to the landing zone.

Harley stepped to her side. "What are you thinking?"

Chance pointed to the area right at the driver's door. "Those are Kenny's boot prints. They're his issued work boots. The tread pattern matches mine." She walked over close to where Kenny had been. Most of the prints were obscured right around where they'd found him. She trailed the beam of her flashlight over to the right. "This set of prints comes from over there. I want them blocked off and casted." She trailed the beam back to another area of the ground, just before the gravel started. There in the dirt, was the imprint of a weapon. She wasn't sure if it was Kenny's or whomever he'd pointed his weapon at. There were boot prints near the weapon's imprint.

"I think Kenny pulled in on something, and he pulled his weapon." Chance moved into a shooter's stance with her hands in position. "I'm betting there was more than one of them. Someone from over there," she pointed to her right, "shot him here." She indicated the blood stain on the ground and pointed to herself where the bullet had entered Kenny's body above his vest. "His weapon is gone; his holster is empty. We'll have to check his hands for residue to see if he fired or not."

Taylor walked up to them. "I didn't want to say this with Jax in hearing distance. There's some blood by Doc's truck. Did you pick her up here or at her house when you headed to Fairmont?"

Chance spun, noticing for the first time that Jax's dually was missing. "We left her truck here." She walked quickly to the old Ford parked at the front of the clinic. She was careful to avoid disturbing anything near the truck. Footprints would be impossible to see in the gravel unless they were bloody. There on the ground, three feet from the door, was a line of blood and several cast-off drops. "Shit, what the hell happened here?"

Taylor shook her head and ran her hand through her sandy-blonde hair. "This is all speculation but, what if someone called Doc about an injured animal to get him here. Once he showed up, they struggled," she pointed to the disturbed gravel, "and someone got injured. Doc's gone, and so is Jax's truck."

"It's all plausible, but from what Jax said, he doesn't normally drive after dark. The porch light to their place wasn't on. That tells me whatever call came in was before dark, and he intended to be back. Taylor, get in touch with the Comm Center and have them contact the phone company. See if there were any incoming calls this afternoon or this evening. We'll have to check with Jax to see if anything valuable is missing from inside. Finding out what the hell he came back here for is priority one. Check Kenny's dash cam see if there is anything on it. Get those boot prints protected right now before someone stumbles over them." Her mind was racing.

"You got it, Sheriff."

Harley stepped to her side. "We both need to wash up. Come over to my cruiser. I've got baby wipes and hand sanitizer."

Chance looked at her hands and rubbed them together. The tacky residue made her sick. "Harley, whoever did this better hope they can grab a space shuttle off this planet, because that's the only way they don't end up in Kenny's cuffs or dead."

Chapter Eighteen

JAX SPREAD HER FEET wide to absorb the movement of the ambulance. Faith temporarily relieved Kenny's breathing issues. Now Jax sat in the airway position and controlled the tube in his throat while she squeezed an Ambu bag to deliver oxygen. Faith and Sarah were securing the intravenous lines she'd managed to start.

Faith looked up at Jax, admiration showing in the determined look on her face. "I don't know how you got those started. His pressure was damn near nonexistent."

"Twenty-five years of putting lines in animals of all sizes pays off. Some of the veins are so small, you can barely see them."

Faith nodded. "I know some really good techs who couldn't have gotten that stick. Getting those fluids in him pulled him out of that downward spiral. His BP is much better." Faith looked through the cab to the front of the ambulance. "We've got about three minutes to the landing zone. I didn't get a good look. How much blood was on the ground?"

"I'd say he lost at least a couple of liters. No telling how much he's losing internally." Jax rhythmically squeezed the bag.

"Sarah, we need to keep all his clothes, I'm sure Chance will want them as evidence. Anything in here we can use to bag them up in, so they won't get thrown away?" Faith adjusted the flow of the running IV line.

Sarah reached into a compartment and pulled out a few clear plastic bags. "With these, they'll be able to see what they are. I'm sure there will be a law enforcement presence over at the landing zone. I'll pass them on to an officer." She began gathering the remnants of the uniform they'd cut off Kenny.

They'd made quick work of checking for any hidden injuries. Kenny lay completely naked on the cot, covered by a sheet. Faith ran an EKG strip and attached it to the run form. "Can you remember what his vitals were on scene?" Faith was filling in the bottom part of the form.

Jax rattled off her findings, and Faith's pen scratched along the sheet on the clipboard. "He'd had about 250 milliliters of lactated Ringer's before you guys got there."

They'd already changed out one bag halfway into the trip. The sheet beneath their patient was crimson, as blood continued to ooze out of the wound in his chest.

Sarah finished collecting the clothing and looked up. "We're here."

The next few moments were a blur, as Faith and Jax relayed everything they could to the flight crew, who began to package Kenny for the trip. Within minutes, Kenny was being loaded into the helicopter. One of the flight crew looked at Faith. "He's pretty unstable, want to tag along?"

Faith nodded and climbed in, pulling on a helmet they handed her. She looked out at Jax. "Tell her I've got him."

Jax nodded and ran back to the fire truck that sat a safe distance from the helicopter, Sarah right at her heels. She knew the takeoff would throw rocks and dirt. Once the massive machine lifted into the air and headed toward the hospital, they walked back to the ambulance.

"I need to give someone his clothes. I think I saw one of the troopers where we parked the ambulance," Sarah said.

"Okay, I'll wait for you there. Can you take me back to the scene so I can find Chance? Uncle Marty is still missing."

"Of course. Let me take care of this and we'll go."

Jax looked at the ambulance. Long continuous tracks of blood covered the floor, where the gurney's wheels had traveled through the pool. Packaging for the supplies they'd used lay strewn on the floor and seats. It looked like a war zone. The reality that she'd had a part in giving Kenny his best chances for survival gave her a chill. Her love would always be with the animals, but being a paramedic allowed her to touch the fringes of human medicine. Tonight, she'd made a difference for the two-legged kind.

She climbed in and gathered the discarded trash, making sure that none of it was evidence. She shoved it all into a biohazard bag. Sarah came back, pushing the gurney they'd transferred Kenny from. She loaded it herself, with the assistance of the motorized wheelbase. Once inside, she grabbed Jax's hand.

"Hey, are you okay?"

"A little shell-shocked," Jax admitted. "It's been a while since I was this close and personal with a serious trauma. I haven't ridden an ambulance in years. Most of the time, I handled field care on the rescuers from our group and acted as a tactical medic for the SWAT team. I can only hope I didn't screw up.

"Jax, you probably saved Kenny's life. I'd ride the bus with you any day. You did great under pretty rough circumstances. Thank God for your jump bag. I'd like to get you signed up as a volunteer for us. You don't necessarily have to do any ambulance duty. With the affiliation, any care you give would be under our medical license as well. I know you fall under the equine squad, with this, all your bases would be covered."

"I'll think about it. Right now, all I can focus on is the fact that Uncle Marty is gone, and I have no idea where he is."

"Every law enforcement agent in the county is going to be looking for him. Even if they weren't, you've got the very best officer on it, with the biggest reason to find him. She'll do it for the woman she loves."

Sarah stepped out to find the driver. Jax thought about the fact she'd worked with both Faith and Sarah to save Kenny's life. There'd been no time to be awkward with Chance's ex-lover. Faith was on a helicopter headed to the hospital, and the elephant in the room hadn't had time to trumpet. The door opened and Sarah climbed back in to sit on the bench beside Jax.

"Let's get you back to the scene. Faith will text me with any updates."

"Okay." Jax sat quietly and cleaned off her hands as best she could with antiseptic wipes. Sarah doused them with hand sanitizer. Jax would clean up at the clinic, if they'd let her. Part of her brain kept trying to come up with some idea of where her uncle might be. The other part was busy trying to figure out how best to comfort Chance over her injured deputy. Like any good commander, Chance would be taking the responsibility all on herself. She remembered watching Taylor in those hours after Chance's injury and the juggling act she'd tried to perform. Chance had two major incidents going that were tied into one, an officer down and a missing person. Jax wanted to scream at her own feelings of guilt. *Uncle Marty was covering for me. If I'd just waited until Saturday to get the truck, maybe none of this would have happened. Nope, had to get it today. The truth is, I wanted some time with Chance. My libido made me ask a retired man in his eighties to do my fucking job.*

Sarah put a hand on her arm. "Hey, what's going on in that head?"

Jax swiped her face with her hands and accidentally got the alcohol residue in her eyes. "Damn, that burns."

"Do you need me to flush it?"

Jax held her eyes tightly together and forced them to water. "No, it's okay. It's mostly gone now." As she clinched her eyes, she was able to hide some of the anguish in the tears brimming behind her lids. Sarah ran a comforting hand across her back.

"Chance will find him. You know she'll move heaven and earth for you."

The choking emotions Jax felt were like someone having their hands around her neck. She couldn't speak and only nodded an acknowledgment. It felt like hours before they pulled back into the scene and exited to stand outside the crime-scene tape.

Chance came over, took Jax's hand, and looked to Sarah. "How's he doing?"

Sarah pulled out her phone. "Faith just texted that they're rushing him to surgery. He's lost a lot of blood. They took a quick X-ray, and the bullet is sitting close to a major artery."

Jax watched, as Chance visibly tamped down the growing anger.

"Taylor's going to head to his house, pick up his wife, and take her over to the hospital. I'll get over there as soon as I can. We've got two sides of this investigation that need attention. For now, it's all one. Harley and her troopers are going to head up Kenny's shooting, while we concentrate on finding Doc Hendricks. We'll be coordinating everything as a joint command." She stopped and pulled Jax to her. "We'll find him. Right now, I need you to come with me and see what, if anything, was taken from the clinic. Be careful and step only where I do. Sarah, keep me updated please and—"

Sarah held up a hand. "I know, tell Faith thanks. I'm going to see if Kristi can head to the hospital. She's friends with Becky."

Chance held up the tape, allowing Jax to duck under. "Taylor's planning on picking up Penny. Becky might need a babysitter for the kids. Maybe Kristi could offer that instead."

"Good idea. We'll handle it. You two go on. We've got another crew taking county calls, so we can stay here in case you find Doc in need of medical attention."

Jax grasped Sarah's hand. "Thanks, Sarah."

Chance escorted Jax to the clinic. "Be careful. Do you have your keys for the side door? We're trying to avoid that front entrance where there are tracks we want to preserve."

Jax reached for her keychain. "I do." Once they were inside, she looked around.

Chance put a reassuring hand on her back. "I want you to pay close attention to anything that's out of place. Let me know if something looks disturbed, that's open and should be shut, or unlocked when it should be locked."

Jax nodded and looked around. The pet-safety display was knocked over. She pointed that out to Chance. She closed her eyes for a second and tried to picture if she'd hit it when she ran in for supplies. "I can't remember if I knocked that over running in for my jump bag or not."

"Okay, anything else in here?"

Jax looked around trying to focus. "Lindsey's office chair is overturned."

Chance took out a notebook from her back pocket and made a notation. They walked along the edge of the room, careful to stay out of what would be the normal paths of travel, to catch anything out of place. They walked down the hallway toward the exam room. Chance stopped and pointed to an open door.

Jax saw it too. "That's the pharmacy and sterile supply room. It shouldn't be open. I didn't go in there. I pulled things out of the small exam room."

They walked over to the door, and Jax peered into the room. Drawers were askew and medicines were spilled on the floor. A set of keys dangled from the narcotics vault. "Those are Uncle Marty's keys. That's where we keep things like ketamine." She looked at some of the inventory. "It looks like antibiotics were taken too." She kept moving across the room, trying to see if anything else was missing. "I can't tell about anything else."

"Good girl. Okay, let's check the rest of the place." Chance led her back through the rooms.

In the surgical area, Jax noticed a few suture trays and small instruments that would be used during surgery were missing. Jax rattled off what she could tell had been taken. She heard a set of footsteps coming toward them. It was Harley.

"Chance, we've got some significant blood out in the parking lot in an empty spot. You need to see Kenny's dash cam footage."

Jax's stomach turned, and she felt Chance's arms around her. "Don't jump to conclusions. Let's see what happened."

Harley shook her head. "Damn. Sorry, Jax. Not from Doc Hendricks. Probably one of our suspects. Kenny might have hit him when he fired his weapon. Tyson got a piece of someone too. "

"We've got some missing medical supplies. Things that might be needed to patch someone up, drugs to fight off an infection and pain meds. Still doesn't explain Marty's disappearance though."

"Whoever's on the tape has him. We saw them shove him into Jax's dually and take off after they came out of the clinic. That's on the tape." Harley explained.

When they made it back out, Chance and Jax sat in Kenny's cruiser and listened to the audio while they watched Kenny pull up and put his headlights on one subject pushing Marty toward the door. Jax covered her mouth as she watched her uncle stumble and go to his knees. Kenny got out of the vehicle and released Tyson, who stood at his side. Kenny ordered the man with Marty to show his hands, advising if he didn't the dog would be released. The man raised a gun, then grabbed his leg as Kenny fired his weapon. Another shot rang out from off screen, and Kenny fell to the ground. Tyson disappeared from the screen before a great deal of barking and snarling could be heard.

Jax watched as the individual near her uncle tied something around his thigh and roughly pulled Marty to his feet, before he opened the door to the clinic and shoved Marty in. Minutes later, they heard Tyson whimper. Something happened off screen. A man ran over to Jax's truck and busted the window. He pulled the door open and lay on his side on the floorboards.

"He's hot-wiring your truck." Chance pointed to the screen. "Where that guy's at, there's a small blood trail. Somehow, he got away from Tyson. We need to check Tyson for injuries. That dog wouldn't have given up unless he was knocked out or hurt."

The next footage showed the first man with a leg injury coming back out of the clinic. He was pointing a gun at Marty, who had a box in his arms. Doc was forced into the truck. The man who'd shot Kenny walked over and picked up the deputy's service weapon. He pointed it at Kenny, but a shout from the truck drew him back over. Soon after, the truck backed out of the screen.

Jax put her hand over her mouth to stifle a scream at her uncle's kidnapping. *This is my fault. He should never have been here.*

"That bastard was going to execute him." Chance struck the dashboard with her fist. "Harley, I'm going to assume there's a BOLO alert for Jax's truck?"

"There is. If it's in the open, we'll find it. The California plates should make it stick out."

Jax looked at Chance. "That truck has OnStar. I can call and report it stolen. They should be able to track it. If whatever that guy did to hot-wire it didn't disable it."

Chance looked at her. "Do it. The quicker we find that truck, the sooner we find Marty. He's going to be okay, honey. With those injuries, they need him alive. I'm guessing that's why they took the meds and equipment they did. That one suspect has a bullet wound in his leg and the other a set of teeth marks somewhere. They're going to use Marty like a doctor. Make that call."

Jax reported it then passed the phone to Chance. "They need to ask you some questions. I figure if its location information, you'll understand it better."

Chance rattled off her law enforcement credentials and advised that she'd have the communication center call OnStar's emergency number to confirm everything.

"Thank you, we need that as soon as possible. A deputy's been shot, and another individual's been taken captive. Anything you can do to get that information to us yesterday, would be greatly appreciated." Chance handed the phone back.

"Now what?" Jax asked.

"Now we run by my place. I called Maggie and Dee to sit with you, while we go kick the crap out of some bad guys to get Marty back."

"Oh. No. You. Don't. You aren't leaving me behind anywhere. Get that out of your head right now. Wherever you go, I go. Don't argue with me. If you do, I'll borrow a vehicle and follow you. Chance, he's my uncle, and he's in this because of me. They should have me, not my eighty-two-year-old uncle."

Jax let Chance pull her close, as the tears began to roll. Great sobs echoed between the silent screams she couldn't let go. She had to hold it together.

"It's going to be okay. I need to go to the house and get Zeus and my vest. I'm only carrying one weapon. It won't be enough. Whatever we're going into, I don't want to be underprotected. Now, you can't argue with me about this one thing. We're going to have an ambulance standing by at a safe distance. You will stay with Sarah, period. You can't be involved in whatever we have to do. You aren't law enforcement, and the risks are too great. These guys shot a deputy. They'll think nothing of shooting a civilian."

"I was a medic on a SWAT team. I know what I'm doing."

"Honey, you haven't trained with any of us. I love you with all my heart. You have to stay with Sarah for my piece of mind. Marty is a tough old bird. He'll do what he has to do to survive, and they need him with those wounds. I want you to know we're going to do everything we can. If he was sitting in this cruiser with me, he'd be just as upset thinking it should have been him and not you. I know him that well."

Jax thought about Chance's words and knew they were right. Chance would be worried about keeping her safe instead of focusing on rescuing Marty. She nodded. "Okay, on one condition. I want a radio so I can listen to what's happening. I mean it, Chance. Not knowing will worry me more."

Chance grabbed Kenny's portable and handed it to her. "I'll let you know what channel we'll be on. Sarah can help you find it." As they stepped from the vehicle, Chance's cell phone rang. She answered it and waved Harley over, as she put it on speakerphone.

"Sheriff, this is Willa at the Comm Center, OnStar has a general location. The truck is up Camp 70 Road and stationary."

"Willa, you keep OnStar on the phone. If that vehicle moves one foot, you call me back. I'm going to have Harley bring in her tactical unit. I'm going to go to the house to gear up, and we'll let you know where we'll set up a command post. Probably in the Davis Fire Department. Call the Chief and ask him if we can use the event hall."

"Okay, Sheriff, you got it. Watch your back."

"Always, Willa." Chance hung up and looked at Harley, who was on her own cell phone. When Harley completed her call, she stepped back over to them.

Harley rested her hands on her gun belt. "Okay, the tactical team is assembling and will be headed this way from Elkins. It's probably going to take us an hour to get them over here."

Jax went wide-eyed. "You're not going to do anything for a damn hour?" Jax threw her arms in the air. "They could kill him in an hour!"

Chance gathered her into her arms. "Jax, honey, calm down. Yes, we are going to do something, with or without the tactical team. We need them to get ready and over here in case this turns into something bigger. I'm trained in hostage negotiation and so is Harley. We don't need to wait on them to move forward. It's all part of the standard operating procedure. Covering all the bases. Come on, we need to go." Chance turned back to Harley. "I'll meet you at Davis Fire Hall in forty. Maggie is bringing Zeus to my house. I need to make some calls...to Taylor and to get a location on Randy. I know it's killing him to handle the other incidents while this is going on. I'm sure you have every trooper this side of the state on their way over here. I got word the Feds are coming in too. We've got to get a handle on this before it becomes a huge cluster fuck with no organization."

Chance led Jax to the truck and they hustled in to make their way to Chance's house. Jax was trying to process it all and failing miserably. What would she do if something happened to Marty? Her mother was going to go ballistic when she found out. She was trying to decide if she should call her or rely on her mother's local grapevine spies. If Jax didn't call, the wrath of Hurricane Jacqueline would destroy everything in her wake. On the other hand, there was nothing she could tell her. They didn't know where Uncle Marty was, or if he was still alive.

"No, I'll wait," Jax murmured.

"You want to wait at the house?" Chance questioned.

"No way in hell that's happening," Jax snapped.

"Hey, hey. Settle down. I heard you say you'd wait."

"I was talking to myself. I was trying to figure out if I should call my mother. I'm sure, with all the scanner traffic, she already knows. I'm amazed my phone hasn't..." Jax looked down at her phone and shut her eyes. "Speak of the devil and she shows up."

"Jax, you can't tell her much at all. You can tell her he's missing and we're looking for him. Tell her you'll call her when you have more information. Leave it at that."

Jax pushed the answer button. "Mother."

***

Chance tried to give Jax as much privacy as she could. She concentrated on what she needed to get at the house. When they'd emptied out her wrecked cruiser, she'd put all her equipment in her personal armory. Her semiautomatic rifle and ammunition were in there. When she pulled into the driveway, Jax was still on the phone being berated by her mother. Chance's patience was wearing thin. After a few more seconds, Chance reached over and grabbed the phone.

"Mrs. St. Claire, this is Sheriff Chance Fitzsimmons. I assure you, we're doing everything we can to locate your brother. We have local, state, and federal officers working jointly on the operation. When we have more information that I can release, I will call you personally. Jax had nothing to do with his disappearance, and he did not wander off on his own. At this time, that's all I can tell you. Please keep your phone near you so that I can contact you. We are currently en route to an operational command meeting and Jax is needed." She hit *END* on Jax's phone and placed it in the consol. "Come on, I need your help. I won't let her talk to you like that when the fault lies clearly with the men who took him. If she calls back, let it go to voice mail. There is nothing more we can tell her until this is all over."

Jax climbed out of the car and grabbed Chance, pulling her close. She reached up and framed Chance's face with her hands. "I love you more than I will ever be able to say for all the things that make you extraordinary, Sheriff Chance Fitzsimmons. Now, let's go get Marty."

Chance kissed her and grabbed her hand, bringing her into the house where Zeus was waiting. Maggie jumped up and grabbed Jax, hugging her tightly. Dee came from the other room. "Is there anything we can do?"

Chance shook her head. "Not at this point. I have to get ready." She trudged into the basement of the house and punched in the code. Dee was right behind her and Zeus at their heels.

"I'll give you a hand."

She smiled. "Thanks Momma D, I can always count on you."

"Five Points, all I'm going to ask is you be careful. I know you will, but I wanted to give you that order, personally. Now, let me help you carry what you'll need."

Chance squeezed her hand and entered the armory. "Grab that ammo on the shelf there. I need to get my tactical gear on."

Dee grabbed several magazines for Chance and held out her hand to hold the weapon, as Chance shed her sweatshirt and slid on the tactical body armor with items she might need. She grabbed her ballistics helmet and yellow, vision-enhancing glasses. Chance's cell phone rang, and she looked at the number. Mya Knolls. Chance sent the call directly to voice mail, only to see the number reappear on the display. Chance again sent it to voicemail.

"I don't have time for your shit, Mya," Chance mumbled, as she and Dee left the armory. Chance kicked the door shut.

They made it back upstairs and Chance walked to the closet and pulled out Zeus's tactical vest. It was slightly different from his everyday vest, with increased protection and a place for a body camera. She bent down and slid the camera into place. "Let's go to work, boy." Zeus barked, and she met Maggie and Jax in the kitchen.

Maggie stepped forward and put a hand over Chance's heart. "Your mother named you Chance. I'm only asking that you don't take any unnecessary ones, okay? I know you're healed up. I also remember, it wasn't that long ago you were lying in a hospital bed. Let's avoid a repeat, shall we?" She leaned forward and hugged Chance before she kissed her on the cheek. She bent to talk to Zeus, who stood expectantly at Chance's side. "That goes for you, too, granddog. You take care of her and you both come home in one piece. That's an order."

Chance saluted. "Yes, ma'am. Okay, we've got to go. Try not to worry, even though you will." She leaned in to kiss Maggie and whispered to her. "Call Jax's mother and try to calm her down. You don't know what's going on, so there's nothing to tell her. Try and keep her off Jax's back, please?"

Maggie shook her head. "Now, all three of you be careful. I expect details later over a beer. "

Chance linked hands with Jax, who was now holding the ammunition. "We will. Now, Team Mom, try not to worry. We'll be back."

Ten minutes later, they pulled into the fire hall where the parking lot looked like a Fraternal Order of Police meeting. Her phone rang with a call from Taylor.

"How is he?"

"He's still in surgery. They came out a few minutes ago and gave us an update. The bullet punctured his lung and did some damage inside. All his vitals are now stable, and they've replaced almost all of his blood. Carl's making calls for a blood drive and arranging a hotel for Becky over here. All the wives are on babysitting duty until family can take over. Everything's covered there. I talked to Harley. She told me about the truck. Randy is stopping by the BFS convenience store to look at their surveillance camera footage. There's also one at the water plant, outside of town, that we can check for vehicles that might have headed out to the valley. Maybe they have one stashed somewhere they jumped into. If they're still up at Camp Seventy, remember that there's an old hunting shack back in there about three miles. I wonder if that's where these assholes are holed up?"

Chance thought about it. "Very possible. It doesn't have any electricity or running water, but if you're on the run, it's not a bad place to lay low. We'll check it out. Tell Randy to call me if he sees anything on the surveillance tapes."

"You got it. You handle things there. I'll take care of Becky and coordinate from here. The emergency room had an unused office I'm working out of. You be careful, Chance. I'll be over there as soon as I know he's out of surgery."

"If anyone ever doubts why you're my second in command, I'll remind them of how well you read my mind and handle things. We'll get these assholes. Count on it. "

They hung up and Chance put her phone on vibrate before she slipped it in her back pocket as she walked in. One of Harley's troopers had Kenny's camera hooked up to a computer. Two images of the suspects were being projected onto the wall. The photos were slightly grainy. Two males, one Caucasian and one African American. An operational meeting was about to begin.

Chance sat Jax down in a chair and kissed the top of her head. "It's going to be okay."

A large whiteboard was rolled to the front, and Harley drew out an organizational command chart with the individual players and their assignments. As they finished the delegation of positions, Chance stepped forward.

"I appreciate each and every one of you being here. I've heard from Taylor at the hospital. Kenny is still in surgery. They feel sure he's going to pull through. Now with that being said, Kenny wouldn't want anyone to get a splinter. Please be careful. The Comm Center says Jax's Silverado hasn't moved from out at Camp 70 Road. It's dark blue with California plates. Taylor and I were talking." She pulled up an aerial map and drew a circle with her finger around a particular area. "There's a hunting cabin someplace out here. It's pretty primitive, no electricity or running water. I haven't seen it in years. It's possible they've rigged up solar or a generator. There was a lot of brush around it when I saw it last. Anyone else been out there?"

A hand went up in the back of the room from one of the Fish and Wildlife officers. "We had some issues out there last year, on government property that joins up with that tract. There are a ton of ATV trails out there. They could be long gone."

Harley nodded. Quade Peters stood up. "We can take some of my guys and come out of the Timberline area at that gate and work our way to the cabin from that direction. Maybe cut them off if they try to run."

"Good idea, Quade. I hadn't even thought about that."

"Okay, that will take us a while. We'll head out. Call me if there is anything else I need to know." Quade stood and gathered his people.

Chance looked out at the officers. "Everybody got their assignments? Everybody know what they're doing? Last chance to ask questions." No one said a word. "Okay, let's go find Doc Hendricks." She pointed back to a black-and-white still shot from the dash cam. "We have nothing to show that he's unable to move under his own power, and he's still a pretty tough bastard—even at eighty-two. I'm betting he's giving them hell. He won't make it easy on them, if I know him. Be careful of crossfire. Let's roll."

The din of voices and scraping chairs bounced off the walls, as everyone got to their feet. Chance found Jax, who rose to meet her. She pulled her over to a quiet corner.

"I want you to stay here. Sarah and the ambulance crew will be with you. Are you sure you want to listen?" Chance watched her nod. "You may not hear much for a while. I'm putting this radio on the encrypted tactical channel we'll be working on. Don't transmit. Listen only. Remember, you won't understand a lot of what you might hear. As soon as I'm done, we'll either call for you to meet us with the ambulance, or I'll meet you back here. No matter what you hear," Chance pointed to the ground, "you stay put. Do you understand? Under no circumstances do you leave this fire hall."

Chance watched Jax's eyes tear up. She wrapped her in a hug and held her tightly. "We'll find him baby, believe me. We'll get him back."

Jax looked up at her. "You'd better make sure when you get him that you come back to me without any more battle scars. I've already missed too much time with you. I don't plan to miss one single minute more." Jax grabbed her by the vest. "I've been in love with you for over thirty years, and I plan to be in love with you for another forty. You hear me?"

Chance kissed her, kissed her like she hadn't seen her in a month of Sundays. She kissed her for all the missed Sundays. She had no intention of missing another one either. All the years apart melted away. All that mattered was merging the memories of yesterday with those to be created tomorrow. "I hear you. I'll be back, intact, with Marty. Believe that here." She kissed her forehead. "And here." She placed her hand over Jax's heart and kissed her softly this time, her lips lingering until they separated, breathing each other in. "I will be back."

Jax looked down at Zeus. "Both of you."

Chance pulled away from her and felt Jax hold tightly to her hand.

"You've always kept your promises to me. I expect you to do the same this time. No exceptions."

Chance drew her arm across her chest with her hand resting on her heart. She turned and met Harley at the door. "Let's do this."

Chapter Nineteen

CHANCE RODE WITH HARLEY, out Camp 70 Road. They were in constant contact with the Comm Center, who had advised them OnStar was still reporting the vehicle to be stationary. They were about two and a half miles from the location. It was dark, and intermittent cloud cover kept obscuring the moonlight. The cover of darkness hid the sides of the narrow dirt road. "We're about five hundred feet from the site. Kill the engine, and let's go on foot."

Harley raised the other units behind them and advised them to do the same. The quiet click of doors opening and shutting sounded like gunfire cracking in the silence. Weapons drawn, the officers fanned out and approached the Silverado.

Chance reached it first and used her flashlight to check the bed of the truck, then the interior. She shook her head. There was no sign of anyone. She spoke quietly to Harley. "There's blood on both the passenger and driver's sides. Check around. Let's see if there's a blood trail. Maybe Zeus can pick it up. It's not his strongest skill, but it won't surprise me if he can do it."

"I have no doubt." Harley spread the word about what they were looking for. They were drawn to several blood trail cast offs near a path to the right of the road. "Chance, over here."

Zeus followed Chance, as she bent near the dark drops illuminated by a flashlight. She aimed her own beam of light along the trail that disappeared into the wood line. She took Zeus back to the truck and opened the door, allowing him to smell the interior. Chance was aware that the part of a dog's brain devoted to the analysis of smells, was greater than a human's capacity. The scent of fear sweat was particularly pungent. Combined with the smell of blood, it translated to prey for a dog like Zeus. "*Zoek*, Zeus, *zoek*." When she gave the command for him to track, she knew he would follow the scent to its source. The dog looked at her, his bright eyes gleaming, and took off in the direction of the blood trails.

"Hope you guys can keep up." She took off at a fast jog, watching Zeus keep his nose near the ground.

Chance was sure they'd gone close to a half mile, when the small shack came into view. She could hear the sound of a generator running. In an urgent whisper, she called to Zeus, "*Hou op. Hier.*" The dog returned to her side, his tongue darting in and out as he panted beside her. "*Goede jongen.*" Chance quietly praised Zeus as he crouched in the dark, looking and listening for anything from the cabin. She turned her flashlight backwards to mark her position to the officers who were rapidly approaching.

Harley knelt behind her with a cadre of ten other officers. "Wonder how many are in there?"

"The place is pretty small. We know of two perps and Doc. Hard to say. Comfortably, maybe one or two more. I wish I'd remembered to grab the thermal imager at the fire hall."

Harley nodded. "We could send someone back for it."

"Place isn't that big, and I don't want to wait anymore. Doc's on borrowed time. He's seen their faces. They'll keep him as long as they need him, then he'll be disposable."

Harley put a hand on her shoulder. "We'll make sure that doesn't happen. Let's spread the troops out and surround the place. If they don't have a way out, it'll come down to negotiation. Doc will be their biggest bargaining chip. Let me handle the communication with them. I'm going to head for that tree and shut that generator down."

Chance knew what Harley was doing. She was taking the responsibility for Doc. If it went wrong, Harley would answer Jax's questions. "Fine, I'm taking the shot."

Harley nodded and turned back to the troops behind her. She coordinated who would go where and do what. Chance watched as everyone touched their earpieces. The curly wires that came out of their radios and snaked up their necks, would keep any communications from alerting the occupants of the cabin to their presence. Harley pointed, and the officers fanned out to surround the structure.

Chance found a side-by-side UTV at the edge of the woods, with the key in it. She removed the key and put it in her pocket. She watched another officer do the same to another one. She nodded to Harley after every officer found cover behind the trees, their weapons trained on the cabin. The generator hummed softly. It was chained to a large tree, which would offer Harley a modicum of protection.

Harley raised her arm to indicate she was ready to kill it. When that happened, the officers would be behind cover substantial enough to eliminate themselves as a target. When she dropped her arm, the generator went quiet.

Voices rang out from the cabin.

"What the fuck? You forget to put gas in the damn thing?"

"Where's the flashlight, you stupid fuck?"

"Don't call me stupid. Who's got the old man?"

"My gun is in his neck. Get the fucking lights back on."

The argument continued back and forth. Chance noted two voices, neither of which were Doc's. A flashlight bounced around the cabin. Harley announced her presence.

"This is Sergeant Harley Kincaid of the West Virginia State Police. The cabin is surrounded by law enforcement officers. Drop your weapons and file out of the cabin with your hands in the air."

A shot rang out in Harley's direction. Chance and Zeus took cover. Slowly, she inched her way back up to get a visual on the cabin. The flashlight had been turned off, and she could hear shuffling inside the structure. To her left, Randy appeared with Vader and she acknowledged him.

Doc shouted with irritation. "You son of a bitch get that gun out of my ear. You're making my hearing aid squeal."

"Shut up, old man, before it's a bullet instead."

"You don't want to do that," Harley cautioned. "You're in a tough spot right now. If the deputy in surgery dies, you're looking at one count of murder. You shoot Doc Hendricks and it'll be two. You're in a no-win situation. Make this easy on yourself and come out."

"Fuck you, bitch. You back off or the old man dies right now."

"And then you've got no bargaining chip. The only reason you've got a shot at cutting a deal is because he's still alive." She melted against the tree, as another shot came from inside the cabin. Harley tried again. "If you guys think you can outshoot us, you're wrong. Right now, you're like fish in a barrel. There are officers all around the perimeter of this cabin.

Before the shooting started, Chance had made a lap around the cabin and found only the one exit, along with a few windows too small for anyone to crawl out of. She made her way to the side where the door was and positioned herself and Zeus low behind a large rock. "*Blijf*," she whispered, telling him to stay, as she peered around the rock at the illuminated door. "*Bewaken*." Zeus became tense and hyper alert at her side, waiting for her command.

Harley tried again. "Come on, let's make a deal. You let Doc go, and you can come out. We'll take you in without incident. The longer this goes on, the worse this is going to get. We need to end this without any more blood being shed. There is no way out of this without working with me. We have a dozen officers here. In minutes, there will be another twenty officers here. Let's end this now."

"No fucking way are we coming out there. You back the fuck off, or the shit's gonna get real. I'll put a bullet in this guy and not shed a tear."

"Oh, you'll shed a tear, trust me, you will. The clock's ticking."

Another shot rang wild, followed by a barrage of gunfire coming from the cabin. Chance could hear them striking the trees and rocks around them.

Chance keyed her mic. "Harley, I'm going to try and work my way around to that other corner. We've got two dogs, now that Randy's here with Vader. We need to flush them. I think I can get to that window, bust it, and drop in a smoke bomb."

She watched as Harley raised her thumb to avoid giving away her position by transmitting. *Thank God for a second of moonlight.* "Randy, make your way to the right of the door with me. That thing swings in and to the left. Click your mic if you receive." She heard a single click and removed the CS-gas grenade from her tactical vest. Within seconds, Randy and Vader were by her side. She signaled to him that she'd drop the grenade on three.

As small as the cabin was, the perps would likely rush the front door. When that happened, she and Randy would release the dogs. With one word, they would order Zeus and Vader to launch at anyone that came out the door with a gun. She could only hope that Marty would be unharmed by the grenade or the men who'd taken him.

An angry voice inside the cabin pierced the silence of the night. "Where you going, old man? Sit the fuck down, or I'll drop you where you stand."

"He's bleeding again. That's the whole reason you dragged me out here. You want him to bleed out? Fine by me."

"Fucking shut up and do what you gotta do. No sudden moves or you're dead, you fucking hear me? You think I'm joking, try me."

Chance could see a flashlight beam moving around and hoped that meant Marty was going to be farther away from the man with a gun. She pulled the pin while keeping the switch depressed, then held up three fingers and silently ticked them off until she'd bent the final finger. She jammed her gloved hand and the grenade through the window. Two seconds after the grenade hit the floor, a hissing sound told her the gas was doing its job. The men began coughing and cussing.

"What the fuck?" Gunfire cracked the air, and she heard wood splinter near her. The door swung open. Beams from the officers' bright, tactical flashlights blinded the man holding an automatic rifle. He fell through the door. A second man tried to run past him.

"*Stellen!*" Chance and Randy yelled simultaneously, and both dogs went into attack mode. They launched themselves, as Chance trained her gun on the man Zeus engaged. Zeus shook his head with a bite grip on the man's arm, as the man tried to turn the pistol held in that hand. Chance swept the man's leg, dropping him to the ground with her gun in his face.

"Show me your hands! Show me your hands! Drop the weapon!"

The man flipped open a blade and swiped at Chance's leg, making contact just above her boot before she could jump away. He swung the knife at Zeus, while he tried to hold onto his pistol. Chance pulled the trigger before she fell to the ground, the pain of the knife wound finally registering. The man didn't move again, even as Zeus shook his arm violently. "Zeus, *kom hier.*" Zeus disengaged from the subject and came to her side. She crawled to the man and pushed the gun away, then swept the knife out of his reach. He was incapable of using those weapons. There was a bullet hole between his eyes.

Harley was on the man Randy and Vader had engaged. She pointed her weapon and screamed at him. "Drop the gun! Drop the gun!"

Randy tried to secure the suspect, while his dog kept his jaws closed on the arm already wrapped in a white bandage tinged with red. Every officer trained the beams of their flashlights on the struggle.

With great effort, Chance stood and made her way to the cabin door. Putting pressure on her leg was excruciating. Zeus panted at her side. She coughed as she pushed through the bodies standing around a pale man on the cot, unconscious and oblivious to what was going on around him. She coughed again at the bitter gas still lingering in the air. Marty lay on the floor, one of Harley's troopers tending to him. The officer looked up at her. "He's alive, but we need to get him out of here."

Chance saw blood on Marty's shoulder. She bent down and lifted the thin man, the pain in her leg forgotten. She carried Jax's uncle away from the suspects, over to the utility vehicle. "I need some lights over here, now! Bring the trauma kit!" She knew they had an equipped paramedic officer with them. The Parsons officer ran up to her and pulled his kit off his shoulder.

"Let me in to him, Chance." Ethan Gibson unzipped his bag and grabbed a pressure dressing, holding it to Marty's shoulder. He peered at the wound. "Doesn't look bad. A chunk of flesh missing, doesn't seem like much more. I'm more worried about him being unconscious than this graze on his shoulder. How old is Doc?"

Chance wiped her face. "He's eighty-two. Pretty good health for his age. Nothing that I've heard Jax mention." She turned a circle and looked at the side-by-side. "Can we get him out of here in this, out to the ambulance? I just heard traffic that they're at the entrance to Camp Seventy."

Ethan pulled the blood pressure cuff off Marty's arm. "Yeah, we can. Unless you think he might have a spinal injury. I've seen him moving all fours. He's just not coming to."

Chance pinched the bridge of her nose. She had no idea what had happened inside that cabin, what he might have endured before they got to him. She didn't want to risk it. If he was stable, they needed to wait for equipment to come in. They could use the side-by-side to get the crew. She looked up and saw the U.S. Fish and Wildlife contingency. "Quade! Can you take this out and pick up Sarah and the equipment to transport Doc?"

Quade jogged over. "I'm on it. Anyone got the keys?"

Chance dug through her pocket and handed the fob to him. It took only a few seconds for him to disappear into the woods. She pulled her radio out and switched channels. "SD-1 to Comm Center."

"Go ahead, SD-1."

"Tell the EMS crew the scene is secure. We're sending a side-by-side out to bring them back here. Tell them they'll need their spinal immobilization kit. Tactical team medic is treating the patient."

"Comm Center to SD-1. That's received."

Chance switched back over to the encrypted tactical channel. She knew Jax would be listening. "Doc Hendricks is alive. I repeat Doc Hendricks is alive."

She went back to Harley, who was making a call.

"Yes sir, three subjects." Harley paused. "One deceased, two in custody." She was silent for a moment, then looked around. "Not that I know of, sir, none reported at least. Yes sir, I'll handle until you bring in an unbiased investigator. Sir, if I may, it was a good shoot. He had a gun and we found an open switchblade. There are about six people who witnessed his refusal to drop his weapon and a camera on one of the K9s. Hostage was injured, but it doesn't appear fatal. Harley paused again. "An EMS crew is on their way in. Our tactical medic is treating him currently. Both of the suspects we have in custody will need medical attention. EMS has been notified for them as well. Two of our troopers will accompany them, while I remain at the scene. We're going to need some lights out here to do the investigation. This place is off the grid." She looked up at Chance. "Thank you, sir. I'll call with more information when I have it."

"Thanks, Harley." Chance handed her the Glock she'd used to defend herself and Zeus against the man, as was standard protocol. "I didn't want to shoot that bastard. He just wouldn't put the weapon down. He had the knife in one hand and a gun in the other."

Harley put a hand on Chance's shoulder. "I meant it when I told Captain Warren it was a good shoot. Period."

Chance let out a humorless laugh. "I've spent close to fifteen years in law enforcement. I've pulled my weapon a dozen times in all those years. In the last two months, I've taken two lives."

"Both were justified, Chance, and you know it. If it was reversed, what would you say to me?"

Chance stood looking at Harley. "The same thing. I get it. It doesn't make it any easier."

"No, it doesn't. What it does mean is you were justified in taking the life of someone who was trying to take yours. If it was one of your deputies, you'd be telling them the same thing, so take a bit of your own medicine. Okay?"

Chance shook her head and turned at the sound of the side-by-side. "That'll be the EMS crew. We need to get Marty packaged and loaded up. I don't think he's regained consciousness yet. Jax will want to get him to the hospital. We may even need a chopper. That guy in the cabin with the busted leg didn't look too good. What the hell were they doing here that they take him in the first place? What in heaven's name could they have wanted with an eighty-two-year old, retired veterinarian?"

Harley pulled off her helmet and scrubbed her hand through her hair. "My guess, that guy in there, needed medical attention by the looks of him. He's got bone coming through the skin on that leg. Next best thing to a doctor is a vet." Harley nodded. "There's your girl. You'd better go show her you're still standing."

Chance winced, as she turned to see Jax jump out of the UTV and to her uncle's side. Biting the side of her jaw against the pain in her leg, Chance made her way over. She'd wait until they loaded Marty up, then she'd have Ethan look at the knife wound in her leg. She didn't want Jax to know she was injured. An unconscious uncle was enough to worry about. Right then, she wanted to hold Jax more than anything. She wanted to make a nightmare of a day go away. *Later.*

Chapter Twenty

THE OFF-ROAD VEHICLE was still in motion when Jax jumped out and ran to where her uncle lay on the ground. Tears streamed down her face. *He's alive. That's all that matters right now.* Trying to convince herself that anything else could be fixed, she centered her emotions and looked at him with her paramedic training. *A.B.C. Airway, breathing, circulation.*

Sarah was at her side in a minute and put her hand on his wrist at the pulse point. "Ethan, can you give me an assessment?"

Ethan rattled off the pertinent information and slowly, the vice around Jax's chest released. Yes, he was unconscious, and that was worrisome at his age. But he was breathing normally, and Sarah told her his pulse was strong. He had a flesh wound in his shoulder, and blood oozed through the bandage. He was alive. She needed to focus on that. She looked to Sarah. "Load and go?"

Sarah nodded. "Since they don't know what happened to him, we've got to protect his spinal integrity until we know there is no trauma. We can put the spine board in the bed of the UTV and transport him back to the ambulance. We've got a chopper landing, so let's get him out of here."

The agreement Jax tried to choke out was drowned by the bile rising in her throat. The rush of hot water in her mouth warned her she was about to throw up. She crawled away from her uncle and heaved into the tall grass at the edge of the path. Briers pierced her palms as her stomach violently emptied. She felt a hand sweep her hair back and hold it, while a cool palm came to rest on her forehead. Zeus whined and tried to get close to her.

"It's okay, baby. Let it go."

Chance. The voice she'd heard in her dreams was comforting her while the stress left her body along with her stomach contents. When she had nothing left to bring up, she dry heaved while Chance held her. When she'd finished, she wiped her mouth with the back of her hand and sat back on her heels. "Oh my God."

Chance encircled Jax with her arms. "I've got you. He's going to be okay. We need to get you both out of here." Chance took a bottle of water from someone passing by and opened it. Jax drank while Zeus nuzzled under her empty hand, and she gratefully accepted his comfort. She took a large swig, swished it around her mouth, and spat it on the ground. Jax groaned and took another mouthful, only to repeat her earlier action. She handed the bottle back to Chance and wiped her mouth again. When she felt strong enough, she let Chance help her up.

They stood, and she felt Chance stumble. For the first time, Jax looked up at her. "Are you okay?"

Chance nodded and took her hand. "I'm okay, just coming down from the adrenaline rush. Come on, we'll talk at the hospital. I'm going to have to stay for a bit. I'll meet you there as soon as I can."

Jax threw her arms around Chance and let the tears pour out. What little radio traffic she'd heard had terrified her. Only when she'd heard Chance's voice telling that Marty was alive did she take her first full breath. It had burned in her chest. She knew both her uncle and the woman she was in love with were still alive. "Thank you, Chance. Thank you seems so inadequate for what I feel right now, but I don't have the words."

Chance held her with one arm and pushed a lock of hair out of her eyes. "No thanks needed, my love. Now go. I'll see you at the hospital. Call me if you need me to stop by and bring you anything, okay?"

Jax nodded and squeezed Chance one more time, before she released her to bend and kiss Zeus between the eyes. "Thank you, boy, for making sure both of them came back to me." She kissed him again. Zeus licked her face, clearing away her tears. She put her arms around his neck and squeezed, before she rose and walked back to where her uncle lay on the backboard.

"We're ready to go. I'm guessing you're going with us?" Sarah's concern was written all over her face.

Jax took a deep breath and climbed into the bed of the side-by-side. "I am. Let's get him out of here." She looked back at Chance, kissed her fingers, then slapped the plexiglass that separated the cab from the bed to let the driver know they were ready to move. She reached down and held her uncle's hand.

"He's going to be okay, Jax," Sarah reassured her. "I found a lump on his head. How he got it is a mystery. I'm guessing that's the source of his unconsciousness. Vitals are all good, and I've got a line going. The monitor shows a steady heart rate and the bleeding on his shoulder is controlled. There's a chopper available, but I think he's stable enough for an ambulance ride to Garrett. Ethan told me the other guy in the cabin might not make it. I don't want you to think Marty isn't more important, but I want those bastards to pay for what they did. The best way to make sure he lives to see a courtroom is to fly him out."

Jax understood Sarah's need to explain, but it wasn't necessary. Her own clinical mind had triaged the patients with an experienced view of her surroundings. The other man was critical; Uncle Marty didn't seem to be. Forty minutes later, they pulled into the emergency room, where they were met by a few nurses and a doctor who ushered them into the treatment area.

Sarah looked at Jax. "They're going to need his information, Jax. I promise, I'll stay with him and come get you as soon as I can. I promise, I won't leave him."

Jax could do little more than nod.

"Jax, he's going to be okay. Call Maggie and give her the heads up that they are okay. I think Chance said she was calling your mom."

Jax pushed both hands into her hair and pushed it back from her face. "Yeah, I should do that. Thanks, Sarah." She made her way to the reception desk and started to give her uncle's medical history and personal information. When she'd completed that, she called Maggie. The phone rang only once.

"Hey, Maggie, it's Jax. Chance found him, and we've got him at the emergency room."

"Oh, Jax. I'm so happy to hear that. I know your mom will be too. You need to call her as soon as you have an update on him. She's been worried sick about both of you."

Jax tried to keep from saying anything insulting. Her mother had never worried about anything but her reputation. To try and believe that it would be any different now would be impossible, even if it were true. "I'll call her. I just wanted to let you know it was over."

"And Chance?"

"She was walking and talking when I left. I assume she's the same as when I left her. To tell you the truth, I was so focused on Uncle Marty, I really didn't get a chance to check her over. We needed to get him out of there. I'm sure she'll be on her way to the hospital as soon as things settle down there."

"How are you, honey?"

"Me? I didn't have anything happen to me. I wasn't anywhere near what happened."

"I know you were listening to the traffic. Only hearing half of what was going on and not being able to see it for yourself creates a completely different kind of terror. Not to mention how close you and your Uncle Marty are."

Jax took a few seconds and let her feelings surface. "I was terrified I might lose both of them. Uncle Marty is far from being a young man. I'll lose him someday in the near future. I know that's inevitable. The thought of losing Chance before we've had decades together scared me more than anything I've ever felt."

"The difference between you and Faith is, when the time came, you were able to let Chance do her job. That's why I have no trouble seeing you two together for the long haul. As much as I worry about her, to hold her back would kill her spirit and put out the fire that drives her. I beg her to be careful. What I don't do is ask her to bleed for me. That's what it would be, Jax. It would involve cutting out part of her soul. When she was in the burn ward, I prayed for her to live. I'm pretty sure she was praying to die. I asked her to fight, to fight with everything she had to come back to us and she did. That's why I don't ask her to quit. She's already been to the gates of hell, walked through them, and put the damn place out."

Jax rubbed her arm at the chill that rushed over her. "I wish I'd known. I'd have been there."

"I have no doubt you would have, and she'd have fought just as hard to come back to you."

They said nothing for a few moments, Jax leaned against a wall trying to absorb everything. "I probably need to go get an update and call Mom. She'll have a million questions about her older brother."

"Honey, she may not say it to you, but she's just as concerned about her daughter. It could have been you they took. It scared her."

"All those years I spent out in California and never once did she express any concern for my safety. I move back here to a sleepy little county in West Virginia and all hell breaks loose."

Maggie laughed. "I'm betting that no matter where you were, she worried. Your mom was always wrapped tightly within herself. It was hard for her to let anything shine out of that hard exterior. Trust me, I remember a young lady who was very different. Someday, I'll tell you all about her. I love you, Jax, for who you are and because you love my daughter exactly the way she is. Call me with an update if you get the time."

Jax felt her heart swell with Maggie's declaration. Strange how less than a gallon bucketful of time with the woman made Jax feel like she'd missed out on an ocean's worth. "Love you too, Maggie. Tell Dee not to worry either."

"Easier said than done, but I'll try."

They hung up as Sarah opened the door that separated the waiting room from the treatment area and beckoned her in.

"Jax, this is Dr. Amy Halston. She's the attending physician tonight." Sarah pointed to a woman standing in scrubs. "Amy, this is Jax St. Claire, Martin Hendricks's niece."

The tall slender woman reached for Jax's hand. "Sorry to meet you under these circumstances. I hear you're a paramedic that I hadn't yet had the pleasure of meeting."

"Nice to meet you, Dr. Halston. Trust me, I'd rather meet you any other way than this. How is he?"

Dr. Halston put one hand in her pocket and waved her toward a treatment area. "He's come around once or twice. Not really coherent or orientated at this point. His eyes have opened a time or two to verbal commands, which is a good sign. We're sending him up for a CT. His vitals are stable, and fortunately, the bullet only grazed that shoulder. He'll have an impressive scar to show for it. I don't expect any lasting deficiencies. I wasn't able to find anything more than a variety of abrasions. He's obviously been through the wringer. As long as nothing serious shows up on the scans, we'll keep him a day or two for observation. It's all precautionary due to his age. After that we'll send him home with instructions to rest. Trauma like this is more difficult to recover from at his age. The good thing is it's not impossible."

"He's always been one of the strongest men I've ever known, despite his stature. No major health issues beyond some night blindness." Jax ran her hands through her hair.

"Well then, I'd say some rest and a little less action, and he'll be right as rain. They're just readying him for transport to the scan. Do you have any questions for me?"

Jax shook her head. "Not until we get the scan, I guess."

"He's responding and moving all his extremities with stimuli. I think he took a pretty good knock on the head. Likely a concussion, and you know what those can do." Dr. Halston signed a clipboard for the transport team. "You can either wait out in the reception area for him or there's a waiting room upstairs. Likely, he'll go straight to a room after the scan. I'll see him there once the radiologist reads it."

Jax stood by Sarah. "I'll go with him, if that's okay. If he comes to, I want to be there. Will I be able to make a phone call from there?"

"Yes, there's a phone in the room if you don't have a cell phone." Dr. Halston walked with them to the elevator.

"Thank you, Dr. Halston."

She smiled. "Call me Amy. I'm not big on formalities. I heard you're a doctor of a different kind." Amy winked. "And any person special to Chance Fitzsimmons has to be good people.

Jax laughed. "Thank you, Amy."

The elevator carried Jax and Sarah up to the radiology floor with the transport team. Her uncle lay on the gurney looking frail and, to Jax, very much his age for the first time.

Sarah squeezed her hand. "He's going to be okay."

Jax stared at the pale form under the starched, white sheets. "From your lips to God's ears." Sarah left to check on Kenny's condition and promised to be back.

Pale grey walls were closing in on Jax after twenty minutes of wearing a path from the seats to the window, waiting for Marty to return. With great trepidation, she called her mother. The dread in her stomach threatened to expel the cold coffee she'd forced down. The phone rang only once, before the clipped tones of her mother's exaggerated posh accent came across the line.

"Well?"

Jax took a deep breath and put her hand on her stomach to calm the butterflies. *You're not ten anymore. She can't ground you.* "Hello, Mother. He's currently undergoing a CAT scan. All his vitals are within acceptable ranges. He hasn't come around yet." She went on to clinically lay out his assessment to her mother, using great care to measure her tone.

"How old is his doctor?" Jacqueline St. Claire requested.

"About my age. I didn't ask her for specifics."

"Is she married?"

"What in the hell does that have to do with Uncle Martin's condition?"

"From your defensiveness, I take it she's gay."

Jax felt the raw anger raise her blood pressure but answered her mother with a measured tone. "What in the hell, Mother? I have no idea, and even if she is, it's not relevant to his treatment."

"I raised you better than to swear at me. I thought that radar thing all lesbians are supposed to possess would tell you her particular persuasion."

"Mother, are you at all interested in his condition, or did I call you by mistake thinking that you give a shit? You can take your homophobic rhetoric and press it between the pages of your well-read Bible. Put it in Leviticus, I know that's your favorite book of scripture. You've quoted the verses at me often enough. Don't forget to condemn yourself when you eat lobster or wear your cotton polyester blends. I'll call Dad with the results of Uncle Marty's scan. If you're interested in knowing what the diagnosis is, ask him."

She pushed the *END* button. She contemplated turning off her cell phone but thought better of it. *Chance might call.* She slid the phone in her back pocket and resumed her pacing. Jax looked at the clock and prayed the scan would be almost done. Her cell phone vibrated. Positive it was her mother, she ignored it. The woman hated being hung up on. Jax had done it enough times to know. She took it out of her pocket when it buzzed again. Her mother's picture appeared on the screen. Frustrated, she sent it directly to voice mail and texted her father. *She can go to hell.*

She watched the ellipsis dance up and down. Her father was all thumbs when it came to texting. A sentence containing less than five words would have at least one spelling error and no punctuation. He was seventy, and his lack of technology skill often amused her. When the message came through, she laughed out loud.

Devils fraid shelltake over

She shook her head at the spacing issue. *Thanks, I needed that. Can you talk?*

The ellipsis went through its stair step scale half a dozen times before the short message popped up.

I call u

Jax sat down in the uncomfortable, industrial chair meant to last through thousands of hours of abuse. She held her phone to her forehead. She wished Chance were with her. Her phone vibrated and the caller ID indicated it was her father.

"Hey, Dad."

"Jibber Jack? You all right?"

The nickname broke her. She let the tears fall. If only he'd have stood up to her mother all those years ago, things between all of them could have been so different. "Not really, Dad. I'm worried about Uncle Marty. I'm also sick and tired of feeling the wrath of your wife for being a lesbian. Why do you think I stayed in California for so long?"

The silence stretched between them for several uncomfortable seconds before he spoke. "I wish I could go back and speak up for you like I should have, Jax. I'm a retired old cop, who clings to what I have. We missed out on so many years with you, still are. Your mother is a complicated creature. Beautifully complicated, and she still makes my heart race when she looks at me. I've spent the last fifty years feeling blessed she picked me. Sins of the past, my dear one. Now, how is Marty?"

She relayed to him what she'd tried to tell her mother. She looked up to see her uncle being wheeled past the waiting area.

"Dad, they're taking him to his room. When I know more, I'll call you. You need to tell her I won't answer her calls. If she wants to know anything, she can show up here and ask for herself or wait for you to relay what I tell you. I've got to go. I love you."

"I love you too, Jibber Jack. Get some sleep if you can. You sound exhausted. Martin will need you."

"I'll sleep sometime. Right now, I need to go."

After Martin was transferred into his room, nurses bustled about him going through all the admitting procedures. Amy came in and told her that the scans confirmed Marty had a concussion that would require monitoring.

At some point, she dozed off until she heard him moan. She shot across the room to his bedside. "Uncle Marty, can you open your eyes for me?"

Slowly, pale-green eyes, so much like her own, met hers. "Hey, kitten. You okay?"

Jax sobbed out a laugh. "Am I okay? I think that question is one you need to answer for me. I'm so sorry."

He took a deep breath and winced. "Sorry? Did you pistol whip me?"

She held his hand to her cheek, as she sat down on the chair by his bed. "No, but it should have been me."

With force she wasn't expecting, he squeezed her hand. "Jax, I'd be in jail right now if they'd taken you instead of me." He labored a few breaths. "I'd have killed 'em."

"Easy now, those monitors over there are jumping all over the place. I'd like to be allowed to stay for a bit."

Marty slowed down and used broken sentences to relay the information. "Call came. Wanted you. Sick horse." He stopped for a minute and shook his head.

"Don't talk. We can do all that after you've rested."

"Need to...get it out."

She closed her eyes and drew on the strength he'd taught her to have when she needed to treat a wounded animal. "Go ahead."

"Thought it'd be simple. In and out. They jumped me. Took me...that cabin. Needed more supplies."

He lay there for a few minutes, and Jax could tell he was trying to gather some strength. "Uncle Marty, it can wait. They got them all."

He opened his eyes again. "Tomorrow's not a promise, kitten. Let me get it out."

"You'd better not be going anywhere. I need you."

"Doin' my best. Told 'em I needed stuff they wouldn't understand. Hoped someone would see us...when we came back. Kenny came. It hit the fan."

"They got them all, Uncle Marty. Chance and the others figured it out. Two of the guys who took you are still alive. The one you were treating, and the one Tyson bit."

Martin let out a long breath. "Happy 'bout that. They was gonna shoot Kenny again. I stopped them."

"I think we've got the gist of it, Uncle Marty. Rest now." She'd have to call her father to relay the scan results Dr. Halston had given her. Jax hadn't noticed Taylor standing in the room, until she spoke into her radio. Jax recognized Chance's voice advising she was on her way in the door of the emergency room to get looked at. *Looked at? Why? What happened?*

Taylor stepped closer to her. "Kenny's alive because of him. That guy's as tough as John Wayne's toilet paper."

Jax screwed up her brow in confusion. "What the hell is John Wayne toilet paper?"

"Rough, tough, and don't take shit off of nobody."

Jax nearly doubled over at the fairly accurate character assessment of her favorite family member. "Tell Chance I'll be down in a minute. I'm going to call Maggie."

Taylor tipped her hat and left the room.

She leaned over the bed railing and kissed the sleeping man. "Shortest John Wayne look alike I've ever seen."

Chapter Twenty-one

CHANCE LIMPED INTO THE emergency room at Garrett Memorial. Zeus was in a K9 cruiser in the parking lot. She'd need to make arrangements for him. She recognized Bailey, a nurse from Tucker County, who had her hand on a flat, green button, ready to walk back through the swinging doors into the treatment area. Bailey's eyes grew wide at the sight of Chance's leg, and she quickly grabbed a wheelchair. She said something to the receptionist, which caused the woman behind the glass to pick up the phone and dial.

"What the hell, Chance, you're bleeding all over my waiting room. What happened?" Bailey pushed the chair to her.

Chance eased herself down. "I took a gun to a knife fight."

"You're as pale as a hospital sheet. How long ago?

"Hours. I'm okay, Bailey. It's just a scratch."

"A scratch as big as the Grand Canyon. You cops are all alike, ten foot tall and bulletproof."

Chance tapped her chest. "Bulletproof maybe. I will admit black BDUs don't form a very effective knife barrier."

Bailey pushed her into an exam room. "Get up on that bed. I'll get the doctor."

"Thanks, Bailey." She climbed from the chair, as Bailey pulled the curtain. She removed her vest and bent to untie her boot. Within seconds, the curtain was ripped back and Faith appeared before her.

Faith's eyes raged. "Where are you hurt?"

Chance stopped what she was doing and looked at Bailey. "Bailey, who's on duty tonight?"

"Amy's the attending. I saw Faith come around the corner. I thought..."

Chance looked directly at Bailey and ignored Faith. She held up a hand when Faith came near. "Bailey, can you please find Amy for me?" Chance controlled her voice as much as possible and put a strong emphasis on please.

Bailey nodded and left. Faith approached the bed and reached out for Chance's leg.

"Faith, stop. You aren't on duty, and you won't be treating me. Do you understand?"

"Get off your high horse and let me see what you've done this time." Faith pushed her hand aside.

Chance stood, ignoring the pain in her leg. She was walking through the curtain just as Dr. Halston came around the corner and nearly ran into her.

"Whoa, whoa there, Terminator. Get your ass back on the table. You've strung blood all over the place, and I don't plan on having to declare a biodisaster for any more bloodshed." Dr. Halston stepped into the room "Dr. Riker, can you give us a few minutes, please? On the bed now, Chance." She pushed past a stunned Faith and stepped between her and Chance.

Faith crossed her arms. "I will n—"

Chance stood to her full height and looked at Faith with the intensity she used when intimidating criminals. "You will, or I will leave this hospital faster than Zeus goes into attack mode on my command."

Bailey took Faith's arm and physically pulled her back. She closed the curtain behind them.

Dr. Amy Halston looked at Chance, and then glanced toward the fabric of the privacy curtain. She raised her eyebrows then pointed to the bed. "Come on, let's see what you've got going on."

Chance unlaced her boot and pulled it off. Blood continued to trickle from beneath the pressure bandage Ethan had applied at the scene. She felt slightly woozy, as she dropped the boot to the tile floor and pulled off her sock. She climbed up onto the bed. After Amy washed her hands and donned gloves, she cut off the Ace wrap and removed the dressing. A deep, three-and-a-half-inch slice to her calf said hello.

"Damn it, Chance. How much blood have you lost?"

"Not enough to kill me. It started back up when I walked in here." She raised her hand. "And before you threaten to pull someone's medic license for letting me, it was my choice. I was walking into this ER under my own power. If the bleeding hadn't gotten worse, I'd have walked all the way back here. Bailey nixed that."

"Damn. You've got a bleeder in here." She pressed a fresh dressing to the wound. "Hold that. She went to the curtain and leaned out. "Bailey, I need you."

Bailey reappeared and immediately reached into the cabinet beside the sink. She pulled out a suture tray and some sterile saline. She washed her own hands and donned a fresh pair of gloves. "Damn, woman. Someone tried to make this leg a little shorter."

"Yeah, what he wanted was something a little more permanent."

Amy looked up at her, as she irrigated the wound. "Looks pretty clean. I need to tie a few things off quickly. Hang on, there's no time for lidocaine."

Chance squeezed the side of the bed, as Amy quickly sutured small, severed vessels. The bleeding slowed.

"Okay, let me get a better look at this. He didn't break off a tip or anything did he?"

"No. One clean swipe. Now, what he'd done with the knife before he decided to shave my leg, that's unknown."

Amy poked and prodded the wound. "Okay, lets numb it up so I can stitch it. Draw the normal bloods so we can get a baseline on her."

"Yeah, you'll need to do that anyway. Someone will show up here soon and have you sign an evidence log."

Amy stood up and looked at her. "Why would your blood tests be considered evidence?"

Chance pointed to her leg. "To put it bluntly, this is the last assault on an officer that guy will ever commit."

Amy shook her head and started to inject the numbing medication. "I'm guessing someone else with a gun and badge will need to see the results?" She looked over her glasses at Chance.

Chance nodded and bit her lip at the burn of the medication. "Why the hell does that stuff have to hurt so much to make it numb?"

"Price of doing business with me, Sheriff." Amy finished numbing the wound, and then dropped the needle into a sharps container. "Sit still for a few minutes and give that medicine time to work. I'll be right back. Bailey, get her vitals and the blood samples. Start a line with Ringer's. She looks a little pale." Amy left the curtained off-exam area, leaving Bailey in the room with Chance.

Bailey propped up the head of the bed and grabbed a blood pressure cuff. After recording Chance's pulse, blood pressure, and respirations, she pulled out several tubes from a drawer. "Okay, time for me to play Monica Bellucci." She wrapped a rubber strip around her arm and pulled it tight. "Make a fist."

"Dracula's bride, huh?"

"What can I say? I like horror flicks. Should I ask what the deal was between you and Faith just now?" She palpated Chance's arm. "Got one, hold still."

Chance put her head back and felt a quick pinch, as Bailey slid the needle into her arm and pushed a rubber-topped tube into the plastic sleeve. Thick, red blood filled the tube rapidly, and Bailey replaced it with another.

"Faith is no longer my doctor."

"You guys have been broken up a long time. Last time when you came in here hurt, she refused to let anyone else work on you. She was the attending that night. I'm sorry if I overstepped tonight. She came in with your deputy on the chopper. Didn't know there'd be an issue."

"I'm not the one with the issue, Bailey. She has no objectivity when it comes to me. If she'd been on duty, I probably would have let her do her job without fussing. The fact is, I've had a pretty rough night. The last thing I need is to be read the riot act by my physician. What I need is someone to sew up my leg so I can go check on Kenny and Doc Hendricks."

"Chance, it's Taylor." A voice spoke through the curtain without entering.

"Come on in. Join the party."

Taylor pushed back the edge and stepped in. "Kenny's doing fine. Doc Hendricks is in a room and stable, with Jax by his side." Taylor looked wide-eyed at Chance's leg. "What the hell happened to you?"

"One of them took a swipe at me and Zeus."

Bailey hung a clear fluid bag from the pole behind Chance's head. "I'm going to let this run in slowly. Amy's right. You're a little pale. Your pressure could use a little pick me up. She'll be fine, Taylor. Amy will be back to sew her up in a minute." Bailey finished hanging the intravenous line. She labeled the blood vials and placed them in a transport bag. "I need to send these out." She pointed to Taylor, and then to Chance. "You, make sure she stays put."

Taylor nodded. "She's got her own personal babysitter until Maggie can get here."

"Dammit, Taylor. Did you call her?" Chance rubbed her face. Having Maggie and Dee worried about her was an even bigger thing she didn't need. In her estimation, she'd already caused them three lifetimes worth of grief, and her regret over that was overwhelming.

Taylor held up both hands. "Don't be pissed at me. Jax still has that radio you gave her. She heard you were coming in. As soon as she's sure Doc's settled, she's coming down here. She called Maggie." Taylor pointed to herself. "Not me."

Chance pinched the bridge of her nose. "Has Marty regained

consciousness?"

"A bit. Everything looks good. Kenny's up in the surgical intensive care, and Becky's with him. Surgeons say he'll be fine. Unfortunately, they had to replace almost his entire blood volume. It's going to be a long recovery."

"He's lucky to be alive, Taylor. The video showed the guy I killed stood over him with the gun like he was going to execute him."

Taylor nodded. "I heard. Doc told them if they killed Kenny he wouldn't treat them."

"I'll have to thank him personally."

"What happened out there? I've heard bits and pieces."

Chance proceeded to quietly give her the down and dirty version of the night's events.

"I'm sorry it came to that, Chance. It couldn't have been easy."

"I didn't think about it. You know as well as I do, the thinking comes after. Before that, it's our training and our instincts that save our life or that of another. He refused to drop the gun. He pulled a knife. He refused commands even with Zeus's teeth in him. If I had to make a guess, he was high on something. Until they question the survivors, we won't know exactly what went down. Hopefully Doc will be able to give us the full account."

"No hopefully about it. He's awake and told me everything." Jax strode into the area and came to a stop at Chance's side. She looked down at her leg. "I think I asked you not to come back with anymore scars. What am I going to do with you, Sheriff?" Jax leaned over and kissed Chance softly.

Chance reached up and pulled Jax down into her embrace. "More of that I hope."

Taylor chuckled. "I'll leave you two alone for a bit. I'm going to go see if Penny wants to head home. I'll be back." Taylor pointed to Jax. "You're in charge. You hear me?"

Jax stood and saluted. "She's in good hands."

Taylor nodded as she left. "I have no doubt."

Jax pulled up a chair and sat by Chance. She nodded to Chance's leg. "How bad is it?"

"Not as bad as it looks." Chance reached for Jax's hand and kissed the knuckles. Jax was exactly the medicine she needed.

"You didn't tell me out there. I'm guessing this had already happened?"

Chance didn't say anything and dropped her head, not wanting to meet Jax's eyes.

"And you didn't tell me, because you didn't want me worrying about you while I was sick with fear over Uncle Marty."

Chance confirmed Jax's suspicions with a nod.

Jax held her hand. "Honey, I know getting hurt is one of the risks of your job. I don't want you to be afraid to tell me, for any reason. Not telling me, because you think it will freak me out or you don't want to worry me, will only cause me to worry more about what you might be hiding." She reached out and tilted Chance's head up until their eyes met. "I'll never ask you to stop doing what you do. It's not going to scare me away. A long time ago, I let someone tell me the way I felt about you was wrong. I won't make that mistake again. I love you, Chance, for everything you are, and because of what you are. You being a police officer doesn't scare me half as much as what my life would be without you. Because of that, I know you'll do everything you can," she rose and leaned near to Chance, "to always come home to me. That's all I ask." Jax kissed her sweetly, then sat back down holding her hand, saying nothing more.

Amy came back in. "Okay, let's see about putting Humpty Dumpty back together again."

For the next few minutes, Amy cleaned and sutured the wound. She put internal, absorbable stitches in to help hold the tissue together and closed the skin. When she was done, Chance sported eighteen blue stitches across her calf.

"Bailey, put a dressing on that and get her vitals again. If they're in normal limits," Amy looked at Jax as she pulled off her gloves, "she can go home."

"Which is exactly where she's going." The curtain swished aside, and Maggie Fitzsimmons stepped inside. She held up her left hand, all five fingers extended. On her right, only her index finger was in view.

Chance let a grin slip out. She knew Maggie was ticking off another of her cat-like lives. "Hey, Mom. Amy can tell you, I'm nowhere close to death's door. And, before you have a fit, I need to go up and check on Kenny before I go anywhere. He's my deputy. Becky's sitting at his bedside in a hospital, because he works for me."

Maggie shook her head and walked over to hug Jax. "How's Martin?"

Jax nodded. "Good. Better than expected. He regained consciousness a little bit ago. He's battling a killer headache, but that old bird is as tough as the turkey I used to eat in the UC Davis cafeteria.

His doctors say he'll be fine. They're going to keep him a few days, just to watch that bump on his head and make sure there are no lingering effects from the CS-gas." She held up a hand and stopped Chance from speaking. "You saved his life. He told me the stuff you threw in that window was mild compared to what they put him through when he was in Vietnam. Said to tell you not to blame yourself."

Chance relaxed back into the bed. Bailey came back in and unhooked her IV. Amy entered right behind her. "Okay, here are your orders. I'm giving you a broad-spectrum antibiotic. One shot now, pills for when you're home. Your records show you've recently had a tetanus booster. We'll call you in a few months to do blood work. Keep that thing clean and dry for a few days. I've left some items you can use to help you shower. I could give you some narcotics for the pain, if you want them?"

Chance shook her head. "No, over the counter will be fine."

"Chance, I'm also giving you some crutches for a few days. That knife wound hit muscle. It needs to heal. I know you won't sit your ass on your couch and watch TV, so use the crutches for a few days."

Maggie crossed her arms. "Don't worry, Dr. Halston." She narrowed her eyes, "She'll be a very good girl. Count on it."

The doctor tore the written prescription off her pad and handed it to Maggie. "I've got no doubt she'll have lots of help being just that. Let's not meet again this way, shall we?"

Chance saluted and took the crutches from Bailey. "Not if I can help it."

Bailey and Dr. Halston left the room. "Mom, let me go see Kenny and Marty. After that, I promise to let you take us home. Please? And could one of you get Zeus from the cruiser outside?" Jax left the room ahead of her.

Maggie nodded. "I'll be waiting down here with Dee when you're ready."

"Okay, I'll run up and be down in a bit."

Jax was waiting on the other side of the curtain with a wheelchair. "Don't put your track shoes on yet. Sit your ass down in this and I'll take you. No arguments."

Chance looked at the chair and decided to pick her battles wisely. She was exhausted from the events of the day. It was close to one in the morning, and the adrenaline rush was long gone from her system. She turned around and let Jax bring the chair close so she could sit in it easily.

Maggie leaned over and kissed her head. "Kid, you'd better start buying that Scotch by the gallon. I'm going to need it."

Chance squeezed her hand, as they moved toward the elevator. Faith sat behind the charge nurse's desk. Her eyes were puffy and void of makeup. It was evident she'd been crying. She watched the group without saying a word.

Chance reached down and stopped the chair. She looked up at Jax with an unspoken request. Jax nodded her head and moved past her with Maggie, allowing for some privacy.

"Is there an empty office here somewhere?" Chance asked.

Faith nodded and came out from behind the desk. She took the handles of the wheelchair, moving Chance into an unused treatment room with a door. She closed it behind her and took a seat on a rolling stool in front of Chance.

Chance held up her hand to stop her from speaking. "You listen first. If you interrupt me, I'll wheel myself out of here and we won't speak again. Do you understand?"

Faith appeared to hold back a sob, as she nodded and looked at the floor.

"Tonight, I took another man's life because he was a threat to me, Zeus, and every other officer at the incident. That man did this." She pointed to her leg. "It's true. This could have been much worse. He had a gun as well as a knife. He took an eighty-two-year-old man hostage. Had we not stopped him, he'd likely have killed Martin Hendricks tonight. My badge gave me the authority to stop him. My gun provided me with the means to do so, and my training made the difference in his life or mine. Yes, it's possible someone else could have done what I did. There's no way to tell what the outcome would have been. I'm a duly sworn officer of the law, and I acted appropriately to the threat."

Chance stopped and gathered her thoughts, hands shaking with anger, adrenaline surging through her. "That same group of men shot my deputy, someone I consider a friend. There are bad people in this world, and someone has to stand up and say 'not on my watch.' That someone in this county is me." Chance pointed to her chest, where the T-shirt she wore displayed an embroidered five-point badge. "Many others have done it before me, and there will be others, like Kendra and Daniel, who will be there to do it after I'm dead and gone. The point is someone," she bent her head and forced Faith to look at her, "has to do it. The laws don't enforce themselves. Without consequence for breaking those laws, there is anarchy. I took an oath to protect and serve like generations of officers before I was born have. One that my father took as well. I don't do so without merit or with reckless intent. Neither did my father. He upheld that oath with his life."

She stopped, centering herself, as she watched Faith wipe away a tear. Chance put her head back and remembered all those nights she'd fallen asleep with the woman in front of her. She'd loved Faith, still did to some extent, but not the way she had in the past. *How do I get through to her?*

"Faith, all those first-edition books you treasure and collect sit on a shelf. No one is ever allowed to touch them. You told me you didn't want the spines cracked or a single page dog-eared. Priceless, you called them. Daniel and Kendra wanted so badly to hold them, but you were worried they'd damage them. They weren't five. They were teenagers. They wanted to see what you saw, why those books were so important. You tried to treat me like those books. You wanted to put me on a shelf inside a cabinet, to keep me exactly like that, unread and untouched. Books aren't meant to sit on a shelf to be looked at. They have a story to tell. Those pages can crumble, be eaten by moths, or destroyed by water. You know how those stories stay alive? The people who've read them tell the story to others, and someone else writes another book. Putting something out of reach so it can't be harmed doesn't make it a beloved story. It makes it an object. I'm like that. Making me be anything other than who I am, trying to preserve me, would destroy me. Maybe more slowly than if something happened to me on the job, but in time, it would destroy me."

Once more, Chance stopped to ramp down her vitriol. She didn't want to hurt Faith any more than she already had. Something had to give. "You made the decision you couldn't live with the uncertainty of my life. You left, found a love that was what you said you needed. Still, you can't let go of the control you want to have over my life. That's why I removed you as my physician. Your concern obscures the lines. If you only acted with your skill and training, it would be different, but you bring your broken heart as well. That isn't healthy for either of us. If all of that isn't enough, you're married. You've got gold bands and happy-ever-after I do's in place!" Chance pointed to Faith's left hand, where a thin gold band and a diamond ring were seated.

Faith choked back a sob. "Theresa left."

Faith said it so quietly, Chance nearly missed it. She reached out and lifted her ex-girlfriend's chin. Faith stood so quickly the stool hit the wall. She wiped at the tears, as she turned her back on Chance.

Chance shook her head in confusion. "Why?"

Faith threw her hands in the air. "You're why! All these years later, I'm still in love with you. Trust me, I wish to God I wasn't." Faith stood with her hands on her hips, her back still turned to Chance. "I fucked it up. I fucked it all up. And now, Theresa's walked away until I can make up my fucking mind what's important to me, who matters more. Go ahead and walk out, because I spoke before you gave me permission."

"Faith, sit down and look at me."

"Not now, Chance. I barely have a shred of dignity left to my name. Let me keep it. I walked away from you, because I was afraid of losing you forever. I didn't want to feel that pain. I poured my heart and soul into a relationship with Theresa. I love her, Chance, I do. I can't help that I've never stopped being in love with you. God knows I've tried. I wanted to hate you. I can't. I just can't. When you got hurt, I thought it was a sign I was still supposed to take care of you. Jax showed up at the hospital, and my possessive instincts took over. If I had a dollar for every time I heard Sarah or Kristi talk about the good old days, I'd be filthy rich. It wasn't me they were talking about when they said how star struck you were. It wasn't me that took your breath. It was her and now she shows up out of the blue. The mythical unicorn did exist!"

"Faith, I've dated other women since we broke up. A few in fact."

Faith turned and grabbed the sink counter so tightly, her knuckles turned white. "And not one of them had a snowball's chance in hell with you. I knew that. I think, subconsciously, I reveled in the fact you were choosing women who were disposable in some way. Somehow, I thought you'd miss me enough that you'd quit your job and ask me to come home. Then the myth, the legend, came back here. The only woman you'd truly ever given yourself to. Now my whole world sits in flames around me, and I'm in the middle of Death Valley with no water in sight."

"Faith, I really don't know what to say or how to help you. When we broke up, I let you go because I wanted you to find the happiness and security you needed to be whole. You were never going to be that with me."

"Don't speak for me, Chance. You don't know what I need to be whole. I have to live in a town where my sister is best friends with my ex-lover. In a town where my nephew is her godson and wants to be just fucking like you. Theresa has to live in your shadow, scratching and clawing for her place at my side, while I silently pine away for you even though I made a solemn vow to forsake all others. Well, apparently, I had my fingers crossed when I made that promise." She dropped down to her knees in front of Chance and put her head on her lap. "Can't you see that I still love you?"

Chance put her hand on Faith's head. She tried to find the words to both comfort and let her down as easily as possible. She didn't have any. There wasn't a single word she could offer to give Faith respite from her torment. Faith was still in love with her. Chance could see that now. Unfortunately for Faith, Chance was in love with Jax. That wouldn't change. She'd waited a long time for the love of her life to come back.

"Faith, look at me." The blue eyes that Chance had always been able to read were too clouded with tears. "When we were together, I loved you with my whole heart and soul, no matter what you believe. I won't lie and tell you I didn't love Jax somewhere, but she was part of my past. A very good part of my past. When she left and didn't come back, I moved on. I never believed she'd be back in my life. She went to the other side of the country, because she didn't want a life under her mother's thumb. She wanted to be free to love whomever she wanted, regardless of their gender. Out there, she built a life free of those chains. If she'd asked me to go, I might have. It didn't work out that way, and life went on."

Chance took a breath and started again. "You and I had our moment in the sun. There's no mystery to why it didn't last. I'm still the person you left, because you couldn't live with my job. Nothing about that has changed or will for a very long time. You say you want me back because you love me. To me, it feels like you want to put me back on that shelf with those first editions. I want to be a dog-eared paperback copy of *Pride and Prejudice*, well-loved and held daily in the hands of its reader. Faith, you'd never be happy with that version on your nightstand, and I won't be happy on the shelf."

Faith wiped her eyes and stood. "I'm not giving up, Chance. I won't. I can't."

Chance put her head back and closed her eyes for a moment. *This isn't happening. Not now when I'm finally happy again.* "Faith, I'm going to say this one more time, more slowly if I must, so you understand. After that, I'm going to go see Kenny and Marty. You and I are not a couple anymore. You have no say over my life, no matter how much you want to. My heart and soul belong to Jax. Unless she tells me different, I'm planning a life with her. The one thing you know about me, without fail, is that I'm faithful. If you can't respect that, then we have nothing more to say. I wish you well, Faith. Theresa is a good woman, and she loves you. Think very carefully about what you're doing before you burn that bridge." She stood and winced.

"Sit down, Chance. I'll take you back out. You can say whatever you want. That doesn't mean I'm done trying."

Chance grabbed her crutches that were hanging from the handle of the wheelchair. "Yes, you are." She turned, pulled open the door, caught it with a crutch, and stepped into the hallway. "I'm ready to go."

Jax moved quickly to her side, her brow furrowed. "Where's your wheelchair?"

Faith came out from the room. "This isn't over." She placed the wheelchair beside Chance and walked away without looking at either of them.

"It is for me." Chance headed toward the elevator on her crutches, as Jax pushed the wheelchair by her side.

"Do I want to know?" Jax asked as they stepped in.

"Not right now, you don't."

Jax nodded. "Will you at least sit down for me? I know you want to walk off that anger, but your leg could use the ride."

Chance took several deep, cleansing breaths, trying to rid herself of Faith's possessive obstinance. She met Jax's eyes. "I'd do almost anything for you."

"Then I'll only ask that you decide this is something you will do for me." She turned the wheelchair sideways and held it.

"This could get ugly." Chance sat down.

"Not my first rodeo, honey. I've faced down worse." Jax leaned over and kissed the side of her neck. When the elevator stopped, they exited.

"Good, because my heart belongs to you. Remember that, no matter what."

Chapter Twenty-two

ONCE AGAIN, CHANCE WAS grounded to desk duty. There was no way she could run without tearing out the stitches. She'd been cleared by the investigating officers on the shooting at the cabin. July's festivities came. She'd done everything she could to behave and still do the parts of her job that she was capable of.

"Hey, you." Chance looked up to find Jax standing in the open doorway. "Well, aren't you a sight for sore eyes."

Jax pointed to her scrubs. "Don't look too hard. I'm a mess of animal hair and God knows what else."

Chance rose and came to stand in front of her. She sighed, as she pulled Jax into her arms. "You're the most beautiful mess I've ever seen. Hi." Chance leaned down and kissed her. When she felt Jax melt under her touch, she held on tighter. It never got old.

"Whew. Now I'm a hot mess for other reasons." Jax traced Chance's jaw line.

Chance stepped completely into her office and closed the door behind them.

Jax followed her across the room and sat on her lap. "Any news?"

Chance nodded. "Some. There are still questions to be answered about the men who took Marty. Two of the three had Baltimore addresses I think connect somehow to the Kurst family. I can't prove it yet. What Martin said about the broken leg matches up with what the suspects told us. They're pretty tight lipped, under advice of their lawyers. We still don't know why they were in the woods in the first place, or how the one guy was injured. I'm positive it's drug related. I won't be surprised if the whole mess ties into the guy who tried to make roadkill out of me. How's Marty doing?"

"Fewer nightmares. Still jumping at shadows. He's taken to turning his hearing aids down so that loud noises don't startle him as much. He's going to be okay. He just needs to see the guys who did this go away for a long time."

Chance ground her teeth together, thinking about what Marty had been through. "With everything that has to be investigated, I'll be surprised if they go to trial this year. Trust me, no matter how long it takes, justice will be served. Harley's assured me of that." She took a deep breath and tried to lighten the mood. "Speaking of Harley, Meg graduates the academy soon."

Jax's smile lit up her face. "She does. Lindsey is ecstatic to have her coming home. Only seeing her on the weekends has been hard. Thankfully for them, I don't have weekend hours. Lindsey's thinking about applying for Uncle Marty's scholarship to go to veterinarian school at WVU. I think she should. She's phenomenal as a technician and about as good at diagnosis as I am. I'll support her in any way I can."

"The guys out at the farmhouse working today?"

Jax sighed and leaned into Chance. "I think it would've been easier to tear the damn place down than the total remodel I'm doing. Once they found that termite damage, it meant replacing some of the major floor beams. The water running down the foundation has to be channeled away, or it's going to start causing major issues. I'd have still bought it. The move-in date will be a little fluid for a while."

"What a shame." Chance couldn't hold back her grin.

"Yeah, I know it's been a real hardship having me live with you. I can tell. I'd rather have it done correctly than fast. At least the barns are usable. I love having Macallan and Glenlivet close to me. Moving your Kelly in with them was a bonus. An evening ride is just what the doctor ordered for a weary vet and a cranky sheriff."

Chance looked deep into Jax's eyes. "It's been a bit challenging getting on and off with this leg, but we've managed. It's not only the horses that make me a lot less cranky. Waking up beside you every morning has done wonders for my disposition."

"Rather enjoy that myself. What happens when the house is done? I don't want to think about waking up without you. If Faith hears we aren't sleeping in the same bed every night, she'll jump you in a New York minute."

Chance put her forehead on Jax's. "Doesn't matter what she does. I'm with you and only you. I've loved you forever, and I intend to love you for the rest of my life. Chance pulled Jax closer and braced herself. "What would you think if I moved in with you? Taylor and Penny have been looking for a bigger place."

Jax's smile swallowed her face. "Penny told me they're trying to get pregnant. The place they're living in now is too small to even add a thimble."

"I can't bring myself to sell the property, especially now that it borders yours. I think it might be a good fit for them, considering the rent break I'd give them. They might eventually want to build a place of their own. For now, I think it's a good solution to both our problems. I want to be with you, and they need space."

"I don't care which house we live in, as long as I'm living with you." She bent down and kissed Chance with a passion full of promise.

Chance nearly melted into her chair. She was absolutely sure of at least one thing at this point in her life. She'd be sharing whatever years she had left with the woman seated in her lap.

"I've got to get out of here before I strip you down and make love to you on your desk." Jax kissed her again and got up. She fanned herself. "And now for an abrupt right turn and a bucket of ice water. I'm cooking at Uncle Marty's tonight. I expect to see you there at six, Sheriff." Jax winked, as she went through the door.

"I'll be there." Chance looked down at Zeus. "We are some lucky fucks, my boy." Her cell phone rang, and she watched Faith's number display on her screen. She sent it immediately to voicemail and grabbed a bottle of Advil. She needed quick relief from the headache that would surely follow.

Penny showed up in the door. "I just told Faith you were in a meeting."

Chance nodded to her phone. "That was her. I sent the call to voicemail."

"What are you going to do?"

"I don't know."

Penny crossed her legs and leaned forward. "What does Sarah say?"

Chance put her head back and closed her eyes, willing the pain meds to take effect. "She's worried about her sister. Faith's drinking heavily. She sobers up for work, then sits in her house and kills a bottle or two of wine a night. I have no idea what to do. I think it's time I go see Theresa."

Penny looked at her with shock. "Think she'll see you?"

"I have no idea. Only one way to find out."

***

Chance knocked on the screen door to the ranch-style home. Theresa's sister, Nadine, came into view. "You're probably the last person she wants to see, Sheriff."

Chance stood turning her hat around in her hands. "I don't doubt that. I'm also the person she needs to see."

"Maybe. Come in. Coffee?" Nadine held the door open for her.

"Thanks, black is fine."

"Okay, have a seat." She poured the coffee and set it on the table. "I'll go get her. For the record, I know it's not your fault, Chance."

Chance nodded. "That's one of you." She watched Nadine leave and took a moment to steel herself for the coming conversation.

Slow steps brought Theresa to the doorway, where she hesitated with her hand on the wall before entering the room. Chance noticed the dark circles under her eyes.

"Didn't expect to see you here." Theresa turned a chair around and straddled it.

"I know you didn't. I want to tell you a few things. You don't have to believe any of them; it's your choice. On my father's badge, I swear to you they're true."

Theresa sighed deeply. "Go ahead, Chance. Say what you have to say." She sat turning her wedding ring around her finger.

"The long and the short of it is this. I was happy for you and Faith when you found each other. You were able to give her what she said she wanted—a stable home life—someone who came home at four o'clock every night and didn't have to jump and run at a moment's notice. Getting ready for work didn't involve putting on a bulletproof vest every day. You command an audience with a whistle around your neck and give kids an opportunity to feel what we did when we won the championship. You are exactly what she needs, even if she's lost her way."

Theresa slowly spun a spoon in a circle on the table. "She lost her way chasing after you."

Chance pointed to her chest. "Not with my encouragement, Theresa, or at my request. I let her stay as my physician, because she asked to. We stayed amicable, because I didn't want tension. If anyone had a right to be pissed, it was me. She left me for you. I'm not a fool, Theresa. I knew she was interested in you before she left me. I let her go without a blowup because we are Daniel's godparents and I want her to be happy. The rest didn't matter. She moved on, and now I'm doing the same. I'm head over heels in love with Jax St. Claire, and I will be until the end of time. We're living together, and as long as that makes her happy, I'll be right by her side. I was never what Faith needed beyond the surface. God knows I tried to find a way to walk away from who I am. Lucky for her, you gave her a chance at a different life. I don't know if you can salvage your marriage. Only you know that. I hope, for both of your sakes, you can. If you can't, I want you to know that I've done everything in my power except slap a restraining order on her. Short of leaving town, I'll do anything you ask me to."

Chance had almost reached the door, before Theresa finally spoke up. "I made peace with the fact you'd always be in our lives. I even made space for you. The problem was she kept making my space smaller and yours bigger. Her love for you didn't stop when she walked away. I was hoping I would eventually be enough. I've done everything I can to be what she wants. Your shadow was too impossible to shine through. I want to hate you. Trust me I do. I can't. It's not your fault, and no, I don't want a restraining order on her. It'll hurt her career. She can't lose that too."

"I don't think she's lost you."

Theresa looked up at her, eyes full of pain. "Not for lack of trying, Chance. Not for lack of trying."

"I'm worried about her drinking. Sarah says it's getting worse. She can't seem to reach her."

"I'm not sure what I can do. I keep trying to get her to meet with me, go to counseling. She keeps refusing."

"Don't give up. She needs you more than she knows."

"Thanks for stopping by."

"Remember this, Theresa. You don't need to fill my shoes. You have an extraordinary pair of your own. If she can't see that, lay the blame where it squarely belongs."

***

Chance drove to Marty's, where dinner preparations were under way. She sat with a glass of iced tea in her hands, staring off into space.

Jax put a hand on her lower back. "Hey, where are you?"

"I was thinking about my conversation with Theresa. I don't know when I've ever felt that bad for someone. Faith is killing her."

"This isn't your fault, Chance. You have to stop taking this on yourself. Come on, help me grill the pork chops. The glaze is by the grill."

"I love you, Jax St. Claire. Don't ever forget that."

***

The next morning, Taylor sat in Chance's office with her, going over the coming week's schedule.

Taylor stretched her back. "I think Kenny's stopping by the office for a visit next week. He's going to put in for retirement."

Chance nodded. "Penny told me that the other day. He's doing really well in therapy. It's yet to be determined whether he'll ever be able to come back to law enforcement. The bullet caused some major nerve damage. He still can't get his arm into a shooting position. I know he's been thinking about going back to law school."

"I hate to lose him as an officer. Only time will tell if he takes some other position when he's fully recovered."

Chance nodded. "I'm going to retire Tyson with Kenny. It's his dog, and they should be together. Kendra is fighting me tooth and nail to take the test next month. Swears to me she'll finish her degree online. Maggie had me write a promise I wouldn't let her, in blood."

Taylor chuckled. "Daniel's chomping at the bit for you to give that test."

"I know. I'm not sure who's going to kill me first, Maggie and Dee or Sarah and Kristi. He's bound and determined to be on the top of that list. I have no doubt he'll ace it all."

Taylor nodded in agreement. "He'll be a great officer, because I know his mentor. She's the example we all strive for."

Chance rocked in her chair. "Thank you, Taylor. Coming from you, that means a great deal. Once Kenny officially retires, we can post the test date. Daniel's young, but unless someone comes out of left field, I expect he'll be our new hire. Enough about that. I want to talk with you about something else.

Taylor looked concerned. "Something with the schedule?"

"No. Not work. The remodel at Jax's is almost finished. When it's done, I'm going to move in with her. I'd like you to consider renting my place. You're going to need more room, my friend."

Taylor sat forward, resting her elbows on her knees. "I don't know that we could afford a place like yours. You know what our salary is, and well, with the fertility treatment bills, there isn't a lot left at the end of the month."

"I know all that. You haven't even heard what the rent is. How about you let me make my offer before you turn it down?"

Taylor nodded.

"We make hay for the horses on my place, and now we'll have Jax's too. I need a lot of help when its time. My place is going to need the logs treated soon. What I'm offering is two hundred dollars a month rent, along with your promise to help with the maintenance on both places. Don't argue with me. I need the help more than I need the money. You guys will need the room for that little one you're trying to have.

Penny walked in, handing them each a cup of coffee. "It's not a question of trying anymore." She ran her hand over her stomach and stood by Taylor, who was grinning like a Cheshire cat. "It's the little one we're having."

Chance's eyes went wide. "You're pregnant?"

"Glad to know you haven't noticed me tossing my cookies every three minutes. This morning sickness should be renamed all-day-and-all-night sickness."

Chance came around the desk and Taylor stood. Chance wrapped them both in a hug. "I'm so happy for you two! You're going to make great parents."

Penny cried into Chance's shirt. Taylor drew her wife into her arms. Tears streamed down Penny's face, as she tried to wipe them away. "Damn hormones."

Chance put her hands on the shoulders of the two women before her. "As soon as Jax's place is done, I want you guys to move in, okay? No arguments. Let me do this for you, so I can watch that little one grow up."

Taylor looked directly at Chance. "We wanted to talk to you and Jax about being the baby's godparents. Since Daniel is old enough to take care of himself, we were hoping you'd have a vacancy?"

Chance was taken aback and was barely able to choke out words. It hadn't been in the cards for her to have her own children. She was overwhelmed that those closest to her felt her worthy enough to be a stand in, if needed. "I'd be honored, and I'm sure Jax will feel the same."

***

Chance backed her truck down to a secluded place on the riverbank.

"This is a great spot." Jax stepped out of the truck, and Zeus bounded out behind her.

Chance drew Jax close. "Reserved for you, my love."

They walked to the tailgate and pulled out the cooler and other things they'd brought with them. Chance spread the air mattress in the bed of the truck and attached the pump. It was made to fit between the wheel wells.

Jax chuckled. "All those years ago, we put a sleeping bag down in the bed of a truck."

Chance looked above her sunglasses. "We're over fifty, and neither of us would be able to walk if we did that today. When I make love to you under the stars, I want your back to be comfortable."

Jax threw a bag of marshmallows at her and glared.

Chance shrugged. "Truth hurts, honey."

"Your back is going to be complaining when you're lying outside on the ground beside the truck."

Chance put on her shocked face. "You wouldn't kick me out of your bed, would you?"

Jax walked up to her and kissed her passionately. "Not for even a single night. Faith's probably hiding in the bushes waiting for her opportunity."

"If that's so, she's going to get one hell of a show."

Jax blushed. "Oh really. That sure of yourself, huh?"

"Let's just say I like my odds."

"I'd say the odds are in your favor."

"Then I'm all in." Chance pulled Jax to her again. Jax's lips opened with their kiss, and Chance grew wet as she explored the depths of Jax's mouth. She loved this woman with everything she had. *Tonight, I'll show her how much.*

***

Later that evening, they lay in the truck bed watching fireworks. One of Harley's troopers doubled as a bomb tech. He needed to 'dispose' of some illegal pyrotechnics. The quarry where he set them off, allowed for a spectacular show from the spot Chance had parked the truck.

"Comfortable?"

Jax snuggled in close. "Very."

With each colorful display, Chance saw flashes of her life: her teenage years with Jax on a riverbank, her smoke jumping career, the scars she still bore on her body, and her former law enforcement position. It was hard to compare those times to the life she led now as small-county sheriff. She thought about the people she'd met and feelings she'd once had. They all paled in comparison to what she felt with Jax. Quiet music played through the truck's speakers; the soft lyrics of Staind's "Tangled Up in You" said all the things Chance was feeling. All these years later, she was still so deeply in love. When Aaron Lewis crooned about the hand he wanted to hold while he grew old, Chance knew it was time.

Jax drew lazy circles on Chance's chest. "What are you thinking about? Your heart is beating a mile a minute."

Chance pulled Jax on top of her and kissed her. "You. I'm thinking about you and how much my life has changed."

"I'm sorry it took me so long to find my way back."

"None of that matters now. That's all in the past. What does matter is the here and now."

Jax ran her fingers down the scars on Chance's side. "I agree."

"All those years ago, on a riverbank just like this, I knew I'd never love another woman the way I did you. I'd never met someone so beautiful, so smart, and so damn sexy. I couldn't believe you were mine, and somehow, I let you slip away. I know we had journeys to take in order to become who we are today. If I had to go through all that pain again to know you'd be here with me now, I'd do it without thinking twice. I don't want to miss another minute with you."

Jax crossed her hands over Chance's chest and rested her chin on them. She looked Chance directly in the eyes. "I can tell you, you won't ever have to. I'm staying right here."

"Permanently?"

Jax furrowed her brow. "I thought you knew that. How can you doubt it? I said I want to be with you forever and I meant it."

Chance held up a diamond solitaire and let the moonlight catch the perfectly polished facets. "Then marry me."

Jax covered her mouth, shock showing in her eyes.

Chance rolled them over and held herself above Jax. "We've lost out on far too many years of being together, Jax. When you left, you took a part of me with you. By the grace of God, and the miracle of a gold-star chance, you're back here in my world. I want everyone to know that I belong to you and only you. There is nothing in this world I want more than to wake up every morning looking into those green eyes to see the love that I've longed for my entire life. Maggie will tell you I should have died all those years ago when I got burned. I lived through it, because she begged me to fight."

Jax wiped at tears running down Chance's face.

"Do you know what I kept thinking through that hell?"

Jax shook her head.

"If I gave up, I might never see you again. I know we weren't in touch. I didn't even know where you were. I lay there in agony, praying for a moment's peace without pain. I found that moment when I remembered floating down the Cheat River with you. I could see you in my ball cap, so beautiful it hurt. When I was at my worst, I'd remember hearing you say how much you loved me. I'd remember touching you and how buzzed I'd feel at the touch of your lips on mine. You kept me going when all I wanted to do was die. My dad told me my own gold-star chance at love would come one day. I'm grabbing it like he said and asking you to give us something long overdue." Chance held up the ring again. "Marry me, Jax. Marry me and take that second chance at a love I promise you'll never regret."

***

Jax lay beneath Chance, stunned. She'd never expected to hear Chance say those words. Now she stood on the edge of the unknown. *No, not the unknown.* She stood on the threshold of the life she'd walked away from all those years ago. One word would erase all those wishes she'd made as she drove from California to West Virginia. One word would give her the opportunity for a do-over, the chance to wear the gold band of the woman she'd loved for over thirty years. One word. A single syllable that would change her life forever and give them what they'd apparently both been dreaming of. One syllable, three letters.

"Yes." The word came out as a whispered echo of a prayer said long ago. She felt her world right itself. With conviction, she answered again. "Yes, Chance Raylynn Fitzsimmons, I will marry you whenever and wherever you want."

Chance's whoop into the night caused an eruption of Jax's laughter. She smiled, as Chance pumped her fist in the air then sat up, letting the blanket fall away from their naked bodies. Chance drew Jax's left hand into hers and slid the shining symbol of devotion onto her left ring finger. The ring felt like a part of her the second it settled into place, as if it had always been there.

Jax reached up and cupped Chance's face with her hands. "I love you, Chance. Now and forever."

***

Chance put her arms around Jax and supported her as they lay back. She let her lips fall to Jax's, absorbing the heat and the taste of the strawberries they'd shared. She melted into the feeling of belonging to someone on a soul-deep level.

"I love you, Jax. I'm never letting you go, never again. Thank you for coming back to me."

Jax kissed her again and pulled her even closer.

***

Tomorrow, there'd be another emergency, another call, another case to solve. Tonight, there was nothing but the memory of something her father had told her that her mother said on the day she found out she was pregnant. Life was all about opportunities and what we did with them. Chance had been named for all the things her parents wished for. In her mind, she'd been given more than most. She thought about the woman who would become her wife. She knew she'd been blessed. With all the tragedies she'd experienced in her life, she remembered her mantra. *Steel is tempered by fire, and gold is refined by it*. She'd lived through it all and now would live with Jax by her side. Their story wasn't over; it had only just begun. She was ready for whatever life threw at her, as long as the woman she held in her arms was at her side.

And the story continues

Forever Chance

Chapter One

SHERIFF CHANCE FITZSIMMONS SAT on the desk in the front of the auditorium style classroom at West Virginia University. Her good friend, Professor Scott Ross, recruited her to speak on rural law enforcement challenges. She looked over her audience, the number of male students far outweighing the female by nearly three to one. She was proud to see that one of those females, was her little sister Kendra. Her near carbon copy sat front and center, a miracle of anything but genetics.

"Rural law enforcement differs a great deal from being an officer in a municipal setting. For instance, in a municipality, the distance between where you are and where your dispatched to, can be a matter of a few minutes or blocks. In my jurisdiction, it could be twenty to forty minutes for me to reach a call location, more if its bad weather. What's worse is your available backup could be on the other side of the county. There are times that reality can have deadly consequences."

Chance used her clicker to advance her presentation. A large picture of her father in his uniform appeared on screen. "This officer died in the line of duty on a domestic call. His back up was very far away as an enraged husband threatened his wife with a gun. " She turned to the audience again. "Deputy Ray Fitzsimmons died when he shielded the female victim from gunfire. That deputy was my father and he died on scene from a gunshot wound to the head. He was doing all the things he'd been taught, including wearing a vest and using caution. Unfortunately, humans rarely survive gunshot wounds to the head. My dad saved a life that day. It cost him his."

Chance watched as the students stared at the screen. She could see that Kendra's were directed firmly at her. "Firefighters have a saying. You risk a lot, to save a lot. You risk little, to save little. Now, I spent many years jumping out of a perfectly good airplane into wildfires. I know what that means. I also know the cost of putting your body between an innocent and a bullet. It's one of the reasons all of my road deputies have a K9 unit with them. They are never alone."

A hand went up in the back of the room and Chance pointed to him as she nodded for the student to go ahead with his question. A young man that couldn't have been more than nineteen, stood. "Didn't it worry you when you became an officer that you might face that same fate as your father?"

Chance sat on the edge of the desk and took a calming breath. She thought about her father every day she put on her badge. It was a part of her morning ritual as she stretched her scar tissue and repeated something Maggie had said to her when she'd been in the burn ward. *'Steel is tempered by fire and gold is refined by it.'* How do you explain what she felt about being an officer?

"My dad was my hero. Every day, I watched him put on his uniform and pin his badge over his heart. Ray Fitzsimmons believed in honor and duty and he taught me those same values. In life, you have to find something you believe in from inside the marrow of your bones, something that's elemental." Her hands reached up and unpinned her badge. "My dad told me there are five points to this badge," she placed her finger on one of them and touched the next point with each word she spoke, "honor, duty, courage, integrity, and empathy. His belief was that the empathy part was the hardest as an officer, because it required finding balance. He also said I'd clearly understand that when I was wearing the badge. His words hold even greater truth today."

Chance made eye contact with the students in the room before stopping at Kendra. "Some of you will become officers, some lawyers, and maybe some will find this field isn't for you at all. What I can tell you is this, the day you make the decision to enforce the laws of our land, you will use each of these five points in the performance of your duties."

She touched one of the points again, "Some of you will rely on your courage and some will heavily on duty. I encourage you to lean on the one my father said would be the most difficult, empathy. When you've dealt with the same addict for the third time in as many days, when you've arrested the same abusive partner over and over only to have the other party file resend a domestic violence petition again, when you've put the same thief in jail for the fifth time, you'll find that empathy the most tenuous to achieve. You'll feel like you're getting nowhere more often than you'll feel like you've made a difference. I can only hope that one day," Chance held her badge in the air, "that someone will walk up to you and says you've been their role model and their reason for choosing this profession."

She let her eyes settle on Kendra for only a moment. It was enough to feel the connection she and her adopted sister shared. She fastened the badge back on her uniform. "You'll remember why you pin the badge on every day and stand as the thin blue line between order and anarchy." Zeus barked his approval and the class released a small laugh. Chance reached down to pet him. "He's listened to this speech enough he could give it himself. Thank you for your attention today. I'll leave a stack of business cards with Professor Ross if you have any other questions."

A round of applause came from those in attendance as chairs shuffled and backpacks were hefted. Scott Ross stepped to her side and held out his hand. "Thanks, Chance. Having you come in and talk with them as a current law enforcement officer, really makes an impact."

Chance pulled on his hand and embraced him in a hug. "It's always a pleasure." She pushed him back but held him by his shoulder. "What really makes an impact is having a professor like you that's been neck deep in the trenches. You can tell them the truth beyond what the recruiting posters portray."

Scott chuckled softly. "It does differ slightly. Regardless, I am in your debt for so many reasons."

Chance shook her head. "Scott, there's no debt between us, ever. I mean that. I enjoy coming down here. Gives me a chance to take Kendra to lunch and get an eyes on report for the mom squared. Isn't that right, pain in my ass?"

"You're buying, so I'll agree." Kendra smiled with a look of genuine mirth.

Chance pointed to her. "See what having a kid sister thirty years younger gets you? An empty wallet and a dump truck load of sarcasm." She playfully shoved Kendra.

Scott's laughter was contagious. "Hell, having a brother two years younger gets you the same thing."

Chance was aware of Scott's brother Miles, who'd been in and out of rehab several times. Scott's parents had died over a dozen years ago and he'd taken it upon himself to try and keep his younger brother on the straight and narrow. "I have no doubt."

Scott put his foot up on a chair and leaned forward, exposing the ankle section of his prothesis. "And the debt goes beyond your guest lecture and you know it."

Chance lowered her gaze for a fraction of a second before meeting his eyes. "We'll have to continue to agree to disagree on that point, my friend. Any time you need a lecturer for a day, give me a call." She snickered when Kendra's stomach growled out a protest. "For now, I think I need to feed the beast over there. I'm pretty sure there's a lion in there trying to claw its way out."

Kendra blushed.

Scott shook her hand. "Don't think I won't. I'm glad you're doing alright after the events of earlier this summer. We've both had enough knocks for a lifetime I think."

"Mags and Dee will certainly agree." Chance nodded.

"I'd say you better include your fiancé or she's likely to give you another. I don't mess with Jax. She's tough." Kendra pointed a finger at her.

Scott snapped his fingers. "That's right. You're finally taking the plunge. Congratulations. I hope to meet this miracle worker someday."

"We'll have to do dinner sometime with you and your wife. I

venture to say they'd get alone great. Really, it was great to see you Scott. Call me anytime and if I can work it in, I'm there." Chance hugged him again.

"Dr. Ross is busy delivering babies today. I don't know how she does it. She's the most sought after OBGYN in the area and I have no idea what she ever saw in me. Kendra, I'll see you next week."

"Thanks, Professor Ross. I'm looking forward to the session."

Scott pointed to Kendra. "She reminds me so much of you, it's scary. Kendra's going to be a fantastic officer someday. She's got a great role model to follow."

Chance blushed. "I think her professors have a bit to do with that as well."

"You two are embarrassing me and I'm starving. See you next week, Professor Ross." Kendra hefted her backpack to her shoulder and grabbed Chance's sleeve.

Chance "I think that's my que to leave. Call me, Scott."

Once they'd left the classroom, Chance asked the obvious question. "Where do you want to go?"

Kendra didn't even hesitate. "Colasantes."

"Okay, you're on."

"And I have a favor, well more of request really." Kendra dropped her eyes.

"I can't say yes or no until you tell me what you want." Chance rolled her hat around in her hand.

"Can I bring a guest?"

"I don't see why not. Who do you want to join us?" Chance watched Kendra. She was sure she was about to learn who her sister had been spending an inordinate amount of time with. Try as she might, she struggled for the name she'd heard Kendra use in one or two of their phone conversations.

"Brandi."

"Do we need to pick her up somewhere or is she close by?"

Kendra cleared her throat and rubbed a hand across the back of her neck. Chance grinned at the blush her little sister was sporting.

Kendra pulled out her phone and tapped the screen a few times and waited. "She's over at the Mountain Lair, she can meet us at your vehicle in ten minutes."

Chance put a hand on the younger woman's shoulder. "Breathe, Bullseye. I promise, I won't interrogate her."

Kendra's nervous laughter made Chance smile. One deep breath later and Kendra met her eyes.

"I've been wanting to introduce her to everyone for a while. She's...well, special."

"I gathered that."

They started walking toward the parking garage, Zeus on their heels. They passed hordes of students rushing from one place to another, earbuds in place while they stared blankly at their phones. It amazed Chance how they were able to navigate without falling over something. One second later, she corrected that thought as one of the enraptured students walked into a glass wall and banged their nose. Books scattered across the floor as the young man stood and picked his things up while he held a hand to his face.

"I hope you aren't so consumed with your phone or anything else, that you lose sight of the objects in front of you. When you're an officer," she pointed her hat to indicate the student to Kendra, "that will get you killed."

Kendra nodded and voiced her understanding. "I try to know what's going on around me all the time. You taught me that and it serves me well with this madhouse down here."

They continued their way through the throng until they reached the open concrete structure. A petite girl about Kendra's age, paced near her vehicle. Short dark hair cut in a pixie style framed delicate features. Chance assumed this was Brandi. Chance extended her hand. "Hi, I'm Chance, Kendra's sister."

With a voice belying her small stature, Brandi answered in kind. "Brandi, Brandi Antolini." Her eyes were an unusual green.

Kendra shook her head and laughed. "Don't mind me, I think I was supposed to make that introduction."

Brandi cocked her head. "Then speak up, you know I don't have a shy bone in my body. If I did, we still would be waving at each other in biology class."

Chance nearly burst out laughing. *She's got Kendra's number.* "How about we make our way to the restaurant? That way, we can order while we get better acquainted. This one," Chance pointed a thumb at Kendra, "gets hangry if she doesn't eat every two hours."

Brandi looked down at Zeus. "Especially in the morning, she's really cranky before coffee and sustenance."

Kendra cleared her throat and raised her hand. "Kendra here, present and accounted for, don't mind me."

Brandi knelt. "Who is this beautiful creature? And I never mind you."

"No, you don't, even when it's in your best interest. Brandi meet Zeus, Chance's K9 partner." Kendra extended her hand and scratched Zeus.

Brandi looked to Chance. "Is it okay if I pet him?"

Chance nodded her consent. "I'm sure he'd like that."

Brandi presented the Malinois her hand. Zeus leaned forward and sniffed it before looking to Chance who nodded again. He put his nose under Brandi's hand and bumped it. She stroked over his head and ears. "Wow, he's all muscle."

"He and I spend a lot of time keeping in shape. It's important for our job and he's all about the job."

Kendra leaned down. "When I go to work for Chance, I'll have a K9 too."

Chance watched as the smile on Brandi's face lit up.

"And I'll take care of it."

Kendra stood. "Brandi's a veterinary medicine student from California."

Chance couldn't help laughing, the irony not lost on her.

Brandi stood and furrowed her brow, "What's so funny about that?"

Chance stared gap mouthed at Kendra. "You didn't tell her?"

Brandi too looked at Kendra. "Tell me what?"

"That my fiancé is a vet that moved back to West Virginia after a twenty-year practice in Northern California."

Brandi punched Kendra in the upper arm. "How did you forget to mention that?"

Kendra winced and smiled. "Ow, and I didn't think about it."

Brandi put a hand on her hip. "Start using that head for something other than your good looks. You're getting a sister-in-law that's a vet? Kendra, that's pertinent information. Good thing you're as good looking as you are."

Kendra furrowed her brow. "What's that supposed to mean?"

Chance cleared her throat this time and leaned close to Kendra. "Let me help you out here before you dig that hole so deep, you'll need the rope rescue team to get you out." She turned to Brandi. "Let's chalk that up to being starstruck by your charm. I say we go eat."

Kendra shut her eyes and put her head back. "Please, God, save me?"

Brandi leaned over and kissed Kendra on the cheek. "I'll let you make it up to me later. Can we go? I'm starving."

Chance hit the locks on the door and opened the rear hatch for Zeus to load. "That we can."

* * *

Two hours later, Chance was on her way back to Tucker County, a smile playing across her face. She made a call to Jax who answered in the first two rings.

"Hey, you. On your way back yet?"

"I have one more stop, beautiful. Anything you'd like me to bring home for supper or do you want me to grill?"

"Such a sweet talker. Any chance you're coming home by Clarksburg?"

"Going right through there. I need to stop in at the Sheriff's office for some information."

"Then I say you bring home Los Loco's tamales and chips with salsa."

Chance would be happy to stop in and see how Anita is doing. "Your wish is my command."

"Be careful on your way home. I love you. Tell Anita hi for me."

The words Jax spoke never failed to warm Chance from the inside out. How her life had changed. "Will do and I love you too. See you at home."

It took forty minutes to make it to downtown Clarksburg. Chance wanted to check with her fellow sheriff and friend, William Andrews, about the heroin pipeline that seemed to be streaming into their state. The overdose rate in his county was much higher than her own. She knew that part of it was the fact he had a major city in his jurisdiction and two major roadways that intersected. Interstate 79 traversed the state north and south and Route 50 east to west. The natural gas business had brought in more than economic growth with their out of state employees. Thousands of gas well workers were staying up to fifty miles away from the well sights. When those workers were present, the opportunity for illicit drug sales and prostitution skyrocketed. She parked her new Suburban in a lot close to the courthouse where the Sheriff's personal office was. The road officers and detectives were in another location.

Chance and Zeus entered the courthouse. An old colleague was acting as security and ushered her through the array of metal detectors and X-ray machines. She stopped at the receptionist's desk and announced herself. Minutes later, William appeared and ushered her into his office.

"How the hell are you, Chance? When we got the word what happened up there, we were all ready to load up and bring in reinforcements." Will sat behind his desk and rocked back in his chair.

Chance rubbed a hand through her hair. "I'm doing really well. No lingering injuries from either dust up. It's been back to being a sleepy little county for a few months. With the Leaf Peepers Festival coming up, I'll get busier than I'd like to be."

Will reached into his desk and pulled out a pack of nicotine gum.

Chance pointed to the gum he held. "You still trying to quit smoking?

"Yeah, for the ninety-seventh time. My doctor chews my ass and my wife threatens pieces of it if I don't. Hard habit to break when you started at sixteen. I'm still not sure how I made it through the academy some days."

"I'm grateful that's one vice I never indulged in. Got a few questions for you. Anyone have a bead on the flood of heroin that's floating around? I've got a suspicion mine's coming out of Baltimore, but no real proof."

Will reached for the keyboard of his computer and hit several keys, while he motioned for her to come around. "We've been tracking the overdoses and trying to pinpoint when this shit is coming in for sale. Problem is, these folks are getting it from all over. Gas well workers from out of state with too much money and not enough sense. We've had a few traffic stops with them coming back from Texas or Oklahoma that have yielded some significant product. The bulk is coming out of Pittsburgh by the usual suspects with a few more heavy hitters pulling the strings. Huntington's pipeline is out of Detroit. The only guys that get caught, are the low-level guys below the middleman. Our taskforce squeezes them. Unfortunately, they're more afraid of ratting out the kingpins than they are going to jail."

Chance rolled her hat around in her hands. "I'm worried what ski season will bring. Like your visiting cowboys, we'll have the mountain crawling with idiots with too much money far away from home."

"I think I'd still take your crazy over mine. The view alone is worth it."

"I can't argue with you. I wish I had a better handle on this heroin thing. We've beefed up our emergency medical service with extra

Narcan and will have heavy police presence during the festival. No way to keep track of the amount of out of state visitors, though I'd really like to put up the license plate reader that came in. I've got the money from a grant, it's more the privacy issues I'm currently tiptoeing around. No matter how many times I explain that this camera isn't being used for traffic violations, it's a hard sell. I've explained over and over that the only thing it keys in on is a plate already in the system for a warrant or a be-on-the-lookout. I still have resistance. Hell, I've got sovereign citizens as residents of my county that are calling it unconstitutional even though they don't believe in a single law, constitutional or not."

Will chewed his gum furiously with pop and cracking sounds coming from his mouth. "Those citizens," he made air quotes, "are nut jobs. Remember that class we took last year at that law enforcement convention? They don't think anyone has rule over them. One of my deputies stopped one a few years ago for having no tags on a vehicle. The guy had no registration and no insurance. I'm still fighting all that in court. The amount of discovery he requested is far outweighing what the fine would have brought. Makes no sense except that they like to fuck with law enforcement. Dangerous as hell too. You be careful."

Chance rose from her seat and Zeus stepped to her side. She reached out her hand to shake Will's. "I'll do just that. Now I've got to get out of here and over to Los Loco to pick up dinner or I may be sleeping on the couch."

Will rose and shook her hands. "I may run over there and do the same. Congratulations, by the way. I thought you'd end up marrying that doctor but looks like you found someone that will put up with you and your K9 there." He nodded toward Zeus.

Chance brushed a hand across Zeus' well healed ear and thought of the care Jax had given them both when they'd been injured. "Sometimes, things work out for the best. Thanks, Will. Keep in touch."

Will waved her out of his office and Jax made her way back to the vehicle. "Let's go make momma happy."

Available in Autumn 2019

About CJ Murphy

I began to create lesbian fiction after my wife suggested I write her a story as a personalized gift. I was privileged to be mentored by another published author who helped turn a raw manuscript, into an actual novel. Upon completion, she encouraged me to submit to Desert Palm Press. DPP offered me a contract for my first novel, 'frame by frame' in 2017. My second novel, The Bucket List, was published in late 2018. I credit my story telling ability to being an avid reader and having an adventure filled occupation for twenty-five years as a career firefighter.

Connect with CJ:

Email: cptcjldypyro@gmail.com

Facebook: CJ Murphy (Murphy's Law)

Blog: Murphy's Law Ink

Note to Readers:

Thank you for reading a book from Desert Palm Press. We have made every effort to edit this book. However, typos do slip in. If you find an error in the text, please email lee@desertpalmpress.com so the issue can be corrected.

We appreciate you as a reader and want to ensure you enjoy the reading process. We would like you to consider posting a review on your preferred media sites and/or your blog or website.

For more information on upcoming releases, author interviews, contest, giveaways and more, please sign up for our newsletter and visit us as at Desert Palm Press: www.desertpalmpress.com and "Like" us on Facebook: Desert Palm Press.

Bright Blessings

Made in the USA
Columbia, SC
24 June 2019